THE DEFENDER OF THE LIGHT

BOOK 9 OF THE SYLVAN CHRONICLES

PETER WACHT

Kestrel
Media Group, LLC

The Defender of the Light

By Peter Wacht

Book 9 of The Sylvan Chronicles

This book is a work of fiction. Names, characters, places, and incidents are the product of the author's imagination or are used fictitiously. Any resemblance to actual events, locales, or persons, living or dead, is coincidental.

Published in the United States by Kestrel Media Group LLC.

ISBN: 978-1-950236-16-9

eBook ISBN: 978-1-950236-17-6

Library of Congress Control Number: 9781950236169

❀ Created with Vellum

ALSO BY PETER WACHT

* Free short stories can be downloaded from www.kestrelmg.com

YOUR FREE SHORT STORY IS WAITING
BLOOD ON THE WHITE SAND BY PETER WACHT

Sold into slavery as a child Bryen created a name for himself fighting on the white sand of the Pit. Now someone wants him dead. **Will his latest challenge be his last?**

Download your copy at www.kestrelmg.com

He has vanquished man and beast, earning him the name of the Wolf. Yet all his success has given him is more opportunities to bleed and die for the pleasure of the crowd.

Bryen now faces his greatest challenge. The Champion of Sharston, a mountain of a man who has never lost a combat, has come to the Colosseum. His sole purpose is to skin the Wolf.

Bryen quickly realizes there is more at play than the usual combat. For some reason a darker power wants him dead.

Note to Readers: This short story precludes the events in *The Tales of Caledonia.* And at the end of this book you'll find an excerpt from Book 1 of this new series, *The Protector.*

1

A BEGINNING

It was only early morning, but it already appeared to be dusk. The brightly shining sun didn't have the power to force its way through the murk that had draped itself over the desolate land. Most people refused to enter the Charnel Mountains, and those foolhardy enough to do so rarely returned. Any who traveled within ten miles of the forbidding peaks could sense the evil lurking there, the wickedness hidden away from the sight of man, but always there, always watching, always waiting for the unsuspecting to come just a little bit closer. To push their luck just a bit too far, until it was too late. Because darkness lurked in the Charnel Mountains, a darkness that had transformed what had once been the vibrant and green landscape of the Northern Peaks into a cinder-covered wilderness that was home to a terrifying swarm of dark creatures. A darkness that was preparing to break free from its bonds and consume the Kingdoms in one fell swoop.

Yet that reek of evil, so prevalent and overpowering, did not prevent the flight of five kestrels from soaring across the

Northern Steppes, their strong wings pushing them higher
into the sky in search of the warmer drafts that were so difficult to find in the north. For here, where the blackened,
imposing fangs of the Charnel Mountains rose above the
always present clouds and gloom, a cold had begun to seep
down toward the south, a cold that brought to mind the days
of old when an army of Ogren, Shades and other monstrous
creatures had marched from these terrifying peaks and had
threatened to conquer the Kingdoms, held back only by the
valiant efforts of the men and women who had risked their
lives so long ago. Despite their best efforts to find an easier
route, the kestrels found little to aid them at the higher
elevation they achieved as cold gusts blasted down from the
mountains and across the grass-covered lea to slam against
the northern Highlands.

The shrill squawk of the lead kestrel broke the unnatural silence that lay heavy upon the flat land below. There
was no movement within the long stalks. Not even a hare.
There was only dry, brown, sickly grass that flowed
according to the whims of the unceasing wind. Long lines of
black ash and soot that had given the Charnel Mountains its
name crisscrossed the plateau and ran from the Highlands
to the passes that led north toward the Shadow Lord's lair.
The raptors tracked those blackened trails, some hundreds
of yards wide, across the grasslands, understanding that
these paths of befouled and dead grass had formed because
of the dark creatures that favored these routes as they
sought to cross the Northern Steppes and then invade the
Highlands, attempting to build up their numbers in that
mountainous Kingdom so that they could make it their own
and thereby avoid the Breaker when it came time to descend
once more upon the Kingdoms. An understandable strategy,
although the Marchers certainly had something to say

about it. The Highland Lord had set three of his chiefs and a very determined young woman the task of preventing the Ogren and other dark creatures from entering the Kingdom, knowing that if the beasts gained a foothold the marauders might never be dislodged. Nevertheless, even though the Marchers had proven successful in keeping the dark creatures from obtaining purchase in their homeland, there was still a price to pay. Dark creatures, the spawn of the Shadow Lord, destroyed nature. Not immediately, but over time. The corruption of these beasts, even just their steps crushing the grass, slowly ate away at the vitality of the world. The first Ogren, Shades and other beasts so important to the Shadow Lord's designs that had stomped through the chest-high grass had created their own paths across the grasslands with the bands of dark creatures that followed benefiting from their efforts. As had happened in the Charnel Mountains, the once verdant and vital steppe had begun to suffer, the green grass becoming brittle as it turned a dried-out brown before settling for a blackened, burnt crisp that would eventually wither away into a flaky soot.

The large raptors followed those sterile trails for a time, as the peaks of the Charnel Mountains gained in clarity and size. Some said that the Charnel Mountains were an abomination, caused by a tremendous magical battle between the forces of good and evil. Those who followed the light had won, but the cost for their effort had been almost too much to bear. Because even then they could not destroy the dark, instead imprisoning their enemies in the mountains and sealing them away for eternity, or so they thought. Dark grey stone formed the jagged spires, the very tips of the monstrous peaks a sooty black to match that of the tracks used so often by the Shadow Lord's dark creatures seeking access to the Highlands.

The kestrels' powerful wings spanned seven feet, and the white feathers speckled with grey on the bird's under-side blended perfectly with the sky. When visible, the raptor was a dangerous predator. When hidden, it was deadly, shooting down through the thin air like an arrow, its sharp claws outstretched for the kill. The Highlands was the raptor's domain, now its only home. Once, not too many years before, kestrels lived in every Kingdom from the Western Ocean to the Sea of Mist. But no more. Nobles and wealthy merchants paid dearly for the feathers of the mighty bird. Rumors of their magical powers abounded. Some believed the feathers, when ground down and mixed with a few select ingredients, served as an aphrodisiac. Others insisted that drinking the strange brew gave wisdom. Still others thought that it brought riches. Though no one had ever proven the truth of these myths, the old beliefs died hard. As the years passed, so did these majestic birds, until none remained except those in the Highlands, protected by the harsh weather, the rough landscape and the Highlanders themselves, for the raptors had a special place in their hearts. The kestrel was the symbol of the Highland Lord, and for the new Highland Lord perhaps something more.

Just as the Highland Lord had begun to flex the muscles of the Marchers after almost a decade of fighting to free their homeland from the enslavement that the reivers sought to impose, the kestrels had begun to expand their territory as well, once more flying from their roosts in the Highland peaks to stake their claim to the territories bordering their mountain home. They were aggressive birds to begin with and savage when they came upon dark creatures.

As the begrimed smudges of the Charnel Mountains

solidified into rocky, soot-covered peaks, the five kestrels as one squawked a challenge, spying two Dragas gliding above the closest summit. Almost four times the size of the raptor, the Dragas were a significant threat. The flying dark creatures enjoyed a clear advantage over the raptors, their scaled hides offering them additional protection, although that benefit did cost the beasts the speed that the raptors put to good use during their aerial combats. The kestrels understood the dangers presented by the dark creatures' long, spike-like claws and sharp teeth, but they also knew the weaknesses of the Dragas, their leathery wings and soft underbellies the raptors' preferred targets when engaged in a skirmish.

Startled by the challenge, the Dragas at first sought to respond violently. The two dark creatures roared in anger at the temerity of the kestrels for encroaching on their domain. But then, strangely, rather than attacking, the two dark creatures tilted their sinewy wings and quickly caught a downdraft that pushed them around the mountaintop and deeper among the towering peaks.

At first the kestrels thought to pursue, having little fear of the two Dragas because of their superior numbers, but then they considered the danger of taking such a risk. Perhaps the two Dragas did fear the five kestrels, acknowledging how deadly the large raptors could be when their sharp claws tore into unprotected wing or gut. Or maybe there was more going on than what the naked eye could see. Perhaps the two Dragas served as bait with more of the deadly dark creatures waiting among the lofty spires for any raptor foolish enough to follow.

Ignoring their instinct to attack, though not without expending some effort in doing so, the kestrels instead settled into a lazy patrol. They drifted along the border of the Northern Steppes and the Charnel Mountains, sharp eyes constantly searching for movement, for any sign of the next Ogren raiding party seeking to make its way across the grassland and then into the lower Highlands.

The tallest of the mountains in the northern range could not be seen completely, as fully a third of its mass reached up into the clouds. Known as Blackstone, that single peak had an even older name, Shadow's Reach. On certain winter days, when the sun was just right, the shadow of Blackstone reached out across much of the Northern Steppes, turning day into night and, for those unlucky travelers caught in that desolate land, life into a nightmare.

As the kestrels maintained their patrol, they couldn't help but watch an event that would have been unheard of just a few years before. But today's occurrence was becoming more commonplace. A single ray of sunshine had fought its way through the thick clouds, shining down on Blackstone, illuminating the abandoned city named for the peak on which it had been built. The sunlight flickered, struggling against the leaden gloom. The shadow fought hard, but the light refused to yield, increasing in intensity with each passing second. And then surprisingly another ray of light broke through the pall, and then another, and another, until the bright sunlight burned through the fog that normally hid the ash-covered and broken down buildings and towers, most no more than ruins, the bricks and stones having collapsed long ago.

As the streams of sunshine blasted through the thick overcast, several rays of light shone down through a hole where a glass dome had once resided on top of the largest building in the city that still stood, a monstrous castle with gargoyles and other hideous beasts in gruesome poses standing guard atop the crenellations. As the darkness reluctantly dissipated, the room revealed its secrets. Gigantic marble columns stationed around its perimeter appeared. Black and white tiles as wide as a tall man covered the floor. If there were any doors, they remained hidden in the darkness that prowled at the distant edges of the chamber.

The beams of blazing light settled on the room's most unique characteristic, a stone disc with an intricate design set in the very center of the floor. Two figures emerged from the cuts in the block, done with such excellent workmanship that they appeared lifelike. The first resembled a young man with a blazing sword of light. Opposing him was a tall man with a cruel face wielding a sword that swallowed the light. They were locked blade to blade, their faces no more than the breadth of a finger apart. The boy wore a look of determination, the man a grin of arrogance and sure victory.

As the sun touched the stone it grew warm. A rumble began in the room, drifting out to the very fringes of Blackstone, and from there it traveled through the Charnel Mountains and across the Northern Steppes. It was not an earthquake, for that was something of an end. Instead, it was a beginning.

As the earth began to heave to and fro violently, in some places the sides of entire mountains sheared off and tumbled into the stunted, twisted forests far below. The kestrels observed from far above, unaffected by the rumbling ground that ignited the rockslides among the peaks. But only for a few seconds, because the kestrels' attention remained focused on the northern skies, watching, waiting, hoping that their blood enemies, the Dragas, would reappear. These raptors wanted to hunt, and there was no better prey than the servants of the Shadow Lord.

For these majestic birds had become infused with the

energy now surging within the Highlands, the people now free from the bonds that had threatened to destroy their rugged, mountainous Kingdom for almost a decade. There was a change moving through the Highlands, a power, a force, that offered new hope, new blood, and a new defiance.

DANGER FROM ABOVE

"Rynlin, above you!"

Even with Anara's warning shout, the tall Sylvan Warrior didn't have time to glance at the top of the crest that loomed above him. His piercing green eyes held an intensity that would have frightened most men and were accentuated by the sharp features of his face. The short black beard flecked with grey gave him an almost dastardly appearance. If anyone had the courage to tell him so, he would have smiled and thanked them for the compliment. But now it was all that he could do to keep the Mongrel swaggering in front of him from sinking its long teeth into his throat.

The Ogren and Shades so common to these dark creature raiding parties were bad enough, but now Mongrels had been added to the mix. Ogren, their heavily muscled bodies covered in short fur, were twice the size of a man and truly hideous creatures. Their frightening strength more than made up for their lack of intelligence, though their massive shoulders and upper body that gave them that strength sometimes proved too heavy for their spines, forcing them to walk hunched over. Their chiseled, beast-like faces looked as if they had been carved from rock. Long sharp tusks protruded from their lower lips to curl around their cheeks. Ogren were efficient soldiers. They enjoyed killing, and they ate what they killed. A single soldier did not willingly fight an Ogren, not if he or she wanted to live.

The same could be said when a soldier came up against a Shade, which was often charged by the Shadow Lord with leading an Ogren raiding party. Sinuous and graceful, its movement resembled that of a snake. Stories said that Shades had once been men who had sold their souls to the Shadow Lord. In return for the benefits afforded to them by their master, they had also paid a price, their skin taking on a ghoulish cast, their hair becoming lank and greasy, and their eyes turning a milky white. Their needs had changed as well, as they no longer required food for sustenance. Rather, they drank the souls of their victims to maintain their vitality.

Mongrels towered over Fearhounds, many reaching the size of draft horses, and their size meant that they had few things to fear. Black or grey in coloring, their sharp, hardened claws could cut through rock like a knife through paper. Their incisors, almost as long as a child's forearm, could bite through a soldier's steel breastplate with ease. Yet despite their muscular bulk, they were fast and could outrun a horse over a short distance. Not unexpectedly, they were aggressive. Once they had their prey in sight, they never stopped their pursuit, even when outnumbered, as they tried to take their quarry even if doing so meant that it would cost them their lives as well. For there was only one thing that mattered to a Mongrel, and that was the kill.

That certainly proved to be the case for the huge beast that stalked toward Rynlin now. The shafts of several Marcher arrows stuck out from its rough hide, but the steel-tipped quarrels apparently had no effect on the deadly dark creature. The beast continued to move with a dexterity and speed that few other animals could match. Although Rynlin couldn't see what waited above him, he could guess. He and several other Sylvan Warriors had tracked the Mongrel pack as it crossed the Northern Steppes and entered the lower Highlands. Normally, because of the large number of Mongrels, Anara would have called together Nestor, Renn and Seneca, the Highland chiefs charged with defending the northern Highlands from the encroachments of the Shadow Lord's minions, combining their forces to take on the several hundred dark creatures.

But this time, she couldn't. Ogren and Shades also had tried to climb from the lower passes to the west and east of where the Mongrels had chosen to enter the Highlands, forcing Renn and Seneca to hold their ground. Anara, charged by Thomas with coordinating the Marcher defense, could only bring the small reserve that she maintained to Nestor's aid, since he faced the greater menace as the Mongrels threatened to break through the center of the Marcher line. If the Mongrels did get past Nestor and his Marchers, even if Renn and Seneca proved successful at eliminating the dark creatures coming their way, it would still be the beginning of the end. The Mongrels would have gotten behind the Marcher perimeter and would be free to range deep into the Highlands.

Hearing a deep growl just a few feet above his head, Rynlin knew that his time had run out. The two Mongrels were working together. The one in front of him charged forward, its sharp claws digging up the rock and dirt, and Rynlin could sense the one above him preparing to leap. Better to face the danger in front of you, he thought. But he only had one chance, and he could only hope that he was fast enough. Sprinting toward the charging Mongrel, he ignored the beast above him. Just before the onrushing Mongrel's slavering jaws clamped down on his chest, he rolled to the side, trailing his Talent-infused blade across the side of the dark creature. A steel blade would have just skittered across the rough hide of the Mongrel, but not one blazing with the power of the natural world. The glowing steel sliced through the Mongrel's toughened exterior and bit deeply into its flesh, the creature's innards spilling out as the beast toppled to the rocky ground.

Yet even with his success against the attacking Mongrel, he knew that it was too little too late. He could never turn in time to face the second Mongrel that he sensed had launched itself from the crest above him into the air, less than a second from tearing into him from behind.

"Down!"

Rynlin obeyed the shouted command instinctively, dropping flat on the ground as a blast of white hot energy shot through the space where he had been crouching. The energy sizzled through the air and tore open the chest of the Mongrel that had tried to attack him from behind, leaving a smoking husk in its wake as the dead beast crashed onto the stone and dirt.

"Thank you, my love," said Rynlin, pushing himself up from the soil and dusting himself off. "I don't know what I'd do without you."

"Let's hope it never comes to that," replied Rya Keldragan, Rynlin's wife, who examined her husband with a critical eye to ensure that he wasn't injured. "I doubt that you'd do well managing things on your own."

No more than five feet tall, Rya carried herself like a giant. Her dark chestnut hair covered one side of her face, pushed there by the strong, cold mountain breeze. As she swept her hair out of the way with a quick swipe of her hand, she revealed deep blue eyes. Eyes that Rynlin had gotten lost in time and time again, much to his pleasure.

"The others?" asked Rynlin.

"Well," replied Anara. "Maden Grenis held the left flank in support of Nestor. The twins aided me on the right. Those two seemed to take particular pleasure in destroying the last of the Mongrels."

"Yes, they certainly would," answered Rya. "For them, it's personal." Elisia and Aurelia Valeran, twin Sylvan Warriors from Kashel, one with midnight black hair, the other with shocking white, coordinated their efforts in a way that only those who could apparently read the other's mind could. In fact, several Sylvan Warriors did, indeed, believe that the Valeran sisters could read each other's mind, but the two refused to confirm the suspicion, preferring to keep their peers in suspense. "But you appear to have a knack for it as well, arriving at the most critical time at the most dangerous part of the conflict."

Anara nodded at what she took as a compliment. Not very tall, the red-haired, pixie-faced Marcher had a tenacity that few could match. Rya thought that it had served her well when she was forced to work in the mines and survive the Black Hole when the former High King had maintained his dominance over the Highlands through a regent who was charged with extracting as much wealth as possible from the mountainous Kingdom. Furthermore, the young woman's determination clearly was a major asset as she led the Marcher forces in the north while Thomas Kestrel, new Lord of the Highlands, pursued the Key.

"I'm just doing what's necessary," she answered modestly, flipping a dagger from one hand to the next, a habit that helped to soothe her nerves but often put others on edge. As a result, she always had a blade close at hand. "Renn and Seneca report that the Ogren raiding parties failed to make it out of the lower passes. So, for now, our lines hold. But who can say for how long?"

"As long as necessary," said Rynlin. They all knew that the number of dark creatures seeking to infiltrate the Highlands had grown exponentially in just the last few weeks. They couldn't say for certain as to why the Shadow Lord had expanded his efforts to gain control of the Highlands, but Rynlin and Rya had their suspicions. It all came down to time, which seemed to be running short for the Kingdoms. If these larger raids were any indication, the Shadow Lord would release his Dark Horde soon, whether toward the Breaker or through the Highlands would depend on whether the Marchers could maintain mastery of their homeland.

"As long as necessary," repeated Anara. "Thank you both for your help. Without you, I don't know what would have happened."

"We do what we can," replied Rya. "As others do what they must."

Anara looked at Rya for a moment, the shorter woman's commanding presence intimidating for most, but not for Anara. She had seen too much of the world, good and bad, for Rya to unnerve her as the Sylvan Warrior did to so many others. Rather, she spent a few seconds trying to puzzle out Rya's cryptic comment before deciding that she didn't have the time to stand their thinking, remembering all that needed to be done after this latest battle. Aiding the wounded. Burying the dead. Preparing for the inevitable next attack. Having nothing else to say, Anara nodded and trotted off in search of Nestor.

"An intense young woman," said Rya.

"Yes, she reminds me of someone I know." Rynlin smiled when he said it, understanding that his wife likely wasn't in the mood to be teased. "He's all right, you know, at least for now. We can breathe easy for a while longer."

"I know," replied Rya. "I just worry about him." She held a slim, silver necklace in her hand. She examined the amulet carefully for a moment, taking in the craftsmanship, impressed by the skill required to carve the unicorn's horn so delicately into the soft metal. When she thought about her grandson, it felt warm against her skin, confirming for her that Thomas was well wherever he was off to the west.

The necklaces had been in the Keldragan family for millennia. They were said to be made from the same magic that had created the world, though Rynlin didn't believe it. A nice story, but a false one. He did believe in what the pendants could do, however. These particular necklaces were attuned to the members of the Keldragan family. Each necklace served as a beacon, identifying where the Keldragans were located in the Kingdoms. Moreover, it was these necklaces that the Keldragans had crafted and then given to the Sylvan Warriors shortly after that legendary band of warriors had formed under the direction of Athala with the charge of defending the Kingdoms from the predations of the Shadow Lord the first time that evil creature sought dominion over the continent. In the thousand years since every individual who had passed the tests to become a Sylvan Warrior had received a necklace to acknowledge that accomplishment and serve as a physical reminder of the responsibility that person had assumed.

Rynlin nodded, his thoughts turning to his grandson as well and the prophecy that had ruled Thomas' life since his birth two decades before.

When a child of life and death
Stands on high
Drawn by faith
He shall hold the key to victory in his hand

Swords of fire echo in the burned rock
Balancing the future on their blades

Light dances with dark
Green fire burns in the night
Hopes and dreams follow the wind
To fall in black or white

HE HAD THOUGHT for quite some time that Thomas was the Defender of the Light referenced by the prophecy and fated to battle the Lord of the Shadow in a contest that would determine the fate of the Kingdoms. The events that had followed, Thomas becoming a member of the Sylvana and Lord of the Highlands as well as other occurrences, had confirmed it for him. Yet to do what was required of him, their grandson must find the Key in order to bypass the Dark Magic protections put in place by the Shadow Lord and enter Blackstone unharmed, for without the Key only those foolish enough to have sold their souls to the Lord of the Shadow could set foot in that lost metropolis without dying a horrible death.

That's where Rynlin had been stuck, despite centuries of effort to find some clue as to what the Key might be, an actual Key or something else, as well as where it might be located, as it had been lost during the Great War when the Sylvan Warriors had worked with the Kingdom armies to force the Dark Horde back into the Charnel Mountains.

What had irritated Rynlin all the more was that he, Rya and several other Sylvan Warriors had been there when Athala had crafted the Key and Ollav Fola had used the artifact to fight the Shadow Lord when that evil creature had first tried to conquer the Kingdoms, but neither Athala nor Ollav Fola had ever revealed what it was and where it had been hidden, taking the secrets of the Key and how it could be used to their graves. It was Thomas who had solved the puzzle, that conversation vivid in Rynlin's mind. But the only way to know for certain was to find the Key and try to use it.

Thomas had explained that much like before he became a Sylvan Warrior, the pull that he felt toward the Pinnacle in the Highlands that served as the Sylvana's meeting place kept getting stronger when it was time for him to take the tests to become a Sylvan Warrior. So much so that he knew exactly the direction he needed to go, even if he wasn't quite sure where he was going and when he would get there. If he turned in the right direction, the pull grew stronger. The same feeling had come over him again, but this time whenever he turned his mind toward finding the Key. It was faint, he had admitted. Barely a touch on his consciousness, but still there, nonetheless. The mistake in examining the prophecy was to fail to connect the line preceding the one that referenced the Key. Finding the Key required faith. Thomas had to give up what little control he exercised and allow a greater power to guide him in order to achieve his larger goal.

Rynlin's initial reaction was skepticism, pushing back at his grandson's conclusion. But Thomas' logic made sense, so his grandson had convinced him. And in all honesty, they had little else to go on. Perhaps it was time to take a risk, to allow faith to guide them. And so Thomas had set a course west with a band of Marchers with the goal of finding the Key.

"Drawn by faith," Rynlin murmured, fingering his own necklace, the warmth giving him the confidence that Thomas was on the right path.

"What was that?" asked Rya, used to her husband's distracted looks and comments.

Rynlin looked at his wife, startled, finally coming back to himself. He smiled sheepishly. "Nothing, my love. Nothing at all." He began to walk toward the aid station Anara had set up, wanting to see if he could help those Marchers injured in the fight. "Wasn't Daran supposed to be here?"

"He was," said Rya, walking next to her husband. "We could have used him. It was a close thing for a while."

"It was," Rynlin replied. "Close indeed."

His thoughts began to wander down a darker path. The red-haired Sylvan Warrior, who always had a ready smile, had failed to arrive several times in support of his comrades, despite their repeated requests for assistance. The first time was worrisome. Now, after almost a handful of missed appearances, it was becoming ominous.

TWO COMPETITORS

"Thomas, being a good leader doesn't mean that you always have to be in the lead," said Kaylie. "Sometimes you need to allow others to step forward. You need to give others the chance to demonstrate what they can do."

She stood close to Thomas at the bow of the ship, her left hand resting on his right, their shoulders touching. He knew that what Kaylie was explaining to him was important. And she was right, he had to admit. Not allowing others to step up demonstrated a lack of faith in their abilities. But this had been a topic of conversation for the last few days ever since the attack by the Great Sharks, and he wanted to move past it.

"You don't need to take it all on your shoulders. I'm here. Oso. Aric. Every one of the Marchers, man and woman, will do what is necessary. They understand how important this mission is and the risk involved. They're here because they want to be here. They understand the importance of what they're doing. Please, let them do what they do best and don't place yourself in any unnecessary danger."

Kaylie gripped Thomas' hand when she said the last.

Her anger at the risks that he had taken to this point in their journey, such as launching himself onto the skull of a Great Shark that threatened to capsize their ship, had dissipated to a certain extent and instead been replaced by an intense worry. She understood the hazards that he faced and the burdens that he carried, the task that only he could accomplish. She also expected that he would seek to change the subject and that she would allow it for now. If she pushed too hard, he would ignore what she had to say, but a planted seed could grow with time, something that Rya Keldragan had, in fact, taught her during one of their training sessions.

"Do you really think that it will be as bad as you say?" asked Thomas, smiling to himself. This discussion with Kaylie brought to mind the many conversations that he had engaged in with his grandmother when he was younger, usually after he had done something that had irritated or worried her. There was never really any use in arguing your case whenever Rya had decided that you were in the wrong or had done something foolish. Because she was usually right. It just took him awhile to see that. So better to listen, to take in the advice, and make use of it in the future.

Of course, Thomas wasn't suggesting that Kaylie was like his grandmother, far from it. But there were some similarities, even if just a few. Not only a strength of purpose, but also a certainty in herself, in who she was. Since Kaylie had joined their expedition to the west she had changed in several ways. "More comfortable in her own skin" was how Oso had put it the other day. She had done everything that had been asked of her and more without objection or complaint, using the Talent and her blade whenever needed and with great effect.

If not for Kaylie, Thomas admitted that he likely would have died in Great Falls, murdered by the Wraith. Kaylie's timely intervention and her determination to protect him against a dark creature that the Sylvan Warriors described as the Shadow Lord's most dangerous assassin had not only saved Thomas' life, but also elevated Kaylie in the eyes of the Marchers, her hard-won respect much deserved.

Despite the dangers presented by the Wraith and the other dark creatures that had sought to impede them from achieving their goal, he and his Marchers had reached the northwestern Kingdom buttressed by the Western Ocean and the Winter Sea. As each league had passed beneath the *Waverunner's* keel, the five-masted merchant vessel slicing through the waves, the pull of the Key had grown stronger, more insistent, demanding that he seek out the artifact. That pull had become an ache in his gut, so intense that try as he might he simply couldn't ignore it.

Their thoughts turned to other matters as Laurag, the capital of Inishmore, quickly came into view. The Marchers stood at the rails, admiring the many tall spires that rose into the sky, their white, almost translucent marble reflecting the bright morning sun to the point where these manmade spikes resembled sparkling flames. After the dangers of their voyage, they were ready to step back on to dry land. They had made good time after their harrowing escape from the Great Sharks, and Thomas had little doubt that the captain would be glad to see their backs when they walked down the gangway.

"It'll probably be worse," cautioned Kaylie. "Watch your back and be prepared for anything here. When the last legitimate king of Inishmore was assassinated several centuries ago, none of the other ruling families were strong enough to assume the throne on their own. Alliances became the way to power, but in this Kingdom, alliances have always been fragile at best. They are made out of expedience and the opportunity for gain, so they are always changing. As a result, you never know which family might be for or against another. You won't necessarily know what they're trying to achieve other than the fact that the ruling houses will do whatever is necessary to maintain or expand their power, to gain some advantage, or to ensure that another family does not gain an advantage at their expense."

"We're just here to find a ship," protested Thomas. "And we have no interest in Inishmore's politics."

"It's not a matter of what we're interested in. It's not that straightforward, unfortunately. Rather, it's a matter of what they're interested in."

"Who?"

"Colasa and Eshel," answered Kaylie. "Traditionally half a dozen houses have vied for the throne at any one time. But not anymore. Those two houses have consolidated the other houses behind them. How, I don't know, considering that the loyalty of an Inishmorian lord is worth as much as the sweat on your brow. I expect that those two will do anything, use anyone, if they think it will help them seize the throne."

"And you think that they know we're coming?"

Thomas saw the spires of the city taking shape as the harbor appeared, a massive stone wall curling out into the sea to protect the moored ships and bustling port from the sometimes monstrous waves so common to this part of the world, rogue waves that could swallow their ship whole and leave no trace of their existence as Torlan had explained. Thankfully, they traveled at a time in the year when such waves were rare, though not unheard of.

"I don't know for sure, but my guess is that as soon as we dock those two will learn of our arrival quickly. After what happened on the way here, I'm certain that some of the sailors will begin telling tales in the taverns lining the waterfront. Once that happens, those stories will be all over the city within an hour and travel quickly to the ears of Colasa and Eshel through their network of spies."

"Then we need to be quick," said Thomas. "Find a ship as fast as we can."

"Agreed," said Torlan, captain of the *Waverunner*, who had stomped up the deck to them, yelling commands to his crew all along the way. "I'll keep the men busy for as long as I can, but they'll want to be off this ship just as much as you. They'll spread the word of what happened on our voyage just as fast as the young miss suggested, and the story will grow with each telling, finding its way quickly to the ears of those who will seek to make use of it for their own gain. That's the way of it here in Laurag. Once the lads unload the cargo, I'll have nothing to hold my sailors here."

"Thank you, Torlan. We do appreciate it. And we appreciate everything that you've done for us."

"It's nothing, miss. Some of us remember the stories, the way it was in a darker time. And some of us are willing to do what's necessary to make sure that doesn't happen again. Lord Kestrel, I wish you luck on your business. And if you ever have need of a quick voyage back to the east, call on me. My crew and I would be happy to assist. Look for Brienne in the south docks. She's one of the few captains willing to risk a run to the Distant Islands this time of the year. She can be trusted, take it from me. You can tell her that I recommended her to you."

"Thank you, Torlan."

Torlan nodded, slapping Thomas on the shoulder, then lumbered away to ensure that the sailors managed their tasks smartly as they entered the harbor and tied up to their mooring.

4

RECOVERED

Ragin Tessaril, son of the former High King, a young man born into power and privilege, used to obtaining whatever he wanted whenever he wanted, lay rolled up in a ball, his threadbare cloak pulled tight around him in a desperate attempt for warmth. He was starving and cold, always cold, shivering uncontrollably as the brisk wind blew across the top of the hill, infusing the never-ending chill deep into his emaciated bones.

How long had he been here? Weeks? Months? He didn't know. He had lost track. Nothing had changed except for the sky, shifting from the murky gray of the day to the pitch black of night, and then back again. A continuous, dreary cycle. Ragin surveyed his surroundings for the thousandth time, not bothering to lift his head. In the beginning he had hoped for some change in this cursed land, yet as the days and then weeks passed, he knew that it was a useless wish. He lay on a small hillock with a single, leafless, dead tree at its top, the branches twisted and broken. Sunlight didn't exist in this soul-crushing place. Instead, a dismal haze covered the landscape, the greyish fog billowing and churning at the touch of the breeze. Despite the length of time that he had been here, the smell still made him want to retch, but there was nothing in his stomach to expel. For as far as he could see, a turbid, black water surrounded the knoll and extended all the way to the horizon. In some places the muck roiled, bubbles letting off a noxious, sulfurous odor that spread in the air. In others, wide ripples would appear for just a moment and then disappear just as quickly. Ragin had yet to see the creatures that disturbed the stagnant water, and he wasn't sure that he wanted to, as he had glimpsed on occasion the wide, scaled backs that glided through the mire and suggested the massive size of the beasts that patrolled the swamp.

When first he had been stranded here, his anger had threatened to consume him, the rage roiling in his chest providing him with the little bit of warmth that could be obtained in this disheartening land. Everything that he had worked for had been taken from him in a matter of minutes, all because of an old man. An old man! He had prepared meticulously, accepting the demands of the Shadow Lord so that he could learn the ways of Dark Magic. Giving up his very soul to obtain the power needed to kill his torturer, the boy who played at Lord of the Highlands. But all for naught, as the old man had prevented him from achieving his objective, banishing him from the halls of Eamhain Mhacha before he could strike. And now here he lay in the midst of desolation, no food, no shelter, nothing but a wind that never ceased, a cold that seeped into his very core, and a stench that made him gag if he breathed too deeply.

Ragin had thought that as soon as the old man closed the portal that he had pushed him through, he could create one of his own, mimicking what the Sylvan Warrior had done to return to Eamhain Mhacha and kill first the fool who had dared to oppose him and then the scoundrel who had disfigured him, the boy who had given him a ragged scar on his face that stretched from brow to neck and had altered more than just his appearance. But he had thought wrong. Because wherever the old man had sent him, Ragin couldn't touch the Dark Magic that the Shadow Lord had imbued within him. The power that had once surged through his body, that had given him hope and confirmation that he would gain his revenge, had simply disappeared. Gone. And with it, his hope.

"You have wasted what I gave you," a deep, raspy voice said from behind him. "So much power, yet so little intelligence."

Ragin slowly rolled his body over, his hunger and weakness allowing him to move only so fast. He used the last vestiges of his strength to sit up, and even then, it was more of a slouch, leaning his upper body to the side on his elbow, as he feared that if he tried to elevate himself any further, he'd tumble down the hill and into the slime. He should have felt terror, yet he didn't have the energy for it. A portal of swirling black fog had opened behind him, as tall as a man. Through that portal he picked out a circular chamber mostly hidden by a dark gloom, only a few large black and white tiles on the floor visible. Tilting his head up and seeing what had disturbed him, his fear reignited with a vengeance, making his body shiver even worse than from the cold. Two blood-red eyes studied him, weighed him, and apparently found him wanting.

"I tried," rebutted Ragin, his voice soft and scratchy from the lack of use. He wasn't even sure that it sounded like him any longer. "I tried to ..."

"Trying doesn't matter," hissed the Shadow Lord. "Only success matters. I gave you the power to destroy the boy.

Utterly! Completely! Yet here you are while he continues to be a splinter in my palm."

"I'm sorry, master. I'm sorry."

The Shadow Lord stared down at the quivering Ragin in disgust. He had considered leaving the fool here to die. Now in his rage he wanted to lash out, to destroy the arrogant pup who had failed like so many others to complete the simple task given to him of killing a boy. Not only did the boy still live, but he had grown more powerful, more dangerous. The Lord of the Shadow knew that the Wraith had failed, feeling the final throes of its death somewhere in the western Kingdoms. There were few resources left to impede the boy from challenging him in Blackstone as the prophecy suggested. Would it come down to that? Would the duel between the Lord of the Shadow and the Defender of the Light take place? His servants had failed to put an end to the boy multiple times. It seemed as if the prophecy would have its way no matter how he tried to stop it from coming to fruition. But that didn't mean he couldn't continue in his efforts to kill his nemesis. There was no reason to hold out any hope of success, but there was nothing to lose either. Of course, if the boy did fulfill the requirements of the prophecy and somehow found a way into Blackstone, there also was every reason to have another option in place to aid him in the fight. Just in case. A surprise, perhaps, to throw the boy off at a critical moment. The boy had proven to be stronger and more resilient than expected. So yes, perhaps the sickening wretch in front of him could be put to use after all. Another tool to be applied at the right time, even if it was only to serve as a distraction.

"I did not train you to be a fool, boy," the Shadow Lord said, staring down at Ragin, his blood-red eyes flashing dangerously.

A black mist surged from the Shadow Lord's upraised hand, his fingers thin, clawlike, and spotted with age. The mist surrounded Ragin, spinning faster and faster into a whirl that resembled a tornado. The former Prince of Armagh tried to escape, the haze pricking him in thousands of places at once, sending jolts of pain through his body until he spasmed and flopped around on the hilltop like a fish out of water. He opened his mouth to scream, but he failed to emit a sound, the mist surging down his throat, his insides now threatening to explode as he felt his body being pierced, inside and out. Then, after what seemed like a lifetime but was only a few minutes, the fog dissolved.

Ragin lay on his back, breathing raggedly, sweat soaking his clothes, the cold wind freezing his shirt to his chest. But he ignored the discomfort, the frigid cold, forgetting the pain, the pricks that still sizzled across his skin, and smiled instead. Finally, after how many days he couldn't recall, Dark Magic swirled within him once again. He sensed the power that the Shadow Lord had made a part of him flow through his blood, then laughed weakly as he realized that his master had returned to him the tool that would allow him to achieve his vengeance.

"Against my better judgment, I have given your Dark Magic back to you, boy," said the Shadow Lord. "This is your final chance. Do not fail me again."

5

BLACK OR RED

The Marchers had barely set foot on the docks of Laurag before it seemed as if everyone's eyes were upon them, watching, judging, trying to determine their purpose for coming to the port city and how that knowledge could be turned into some coin if whispered into the right person's ear. It was an unsettling environment, one that sent a prickle of worry down the back of Thomas' neck and made him feel more uncomfortable than when he was being hunted by a Nightstalker.

As they walked up the pier toward the gate to the city, they began to notice the armbands. The sailors didn't wear them, but anyone who appeared to reside in Laurag did. Some people wore black armbands, others red. Any time a person or group of people wearing one color armband came into contact with a person or group of people wearing a different color armband, there were either harsh glares or suspicious gazes. People only conducted business with those merchants and tradespeople wearing bands the same color as theirs. The tension was thick, almost palpable, the threat of violence hanging in the air.

The closer the Marchers came to the gate, the more crowded it became, the men and women of the Highlands pressed together by the many travelers, merchants and townsfolk seeking to enter the city proper. A small table blocked the center of the gate, and to each side an equal number of soldiers stood grasping their weapons tightly, poised on the edge of violence. On one side the soldiers wore black armbands, on the other red.

About to reach the miserly looking man sitting at the table, Thomas turned to Kaylie and asked what was happening.

Kaylie smiled, grasping his forearm warmly. "Not to worry. I'll handle this."

Not fully understanding, Thomas looked at Oso, who towered behind him, and they both shrugged. He and his Marchers apparently had entered a foreign territory.

The Marchers, finally having made their way to the front of the line after several minutes of waiting, sensed more and more eyes upon them. The man at the small table didn't deign to look up, though the soldiers on both sides stared with interest at the newcomers, some gripping the hilts of their swords, others the shafts of their spears, in a stronger grip, a few even shuffling their feet nervously. The reputation of the Marchers had preceded them.

"Black or red?" asked the man in a tired voice, too busy scribbling in the ledger set on the table to acknowledge the people standing before him.

"Neither," said Kaylie. "We take no side."

That comment caught the man's attention. His pencil stopped scratching across the page as he looked up finally, his skepticism plain. Though he wore spectacles perched on the very edge of his long nose, he squinted to take in the young woman and her large companions who crowded around him.

"And you are?"

"Simply travelers from the east, my good sir, seeking a few days of rest before we continue on our way."

The administrator leaned back in his chair, now tapping his pencil against his ledger. He saw that the line behind this fascinating, possibly profitable, group was beginning to back up, but he didn't care, ignoring the complaints that were coming from the now milling crowd.

"Highlanders?"

"Yes, my good sir."

"And why are you out of your Highlands? In my experience, Highlanders rarely leave their Kingdom."

Kaylie could have continued the conversation, but she realized that it was futile. She had taken her measure of this man in seconds. Nothing to his name but the small bit of power that he wielded because of his job. He was an official looking to profit from any useful information that he could obtain while conducting his duties. There was only one way to deal with a man such as this. To take charge.

"You have wasted enough of my time, good sir," stated Kaylie in a strong voice that carried to all around her. She assumed the posture demanded of her when conducting functions in the throne room of Fal Carrach. "As well as the time of all those behind us. Your purpose here is quite simple, is it not? You are to determine the allegiance of any entering the city, and then once identified allow entry so the commerce of this city can continue?"

The man leaned his chair back down, the color in his face rising. "Well, I need ..."

"It is a simple question, is it not? When travelers arrive who have no connection to Inishmore, no allegiance to any lord, it is to be noted and they are to be allowed to pass. Is that not correct, my good sir?" Kaylie bit off the words. Though presented as a question, it clearly wasn't.

"Yes, but ..."

"Then this matter is closed. We have stated our purpose and the fact that we have no allegiance to any of the great houses of Inishmore. You will mark down our number in your ledger and we will be on our way so that we can find a place to stay after weeks on the water. Do we understand one another?" The sharpness of Kaylie's eyes, sparkling with fire, made clear that the bureaucrat's agreement really wasn't expected or even necessary.

"Yes, my lady," the man said weakly. Several of the soldiers on both sides chuckled, enjoying the brief spectacle in what was usually a long and boring day.

Kaylie nodded in satisfaction, striding past the table, under the gate and into the city proper. The Marchers trotted to keep up, Thomas finding his way back to her shoulder.

"Quite impressive. Remind me never to get on your bad side."

Kaylie plunged forward through the crowd, head raised proudly, playing the part she had created for herself as they went in search of an inn. But she couldn't keep a small smile from playing across her lips at Thomas' comment.

6

AN OPPORTUNITY

"News, my lord."

"It had better be good, Orlas. I expect better from my spymaster. Your last few tidbits have been less than useful, and my competitor appears to be gaining an advantage as a result."

Orlas cringed at the words, remembering the recent whipping that he had suffered for the supposedly faulty information that he had passed on to his master. It had come from an impeccable source, a man who knew the cargos that were coming into Laurag weeks ahead of time. The shipment of spices from the Distant Islands would have helped to fund his master's campaign for the Inishmorian throne for several months. And Orlas reminded himself that his man had been right, though he could not say such a thing to his lord, knowing the toll of doing so would be high. The spices arrived exactly on schedule in the early morning of Monday last. It wasn't his fault that his master's man had failed to nick the shipment as they had planned. How was he to know that the spice shipment had been arranged by his master's rival and would be so heavily guarded? His master should have been prepared for that possibility, not him. He was not a strategist. He was a purveyor of information. After that disturbing and painful occurrence, the wounds on his back still raw, he had half a mind to change sides, but knew himself too well. He didn't have the courage to take such a risk, understanding the potential and likely consequences. His current master would put a target on his back with a price on his head that would be so high that his death would only be a matter of time. That bit of knowledge ate at him, irritating him to no end, but he pushed it down, focusing on the task at hand.

"Rumors of the new Highland Lord, Lord Eshel."

Eshel leaned forward in his chair, resting his meaty arms on the large table in front of him. Handsome with a strong jaw and touches of grey coloring his wavy black hair, Eshel's dark eyes gave away his true character. Conniving. Untrustworthy. Predatory. All characteristics of which Orlas had been well aware before tying his fate to that of his master, a decision that he regretted almost every day. True, the money had been good, the influence he exerted addictive, but he had the sneaking suspicion that he had tied his fortunes to the wrong racehorse. Eshel appeared to be a man who would sell out his own mother if it gained him his Kingdom's throne. And who was to say he hadn't done so already? Orlas had never met his master's mother.

Looking beyond Orlas, Eshel peered out at the beautiful day beginning in Laurag, the sun breaking through the clouds to play off the frigid waters of the Winter Sea. He was of a mind to step onto the balcony and enjoy the warmth of the sun, but he quickly rejected giving in to such a dangerous urge. An assassin could be lurking in one of the nearby buildings with a longbow or, more likely, a crossbow, so why take the risk when he was so close to the victory that he craved. All the other noble houses seeking the throne had been destroyed or made to see the error of their ways. Now only Colasa, an upstart young girl with little standing among the more powerful nobles but a great deal of support from the common people of Laurag and the surrounding countryside, stood in his way. Once he eliminated her, Inishmore would be his to do with as he saw fit.

"There are always rumors of the Highland Lord, Orlas. Apparently, he stands ten feet tall, breathes fire like the dragons of ancient times and wields a blazing sword that can slice through steel like a warmed knife through butter. He can talk to animals, and they will do his will. And his fighters are the most fearsome in all the Kingdoms, terrifying all that look upon them and defeating all that oppose them. Oh, and my favorite one of all, they drink the blood of the soldiers they slay."

"Yes, my lord. But these are new rumors. More fact than rumor, actually."

"And what might these 'facts' as you call them be, Orlas?" Keshel leaned back, resting his hands on his ample belly. After the latest escapade based on Orlas' facts he had lost more than a dozen of his best men trying to hijack that spice shipment. News of that failure had strengthened his rival in the eyes of her backers and had emboldened her. She had sent out proposals of alliance to some of the larger noble houses, and much to his dismay and anger he had heard that several of his current allies were beginning to see the girl in a more positive light. So he was loath to act on the advice of his spymaster after such an embarrassment unless he had incontrovertible evidence that the rumor was, indeed, true.

"That the Highland Lord is here, my lord. In Laurag. That he arrived here in just the last day."

Keshel shot to his feet. "How do you know?"

"Spies at the harbor, my lord. The Highland Lord and a band of his Marchers made port yesterday."

"That's not good enough, Orlas. There needs to be more proof than that if I'm ..."

"And the lady, my lord. I brought her to the inn where the Highland Lord is staying. She saw him, my lord, but he didn't see her. She confirmed it. The Highland Lord is in the city."

7

REGRETS

"So, where is Thomas?" Kaylie had knocked on the door to Thomas' room with the sun barely a thought in the sky. Receiving no response, she had begun to fear the worst. Using a trick that Rya had shown her, she had sent several thin streams of the Talent into the lock, manipulating the mechanism so that she could open the door silently and with no one the wiser. She discovered that Thomas had already left for the morning, her initial worry transforming into the beginnings of a simmering anger.

The Marchers had settled into the inn Kaylie had selected, happy to have dry land under their feet once more that didn't roll or sway from one second to the next. The Stonecutter Forge was a small public house, the Marchers taking the top floor all for themselves. It offered a comfortable space, and, most important to Oso, good food. But the Marchers remained wary after the trials of the last few months. The danger seemed to increase with every step that they took on their journey, and they anticipated no less in Laurag or wherever they were headed next. So they would enjoy the quiet and the rest provided at the inn, but they would keep one hand on the hilts of their swords at all times, expecting and preparing for the worst.

"I thought he was with you," replied the big Marcher, who sat on the front porch of the inn, watching the flow of traffic in the street. It was quieter here, away from the harbor and the larger markets, but still made for an interesting experience as he watched the people and goods pass by. He had found an intriguing piece of wood and was whittling it down with his belt knife, thinking that he could craft it into something for Anara. Though he wasn't sure quite yet what it might be. He'd let the wood tell him that. "I haven't seen him all morning. Do you think he ..."

"Went off on his own in search of the captain Torlan recommended," answered Kaylie, clearly exasperated.

Oso jumped to his feet, incredibly nimble for a big man. "Let me get Aric and a few others. We'll join you."

"Assemble all the Marchers, Oso," ordered Kaylie, the command in her voice clear and certain. "We'll leave two Marchers here at the inn at all times in case Thomas returns. But we can search faster if all the other Marchers are out in the streets." Oso nodded, immediately accepting Kaylie's authority and running into the inn to rouse the Highlanders.

Kaylie turned to face the street, watching the steady flow of people. She had spoken to Thomas about this no more than a few days ago. The risks were too high for him to go off on his own. Yet he had still done so. When she found him, she'd strip his hide, Highland Lord or no.

8

HELP REWARDED

Thomas strolled casually through Laurag's streets on the eastern end of the harbor, eyes taking in everything going on around him. Normally he preferred the peace and solitude of the forest, but this morning he actually enjoyed the hustle and bustle of the people crowding around him. Mothers and fathers buying food in the market, merchants negotiating deals as their cargos came into the harbor, tradespeople selling their wares from stalls and shops lining the roads, the black and red armbands ever present and determining who sold to whom. And him just another traveler, invisible in the controlled chaos of the marketplace.

He had risen before the sun appeared, leaving the early morning quiet of the inn behind, driven by the need to get out and explore, not wanting to be cooped up inside as had been the case on the merchant vessel that had taken him and his Marchers west across the Winter Sea. At first, he had thought simply to wander and allow fate to take him where it would through the streets and alleys that formed the honeycomb of Laurag's harbor district. But then as the sun rose in the sky, he decided to pursue the lead that Torlan had given him on the off chance that the captain he had suggested might actually be in port. He did remember his conversation with Kaylie, but he didn't think the task he had given himself would involve much in the way of risk.

Thomas' luck held. After a few inquiries, he had found the right inn. And despite the early morning hour sitting right at the bar was Brienne, just as Torlan had described her. Dark skin, flamboyantly dressed, brightly colored blouse and breeches, broad hat perched jauntily on her head, and a long dagger always in her grasp as she flipped the blade from hand to hand while talking to a few other ship captains. The negotiations had been quick, as Torlan's name held a great deal of weight with Brienne.

In less than ten minutes they had agreed to terms, though the Marchers would have to wait several days before she embarked for the Distant Islands. The seas to the north could be rough this time of year. Rogue waves of a hundred feet or more that could sink a ship such as hers were common. Thus, the need to time the trip as best as possible. That meant relying on Brienne's intuition and experience more than anything else. Thomas was reluctant to do so, but he understood the requirement to depend on her expertise. As each hour passed Thomas felt the crunch of time more acutely. The Key continued to pull at him, a constant tug that grew worse by the day. If he concentrated on the feeling, he knew that once he arrived in Afara, the capital of the Distant Islands, he could make straight for the Key, whatever in fact the Key might be.

As he wandered among the stalls and stores, his mind turned to Kaylie. Something had changed between them. He couldn't put his finger on it, but their time spent together during this journey, and particularly aboard the

Waverunner, had added a new dynamic to their relationship. One that he found both pleasing as well as a bit disconcerting.

With his only task of the morning completed, he had decided to buy Kaylie a small gift as a way to say thank you for her guidance, not ready to admit to himself that there might be more to it than that. That new mission had taken him down a street that more resembled an alley not far from the inn that held several forges and small shops displaying masterfully worked blades. He wasn't sure what to get Kaylie, never having done something like this before. He had thought to ask Oso for his advice based on his relationship with Anara, but his friend seemed to be in the same boat as he was, as neither had much experience dealing with women. What was an appropriate gift to give to someone you cared for? How would Kaylie interpret a scarf or a necklace or a bracelet? What would she read into it? Pondering what he initially thought would be a simple chore had released a swarm of butterflies in his stomach. So he settled on what he knew best, resolving to find a dagger that might appeal to her. Something that he was certain would reflect his feelings for her. Or at least he hoped it would. After exploring several shops, he had finally found what he was looking for. A slim, blue-bladed, foot-long dagger with a bone-white handle and silver-colored crossguard. When the steel caught the light, it flashed much the way Kaylie's blue eyes did when she smiled. Pleased with his acquisition, he tucked the gift into his belt as he headed back to the public house.

Passing by an alley that crossed with his own, he stopped when he heard a cry. Taking a step forward, he peered into the shadows. The alley opened into a small square. A woman hidden by a hooded cloak stood against

the wall, a small blade in her shaking hand. Three large
men stood around her, keeping her back against the wall.
They hadn't drawn their blades yet, but it didn't appear that
they'd need to. Three to one, and the one with an inade-
quate dagger, left little chance of success to the woman.

Ignoring the warning that played across his mind,
including his latest discussion with Kaylie, Thomas
stepped into the alley. He had left his sword at the inn, not
thinking that he would need it this morning and that it
might attract unwanted attention. But now he missed the
comforting feel of the hereditary steel in his hand. Instead
he pulled the two daggers he wore, one on his leg, the
other on his hip, leaving Kaylie's gift tucked safely in his
belt. He approached quietly, the men unaware of his
presence.

"Come now, lassie. Put the blade away. You don't want to
hurt yourself."

Back against the wall, she kept the dagger in front of her,
sweeping it from side to side nervously as the three men
spread out around her, eliminating any avenue for escape.

"Stay back," she said in a frightened voice, the cowl
covering her head muffling her words as Thomas silently
approached.

"Put it away," repeated the man who appeared to be the
leader, large, heavy-set, and with the broken knuckles of an
accomplished brawler. "It could be fun. It'll certainly go
better for you if you listen."

The men tightened the semicircle, but still stayed out of
reach of the woman's blade.

Recognizing how the situation would likely play out, the
odds of breaking free clearly against the woman, Thomas
continued to ignore the warning going off in the back of his
head. Something didn't feel right, something was off. But he

didn't have time to give it more thought. He needed to deal with this quickly.

"Leave her be."

The three men jumped around, startled by Thomas' quiet words.

Realizing that it was only one boy who sought to intervene, the big man's swagger returned, despite the blades in Thomas' hands.

"Run along, lad," said the brawler, contempt dripping from his voice. "This is no business of yours. You don't want to get hurt."

Thomas ignored the dismissal. "I've made it my business. As I said, leave her be."

"And if we don't?"

"Then you deal with me."

The three men stared at Thomas for a moment, taking in his serious, confident expression as he balanced on his toes, reminding them of an animal prepared to strike. At first, they hesitated, sensing something about this quiet intruder that made them uneasy. Then they laughed in an attempt to rebuild their courage, remembering their advantages in numbers and size.

The man closest to Thomas, a hulking fellow with more fat than muscle, tried to end things quickly, lashing out with a metal baton he had been holding against his leg. Designed to crush a man's skull, the baton missed Thomas as he danced back easily and avoided the blow. His attacker had overextended with his swing, and Thomas had no intention of giving him a chance to recover.

Stepping forward in a flash, he drove his dagger between the man's ribs, then slid it across to his belly. The man's eyes expanded first in shock and then debilitating pain. Dropping the baton, his hands went to the wound of blossoming red as he sagged to the cobblestone streets and tried to keep his guts from escaping.

His two companions stood rooted to the courtyard stones in shock, not expecting what had just happened. They didn't have long to ponder it, as Thomas attacked with astonishing speed. The skirmish lasted just seconds, as Thomas' daggers whipped out to mark each man in a half dozen places before the two ruffians, blood dripping from their arms, chests and legs, realized that they had bitten off more than they could chew. Seeing that their opponent had left the way to the alley clear, they each took one of their fallen comrade's arms and dragged him toward the main street, weapons forgotten, as they sought to escape the deadly whirlwind that they had just encountered.

Thomas let them go. He had never intended to kill them, not wanting to become involved with the local authorities. He had simply hoped to drive them away from the woman. His goal achieved, he wiped his daggers with a piece of cloth ripped from the shirt of the attacker who had slid along the wall, then sheathed his blades.

He had barely let go of the hilts of his daggers when he was forced back a step, the woman having dropped the blade with a clatter and rushed to him, her arms encircling his neck, her head, still covered by the cowl, resting against his chest. Her scent, a mixture of honey and lavender, teased at his memory of a time not too long in the past. But he didn't have the chance to focus on that unexpected discovery.

"Thank you," the woman whispered into his chest. "I don't want to think about what would have happened if you hadn't stopped to help."

"I was glad to," replied Thomas, his hands reaching for her wrists as he tried to extricate himself from her grasp in the nicest way possible. But the woman was having none of it, her hold on him actually becoming tighter. The warning in the back of his head grew louder, but he didn't understand the cause because he didn't sense an obvious threat.

"A reward is certainly in order," said the woman. Finally releasing Thomas, her arms slipping from his neck, she stepped back and pushed her hood down.

Thomas gazed at her in surprise. "Corelia?"

Then his hands went to his throat as a misty darkness began to seep into him, one that dulled his senses and sapped his energy. She had latched a collar of black stone around his neck, and he could feel the instrument draining his strength. He tried to pull it off his neck, but the collar held, and with each tug on the shimmering rocks, the black mist that swirled in his head sped faster and faster, becoming a churning mass of darkness that crushed any independent thought that tried to find purchase in Thomas' mind. His strength, both physical and mental, waned. It was as if his consciousness was being pushed into the very back of his brain, and he was looking at himself and the world around him through a thick fog.

"So good to see you, Thomas," laughed the Princess of Armagh. The cowering young woman was gone, replaced by a more commanding presence, a calculating smile curling her lip. "And thank you so much for your help. Why don't you take a nap, my Highland Lord, and we'll talk again later about how I plan to pay you for your kind service."

Her words drifted over him as he sank into the darkness that pulled at him. He struggled desperately against the magic that continued to seep into him, but to no avail, his ability to grab hold of the Talent taken from him. As his eyes closed involuntarily, Thomas fell to the cobblestones, the black mist consuming him.

9

LETTING GO

The clash of steel rang throughout the enclosed courtyard, startling several birds from their nighttime roosts among the joists. The two opponents circled each other warily, a few seconds of blade scraping against blade followed by a longer period of time when the two men tracked each other's movements, knowing one another so well -- their tendencies with the sword, how they preferred to attack and defend -- that these frequent sessions usually ended in a stalemate, as neither could find the opening that they sought.

Gregory Carlomin, King of Fal Carrach and recently named High King, though he hoped that the latter was only a temporary responsibility, was a large man, both tall and broad, and his years of handling a sword were evident. It was on the battlefield that he felt most comfortable, not in a throne room. But what he preferred in life wasn't always his to have. His short beard, once black and now speckled with more salty whiskers than he would care to acknowledge, complemented his short, curly, black hair. Years before he had looked like a rogue, his eyes always smiling and open, his grin frequent. At least, that's what his wife had told him. Upon her death more than a decade before, his eyes had become sad and his smile rarely evident. But in the last few months that had changed somewhat, a spark of fun, of life, returning at certain, perhaps not unexpected, moments.

Kael Bellilil opposed Gregory in the training circle. A head taller than the King of Fal Carrach, he had the grizzled expression of a veteran soldier and the scars to prove it. Completely bald, and with a scar running across one half of his neck from his right ear to his windpipe, the joke among the Fal Carrachian soldiers was that to win a combat Kael simply had to stare at his opponent with his unnerving, flat eyes. A sword wasn't necessary with such a frightening countenance. No one would repeat such a joke to Kael, of course. He was the best swordfighter in Fal Carrach, which was why he was that Kingdom's Swordmaster. He had guarded Gregory's back for twenty years, and Gregory could not think of anyone else who could do a better job.

The two continued to glide in a slow circle, eyes intent on the other's, blades held at the ready. In an instant, Gregory led with his right leg, lunging forward with his blade extended. Kael twisted deftly in response, sweeping his sword down to deflect the blow. But midswing Gregory shifted his attack, bringing his sword up in a low backhanded strike that would have dug into Kael's exposed side. But the slash never connected, Kael spinning out of the way just in time, swinging his blade up with two hands to catch his king's steel on his own.

Gregory and Kael stepped back, nodding to each other in respect, then starting their slow, circling dance once again. Sweat dripped from their brows and their limbs had begun to feel heavy. They had been at it for more than an hour, yet as was the case so often during their training sessions together, neither had yet to gain even a touch on the other, and neither wanted to be the first to ask for a break.

"Are you two done, yet?" asked a strong, husky voice. "The sun is almost up, and we have important matters that need to be addressed."

Sarelle Makarin, Queen of Benewyn, stood in a shaded alcove next to a tall, ascetic man who wore the full-dress uniform of the Armaghian Home Guard. With the removal of Rodric Tessaril from the throne of Armagh, General Brennios had stepped forward to lead the Kingdom and had quickly become a staunch ally of Gregory and Sarelle as they sought to prepare the eastern Kingdoms for the expected onslaught from the north.

Sarelle was a beautiful woman, preferring green dresses that set off her auburn hair. On this day she wore riding skirts, having just returned from her daily circuit of the surrounding countryside. The flush of her cheeks from her early morning ride caught Gregory's attention. It was because of Sarelle and the time that they had been spending together that Gregory's eyes had begun to display the spark of enthusiasm that had been missing for so long.

Gregory grinned at the summons, captured by Sarelle's dazzling smile. Both he and Kael sheathed their swords and approached after grabbing towels to wipe the sweat from their faces and arms.

"Good morning, High King Gregory," said General Brennios.

"I told you not to call me that, Brennios," the Fal Carrachian ruler grumbled.

"Yes, my High King," General Brennios answered, a twist of his lips suggesting a smile.

"My, my," said Sarelle. "It seems that our austere Armaghian regent has a sense of humor after all."

"At my expense," said Gregory.

"Yes, my High King," Brennios confirmed.

Sarelle and Kael couldn't hold back a laugh, Brennios following suit, until Gregory, his face at first a thundercloud, had no choice but to smile as well.

"You seem to be in a good mood this morning, Brennios."

"Indeed, King Gregory," his normally serious expression returning quickly. "I spoke with Toreal just a few moments ago. The final shipment of supplies is due at the docks sometime this afternoon. The Home Guard will be ready to march by the end of the week."

"Excellent," said Gregory. "Toreal is comfortable managing Eamhain Mhacha on his own?"

"Yes, King Gregory," confirmed Brennios. "I'll leave a company of soldiers here in Eamhain Mhacha, but I doubt that he'll have need of them. With Rodric expelled from the Kingdom, the city has changed dramatically in just a few months, and all for the better. The people have enjoyed and made the most of their newfound freedom. Trade has increased fourfold and public works projects under Toreal's direction have restarted."

"That's good to hear," said Sarelle. "And that's good for everyone. All the Kingdoms will benefit from more commerce."

"Indeed, Queen Sarelle," agreed Brennios. "My thanks once again to you, King Gregory, for putting us on this path. Rodric had left Eamhain Mhacha to its own devices, not caring if it crumbled to the ground so long as he achieved his own objectives."

"You give me too much credit, Brennios. I simply offered

a few suggestions, many of which came from Queen Sarelle. You and Toreal have turned these few ideas into reality."

Brennios nodded, though clearly, he thought that the King of Fal Carrach deserved more acknowledgement than he was willing to take.

"I have news from Rendael as well," said Sarelle. "He's already moving south and will meet us in two weeks' time near the Corazon River and the Clanwar Desert."

"That's good to hear," nodded Kael. "Armagh, Kenmare, Benewyn, Fal Carrach and the Highlands. That will give us a fighting chance at the Breaker."

"That's all we can ask for," said Sarelle. "Now gentlemen, if you don't mind, I need a few minutes to speak to King Gregory alone."

Brennios and Kael both offered nods of respect before marching off to their next tasks, though Gregory couldn't help but see the big grin that Kael gave him before he turned on his heel and left the training ground.

"Will you walk me back to my chambers, Gregory?" asked Sarelle, who had placed her hand on his forearm and was already guiding him in that direction. "I need to wash and change clothes before the day truly begins."

"Of course," he replied, his face turning redder from her touch than it had that morning even with his exertions in the training circle with Kael. "What did you want to discuss?"

Sarelle chuckled, her throaty laugh sending a surge of heat to Gregory's chest. "Must we talk about something?" she asked. "I was simply hoping for an early morning stroll."

Gregory smiled and nodded, though he knew that there was more on Sarelle's mind than she had divulged. She never did anything without a purpose. "Of course."

The two monarchs took their time as they meandered

through the halls of Eamhain Mhacha, simply enjoying one another's company, Sarelle's hand sliding from Gregory's forearm to take his hand in her own. But Sarelle could tell that something was bothering Gregory. She could read his moods. When she had first met him upon assuming the throne of Benewyn after the death of her sister, Sarelle had been taken by his quiet stoicism. There was a strength in Gregory that she had found in few others, along with a moral compass that guided him even when following it would make his life more difficult than it needed to be. She had been enamored with him just minutes into their first conversation, but at the time he was dealing with the death of his wife and the need to raise his daughter on his own. Over the years, they had grown closer, and she had learned much to her delight that Gregory, although he initially seemed oblivious to her suggestions, returned her affection. However, he was a bit more reserved than she was and less willing to make his feelings known. Having reached the door to her chambers, she turned to face him, pulling him closer in the same movement.

"What's worrying you, Gregory? I can tell you have something on your mind."

"It's nothing," he replied, not wanting to burden her.

Sarelle gave Gregory a sympathetic smile. "You cannot hide it from me. I know you too well now. Kaylie?"

"Yes," Gregory sighed, his fears for his daughter, so carefully pushed to the back of his mind, now rising to the surface. "I know she can handle herself. Kael tells me she's a more accomplished fighter than most of my soldiers except for perhaps just a handful. I just worry about her. I wish she would have talked to me before she went after Thomas."

"That's understandable," said Sarelle. "She should have spoken with you. And if she did, what would you have said?"

"No, of course," Gregory replied. "That it was too dangerous."

"I may not be a parent, but I understand your fears. I know this is difficult, but remember that your daughter needs to do this. If she is to become the person that you want her to be, the person that she wants to be, this is something that she must do on her own. It's not a matter of proving herself to you. It's more a matter of proving herself to herself."

Gregory nodded reluctantly, his frustration plain. "I understand. It's just not an easy thing to accept knowing the dangers that she faces and what approaches for all of us."

Sarelle smiled again in sympathy. "Your daughter is a capable, strong young woman. And remember, Thomas is with her. He will do all that he can to keep her safe."

"Of that I have no doubt," said Gregory. "I just wish we could do more for them."

"We're doing what we can. Thomas explained why he must find the Key. Kaylie will help him do that. We will be ready for when they return. Once Thomas has the Key, I believe larger events will overtake us, and we must be prepared for what's to come."

"You seem exceedingly confident that Thomas will succeed."

"How could he not?" replied Sarelle. "That young man has a determination that I have yet to come across in anyone else. Besides, with Kaylie at his side, how could he fail?"

"There is that," agreed Gregory, his smile lightening his load.

Seeing the change in his expression, Sarelle smiled as well, but this time for a different reason. Leaning against the King of Fal Carrach, her green eyes sparkling, she brushed her lips first across his cheek and then his lips before stepping back and pushing open the door to her chambers with her hip. Her eyes never left Gregory's as she walked over the threshold. Gregory stood there for a moment, breathing in her scent and remembering the touch of her lips, before following after the Queen of Benewyn and closing the door tightly behind him.

10

UNWILLING ALLY

Kaylie stalked through the streets of Laurag, the ever-present crowd parting before her like a ship's keel cutting through deep water. Oso stuck to her side, Aric and several other Marchers following after and widening her wake with their grim expressions. She had found the ship captain Torlan had spoken of. Brienne had been as described, her colorful clothes and gregarious manner making her easy to locate. The ship captain had confirmed that she had agreed to terms with Thomas that morning. But since then there had been no sign of him anywhere in the surrounding neighborhood, other than a metalsmith who said that a young man matching the description Kaylie had given him had purchased one of his pieces several hours before.

Clearly, Thomas either had forgotten or ignored their conversation aboard the *Waverunner* before docking in Laurag, and that bothered her to no end. But what irritated Kaylie even more at the moment was her confusion about why she had kissed him just a few days gone. She remembered when she first saw Thomas at the Eastern Festival, participating in the archery contest and defeating Ragin Tessaril, son of the former High King, in the final round of the competition. Thomas was not handsome in the traditional sense, and not tall like the other boys and men attracted to her, either because of her looks or more commonly the fact that some day she would assume the throne of Fal Carrach. So why was she so attracted to him when half the things that he did drove her crazy? Yes, he was brave, steadfast, intelligent, even funny. But he was also stubborn, hard-headed, difficult … she growled in irritation. Why couldn't he have done as he had agreed?

"If he doesn't turn up soon, I'll have his hide," muttered Kaylie for what seemed like the hundredth time.

"We'll find him," responded Oso, his sharp eyes scanning the busy streets. Though he said it with confidence, he was worried. Admittedly, Thomas did things his own way. But something about this entire situation didn't sit well with him. "I'm sure he had good cause for taking this on by himself."

"You're certainly quick to support him," snapped Kaylie, allowing her anger and fear to get the better of her for just a second.

"Thomas is the best friend you could have," said Oso, ignoring the sharpness of her words, understanding they came from Kaylie's own worries. "I'd lay down my life for him. He's certainly risked his for mine more times than I can count. And I'd hate to have him as an enemy."

"Why do you say that?"

"Because he's an implacable foe. In my experience, his enemies tend not to live very long."

Oso was going to say more, but they were interrupted by

a short man who stepped abruptly into their path from a side alley. He dressed like a merchant, his jacket and pants conservatively cut and dark in color, but Kaylie's keen eye picked through his appearance in an instant. There was something about this man -- the way that he moved, how his eyes flitted about in every direction in search of what she didn't know -- that suggested that he had been looking for them. Used to the intrigues of a royal court, she assumed immediately that he was one of the many spies loyal to one of the two Inishmore houses competing for this Kingdom's throne, but which one she didn't know ... yet.

"My good sir and lady," began the man, bowing so low it seemed that his head eventually would touch the cobblestones.

"Can we help you?" asked Oso, his irritation clear. He had more important things to focus on at the moment.

"I'm but a simple merchant," the man began. "Nolan is the name. I had heard that some Highlanders had entered the city, and I hoped that I might run across them. There has been so little trade between the Highlands and the Kingdoms of the west. I thought that this might be an opportunity to develop a relationship that would be of value to you, and to me, of course. I seek only a conversation, my good sir."

Kaylie examined Nolan closely. Sweat trickled down his brow, despite the coolness of the day. And there was a wariness about him, his eyes still roving every few seconds, as if he worried that others watched him. He was likely right to do so, as she had no doubt that unseen eyes had tracked them since they had left their inn that morning.

"I have many relationships that would benefit us both, I think," continued Nolan. "Many goods to trade -- some staples, some exotic -- and if I don't have an item of interest,

I can find someone who does. Perhaps we could talk more about your purpose here in Laurag and what you may be seeking? I had heard tell that there was another among your party, another young man, not quite as large as you, though." Nolan gestured toward the bulky Highlander who loomed over him, his slightly shaking hand testifying to his nervousness. "Is he the one I should perhaps be speaking to? I've been told that he's someone of some importance."

A warning bell went off in Oso's head, the large Highlander fixing the smaller Nolan with a honed gaze. He glanced quickly at Kaylie and saw by the tightness of her bearing that her suspicions mirrored his own.

Oso's hand shot forward, grabbing Nolan by the collar. He lifted him off the ground, ignoring the man's startled screech, and brought him into the small alley from which the so-called merchant had just emerged. The large Highlander pushed the trembling Nolan up against the wall, Kaylie crowding close, her dagger in her hand. The other Marchers followed, hands on the hilts of their swords, blocking the alley so that Oso could do what was needed without being disturbed.

"What happened to Thomas?" Oso asked, the menace clear in his voice, the point of Kaylie's dagger digging into the man's side and drawing a thin trickle of blood that stained his shirt.

"I know nothing of this Thomas," sputtered Nolan, the fear in his voice raising it an octave. "Is he the one missing from your party?"

That slip confirmed Oso and Kaylie's suspicions. If Nolan was, indeed, a merchant, he likely traded in information. Her dagger dug more deeply into Nolan's gut. He grew even more terrified, his shaking becoming almost uncontrollable despite the small man's best efforts. Oso's strong grip on the back of his neck had tightened, sending sharp pains down his spine. Nolan struggled a bit, but it was a perfunctory and useless effort, his fear overwhelming him, a single squeeze of the large man's hand eliciting an unprompted but slightly strangled scream.

"What happened to him, little man?" whispered Oso, his fingers shifting to the front of his neck and squeezing more tightly, making it more difficult for Nolan to breathe. "You're asking a lot of questions, wanting answers. We want answers as well, because it seems like you have information that we need."

Kaylie withdrew the knife from Nolan's side, allowing him to see his blood on the tip of the blade. Nolan's eyes fluttered, threatening to roll back in his head, and Kaylie feared that he was about to faint, so she quickly lowered the dagger out of his sight.

"Who do you work for, Nolan? And why are you so interested in Thomas?"

"I'm just a merchant," gasped Nolan. "You have no right ..."

Oso's hand shifted once again, tightening even more around his throat and cutting off his words.

"You're a spy," said Kaylie, her voice hard. "I won't ask again. I'll simply leave you to my large friend." She gestured toward the savagely grinning Oso. "Why are you interested in our friend?"

Nolan was finding it more and more difficult to breathe, his struggles for air becoming obvious. Unable to speak, his face shifting in color from red to purple, finally he nodded his head. Kaylie took it as a sign that he was ready to cooperate, motioning for Oso to release him. Nolan fell back against the wall and slid down to the street, rubbing his throat and struggling for breath. The Marchers closed in around him, and he knew that he had no chance to escape.

"You're right, you're right," croaked Nolan, gulping air hungrily. "But I am not a spy. I am an agent. Spy has such a negative connotation."

"Little difference, little man," rumbled Oso.

"Who do you work for?" asked Kaylie, kneeling down so that she was eye to eye with him. She brought the dagger back into view, reminding Nolan that his blood marred the sleek steel, and that more could be drawn if necessary.

"Lady Colasa," answered Nolan in a croak.

Kaylie stared at the small man a bit more sharply. Lady Colasa was one of the last claimants to the throne of Laurag, strong with the people if not the nobles. They had learned that much from the conversations running through the common room of their inn the night before.

"And she sent you here why?"

This time Nolan didn't hesitate with his answer, seeing the storm cloud on the large Highlander's face about to explode and not wanting to be the cause of it. "Your friend was taken. She wanted to know why, and whether he would be of use or possibly a hindrance to her in her fight for the throne."

Nolan looked at Kaylie and Oso with pleading eyes. "Truly, that's the only reason I approached you. That's all that matters now in Laurag. Two claim the throne. Until only one remains, all that happens in the city could be of value to one or the other as they seek to strengthen their claim."

Kaylie stood, gesturing at Nolan with her knife. "On your feet. It's time to go."

Nolan stared at her, his fear etched across his face. He worried that his usefulness may have come to an end, and that they planned to take him to a part of the city where no one would care what happened to him and where his remains would never be found.

"Where are we going?" he whispered in alarm.

"To the one you serve, of course," said Kaylie. "Take us to Lady Colasa."

11

GAME PIECE

Thomas struggled to open his eyes, his thoughts and dreams spinning in a confusing and undecipherable swirl. It felt like a dark cloud of grey and black had been draped over him, and he couldn't find a way to escape it. His mind darted to wherever it seemed a small opening of light might appear, but each time he thought that he had found a stream of brightness in the gloom, the sought-for ray of opportunity, it disappeared just as he arrived, the heavy weight of the surrounding murk collapsing on him again.

"Wake, Thomas," a voice called from the distance. "Wake, my sweet. I command it, and you must obey."

The words drifted into his consciousness and slowly, ever so slowly, lifted him out of the disorienting, billowing cloud. His eyes opened to a burst of sunlight coming through the open balcony doors, the drapes pulled to the side. Not knowing where he was, he tried to recall the last few items in his memory, but it was a doomed task. Squinting as his eyes adjusted to the bright light, he pushed himself up on the soft bed, leaning back against the headboard. As the sheet was pulled away by his movement, he realized that he was wearing only his underclothes.

Although his eyes were open, the heavy weight that had kept him in darkness remained. He raised his hands to his neck, feeling the collar of black stone that had been slipped onto him in the alley. The darkness that had consumed him had settled there within the necklace. He gave the collar a tug, searching in the back for some clasp, but he found nothing. There was no break or catch in the chain. There was no way to remove it.

"Simply accept it, Thomas. Knowing you and your stubbornness, you will try and try again, and thereby only succeed in frustrating yourself. Once affixed, the collar can never come off. The sooner you understand that the better off we will all be."

Thomas dropped his hands, turning his head toward the voice. The voice that had surprised him in the alley.

Corelia Tessaril, daughter of the former High King, and once a possible heir to the throne of Armagh, walked seductively into the room from the balcony. The morning sun played off her golden hair, the sheer, silk dress she wore flowing across her body with every step and revealing more than it should. For a moment, her beauty transfixed Thomas. But then he remembered that there was more to Corelia than just her elegance and allure. She was dangerous, often ruthless and clearly reckless.

"Why am I here, Corelia?"

His question was sharp, his anger obvious, but it had little impact on the woman as she stopped at the side of his bed. She gazed down at his body, noting the scars on his chest and arms. She smiled appreciatively, her tongue running across her lips as if she gazed down at an object that she had desired desperately and, upon gaining it, had moved on to considering how to use it to her best advantage. Thomas fought the urge to pull the blanket over himself, instead struggling to control the red that threatened to break out on his cheeks. He would not be cowed by Corelia's challenging, suggestive stare.

"It's quite simple," said Corelia, sitting on the side of the bed, her hip pressed against his thigh. Her predatory gaze slowly ran from his toes up his body to finally stop at his eyes. "I play a dangerous but simple game now that father has lost the Kingdom. In this game, if I am to attain what I want, I must play the pieces that I have."

"So I'm now a piece."

"Yes, Thomas. You are, indeed. In fact, you could be the most important piece of all."

"And if I choose not to be played?"

Corelia looked at him for a moment, a twinkle in her eyes, before she let out a husky laugh, her hand rubbing his leg gently.

"Oh, Thomas. You are such a delight. You should know better, shouldn't you? Lord of the Highlands, feared warrior who freed his homeland against all odds, then took the fight into Armagh itself. Sylvan Warrior and master of the Talent. Can't you feel it? Haven't you figured out the trap that you so conveniently fell into?"

Corelia's words cut him to the quick, his fears rising. Unbidden, his hands went back to the collar of shining black onyx. He had failed to remove it physically. Now he tried to do so with the Talent. But that proved to be another exercise in frustration. Though he could sense the Talent, it was just beyond his grasp. He couldn't touch it. It was as if a glass window stood between him and the natural magic of the world, and he couldn't break through no matter how hard he pounded on the barrier.

"What have you done?"

"As I said, Thomas, you are now a piece to be played in my game. Your strength, your cunning, your power ... they are all mine. You will do as I tell you when I tell you."

"And if I don't?"

"Thomas, really? Must we go through this in such excruciating detail? I can see it in your eyes. You know the truth, you simply don't want to accept it." Corelia rose from the bed, straightening her dress. "The black collar was a gift. From someone you know, perhaps? Malachias was quite clear about its power. Once affixed, it cannot be removed. And the one charged with control over the collar controls the wearer. No matter what you may try, no matter how hard you resist, you cannot fight me. You will do whatever I tell you to do when I tell you to do it. You have no choice. Whatever I require, the black collar requires."

Thomas fought to control his emotions, dreading the truth of her words. There had to be a way to remove the collar. There had to be! But he needed to learn more about it before he could even contemplate what options he might have. He decided to turn the focus of the conversation to see if he could discover anything that might be of use to his efforts to escape Corelia's grasp.

"Do you understand the risk that you take, Corelia? Do you understand the consequences of allying yourself to the Shadow Lord?"

For a brief moment, a look of fear passed across her face. But as quickly as it was there it disappeared.

"I understand better than most, Thomas," she said quietly. "Remember, my father made this alliance years ago, so it's nothing new. It's simply more personal now. I know the risks, and I know and look forward to the rewards."

"Maybe so, Corelia. But the Shadow Lord's rewards are

never worth the risk. And there is a difference. Now the one to pay the price for failure is you, not your father."

Corelia stood there for a moment, his words stinging. She sought to reply in a way that didn't reveal how his statement had affected her, but nothing came to mind. She was saved when a door in the far corner opened.

"Ah, the one to lead us to victory has awakened."

A tall, burly man, beard streaked with grey, well-made clothes stretching tightly across his rather large paunch, walked in. The man likely had been handsome when he was younger, but the years had not been kind, his extravagances with wine and food having taken a heavy toll.

Thomas took in everything about the man in seconds, quickly putting together the situation and the role they expected him to play.

"Lord Eshel," he said in a flat voice.

"Yes, young man, you have the pleasure of meeting me." His words came out in a laughing chuckle, but his eyes were hard, calculating.

A tall younger man followed, a sneer marring his handsome visage. He was about to say something, but Thomas' harsh glare blocked the words in his throat. Thomas was not surprised that Maddan Dinnegan had tied his fortunes, or what remained of them, to Corelia's coattails.

"As I said, Thomas, a piece to be played in my game. A difficult game, to be sure, perhaps even deadly." Corelia stepped away from him and back into the light of the balcony. "But a game that offers quite a pot if I win."

Thomas stared at them, unimpressed. Greed ruled them, yet at the same time fear pricked at them because of the partner that they had tied their fortunes to, try as they might to keep it under control.

"So I'm supposed to help Eshel win the throne of Inishmore. That will please the Shadow Lord, as he obviously has some alliance in place with you already. Once done, Corelia plays the harder game. She offers me to the Shadow Lord, and he decides whether to kill me or to allow you to use me to retake your Kingdom."

"The Kingdoms, actually," said Corelia nonchalantly. "Why not a High Queen? Just because it's never been doesn't mean it can't be."

"And you would expect to do that how? Many if not all of the Kingdoms wouldn't accept you."

"Think about it, Thomas. Political marriages are common, are they not? Once the Highlands is allied with Armagh, the other Kingdoms will fall in line. Quite simple, don't you think?"

Thomas nodded. "You seem to have everything figured out, Corelia. But you know what they say. The best laid plans ..."

"Yes, yes, I've heard it all before, Thomas," she replied, a touch of pique coming out in her voice. Corelia walked back toward the bed, Eshel and Maddan watching the exchange with interest. "Remember, Thomas, if you resist me, you will simply be a piece to be played." Her hand trailed along his leg, then up to his chest, tracing his scars. "But you don't have to resist. In fact, we could have a great deal of fun along the way. Political marriages don't always have to be political."

Corelia stepped away, moving toward the door, Eshel at her heels.

"Think about it, Thomas. You have much to gain, and even more to lose. Once Lord Eshel has Inishmore, I'm sure that the Shadow Lord would offer some leniency if he felt confident that you were firmly under my control. And I'd prefer not to waste such a perfect piece to the puzzle."

12

THE CHAR

"Anything we need to worry about?" asked Kaylie. "I wasn't expecting to come to this part of the city."

Kaylie followed right behind the stick-thin Nolan, who walked hunched over, though not from age. Every few paces he glanced back to confirm that Kaylie remained just a step behind him, her hand never far from her dagger. He had led them to the docks, then headed west along the water and beyond the massive warehouses, cranes, markets and merchant houses to a less traveled part of the harbor, a neighborhood to be avoided whenever possible that was known as the Char. Several years before a fire had swept through this section of the port. The remains of many of the destroyed warehouses and offices still stood, charred posts and scorched building frames standing tall as a testament to the tragedy that had occurred. With the leadership of the Kingdom and the city in disarray, and no one able to guess at how the struggle for power would play out, few had thought to rebuild, leaving this part of the city to the gangs, smugglers and less reputable businesspeople to make their way here, a twenty-block square that had become a wasteland with its own set of rules. The most common unofficial edict was also the most obvious: Whenever possible, the strong would prey upon the weak.

Several groups of young ruffians had approached as Kaylie and her party worked their way deeper into the charred remains of the harbor. But these toughs had moved away quickly, deterred by the tall Highlander who walked with a clear purpose and a frightening glare, a contingent of angry Marchers, hands never far from the hilts of their blades, surrounding them.

Oso shifted his gaze quickly from left to right, knowing that his Marchers did the same, looking for anything that could be a threat.

"We're all right for now," he said. "If there's anything to worry about, we'll have warning."

In addition to the Marchers encircling him and Kaylie, he had sent two squads into the Char. They provided more eyes and were close enough to help if there was a need for additional protection or a quick escape.

"You're not planning something you'll regret, are you, Nolan?" Kaylie's voice was brusque, tense. The stillness of the Char but for the inconsistent breeze drifting off the water made her nervous. The only sounds came from their whispered words and the Marchers around her, and though they barely made a noise but for the scrape of a boot on a loose cobblestone, the silence made even the smallest sound seem that much louder.

"No, miss," he replied quietly, cringing at the ice in her voice. "Just a bit farther."

Kaylie glanced around, not quite believing what Nolan had told her. All she saw were the husks of former homes, businesses and storehouses, the jagged beams and joists, the occasional couple of stories still intact but always lacking windows and revealing scorched gashes in the walls, that kept her on edge. After just a few more minutes of walking they arrived at their destination, or wherever Nolan wanted them to be. He had stopped in front of what used to be a tavern. The front door leaned to the side, leaving a gap to peer into the darkness beyond.

"Here? You're certain?"

Oso's suspicion was plain. Nothing seemed to be here but burned wood, ash and rats. His Marchers fanned out around the tavern, swords now in their hands.

"Yes, sir," replied Nolan, unable to keep the fear from his nasally voice. "It's a bit more than it seems."

Wanting to be away from these tall, frightening Highlanders as quickly as possible, Nolan stepped up to the porch that ran across the front of the tavern. Pushing gently on the handle of the broken door, Nolan wedged it aside and stepped into the darkness.

Oso and Kaylie glanced at one another, then Oso shrugged. Sword gripped tightly, he followed Nolan into the tavern. The large Highlander poked his head out of the pitch-black a moment later.

"It's all right," he said with a grin. "Aric, keep an eye out. We shouldn't be long."

Oso disappeared back into the tavern. With nothing else to do but follow, Kaylie sighed and stepped through the doorway, hand on her dagger just in case. A few steps in, she felt a cloth brush against her. Pushing it aside, she walked into a well-lit room. Though the outside of the crumbling tavern appeared dilapidated, the inside had been rebuilt. Several guards stood along the walls, eyeing the two visitors warily.

In the center of the room was a single table with three

chairs. Standing to the side was a waif of a girl, beautiful, graceful, her auburn hair curling at her shoulders.

"Princess Carlomin, you have nothing to fear. Thomas, Oso and I are old friends."

Surprised by the greeting, Kaylie stood there for a moment, shaking her head ever so slightly. Then she sheathed her dagger and grumbled a curse that only Oso could hear. How was it that Thomas seemed to know more lords and ladies in all the Kingdoms than she did?

13

BLADE AT HER THROAT

Thomas fought to maintain his concentration as he danced around the small room that had become his prison cell. Sweat dripped down his body, hair plastered to his forehead, as he slashed and stabbed, lunged and cut, jumping, spinning, and ducking against a series of imaginary enemies, as he sought to keep his skills with a blade razor sharp. But it was a struggle, his mind wandering despite his best efforts to work through the various fighting forms the ghosts of the legendary warriors of the past had taught him. He had been at it for more than an hour, having waited impatiently through much of the morning for the fog to finally lift from his mind to the point where he could actually connect one thought to the next.

First, he had tried for the door, only to discover that he could get no closer than a few feet before the black collar around his neck froze him in place if he tried to advance another step. No matter how hard he pushed himself, he could go no further. His body refused to obey his mind's commands. The same had occurred when he had attempted to walk out onto the balcony that provided a view of a finely mowed lawn, the jump down to the ground looking to be no more than ten or twelve feet. But no luck with that either. He could stand at the edge of the balcony, gaze out upon the dawning of what looked to be a cold, windy day, but that was as far as he could go. He couldn't actually step out onto the balcony. Then he had tried to reach for the Talent, and then again, and again, and again, until it had become no more than an exercise in frustration, the ephemeral barrier in his mind that allowed him to sense the natural power of the world yet prevented him from seizing it remaining firmly in place no matter how he attempted to force his way through. As his failures mounted so did his exasperation. But he could think of nothing else to try, and rather than spend the morning cursing and allowing his anger to paralyze him, instead he had turned his attention to something that he could do, though even that was proving difficult at times as his building bitterness at his own foolishness for ignoring Kaylie's warning played regularly through his thoughts, disrupting what little concentration he could achieve. When next he saw her -- if he saw her -- she had every right to take him to task.

Redoubling his efforts, Thomas increased the pace of his training, ranging about the small space as best as he could, his twin daggers a blur in his hands until he stopped suddenly, daggers still held tightly in his grasp, the sharp steel of both blades less than an inch from cutting through the shapely neck of the Princess of Armagh. Whether he had ceased his attack of his own volition, having sensed his warden entering the room, or because the magic of the collar required it, he wasn't certain.

Corelia Tessaril stood just a few feet into the room, her eyes wide with shock as she examined the steel that threatened to slice into her flesh. Shifting her gaze away from the shining blades, a chill swept through her as she took in Thomas' flinty gaze, his eyes hard, remorseless. Not able to bear the weight of her prisoner's stare, she allowed her eyes to track down his naked, sweat-streaked chest, remembering the many scars that she had traced there with her fingers just the day before. A smile touched her lips. She sensed his struggle, the war occurring within the Highland Lord. The fact that she was the cause of his turmoil absolutely thrilled her.

"Would you have done it if the collar hadn't prevented it?" mused Corelia, pleased with herself because her voice didn't waver.

Thomas stepped back, knuckles white on the dagger hilts, before he eased the blades back into the sheaths that he had placed on a small table next to his bed. "We'll never know."

Corelia smirked. "You certainly keep things lively, Thomas. Perhaps that's why I find you so intriguing. So intoxicating."

Thomas ignored her comment, his hard look measuring her. "Is it worth it, Corelia? The risk that you're taking?"

"It would be less risky if you thought more deeply about what we could achieve if we worked together willingly," said Corelia, who stepped close to Thomas, her hand running lightly down his chest despite the rivulets of sweat. "I understand your anger at the collar. But even if it can't be removed, if we were closer, if we were partners, there would be no need for it. It would have no meaning other than an affectation."

"You think that I would willingly work with you after all this? After what your father did to my family? To my Kingdom?"

"Thomas, you're making this all very personal,"

protested Corelia. "This is simply business on the highest level. If we work together, we can both achieve what we want, for ourselves and for our Kingdoms. Isn't that what you want?"

"There are other ways to protect my Kingdom, Corelia." Thomas remained still, his eyes focused beyond the open balcony doors that allowed a chill breeze to swirl about the room.

"Perhaps," said Corelia. "But you need to think more about yourself and what your future may or may not hold." Corelia reached up with a hand, turning Thomas' chin so that his eyes burned into hers. She ignored the glare, her eyes suggestive. "The path that I'm proposing could be fun for both of us and give you more than you could possibly imagine."

Corelia hoped for something, anything to indicate that he might be thinking about all that she had offered, but Thomas remained silent, his expression unchanging. She sighed. "I know you're taken with Kaylie Carlomin. I can understand why. I admit, she has spirit. But you must see, Thomas, that she can't give you all that I can."

Corelia leaned up, whispering into his ear, her lips touching his cheek. "If you choose the Princess of Fal Carrach, you will die. You cannot defeat the Shadow Lord. With me, you have a chance. What cause would the Shadow Lord have to kill you if you were allied to me? Think about what I can offer you. Power. Privilege. Respect." Corelia's lips trailed down to his neck, sending an uncomfortable shudder through Thomas' body that she couldn't help but notice. "Life. Maybe even love."

"How long did it take you to decide to sell yourself to the Shadow Lord, Corelia?"

Corelia stepped back, her smile disintegrating. "Stubborn. So stubborn that you fail to recognize the forest from the trees."

"And you think you can trust Malachias? Do you know who he really is?" This time Thomas stepped closer to Corelia, his intense eyes capturing her gaze. "He is the right hand of the Shadow Lord and has been so since before the Great War, exercising a dark power that only a few can imagine. He is not in the business of keeping his promises. The only promises he must keep are those that he makes to his master."

"I know who he is," objected Corelia, but Thomas ran right over her words.

"Malachias has but one goal. To remain the right hand of the Shadow Lord. Once he views you as a threat, he will kill you."

"You didn't think that had already crossed my mind?" asked Corelia, her voice growing more strident with every word spoken. "That's why I have you, Thomas. With the collar, you will protect me. You will keep Malachias at bay and aid me as I rise. With you, I will become the right hand of the Lord of the Shadow and rule the Kingdoms in his stead."

"Are you listening to yourself, Corelia?" asked Thomas quietly. "The Shadow Lord doesn't share power."

"No, but he gives power to those who deserve it, and he will give it to me."

Corelia stepped forward, pulling Thomas' lips to hers for a soft, brief kiss that Thomas did not return. She then turned slowly, swaying her hips provocatively as she exited the room. As Thomas watched her go, his grandmother's favorite saying played through his mind: "You must do what you must do." Thomas shook his head in irritation. With the collar affixed to his neck, what could he do?

14

ANOTHER FRIEND

Despite Kaylie's initial misgivings, there was something about Lady Colasa that put her at ease. She knew Eshel by reputation as an older, vain man, full of bluster and with an eye that was easily turned by a beautiful woman. But she didn't know Colasa. She had never even heard of her. She guessed that they were of a similar age. Colasa's eyes glittered in the candlelight, which added an alluring beauty to her features. Kaylie initially thought that those eyes were full of mischief, and perhaps that was the case on occasion, but a relentlessness lay there as well, a determination that had obviously served her well in her struggle for the throne of Inishmore. She decided that Colasa could be a formidable opponent, not only because of what she discerned through her quick, though incomplete, study, but also because of the respect and deference shown to her by her guards, which appeared to result from more than just a sense of loyalty to her family.

"Might I ask how you know Thomas and Oso?"

Colasa turned her penetrating eyes toward Kaylie, having been engaged in a quick conversation with Oso to learn why they had come to Laurag. Through her spies she had discovered that Highlanders were in the city as soon as the first Marcher's boots touched the dock. But she had not known that one of them was Thomas until now.

"My mother is a member of the Sylvana. She is responsible for the Distant Islands. My mother and I were at the Pinnacle when Thomas became a Sylvan Warrior. Although I have some small skill in the Talent, it does not compare to what others, such as you, can do with the natural magic of the world. As a result, I believe that I have been called to a different service."

"You can sense the Talent even when it's not in use?"

"Yes, but unfortunately that's about the limit of my abilities. Thomas is the strongest that I have ever come across, but your ability in the Talent is quite impressive as well, Princess," said Colasa. "Not many are stronger than you, though your strength is a bit untamed."

"I haven't had as much training as I would like."

"That explains it. It's a difficult skill to master, but well worth the effort, my mother likes to say. Have you been called to the Pinnacle yet?"

"Called?"

"Yes, called to become a Sylvan Warrior?"

"No, at least I don't think so. I'm not really sure what you mean." The thought that she could become a member of the Sylvana energized Kaylie, but it frightened her a bit as well. What would it require? She had never spoken to Rya or Thomas about it.

"Don't worry, Princess. I have no doubt that you will be visiting the Pinnacle soon."

"But how do you know? How will I know?"

"You will know, Princess. Have no fear."

The increasing abstractness of their conversation began

to irritate Kaylie, so she decided to shift back to a more important, timely topic.

"And you met Thomas and Oso because of the Talent?"

"Yes, Princess. As I said, my mother took me a few years ago to a gathering of the Sylvana at the Pinnacle. I met Thomas then, and we've visited the Highlands since, so I had the opportunity to meet Oso as well, though just briefly. I must say Thomas' grandparents, Rynlin and Rya, left a lasting impression. Very warm once you get to know them, but also very intense."

"That's a good way to put it. Rya is actually teaching me how to use the Talent. I wish I could spend more time with her." Kaylie chuckled, quickly shifting gears. "So if your mother is a member of the Sylvana, how is it that you're opposing Eshel? I didn't know the Sylvana involved themselves so deeply in the affairs of the Kingdoms."

Colasa's glittering eyes became even sharper. It reminded her of the predatory gaze of a kestrel. "My mother suggested it, actually. We come from a small Inishmorian House, but an ancient one with ties to many of the earlier monarchs before the time of troubles struck several centuries ago and the quest for the throne devolved into a free for all. That's more than can be said for Eshel. He's an upstart from a minor house, no more, but he is a deadly opponent. He prefers to negotiate through intimidation and the quick application of a knife's edge. Eshel has been in league with Rodric for quite some time. That's a dangerous alliance for Inishmore, even if our illustrious High King no longer holds his throne. My mother suspected where Rodric's allegiances truly lay, and she assumed that if Eshel had aligned himself with Armagh, the Shadow Lord wanted to expand his influence in my homeland by having Eshel take the throne. When we saw the stronger houses begin to fall in line with Eshel, we decided to take action. Someone needed to oppose his rise."

"So now it's just you and Eshel," confirmed Kaylie.

"Yes, but we are at a stalemate. Neither of us is strong enough to defeat the other openly, at least not yet."

"Ladies, perhaps we could get to the business at hand," interrupted Oso, his impatience growing. "Finding Thomas."

"We were just getting to that, Oso," replied Kaylie tartly. "Colasa and I needed to get to know one another a bit better before we took the next step." Oso, big as he was, tried to sink into his chair at the reprimand.

"I will help you," said Colasa. "I would do anything for Thomas. But I can't do it blatantly. That could lead to an all-out civil war with Eshel, and I am not ready for that, nor is my Kingdom."

"Not to worry," said Kaylie. "We would never put your claim at risk. If you could tell us where Eshel has taken Thomas, assuming you have some idea, we can take care of this matter on our own. Quickly and decisively."

15

FALSE BRAVERY

Thomas growled in frustration, his temper threatening to get the better of him. He wanted to strike out at something, anything, but he couldn't. He had tried once again to walk out onto the balcony to see if he might be able to jump to the ground and make his escape. But still he couldn't step out onto the stone that was less than a foot away. No matter how much he commanded his body to take that last step, it wouldn't. He could stand there and look out onto the terrace, enjoy the brisk touch of the wind, but go no further. He tried much the same with the door, testing to see how close he could get. He hoped that Corelia would think that a lock would be enough to keep him in his room, and that perhaps the power of the collar diminished if the distance between the one who wore the necklace and the one who controlled it grew greater. But as he strode toward the door, he had been forced to stop short, unable to walk the final step, not even able to extend his arm to reach for the knob. The collar Corelia had affixed around his neck had corralled him more effectively than the cage he had slept in while imprisoned in the Black Hole.

For the thousandth time in the last day, Thomas reached for the Talent. He wanted to howl in anger, but he refused to alert his captors to his distress. The Talent was there. He could feel it. But he could do nothing with it. Thomas closed his eyes and took several deep breaths, struggling to calm himself before finally regaining some semblance of control. He decided to try again. But rather than reaching for the Talent, instead he simply wanted to examine more closely the artifact that was preventing him from using the natural magic of the world. He could touch the thin chain of black, frosted onyx that shone like glass, feel the roughness of its texture, the impressions and imperfections marring each individual stone. But what could he do to try to destroy the barrier? There had to be something that might work.

His focus shifted when the door to his room opened unexpectedly. Thomas turned toward his visitors, taking in the wide bulk of Lord Eshel and the whip-thin Maddan, who kept his hand on the hilt of his sword as if he feared that Thomas could attack him despite the restrictions placed on him by the collar. Perhaps his concern was justified, mused Thomas. These two had visited him once before since he had arrived in this room, and Thomas had charged toward them. But to no avail. He had been forced to stop just feet away as he slid to the stone floor, the collar not allowing him to get any closer. A futile gesture, but certainly worth the effort. Both men had been completely unprepared for the rush, and he wouldn't have been surprised if Maddan had soiled himself. Norin Dinnegan's son played well at the role of brave fighter, but Thomas could tell that there was no substance, no solidity, to his character.

As if to prove that conclusion, Maddan stayed behind Eshel, almost hiding behind the portly lord and clearly demonstrating his discomfort. The Lord of Inishmore ignored the boy who had accompanied him reluctantly and stared at Thomas with an appraising eye. Thomas glared back at him, his expression shorn of emotion.

"You're not much to look at," began Eshel, hooking his thumbs into the belt that was so essential to keeping his breeches up, his expansive gut stretching the cloth dangerously.

"Neither are you," replied Thomas, unable to keep the barbed comment to himself.

Maddan smirked, and Eshel clearly took offense, his face turning a bright red. The Lord of Inishmore was not used to such impertinence. But he remained where he was. Apparently, he, like Maddan, was unwilling to take any chances by moving closer.

"I just don't understand it. Lord of the Highlands, you may be. But why are you so important? What hold do you have on the Princess Corelia?"

"I doubt that anyone has a hold on Corelia," Thomas replied.

"Don't be so sure of that, boy," said Eshel, continuing his assessment of the Highland Lord and confirming for himself that there was nothing remarkable about him. "Don't be so sure."

"We should just kill him now," suggested Maddan. "Be done with it. There's nothing that he can do for Corelia that I can't."

Eshel took a moment to consider the suggestion, unable to hold back a snort of laughter. "I find that highly unlikely," chuckled Eshel. He turned his gaze to the Highland Lord. "The Shadow Lord wants you dead. The boy hiding behind me speaks true about that. So perhaps we should, Corelia be damned. We could gain much by doing so."

"Your own deaths included," said a raspy voice. A black

shadow emerged from the balcony to darken the room. Both Eshel and Maddan took several steps backward, closer to the door. Thomas stood his ground. "The Highland Lord is to remain alive ... for now."

"But Malachias, would it not be better just to ..."

"You forget yourself, Eshel," said Malachias, who tugged the cowl from his bald pate, his black eyes hypnotic in their glow. "I serve at the right hand of our master. And as I said, the boy is to remain alive. For now."

"I understand, Malachias," said Eshel. "All I hope to do is humbly serve. I just think that ..."

Malachias stepped forward faster than a striking snake, his bony, clawlike hand taking hold of Eshel's throat and squeezing tightly. The fat lord gasped for breath. Maddan had pulled the hilt of his sword partway free from its scabbard, but he quickly slammed it back down when Malachias brought his deadening stare to bear on him.

"That was your first mistake, Eshel. You are not to think. You are simply to do. Do you understand?"

Eshel had reached up with both hands for Malachias' clawlike fingers, trying to dislodge them, desperate for air, but failing miserably to remove even a single digit. Unable to speak, he could only nod.

"Good. Now leave us. And stay clear of this room. If either of you are found here again, you will pay a price that may be too steep even for the likes of you."

Malachias released Eshel, pushing him away. Eshel would have tumbled to the granite floor if not for Maddan, who had no choice but to try to catch him otherwise he, too, would have collapsed in a jumble. Despite Eshel's substantial bulk, Maddan succeeded in keeping him upright, if just barely. Before Eshel could say anything else that might offend Malachias, Maddan pulled him from the room and slammed the door behind them, glad to be free of two individuals who terrified him.

The Shadow Lord's servant shifted his unsettling gaze onto Thomas, studying him like he was no more than a tool to be used.

"You resemble your grandmother." Malachias waited a moment to see if his words would lead to a reaction, but the boy's face remained a mask, his body motionless. "She is well, I take it? When last we met, it was not under the best of circumstances."

The Shadow Lord's servant became quiet, his thoughts apparently having drifted elsewhere. Thomas continued to assess his adversary, already knowing the long history between Malachias and Rya Keldragan and wondering how he could make use of it, but Malachias returned to the present before any ideas came to him.

"You have a knack for causing problems, boy."

"So I've been told." Thomas had concluded through his brief study of the wizened creature standing before him that there was a power to the man, if man he still was after serving the Shadow Lord for so long, that could not be denied. But there was a corruption, as well, that had burrowed into his very soul. What appeared to Thomas to be a wasting away. What that could mean, he didn't know. But it suggested a weakness, and that was something that he could employ in the future, if he was still alive to do so.

"A smart mouth won't help you here, boy."

Thomas ignored the comment, seeking to better understand the situation in which he found himself. "Why not get rid of me now? I can't touch the Talent, do anything with it. If I had my sword at hand, I probably couldn't use it against you." He raised his right hand and brushed his fingers across the shiny black onyx encircling his neck to drive home the point. "Your master does want me dead. He's tried often enough to make it so. Right now, I'm an easy kill."

"Yes, and with that collar you will remain so," replied Malachias in a scratchy chuckle. "There is no need to rush. If you must be eliminated, then what will be, will be. But if you prove useful, perhaps my master can be persuaded to employ you for his own purposes."

"You're pulling at straws, Malachias. You and Corelia both."

"Maybe. But then again, perhaps the risk is worth it. Whoever controls the collar, controls you. Controls what you can do."

Thomas stared at Malachias for almost a minute, the pieces finally coming into place. "You think that I can help you supplant your master," he said scornfully.

Malachias cackled, clapping his hands together contemptuously. "Why not? I have served the Shadow Lord for more than a millennium. I may not be as strong as my master, but I am not weaker than him by much. Not after all the centuries I have had to learn the Dark Magic that he gifted me. I am not fool enough to do anything drastic, but if the opportunity presents itself, I'd be a fool not to be ready. If you were to …"

The servant of the Shadow Lord left the remainder of his statement unsaid, knowing that the boy standing before him could complete it for him.

"If I were to defeat the Shadow Lord, then you can assume his place." Thomas shook his head in wonder at the arrogance of such a thought. "You realize, of course, that Corelia would still have control over me. If I can defeat the Shadow Lord, I can defeat you. Corelia will think of that faster than it took Eshel to escape you just a few minutes ago. She won't hesitate to remove any threat that could impede her from achieving her own goals."

"I would expect as much, boy. Thus, the need for her removal at the appropriate time, and with her gone, control of the collar would pass to me, since I'm the one who gave the collar to Corelia."

"Then I become your weapon, to do with as you will, if you don't kill me first."

"Well done, boy. Well done, indeed."

"You play a risky game, Malachias. Do you chafe so under the bonds your master has placed on you?"

Malachias stared at Thomas, his black eyes seething. "I have not been given what I've been promised, boy. I've only received empty words. I can only be patient for so long. After centuries of waiting, there is no guarantee that I will receive what I am owed. So, if it comes to it, I might just have to take what is owed to me, including your grandmother."

"My grandfather will have something to say about that."

"I do hope so. I've been wanting to kill that arrogant fool since before the Great War and look forward to being the one to slide a blade between his ribs."

Thomas' eyes burned brightly with anger, his body taut, ready to spring at his adversary, but knowing, as well, the uselessness of such an action while wearing the collar. It took him several long moments before he regained command of the emotions that churned within him. "Kill me now, Malachias. You're a fool to think such a plan could work."

"It might come to that, boy. I have no qualms about killing you. It's just a matter of when. But for now, I'll let you live."

With a sharp cut of his hand through the air, a swirling portal of black mist appeared before the Shadow Lord's servant. About to step through, he stopped, caught by Thomas' final words.

"You speak of what you're owed. That's all well and good. Just remember, Malachias, that I owe you a debt. For this collar. For so much more. And Marchers always pay their debts. Always."

16

ENTRANCE

"I can't believe that I let you talk me into this," said Oso.

"Be quiet," Kaylie whispered. "We're almost there, and Eshel has eyes and ears everywhere."

Through her network of spies, Colasa had learned that a young man resembling Thomas had been taken to one of Eshel's manors on the very edge of the city. At first Kaylie worried about how to gain access to the villa situated on a walled estate and home to a full company of the Lord of Inishmore's soldiers. Colasa offered a solution both simple and effective. Yes, Eshel's villa was heavily guarded, but she explained that he had begun to act like a king, already playing at the role that he so desperately desired to make a reality. So every evening he welcomed visitors and other hangers-on, solidifying his alliances, searching for new ones, and seeking any advantage that he could find that would put him one step closer to the throne.

With that news, Colasa and Kaylie put together a straight-forward plan. Oso, along with Aric and a few other Marchers, would assume the role of bodyguards, exchanging their fairly well-known Highland garb for something that stood out a bit less. Assuming the role of an emissary from the east, Kaylie would visit Eshel during the evening and attempt to learn Thomas' whereabouts and perhaps even set the stage to free him. Colasa and her soldiers would be near the manor, along with the remaining Marchers, prepared to create a distraction if one proved necessary while keeping any other visitors at bay.

Kaylie and Oso rode in an expensive carriage with no markings that Colasa had acquired, Oso dressed in unaccustomed finery that made his skin itch. The Marchers protected the carriage, their eyes wary, postures stiff, as they approached the main gate and Eshel's soldiers. Once Oso announced who the occupant of the carriage was, however, any concerns about gaining entry to the grounds of the estate disappeared. The soldiers allowed them through with barely a glance, apparently accustomed as Colasa had said to the steady stream of visitors either seeking Eshel's favor or Eshel seeking theirs and unconcerned that anything untoward might happen.

As the horses pulled the carriage into the courtyard at the front of the mansion, Kaylie waited impatiently, but playing her part remained in her seat until the chamberlain trotted down the manor steps to open the carriage door. The Marchers had done as instructed, staying on their mounts, acting like the bodyguards that they were supposed to be.

"My lady, a pleasure to have you join us," said the chamberlain, a small man with wispy hair.

Kaylie ignored him, sweeping past the chamberlain as soon as he opened the door, Oso at her heels. "A pleasure indeed," said Kaylie, striding up the steps and forcing the chamberlain to scurry after her to catch up. "But we have little time for pleasantries, my good man. Take me to Lord Eshel."

The chamberlain ran by her down the long hall, hurrying past works of art affixed to the walls, guards posted in every doorway. The little man had every intention of reaching Eshel's audience chamber first to announce this beautiful and determined visitor, but the effort clearly taxed him.

"You seem to have grown into your role quite easily," whispered Oso.

"It was simple to do," she replied quietly, ignoring the art but taking note of the guards. "I can't tell you how many courtiers I have met in my father's court who have acted just like this."

"Self-important? Officious? Overall, quite annoying?"

"Yes."

Oso chuckled. "Just don't walk too fast. You don't want to give that chamberlain a heart attack."

17

MISCALCULATION

With a final burst of speed that appeared to take the last of his wind, the old chamberlain rushed into Lord Eshel's receiving chamber, Oso and Kaylie right on his heels. Fearing that she might announce herself, the chamberlain gathered what breath he had left to huff out the expected introduction.

"My Lord Eshel, the Lady Lissa of Fal Carrach, emissary of the Lord Norin Dinnegan. My Lady Lissa, the Lord Eshel, rightful ruler and defender of Inishmore."

His task done, the chamberlain backed out of the room wheezing for breath, shutting the large doors behind him.

Eshel stood in front of an ornate desk, bright moonlight streaming into the room from windows that lined the wall behind him. A library of rare books on the wall to the right, the spoils of battles past -- pennants, swords and spears -- on the facing wall, heads of beasts killed during the hunt stationed here and there about the large space. The chamber was designed to impress, to demonstrate his superiority. Eshel meant to take advantage of that, standing silently for almost a minute so that his visitors could take it all in, including himself.

Oso ignored everything around him except for the man who stood before him, assuming that Kaylie was doing the same. Oso measured the Lord of Inishmore in the space of a few seconds. His clothes were expensive, fit for a king, it would seem, but they couldn't hide the fact that he enjoyed the comforts and benefits provided by his wealth more than he should. A bully, spoiled and pompous, based on the arrogant gleam in his eyes. Oso doubted that the man before him had opened any of the books lining the wall, and his desk was not only too clean, but it was immaculate, not a paper to be seen. So he had others rule his lands for him. Eshel had assumed the part laid out for him at his birth, the trophies likely belonging to his father or other forebears. But what did that matter if he played his role to the hilt? He was just one step away from the throne of Inishmore. He didn't have to be a leader. He could simply pretend to be one and all the accoutrements of his rank would flow to him naturally.

Having decided that he had posed long enough, Eshel stepped forward, his swollen fingers leading the way as he ignored Oso and grasped his beautiful visitor's hands with his own.

"My Lady Lissa, a pleasure to have you here in my Kingdom." Kaylie couldn't help but notice what Eshel had said, realizing that it could be taken in more than one way. Although still opposed for the throne, Eshel seemed to have assumed the mantle of power already, at least in his own mind. "A very pleasant and beautiful surprise, if I may be so bold."

Kaylie tried to remove her hands, but Eshel's grasp was

too strong to allow for such a forced break to occur without some awkwardness.

"My Lord Eshel, a pleasure." Kaylie beamed at him, her smile exuding all the charm that she could muster. She presented herself as a courtier, and she knew exactly what to do based on her long experience in her father's court. How she stood, the tilt of her head, a hundred other small things designed to capture Eshel without him even realizing it. "I have heard much about you. To finally meet you in person ... well, all I can say is that the stories don't do you justice."

Oso found it difficult to hide his smirk, lowering his eyes to the stone floor out of necessity.

"That's very kind of you, Lady Lissa. And this gentleman?" Eshel glanced at Oso, a large presence beside the petite envoy, with some hesitation. Though dressed as a servant, he seemed anything but to Eshel, as if the clothes the hulking man wore chafed.

"Kylin, my bodyguard," replied Kaylie with a dazzling smile. "Traveling can be dangerous at times, so better to have someone you can trust at your side."

"Indeed," smiled Eshel, his eyes bright. "I can only imagine the dangers that could befall one of your beauty. Rest assured that here in Inishmore you are safe with me." His mind had already begun traveling down a path where his hopes for a closer connection to the beautiful representative who stood before him now increased by the second. Eshel finally released Kaylie's hands, and she prevented herself from wiping the sweat from the Inishmorian Lord's clammy palms onto her skirts, resigning herself to the discomfort with a barely concealed shudder of disgust.

"That is very kind of you, my Lord Eshel," she said, working hard to stay on task. "I bring you greetings from

Norin Dinnegan of Fal Carrach. He has watched your progress here with great interest. He is quite impressed."

Eshel puffed up like a peacock at her words. All knew of Norin Dinnegan, richest man in all the Kingdoms. His interests were not only economic, but also political. Having the support of a man like Dinnegan could do more for him than the assistance of several of the Kingdoms surrounding Inishmore. Perhaps even help him break the stalemate with his rival for the throne as the costs of his covert battle were becoming more severe and his resources were dwindling.

"Truly? That is a pleasant surprise. Is it because I entertain his son, Maddan? Spending time with that fine young man has been a pleasure." Eshel's lie came out smoothly, as he hoped that the beautiful young lady who could possibly unlock additional funds to support his fight for the crown hadn't noticed his brief delay in responding.

For a moment, Kaylie didn't know what to say. The news surprised her. Why would Maddan be here? At first, she feared that Eshel knew the truth. She and Rya had exposed and helped to thwart Dinnegan's plot to assassinate her father and take the Fal Carrachian throne. As a result, Dinnegan had lost most of his wealth and become a wanted man. But perhaps Maddan had not revealed that information, not wanting to embarrass himself and weaken his position with his host. And it would take quite a while for these rumors to make their way east. For Thomas' sake she needed to carry through with her plan come what may.

"No, Lord Eshel. Though Norin certainly appreciates your generosity in that regard."

Eshel strutted to his immaculate desk, leaning back against the edge and crossing his arms, believing that such a bearing allowed him to exude a sense of ease and power. To

Kaylie, it revealed his rather large belly, which fell well over his belt.

"Why would the great merchant and Lord Norin Dinnegan be interested in me?"

"For the obvious reasons, my lord. Trade, of course. Many of his business ventures are located in the western Kingdoms, Laurag in particular. He is always seeking friends wanting to work with him to the benefit of both."

"I am always in the market for new friends," replied Eshel, chuckling softly at his quip. His predatory leer suggested that at the moment he was more interested in becoming better, much closer friends with Kaylie.

She ignored his stare, though it made her skin crawl. "My lord will be pleased to hear that. I should note as well that he is also seeking friends of a different persuasion."

"What type of friends might those be?" Eshel asked with obvious interest.

Kaylie stepped forward, gliding elegantly across the room, Eshel's eyes fixed on her alluring movement. She placed her hands on Eshel's crossed arms, drawing closer to him. She had evaluated him within seconds of entering the room just as Oso did and she knew exactly which part of his body he thought with the most.

"Friends with grander ambitions," whispered Kaylie.

Eshel stared into Kaylie's eyes, captured by her beauty. For a moment he was speechless, his mind speeding down a thoroughly enjoyable path that proved quite distracting.

"Perhaps we could continue this conversation in private, then. Better to keep such a matter between us. If your man would be so kind as to wait outside?"

Kaylie considered the request for a moment, thinking that she might have overplayed her hand. That she may have been found out. But there was no guarantee that Eshel knew all that had occurred in the east. And the more she thought about it, the more she doubted that Maddan would have divulged his family's waning fortunes, as it would have decreased if not eliminated Eshel's interest in assisting him.

In for a penny, in for a pound, she thought. She had started this ruse. She needed to finish it if she wanted to help Thomas. She looked back to Oso, nodding. His eyes, a bit worried but accepting, flashed as he turned and exited the room.

Hearing the door close, Eshel leaned forward, his lips close to Kaylie's ear. "Now, my dear. You were talking about becoming better friends?"

COMPELLED

T homas awoke with a start from a dreamy haze that he had tried to escape but failed to, time after time. It was only because of the feeling that someone else was in the room that he was able to break through the fog that enveloped his mind and kept his thoughts the unconnected jumble that they had become since he had been collared.

He bolted upright in the bed, feeling a light pressure on his chest. Forcing his eyes open, it took a moment for him to adjust to the dim light of the candles that flickered in the corners of the room. He felt the fingers travel gently down his chest, trailing away as they brushed against his side and the top of his leg. The black onyx chain encircling his neck weighed on him, holding him in place.

"Good evening, Thomas."

He didn't bother to turn his head, recognizing the sultry voice. Corelia sat beside him on the bed, her hip pressed warmly against his own. Her hand went to his leg once again, this time drawing small circles on his thigh.

"Corelia."

He ignored her touch, or at least tried to, instead striving once more to grasp hold of the Talent. Yet despite his best efforts, he failed. Again. His frustration was shifting to despondency. He had yet to find a weakness that he could exploit to break the power of the collar.

"I know what you're doing, Thomas." Corelia spoke softly, almost a whisper. Her breath tickled his ear. "I can sense it through the collar. It won't work. You need to accept your new circumstances. If you do, it will be better for both of us."

"And if I don't?" Thomas' voice barely contained his anger.

Corelia's fingertips moved slowly up and down his thigh. His body began to grow warm, though he tried to ignore the effect his captor's attentions were having on him.

"Then I'll do what's necessary. And you'll do what I want."

The weight of the black chain around his neck felt like it had increased tenfold. Of its own volition, his right arm reached out, his hand settling on the back of Corelia's neck and pulling her closer. He tried to stop himself, to pull back, but he couldn't. He had no control over his actions. It was as if his body and mind had been disconnected. He was powerless against the Dark Magic of the chain. Then he was moving forward, his lips searching for Corelia's. He kissed her, gently. She returned the kiss with passion, crushing herself against him, her hands cupping his face. The heat between them grew. Even though he wanted to, he couldn't withdraw. He had no power over himself. Corelia controlled his actions. Controlled him.

After several long moments, Corelia finally leaned back, her hands still resting on his chest. Thomas felt the weight of the chain lighten. His arm fell to the bed as she rose from where she had been sitting to look down at him. Face flushed, cheeks rosy, a seductive smile played across her lips.

"But remember it doesn't have to be that way. This new relationship could benefit us both, so continue to think about what we discussed earlier. As I said, whether you want to or not, you will do as I command. So better to give in. To accept where things stand now. As you've just experienced, it might be more fun than you think. There is so much more that we can do ... together."

Thomas watched Corelia glide from the room, the silk of her dress clinging to her body. The door closed and he heard the lock click into place. With her gone, the weight of the collar lifted almost entirely, feeling now like no more than a necklace rather than a chain. Taking a deep breath, Thomas tried to clear his mind of the fears that threatened to engulf him. He had not wanted to do what he just did, but he had. If Corelia could make him accede to her wishes in this, she could make him do anything.

He got up from the bed and stood in front of a full-length mirror set near the balcony. There had to be a way to remove the collar. But how? No clasp was visible. Pulling on it had no effect, and it was so tight around his neck that twisting it in an attempt to break it or cut through it wasn't an option. He had already tried with his dagger to no avail. And using the Talent had proven ineffective. The collar didn't let him touch the natural magic that flowed through the world.

Cursing in anger, he struggled to master his rising anxiety. Taking a deep breath, trying to regain his focus, he decided to start over. To approach the problem from a different angle. He examined the black stone, stepping as close to the mirror as he could. The pieces, though imperfectly shaped, appeared flawless, shining brightly in the candlelight. No blemishes. No cracks. No chips. At least none that he could see, and his eyes were better than most.

Then a thought came to him. When he had escaped the Crag on the night of his grandfather's murder, he had been faced with a similar dilemma. He was trapped behind a steel door set in the stone and he was afraid to open it, not knowing if reivers, or something worse, waited for him on the other side. He had used the Talent, extending his senses through the tiny fissures in the stone, the cracks and imperfections invisible to the naked eye, to push the Talent through to the outside, until he had seen the small glade on the other side of the door that was free of danger.

Perhaps he could do the same here. Perhaps there was a solution that he hadn't considered. Corelia had left his mother's necklace, marking him as a member of the Sylvana, in place around his neck, likely not knowing its importance. Shaped like the horn of a unicorn, the very end, crafted into a point, was sharper than any blade he had ever held. Taking hold of the amulet, he tilted his head so that he could get a better view of the collar. Using the mirror as his guide, he went to work.

19

PREDATOR

"So tell me, my Lady Lissa. Your instructions from Norin Dinnegan. What were they?"

Lord Eshel had guided Kaylie to a couch hidden in a dim corner of the room. He sat close to her, his hands holding her right hand, his eyes fixed upon hers. She saw something in those beady orbs that worried her. Though he tried to come across as dignified, as a member of the ruling class, there was something baser to him, a foreboding that made her flesh crawl. She sensed that he was a predator. But not like a warrior. No, Lord Eshel preyed on the weak, on those who couldn't, or didn't, feel as if they could defend themselves. On those who feared the consequences if they came forward with the truth.

"Quite specific, my Lord Eshel." Kaylie tried to shift to her left and put some space between her and the Inishmorian Lord. But to no avail. He simply slid across the couch with her, staying close. "He wishes to offer you aid. He believes that Inishmore needs you, and that your ruling the Kingdom would benefit him as well."

"So he needs me. Isn't that right, my dear?"

"Indeed, my lord. He said as much before I left him."

"And you, my lady?"

"What, my lord?"

Kaylie looked at Eshel in some confusion, not understanding the question. But then she saw what was coming next. Her left hand slipped to her side.

"Need me. Do you need me, my Lady Lissa?" Eshel leaned into Kaylie, pushing his broad, pudgy chest against her, trying to force her down onto the couch.

"No, my lord. I most certainly do not!"

Eshel's movement stopped in an instant, as he felt the blade against his throat, amazement streaking through him. This woman from Fal Carrach had moved faster than he thought anyone could.

"Stand up, my lord. But slowly. I need you not at all, and I'm sure that you don't need my knife slicing your throat by mistake, no matter how much you may deserve it."

20

BEST LAID PLANS

Using the servant's hallway that connected the room that had become Thomas' personal prison to Eshel's private office, Corelia walked slowly, distracted, deep in thought, trying to make sense of the mix of emotions that warred within her. The more time that she spent with the Highland Lord, the more attracted to him she became. She admitted to herself that his response to her kiss could have been driven in large part by the magical collar she had affixed to his neck. But could there be something more to it? A desire of his own that Thomas could not suppress? If the circumstances were different, would the attraction between them be different? More natural?

Corelia scowled as she tried to force those thoughts from her mind. It didn't matter, did it? He was simply a pawn in the larger game that she played. If the time she spent with him proved to be more enjoyable than she expected, well, that was simply an added benefit. She had made her decision, chosen her fate. She was on a path now that she couldn't step off, acknowledging, if only to herself, the severe consequence if she did. She could still have Thomas, she knew. Perhaps not in the way that she might hope, the choice made of his own free will, but he would still be hers.

Still preoccupied and not bothering to knock, Corelia pushed open the door to Eshel's office. She had taken several steps in before she realized that all was not as she had expected.

"You!" Corelia froze in shock, never expecting the heir to Fal Carrach to be in Eshel's manor, much less holding a blade to the Inishmorian Lord's throat.

"You!" The blazing anger in Kaylie's eyes could have set a piece of paper on fire, but there were none to be found in Eshel's office.

Corelia gathered her breath and was about to scream for the guards when Oso slipped in behind her, a blade at her neck.

"Not so fast, Princess." Oso gently pushed his prisoner more to the center of the room. "Should I even call you that? Your father has lost his Kingdom, so what should I call you?"

"My choice would be arrogant bi ..."

"Now, now, Kaylie," interrupted Oso in a measured tone. "No need to go down that road."

"If you think you can escape ..." Eshel tried to add some bluster to his voice, but his fear made his words come out as no more than a squeak, Kaylie's blade digging deeper into his skin, a thin trickle of blood now dripping down his neck and staining the collar of his shirt.

"Escape isn't what they're after, you fool."

"Correct, Princess ..." Oso shook his head in annoyance. "We really need to figure this out. You're not a princess anymore. Former princess? Lady?"

"Oso, some other time," said Kaylie with some exasperation.

"Right, sorry. Take us to him, Corelia."

Noting the seriousness of Oso's expression, the deadness in his eyes, the former Princess of Armagh realized immediately that the large Highlander had no qualms about ending her life if she refused to obey. She knew of this Marcher. How he and Thomas were like brothers. She had no doubt that he would do whatever was necessary to free him.

"Back the way I came ..."

Before she could finish speaking, a hush fell over the room. Maddan Dinnegan, unaware of what was transpiring, entered through the door leading to the front of the manor.

"Lord Eshel, if I might have a moment of your ..."

Maddan stopped in his tracks, frozen for a moment, analyzing the situation. Then foolishly he began to pull his sword from its sheath, and that's when Kaylie's best-laid plans fell apart.

21

CHIPPING AWAY

Thomas stood in front of the mirror for almost twenty minutes, fighting to remain calm as a sense of urgency blossomed within him. He had selected what he perceived to be the weakest piece of onyx, though he really had no good way to tell, chipping at it carefully with the point of his Sylvan Warrior amulet.

At first, nothing happened. Not even a scratch. The point of the unicorn's horn seemed to have no effect, glancing off the hardened surface time after time. But after several dozen strikes, he noticed that his efforts were having some effect. Despite the density of the black stone, it was no match for the magicked silver of his amulet. Examining the necklace in the mirror, he discerned several almost invisible cracks or imperfections now marring the face of the stone. With every well-placed hit, a spark shot from the contact between the natural magic of the Talent and the twisted Dark Magic of the Shadow Lord, the two forces repelling one another.

He stopped for a moment, hearing what he thought were shouts from some other part of the manor. He couldn't really tell, as the room that served as his cell muffled the noise. But that feeling of time running out weighed upon him more heavily.

He closed his eyes and took several deep breaths to center himself, still holding his amulet, the warmth of the silver giving him hope. Reaching for the Talent for what felt like the hundredth time that day, he struggled again to control his irritation. It still felt like he was trying to catch a million drops of water at one time. The Talent was there, beckoning to him, wanting him to take hold, but still it slipped through his fingers. Shaking his head to clear his mounting frustration, he tried again, but this time instead of reaching for the Talent he concentrated on one small piece of the collar, where his amulet had chipped away a tiny, barely perceptible piece of the black onyx. To strengthen his focus, he placed the tip of his amulet against the scarcely perceptible imperfection.

Thomas smiled, wanting to shout with joy. But he controlled himself. He could feel the Talent again, finally, though it was such a minute stream that he could do almost nothing of consequence with it. No matter. He finally had something that he could work with. Maintaining his concentration, he used his amulet to force the tiny stream of the Talent into the small fracture that he had created in the black stone.

Slowly, ever so slowly, with an innumerable number of starts and stops, possible routes of success that ended abruptly and that required constant backtracking and starting over, the Talent wormed its way through the faults of that one small piece of onyx. Once the Talent found a foothold within that shiny, black stone, filling the invisible cracks and crevices, the natural magic of the world began to expand, the pressure building within the onyx as the Talent sought to find a way through.

"Thomas!"

Thomas opened his eyes, reluctantly releasing the Talent. Kaylie stood in the doorway, her hand guiding Corelia by the arm, her dagger pressed against the Princess of Armagh's back.

"Kaylie! Where's Oso?" He had no doubt that his friend would stay very close to her side with Thomas taken.

"In the other room. Eshel's guards are on to us, and Oso is doing his best to keep them off us."

"Then it's time to go." Thomas walked toward Kaylie, seeking his freedom, but he took only a few steps before he froze, unable to move. "Kaylie, the collar," he gasped.

Kaylie briefly glimpsed a flash of black around Thomas' neck, then turned her head at a shout and then a scream coming from Eshel's audience chamber. It sounded like Oso was more than holding his own despite being pressed hard by Eshel's soldiers. Nevertheless, time was of the essence. They needed to get in there to help him.

"Release him, Corelia," demanded Kaylie, needing Thomas free from whatever spell held him in order to make their escape. She pushed the blonde-haired beauty toward Thomas.

Corelia laughed throatily. "It doesn't work that way. Thomas is mine to command. He has no choice but to obey. Once affixed, the collar can never be removed. Never!"

Stepping behind Thomas, Corelia took on a look of concentration. Then she smiled, her eyes burning brightly with spite.

"Your meddling has come to an end, Kaylie," hissed Corelia. "You're going to pay for coming here ... with your life."

Able to move again, Thomas walked calmly to the bed, opening a chest that sat in front of it.

"Thomas, what are you doing? We need to get out of here." Kaylie was perplexed, not understanding why he was so slow to leave.

From the chest, Thomas pulled out his daggers. He slid the one with the white bone hilt into the back of his belt, then flipped the two that remained in his hands, pleased by the balance. Then he turned toward Kaylie, daggers held as he had been trained, walking slowly toward the Princess of Fal Carrach.

"Kaylie, get out," Thomas said through gritted teeth, his face twisted into a snarl. "I can't stop this. I can only slow it down, and not for long."

"What are you talking about?"

Corelia's laughter echoed in the small room. "The collar, you fool. Once affixed, it can never be removed. And it is attuned to me. Which means that Thomas will do as I say, when I say, no matter what it is. He will do whatever I command. Thomas is mine now, and there's nothing that you can do about it."

22

ARROGANCE

Oso took a step back, catching his breath during the short reprieve. The small doorway through which Kaylie had exited with Corelia had proven to be a boon, preventing Eshel's guards from attacking in force.

When Maddan Dinnegan had attacked, Oso had shoved Corelia toward Kaylie. The Princess of Fal Carrach had had no choice but to release Lord Eshel, who had scampered as quickly as his ponderous bulk would allow to safety, flopping into the manor's main hallway and gaining the relative safety provided by his soldiers. As a result, now the Inishmorian Lord directed the attack toward Oso from the safety of the other room.

But Maddan hadn't been so lucky. At first, he had taken several wild swings at Oso, almost as if he were warming up before a bout in the training circle. Then he tried several taunts, thinking that he could incite his towering opponent to do something hasty by offering several lewd thoughts about his mother. Much to Maddan's disappointment, Oso hadn't bitten, simply standing in front of the doorway, keeping an eye on the soldiers who had begun to stream into the chamber behind the Fal Carrachian youth.

Following that, Maddan had danced around in a semicircle, threatening to attack Oso, emboldened by the soldiers behind him, but never getting close enough to actually strike at him. Oso was more than happy to allow the boy who had interrupted their escape to continue doing whatever he was doing. It gave Kaylie more time to free Thomas and, most important to Oso, the fool blocked the soldiers who had responded to Eshel's call to arms from attacking him. And it didn't seem to bother Eshel's guards. In fact, the soldiers hadn't appeared to be in a rush to take him on. Whether because of his size and menacing appearance or the fact that they wanted to see what would happen to the beanpole in front of them waving his sword in the air, he couldn't say. Regardless, Oso was more than content to let the minutes slip by. But then, whether because of pride, arrogance or impatience, Maddan made the mistake of lunging at Oso, sword fully extended, and leaving his side open, not expecting the large Highlander to move so quickly in response. Oso had sidestepped the clumsy attack easily, burying his dagger in Dinnegan's belly. The son of the richest man in Fal Carrach now lay slumped against the wall, his eyes glazing over and his blood seeping out between his fingers onto the thick carpet.

Since then, the large Marcher had killed or wounded six soldiers, the men having no choice but to engage with him once the skinny lord had been eliminated as a threat. Now those soldiers' bodies blocked their fellow guards' path into the fight. And that was fine with Oso. If more than just a couple soldiers could come at him at the same time, his odds of survival would plummet drastically.

But that concern quickly lessened. Oso smiled, his confidence soaring. He could hear it now, coming from the main entrance to the manor. Aric and the other Marchers had figured out what was going on, likely when Eshel started screaming for his soldiers, and had joined the fray, complicating matters for the Inishmorian Lord.

Oso rubbed his sweaty hands on his pants, then grasped his sword once more. He approached the soldier who had just pushed his way into the room, stumbling over one of the bodies that lay across the threshold. With a quick thrust, Oso drove his blade through the flailing man's chest and then returned to his post by the door that led out of the office. He would hold as long as he could, and hopefully Aric would reach him in time. But Kaylie really needed to hurry.

23

PRICE FOR FAILURE

Kaylie stepped back from the advancing Thomas, her eyes never leaving his, dagger to her front. She slid behind a small desk to keep some space between them. She had improved greatly with the dagger thanks to the training proffered by Kael Bellilil. But having seen him fight and win so many times, she knew that she was no match for Thomas, at least not yet.

Thomas approached with an almost unnatural grace, although his face, contorted in a grimace, belied his internal struggle. Even with his strength of will, he couldn't stand up to the Dark Magic of the collar pulsing around his neck. Try as he might, he could not break free from the ensorcellment Corelia had forced upon him. He desperately didn't want to attack Kaylie, but the Dark Magic surging through the collar demanded it.

Thomas' arm whipped out, impossibly fast, despite his attempts to resist what Corelia required of him. Kaylie barely dodged out of the way in time, silently thanking the desk in front of her for impeding Thomas' assault. He attacked again, and again, and once more, his daggers flashing past in a blur, just missing her each time. She could tell that he continued to battle the control Corelia exerted upon him. Otherwise, even with the obstacle in front of her, each of his attacks would have struck home. The thought of cold steel sliding into her flesh sent a shiver through her body. There had to be something that she could do to help Thomas.

"Fight it, Thomas! You can do it. I can see you doing it now. Don't let her do this."

Knowing that her fate was sealed if she stayed where she was, Kaylie rolled away from the desk and underneath a left-handed slash that came so close she thought that Thomas had taken off a few strands of her hair by her right ear. As soon as she regained her feet, she launched a series of lightning fast attacks. Much to her annoyance, Thomas easily defended each one, but each attack gave her a chance to dart past him and gain more space to maneuver in the small room.

"Plead all you want," laughed Corelia, who remained by the wall, enjoying the show. The bloodthirsty curl of her lips reminded Kaylie of Ragin that night on the Tinnakilly battlements. "So long as I control him, Thomas will do as I command. Your end is assured no matter what you do, and with you gone Thomas will be mine body and soul."

Thomas walked toward Kaylie once more, moving away from the desk. His steps were slower now, almost plodding, but nevertheless he could not stop his advance. Sweat poured off his forehead, his jaw clenched. He fought against the compulsion with every ounce of his being, but it just wasn't enough.

"Run, Kaylie! I can't hold myself back much longer. The Dark Magic is too strong."

Kaylie considered the option for just a moment, the

open door right behind her, but she refused to leave Thomas to his fate. Instead she thought about something that Corelia had just said, and then it clicked. She knew what she needed to do, and fighting Thomas wasn't it.

Turning her attention away from Thomas, hoping that he could hold off the Dark Magic for just a moment longer, she flipped the dagger in her hand so that she grasped the point between her thumb and forefinger. Then she flung it to her right. She knew that the steel had struck true when she heard the startled gasp of surprise and pain.

Corelia fell back against the wall, her right leg giving out beneath her. Though not a mortal wound, the blade had sunk hilt deep into her thigh, a stream of bright red blood leaking out.

"You pig-faced bi ... " The Princess of Armagh didn't have time to complete her thought.

Recognizing the opportunity as soon as the blade left Kaylie's hand, Thomas was ready. With Corelia's concentration broken, Thomas grasped the thin tendril of the Talent that he could hold. He forced it back into the seams of the cracked black onyx that he had been chipping away at earlier, pushing as much natural magic as he could into the dense space. The pressure continued to increase, the seams first started with the sharp point of his amulet expanding, the stone now showing visible signs of fissures and flaking. Before Corelia realized the danger of releasing her control of the collar, if only for a second, Thomas pushed one final surge of the Talent into the now yielding spaces within the weakened piece of black stone.

The damaged piece shattered, ripping apart the collar, which fell from Thomas' neck to the floor.

"No, you can't do this. You can't!" Corelia screamed, still slumped against the wall. She had made the mistake of pulling out the blade, and now her injured leg stretched out in front of her, dark red blood pulsing out from the puncture. Her face had become pale as she pressed her hands against the bloody wound. Thomas and Kaylie ignored her.

Kaylie rushed to Thomas, grasping his cheeks with her hands and pulling his lips to hers. It was a brief kiss, but with a deep meaning, and just as passionately returned by Thomas.

"Thank you," said Thomas, grinning. "Quick thinking on your part."

Kaylie stepped back, though her hands remained on his cheeks. She relished the compliment, if only for a very brief moment.

"What do we do with her?" she asked.

Thomas glanced over at Corelia. He took a step toward her, thinking to bind her wound, then thought better of it. A swirling black mist had appeared above the blonde-haired beauty, spinning faster and faster.

Consumed by the pain in her leg and shocked that Thomas had succeeded in destroying the necklace, it took Corelia a few seconds to realize that she faced a greater danger than the loss of blood. She shivered, not knowing why, then felt the first light touches of the inky mist on her skin as pinpricks, quick jabs of pain all across her body. She tried to drag herself across the floor, away from the building darkness that had appeared above her, but her injury prevented it. She opened her mouth to scream for help, but that only gave the swirling black an avenue to intensify its attack, the pitch-black murk surging down her throat, setting her body into a series of convulsions. In only a few seconds it was over. The once beautiful Armaghian Princess was dead, now no more than a withered husk, her energy and life sucked from her by the very Dark Magic that she had tried to harness, forced to pay the ultimate price for her failure.

"Nothing, nothing at all." Thomas stepped away from Corelia's corpse, his daggers still in hand. "We have more important matters to attend to."

24

BLAZING ANGER

Thomas strode down the back hallway, Kaylie watching his back. The clang of steel and screams of battle grew louder as he approached Eshel's office. He stopped in the doorway, staying in the shadows, taking a brief moment to survey what lay before him. Kaylie, in her eagerness to stay with him, stumbled into his back.

"Easy, Kaylie. Keep out of the sharpest of the fight if you can. Daggers can do only so much against the sword."

Oso stood his ground in the room, two guards opposing him, the bodies of at least a half-dozen others strewn about the room, demonstrating how well the large Highlander had been keeping his attackers from advancing and buying time for Kaylie. Thomas could hear Eshel screaming in the hallway beyond the room, telling his men to continue to attack. But he picked up on their reluctance. Aric and his Marchers were pressing Eshel and his soldiers from the other side, giving them little room to maneuver. The confined spaces of the manor played to the Marchers' strengths, reducing the number of guards who could attack at one time.

But Oso was also tiring, the constant attacks sapping his strength. Seeking to help his friend, Thomas stepped lightly into the room, catching the blade of one of the guards by crossing his daggers above his head. The soldier had sought to strike Oso in the back while he engaged the other guard who had attacked the large Highlander with a series of lunges designed to distract him. Hearing the clang of steel behind him, Oso didn't bother to turn around.

"Took you long enough," the big Highlander muttered. Then, knowing that Thomas protected his back, Oso advanced on his opponent, turning his full attention on the soldier who now realized the mistake that he had made by taking on an angry Marcher.

Thomas shouldered the other guard into the wall, then slashed down with the dagger in his right hand, opening up the soldier's belly. The stricken man slumped to the floor, trying to keep his insides from slipping out, but it appeared to be a lost cause. Thomas watched it all dispassionately. His anger was building. His patience was gone. Taking hold of the Talent, relishing once more the power that flowed through him, he infused his twin blades with the magic of nature.

The steel daggers glowed a bright white as Thomas stepped through the office door into the long entry hall. Aric and the handful of Marchers squared off against a dozen guards, who fought desperately to keep them from reaching the Highland Lord despite their greater numbers. Just a handful of guards stood facing Thomas, and from among his soldiers Lord Eshel of Inishmore issued a constant stream of commands as he tried futilely to control a situation that was rapidly spiraling out of hand.

"Eshel!"

Thomas' shout startled the Inishmorian Lord, who

jumped back as his former captive strode toward him, blazing daggers in his grasp. The guards, seeing the Highland Lord approach, the tall Marcher at his back, quickly decided that with these two frightening figures striding toward them, eyes blazing with a deadly intensity, that discretion was the better part of valor. They stepped out of the way, dropping their weapons and not wanting any part of the men stalking toward them.

"Where is Corelia? She has you under her thrall. You belong to her!"

"No more," replied Thomas. He walked inexorably toward the source of his anger, ignoring everything around him but Eshel.

When Thomas was within striking distance, the Inishmorian Lord lunged forward, thinking that a quick attack and his experience with the sword would give him the victory against a pair of daggers. But he had miscalculated terribly. Thomas deflected the strike easily and in a rapid response, brought his Talent-infused daggers together and then apart where Eshel's neck met his shoulders. The blades sliced through cleanly, taking off Eshel's head, which thumped loudly when it hit the granite floor.

Thomas stepped back, letting the steaming corpse fall to the ground. The hall went silent, the fighting having stopped so that all could watch the short-lived spectacle. Thomas stared at the guards still standing, murder in his eyes. Smartly, those who hadn't done so already dropped their swords, having no stomach for continuing the fight. As Aric and the other Marchers secured the surrendering guards, Thomas turned to Oso.

"Thank you, my friend. Now just one more favor before we're done here."

25

QUEEN

L ady Colasa stood in the hallway of Eshel's manor, staring down at the headless body of her former opponent.

"You were really quite thorough, weren't you, Thomas?"

Thomas shrugged sheepishly. "I was a little angry, kind of let it out."

Kaylie stood next to him, holding his hand. The effort to break the collar crafted of Dark Magic and then infuse his daggers with the Talent had tired Thomas, taking more energy than he had expected and leaving him unsteady on his feet. After the unsettling events of the last few days, Kaylie had told him in a tone that brooked no argument that she would be staying at his side for the remainder of their time in Laurag.

"Apparently." The beautiful young woman turned her gaze to Thomas. "Remind me never to get on your bad side."

"Can you make use of this?" Kaylie asked, her mind already racing through the political implications for the only remaining claimant to the throne of Inishmore.

"I can," replied Colasa, smiling deviously. "Thomas' gift

provides the lever to tilt the balance in our favor. But it needs to be seen as my having eliminated Eshel, not a band of Marchers. The stronger houses will respect such a show of strength and decisiveness."

"Mum's the word," said Oso. All the Marchers had gathered their gear from the inn, including Thomas' sword, before they had made their way to Eshel's manor.

"We'll do one better than that. Let's get you on a ship. We still have a few more hours before dawn. If you are all out of Laurag before the sun is up, then I can turn this situation to my advantage and eliminate any questions about who was responsible for Eshel's downfall."

"As you command, Queen Colasa," said Thomas, giving her a warm smile.

26

THINKING OF OTHERS

Lady Colasa, now asserting her right to be the Queen of Inishmore, and likely to have that claim made reality by the end of the day once word of Eshel's demise spread, had worked quickly in the early morning. Her men had roused Brienne, captain of the ship Thomas had bought passage on, and in no uncertain terms told her that she, her crew and her cargo were to be on the first tide out of the harbor before the sun brightened the sky.

Brienne attempted to protest by citing the danger of rogue waves if they left too early, the difficulty of finding all her sailors on such short notice what with all the taverns and houses of ill repute packed into the harbor district, as well as a host of other excuses, all designed to raise the price. Once the transit was guaranteed at double the normal fee for passage to the Distant Islands, and the promise of more business in the future with the Inishmorian crown, the ship captain got moving and guaranteed that they would be free of the port without anyone the wiser. In less than an hour, the ship glided through the rough water well beyond the harbor walls, her crew working furiously as the wind picked up with the rising sun. The Marchers had found space in one of the holds, resting after a long night. Brienne had given her cabin to Kaylie for the few days that it would take to cross the strait to the Distant Islands. A fair trade, the ship captain thought, considering how much she would make on this single, short voyage.

Recognizing Thomas' exhaustion after the events of the last few days, Kaylie had insisted that he join her in the cabin so that he could sleep. It was a small room, the bed barely large enough for one person, the only other pieces of furniture a foldable desk and a washing stand. Kaylie sat on the edge of the bed, watching Thomas. He settled his head against the back of the bunk, but soon realized that Kaylie had an ulterior motive for getting him alone. Thomas' eyes were closed, but he got the feeling that he wouldn't be sleeping any time soon.

"You scared me," she said.

"I'm sorry, it wasn't my intention."

"We had talked about this, Thomas," began Kaylie. "I thought that we had agreed that you would no longer put yourself in danger needlessly."

"Kaylie, we did. You're right ..."

"You're important to the Marchers, to the Highlands, to the Kingdoms. You need to consider how your actions affect others."

"Kaylie, I understand ..."

Kaylie wouldn't allow him to interrupt, intent on making her point. "I don't think you do, Thomas. You must look at the world differently now. Oso. Aric. Any of the Marchers could have found Brienne and arranged for our passage. But instead you left the inn without telling anyone."

"Kaylie, I ..."

"I'm not done, Thomas," her tone sharp, commanding

and cutting off Thomas' protests. "You left the inn, leaving the rest of us unaware of your absence. You put our mission at risk so that you could, what, wander the city? Then you feel the need to involve yourself in what appeared to be an attempted crime, not knowing that it was a setup designed specifically to entrap you." Kaylie's voice had risen an octave as her temper threatened to get the better of her. "What possible reason could you have to ..."

"I wanted to get you something," Thomas interjected in a soft voice, his green eyes glowing in the dim cabin.

"I'm sorry, what?" Kaylie had not expected that answer and didn't know what to say next.

"I wanted to get you something," Thomas repeated, pushing himself off the back of the bunk so that he could look Kaylie directly in her eyes. "When I was out, yes, the thought came to mind to find Brienne. That took less than an hour. Finding you this took a bit longer."

Thomas reached behind his back, pulled free the dagger, and handed it to her hilt first. Kaylie studied the blade she held in her hand, the blue steel catching what little sunlight streamed unevenly through the porthole. The bone-white hilt felt right in her hand, as if it was meant to be there, as if the blade was made for her.

"Thomas, why?" Kaylie's voice had changed, softening.

"I just ..." Why did he feel the urge to buy Kaylie a gift? He had no other explanation other than the fact that it had felt like the right thing to do. "I just wanted to get you something to show you that I cared about you. I looked at bracelets, necklaces, other things. They just didn't seem right. When I found this dagger, I knew it should be yours."

"Thomas, it's perfect," she said, flipping the dagger from one hand to the other. The balance was perfect, but her mind returned to something else that Thomas had said. "I care about you, too." Tears began to streak down Kaylie's face, scared of what she had just revealed, but feeling better for it all the same.

"Kaylie, I didn't mean to make you cry." Thomas sat up. He ran his fingertips through Kaylie's black hair, then wiped away the tears that ran down her cheeks. Leaning forward, Thomas' lips brushed against Kaylie's. Then once more, the kiss growing in passion, both their bodies warming to one another's touch. As Thomas leaned back into the bed, Kaylie followed.

27

AGONY AND HATE

"You must do better, boy! The Highland Lord will tear you apart if this is the best that you can do. Our master gave you a gift greater than you deserve. Do not waste it a second time."

Ragin Tessaril remained on his knees, gulping air. He had sweated through his clothes in the past few hours, struggling to manipulate the Dark Magic that the Shadow Lord had returned to him, trying to master the tremendous power with which he had been gifted in the way that Malachias demanded. Yet no matter whether he accomplished the task set out for him perfectly or he failed, the result always was the same. Pain. A burning agony that shot from his toes through his lower body, then up into his chest and arms until it felt like his hair was on fire. It was all in his mind, he knew, his body remaining unharmed, but it was still all too real. There was nothing that he could do but suffer through Malachias' preferred method of instruction.

"I have done everything you have asked me to do exactly as you have told me to do it," growled Ragin, his anger surfacing, no longer caring about how Malachias would react to his insolence. "Everything!"

Malachias laughed, a raspy sound much like sand scouring stone. "So, you have a spine after all. I doubted it. Especially since an old man banished you. An old man kept you from your task. From your dream. From your revenge."

"I did not know who he was!" screamed Ragin. "I just want to kill the bastard who did this to me! Who destroyed my life!" The former Prince of Armagh gestured to the weeping scar that stretched from where his right eye should have been to his throat.

"And that's the problem," whispered Malachias. The tall, cowled figure, nothing but his bald pate gleaming in the meager torchlight of the chamber, began to walk slowly around Ragin. "You lack knowledge, and you do not have the patience to obtain it."

"I know what I need to know now," protested Ragin. "I am ready for the Highland Lord and anyone who might get in my way. I have been here for weeks with no word of what will happen next. When I will be freed to do what I must do. What I need to do."

"All will be made known to you at the appropriate time," said Malachias. "Perhaps even sooner than you think. But our master did not save you, did not give you the power that you hold now, to simply throw it away. Just like your sister did."

"What do you mean?" asked Ragin, his thoughts of revenge stopping short, if only for a time. What did Corelia have to do with any of this?

"As I said, boy, knowledge is key. Knowledge is power. And this is something you didn't need to know. But I will explain it anyway." Malachias knelt in front of Rodric's son, his hypnotic black orbs demanding Ragin's attention. "Our master prefers to have many options when pursuing a goal. You are simply one tool for achieving his objective of killing the Highland Lord. Your sister was another. She had everything she needed to complete her task. And she had the Highland Lord. She had trapped him. Tried to use him. But she lost control. The Highland Lord is free once more, and she is dead."

Hunched over, Ragin stared at the slick stone. Corelia had been his sister, his competitor as well, but his sister first. Yet he felt nothing at the news of her death. No desire to learn more about what had happened. No emotion. Nothing at all. Except a small sense of relief. She had failed, which meant that he could still succeed.

"I am not my sister," Ragin whispered.

"No, and more's the pity," said Malachias. "Because she, at least, thought about what she was doing. You don't care. You think that just because our master has given you back the Dark Magic you so desperately need and crave, that you are a match for the Highland Lord. You are not! Just because you have the power does not mean you have the ability to defeat him."

Ragin pushed himself off the cold stone of the floor, his body aching, his nerves firing as if they remembered the burning pinpricks of pain that Malachias had extinguished just a few minutes ago. "I am done with your words of advice, Malachias. The Shadow Lord brought me here for a reason. When do I get to kill the upstart?"

Malachias stared at Ragin for quite a long time. He had concluded at the very beginning of these training sessions, so many weeks in the past, that something had broken within Ragin. The Highland Lord had taken more than an eye from him. Yet what was he to do? The Shadow Lord had given Malachias a task, and to fail to complete it would mean paying a price that he could ill afford to pay. All he could do was train the vessel before him as best as he could and hope that the arrogant pup didn't fail again. Maybe the fool would get lucky.

"At a time and place of our master's choosing. But if you let your rage control you, you will be defeated once again, and this time I doubt that the Highland Lord will leave you alive."

"I don't care if I live or die," whispered Ragin. "So long as I kill the Highland Lord first."

28

DEEPER MEANING

After her experiences in Laurag, Kaylie was beginning to understand that what her father had spent so much time teaching her -- politics, persuasion, risk management and decision making, what she thought was boring and tedious actually had a practical application, much like her ability to fight with a blade. It was simply a matter of knowing what skill to apply when.

Kaylie stood next to Thomas on the stern deck of the *Waterborn*, their shoulders touching. What had happened the night before consumed her thoughts. She hadn't expected it. She hadn't planned on it. She certainly didn't regret it. But neither she nor Thomas seemed inclined to discuss it at the moment. She didn't feel the need to do so, preferring instead simply to enjoy the aftermath.

Their ship chasing the sun, they watched as the bright orange ball set in the west, their destination, the Distant Islands, too far off to be seen yet. After all that had occurred in the last few weeks, Kaylie felt much more confident now. Upon first joining the expedition, she had doubted herself, and with good reason she admitted.

But after leading the effort to rescue Thomas from the now deceased Princess of Armagh, the Marchers viewed her as one of their own, something not easily achieved and a sign of great respect. Moreover, they saw what was happening between her and Thomas, something that they apparently approved of, although they kept their opinions to themselves, or at least out of earshot. All except Oso, of course, who whenever he came upon her had a huge grin on his face.

"It's strange," Thomas said jokingly.

"What do you mean?"

"Usually I'm the one getting you out of trouble. Now the shoe is on the other foot."

Kaylie couldn't help but smile, remembering Thomas saving her and her friends from the Ogren in the Burren, and the time he and Beluil protected her and her father from the Fearhounds. Of course, there was also the journey home from Eamhain Mhacha, when Thomas and his Marchers had aided the Fal Carrachians when they were attacked by the Shade and his ensorcelled black-clad soldiers.

"And how does that shoe feel?"

Thomas turned the full weight of his gaze on her, drinking her in, marveling again at her beauty, and also sensing that this was a very important question, one that had several hidden, deeper meanings based on how he responded.

"Very comfortable," answered Thomas, after Kaylie worried that he wouldn't say anything at all. "It's good to have someone you can depend on, trust with your life if necessary."

Kaylie tried to contain the huge smile that threatened to erupt, but she failed miserably. She nudged his shoulder with hers, then reached out and took Thomas' hand. He let her, holding hers tightly, watching the sun slide down below the horizon.

Just as the setting sun kissed the ocean, Thomas turned around and placed his back to the waves, sensing what approached from behind. Three very large sailors, blocking out the light of the lanterns that ran along the rails of the ship, stood in a semicircle, keeping Thomas and Kaylie against the ship's stern. They only wore breeches and were barefoot so that they could navigate the often slick deck more nimbly. They were lean, their muscles hardened from years of hard work at sea. That was to be expected. What worried Thomas was the evil gleam in their eyes. Thomas guessed that they had done this before, shaking down passengers, having selected the moment when his Marchers were belowdecks eating dinner to press their advantage.

"What have we here?" asked the one in the center, a thick braid of dark hair trailing down his back.

"Looks like a bit of fun, Cutter," said the man to his left, the sailor on the right nodding his head and rubbing his hands together in anticipation.

"Could be, could be, Tin." The large sailor in the center took one step forward, his right hand going to his waist, where Thomas saw the handle of a shank peeking out from the top of his trousers. "It's been quite a long time since we've enjoyed the company of such a pretty lass."

Thomas stepped away from the railing, placing Kaylie behind him. But Kaylie had something else in mind, moving to the side so that she stood next to Thomas and she had freedom of movement. Thomas glanced at her, noting the determination on her face. He smiled in approval, seeing the dagger that he had given her already in her hand. He turned his attention back to the sailors.

The three men took an involuntary step backward. Thomas' green eyes glowed brightly in the rapidly encroaching darkness, startling them. Cutter and his boys had done this before. Maybe it was something as simple as charging an additional fee for safe passage on the ship, maybe it was something more, depending on the passenger. He had marked the two young ones when they had wandered to the stern of the large vessel and away from their compatriots. Now, for the first time, he was having second thoughts. Perhaps he had misjudged these two. The brightness of the boy's eyes scared him. They reflected a danger that he had never seen before, not only a sense, but also a promise of impending violence.

"You can return to your duties," said Thomas in a very quiet voice. "Or you can attempt to do what you originally set out to do and know that the consequences will be severe. Likely deadly. I'd suggest that you follow the first path."

Tin and the other sailor took another step back in response to Thomas' cold voice. There was a certainty in his words, what they took to be a guarantee. Cutter had the same urge as his friends. To leave these two be. To find easier prey. But not yet. Not with his mates behind him and the danger of losing his standing on the ship all too real. If he gave up now, someone else in the crew would challenge him. He had worked too hard to risk losing what he had gained just because of some hard words from a boy.

Cutter did the only thing that he could think to do. Escalate the situation by using his size to intimidate. Drawing the shank from his belt, he glanced behind his shoulder to make sure that his men were still there.

"Be careful with that blade, lassie," Cutter warned. "You don't want to cut yourself."

"You're the one who needs to be careful," said Kaylie.

Despite the danger of their circumstances, she felt at ease. The current state of affairs didn't compare to what she had faced the last few weeks while traveling with the Marchers.

Somewhat irritated that he had failed to intimidate the girl, Cutter returned his gaze to the boy. The massive sailor became perplexed. The boy hadn't pulled a knife. His hands held nothing. Yet despite the home-made dagger that Cutter waved in front of him, the boy appeared nonplussed.

"Let's keep things simple, boy," said Cutter, feeling as if he were losing control of the situation, that he had made the wrong decision in approaching this young couple. But he couldn't stop now. Too much was at stake. "I can slice you from top to bottom before you even knew it."

"I could do worse," replied Thomas. Taking hold of the Talent, he concentrated his power on the shank the large sailor continued to flash in front of him.

The blade sparked, and in seconds the hard steel melted to liquid, congealing on the deck, steam billowing up because of the intense heat. The sailors jumped back in shock, fear in their movements, knowing that they had nowhere to run.

"Appearances can be deceiving," said Thomas, now juggling three small balls of fire. The sailors, though terrified, were mesmerized as well, never having seen such a display. Despite their desire to escape, their feet remained rooted to the deck. They couldn't take their eyes from the blazing spheres that the boy spun so quickly that they resembled a circle of flame in the darkening sky. "I'd suggest not making the same mistake twice."

With that Thomas threw the balls of fire into the sea, the hiss of the flame touching the salt water audible despite the creaking sounds of the ship as it sliced through the waves. With that, the spell was broken. The sailors scurried away,

Cutter pushing his mates in front of him, as they hurried belowdecks to get as far away from Thomas as possible.

The sailors gone, Thomas turned to Kaylie, who sheathed her dagger. His eyes were a flat, dark green. She saw death there, and she realized that he had been prepared to kill those sailors in order to protect her.

"I don't think we'll be bothered for the rest of the trip," said Thomas. "Word of what just happened will spread quickly."

"I'm sure that you're right, but you don't always have to be so dramatic," she said, her grin suggesting that she had enjoyed Thomas' demonstration.

Kaylie stepped up to Thomas, putting one hand on his chest, the other behind his neck. Gently, she pulled his lips down to hers. They remained there, hidden in the dark, well past the time the sun finally disappeared into the ocean.

29

GLOWING DOMES

They had made good time upon leaving the port of Laurag, a strong wind at their backs cutting a day off their journey. Brienne, using all of her knowledge and experience, had kept the ship cutting through the waves, some rising as high as fifty feet, and avoided the squalls so common to the waters surrounding the Distant Islands. The sea leading to the harbor strangely calm for that time of year in which colossal waves were so common, they slipped into Afara with nary a worry as the sun began to set.

Standing at the bow, Thomas and Kaylie had never seen such a sight. It was a city of domes with few, if any, straight lines or right angles. As the sun touched the horizon, all the domes appeared to glow as they reflected the last rays of the day's light before it slowly disappeared.

"There's a myth," began Thomas. "Some believe that the city was created with magic, and because of this the domes glow with any touch of the light, even if there is nothing more to see by than the moon."

"That seems quite fanciful."

"It does," replied Thomas, turning to Kaylie. "But the

domes are important to those on the Distant Islands. If you're a lord or a prosperous merchant, you must have a dome atop your home. The larger the dome, the more powerful or richer you are. So in a sense, the domes provide a sense of hierarchy for those living here in Afara. You can tell a person's station by the size of or the materials used to construct their dome."

"I've heard another story as well from Brienne," said Oso, stepping up to the railing. Their ship's captain had taken a liking to Oso, often asking him to come to the helm to speak with her. Although he did so out of nothing more than common courtesy, he knew that Aric and the other Marchers would use it against him for as long as possible. "There was once a ruler here, a caliph I think the title was, who had a harem of more than one hundred women."

"That can't be true," objected Kaylie, bristling at the possibility.

"You're right, Oso. The Caliph Nashir, supposedly with a harem as you said. Seven wives, the remaining women mistresses."

"That sounds like it could be fun," said Oso, smiling at the thought.

"I don't know that Anara would share you willingly with sister wives," said Thomas. "And I doubt that you'd want to risk it with those knives of hers. You'll have a hard enough time explaining why Brienne sought the presence of your company so frequently."

"True," agreed Oso, ignoring Thomas' last comment though it sent a jolt of nervousness through him. "But if she were my wife, she'd have to accede to my wishes. And if I wanted a harem, I would have one."

Thomas knew that Oso was just having fun, and that if Anara were here, she'd stop the conversation immediately with a well-placed punch. But he decided to play along with Oso.

"Well, maybe if you asked her nicely beforehand and explained to her that she was your first wife, the most powerful, responsible for managing the household."

"Yes, that's the way to do it," agreed Oso. "I'll have to think on it."

Kaylie had had enough of the conversation, muttering several curses under her breath as she stalked away. Why did men think that they were funny when they just acted the fool? Oso and Thomas smiled broadly. Clearly, the Princess of Fal Carrach had expanded her vocabulary during her time with the Marchers.

"Was it something I said?" asked Oso in mock consternation.

"Perhaps," said Thomas. "Perhaps."

30

WELL MET

Having arrived in port, and happy to have missed the giant waves and rough weather so common to these waters at this time of year, Thomas and the Marchers bade farewell to Brienne, thanking her for the swift passage, though it took several minutes for Oso to disengage from the ship's captain. Strangely, Cutter and the other sailors who had accosted Thomas and Kaylie on their first night aboard were nowhere to be found. Apparently, as Thomas suggested word had spread of the encounter and within just a few hours of the incident all three sailors had met with accidents that kept them to their hammocks for the remainder of the voyage. Brienne had explained that it was just a few broken bones and bruises. Nothing too serious. Ships could be dangerous places with slick decks and the vessel falling into unexpected troughs. The unwary fall all the time. Whether Brienne or the Marchers had decided to make a point, no one had said. No one really cared either.

"Shall we find an inn?" asked Oso, the sun slowly sinking in the western sky.

"No," replied Thomas. The tug of the Key had become

more demanding with each passing day as he drew nearer to the Distant Islands. The pull now was an ache in his gut, and much as when he had been called to the Pinnacle by the Sylvana, he knew with an absolute certainty where he needed to go to find the Key. "We're close. I'd rather not delay if we can avoid it. Let's head out of town to the north and make for the mountains."

Before beginning this adventure, Thomas had spoken with Rynlin. His grandfather had given him instructions on how to find Ariel, the Sylvan Warrior charged with protecting the Distant Islands, and Colasa's mother, just in case the incessant pull to the west brought Thomas and his Marchers to that island Kingdom. Ariel tended to avoid people in general and only came down into Afara when absolutely necessary.

Taking the main road that ran along the harbor, Thomas and the Marchers quickly made their way out of the quiet city as night fell. The stars began to blossom in the evening sky, giving them some light as they hiked up into the hills that surrounded the port city. They all noticed the difference in climate. It was warmer here, the heat of the day remaining even in the evening. The oppressive humidity made it feel like you were swimming rather than walking, and it wasn't long before the Marchers felt its effects, their clothes sticking to their bodies thanks to a thin layer of sweat. The vegetation differed as well. The evergreens, conifers, maples and white oaks they were all accustomed to in the Highlands were nowhere to be found. The trees here grew to a decent height, though nothing could compare to the heart trees that dominated in their homeland. And, these trees were covered in massive palm fronds, which hid what appeared to be nuts or fruits as big as a person's head.

They walked for another hour under the bright stars of

the northern sky until they happened upon a woman standing in the middle of the road, one hand grasping a walking staff that towered above her. Her grey hair appeared silver in the moonlight, and by the glints coming off the steel situated at various parts of her body, she was heavily armed. Kaylie focused on her necklace, the familiar silver amulet with the twisting spiral of a unicorn's horn marking her as a Sylvan Warrior.

"Thomas, Raptor of the Highlands," said the woman, her voice having a soft, pleasing, lilting quality.

"Well met, Ariel. It has been a long time. You are well?"

"I am. Well met, Raptor." The woman stepped forward, the many steel knives at her belt, larger ones on each hip, and the several tucked into her boots and on her forearms, readily apparent. "I'm sorry that I could not be at the Circle. No offense was intended."

"None was taken, Ariel."

Ariel nodded, pleased by Thomas' response. "Come. I have a camp ready."

Ariel walked off the road in between the trees, Thomas and the others following by the light of the moon.

"Every time we meet someone on the road, Thomas knows them, or they know him," muttered Kaylie. Oso could only shake his head ruefully, noting the truth of her words as they stepped off the road and followed Ariel among the trees.

After the Marchers settled into the camp the Sylvan Warrior had prepared, they set to work cooking a stew with the vegetables that they had purchased in Afara, among other supplies. Kaylie, relaxing into the camaraderie of the Marchers, took the lead for that night's meal, enjoying her newfound status within the party.

"How are you, Thomas? You look tired, and not just

because of your journey." Seeing that everyone was occupied, Thomas had pulled Ariel aside to talk.

Thomas smiled. "Is it that obvious?"

"Maybe not to all, but to those who knew you when you were a child, it is easy to see. You were always a serious child, that was clear, but there's more to it now. An added weight. A greater burden."

"Yes, it's not like when Colasa and I used to play together when you visited Rynlin and Rya."

"I expect not. And how is my daughter?"

"If everything went as planned, she's likely the Queen of Inishmore now."

Ariel nodded, her pride clear. But she didn't appear surprised. "I expected that she would achieve that goal. It was necessary, considering who secretly supported Eshel. If that treacherous blowhard had gained control of the Kingdom, it boded ill for the Distant Islands as well."

"Then you have nothing to worry about in that regard."

"Eshel is no longer a threat?"

"Eshel is no longer with us," confirmed Thomas. "He won't be bothering anyone ever again."

Ariel turned her stern gaze to Thomas. "You helped with this?"

"I had no choice," replied Thomas. "Eshel had formed an alliance with Corelia Tessaril. They put at risk the reason that I am here."

Ariel took a moment to take in Thomas' explanation. "That's something I didn't know. I'm glad you put a stop to it."

Thomas shrugged. "As I said, it was necessary. When we arrived in Laurag, we fell into the middle of their plans. With Eshel gone, it cleared the way for Colasa."

"Fortuitous, then. And a good thing in the end. If Colasa

can create some stability in Inishmore, that will help with what's to come."

"Rynlin told you why I'm here," stated Thomas, having expected as much.

"He did. Though I have to admit that I know even less about what you seek than you do. I have been here for centuries, but I have no idea where to start looking. I can't feel it."

"No need to worry about that," replied Thomas. "I should be able to find it."

"Good, but you need to be careful, Thomas. As I said, I don't know much about what you seek, but I'm told that hidden danger lurks with it."

"What have you heard?"

"I don't know for sure," said Ariel. "It may be more fiction than fact, as this is just from ancient tales, stories that may have only a hint of truth left in them. But these stories suggest that something protects what you seek. Something deadly. Something that I can't sense despite these islands being my responsibility as a Sylvan Warrior."

Thomas shook his head in resignation, grinning slightly. After all that had happened so far on their journey, why should this next task be any different than the others? None of this had been easy. He simply had to continue to move from one challenge to the next.

"I expected as much, Ariel. I'll be as careful as I can."

"Good, I know you will. Just remember, there are many relying on you, many who don't know truly what's at stake."

Thomas nodded, trying to push the additional stress to the side. He could only deal with so much at once.

Ariel looked over to where the Marchers sat and talked. "She's a beautiful young lady," said Ariel, a smile creasing her lips.

"She is, indeed," Thomas agreed, watching Kaylie direct the Marchers as they helped prepare that night's meal.

"I'll go help her. It will be good to know more of the Princess of Fal Carrach." Recognizing the tension building in Thomas, Ariel gave his arm a squeeze in sympathy as she walked off toward the cookpot. She had sensed that he needed some time to himself. Appreciating the opportunity, Thomas disappeared among the palm trees and other plants so different from what he knew in the Highlands. He trailed his fingers along the stalks of a few, enjoying the different texture of the leaves.

As he walked into the forest, he extended his senses. The pull of the Key almost overpowered him. It was close. But Ariel had been right. Because he was so near to the Key, he could also sense some power surrounding it. What that power was he didn't know, getting no feel for whether it was there to harm or to protect. Shaking his head in frustration, he released his hold on the Talent and turned his thoughts to other matters.

Finding the Key was essential. But it held a deeper meaning, including a certainty that frightened him. Once he completed this mission, it would bring him that much closer to fighting the Shadow Lord. Perhaps that much closer to his own death, in the opinion of most who had any knowledge of the prophecies.

Since he was a boy, he knew what he had to do. *You must do what you must do*, as Rya liked to say. Because of that, he never really worried about dying. It wasn't something that appealed to him. But deep down he understood that it was a very real consequence of the path that he walked. That it could prove necessary, essential, in fact, if he were to succeed. He had come to accept that fact grudgingly, even if he didn't like it.

But now he wavered. Perhaps it came from his growing maturity, understanding what was really at risk, at what he might lose. He didn't want to die. Kaylie had changed his perspective, giving him something he had never thought that he could have. He was certain in his feelings for her, but he was afraid to tell her, in part because of his likely fate. Continuing to get close to her now would only make things more difficult for her in the future. As he wandered among the trees he struggled with his dilemma. Yet instead of finding the peace that normally graced his time in nature, he found only more questions with no good answers. More problems for which there were no good solutions.

DARK MAGIC

Night had fallen and Kaylie watched for Thomas to return. Kaylie worried about him, but she knew that he carried some burdens that she couldn't ease. She sat beside Ariel on a log the Marchers had pulled up, enjoying the stew that she had taken the lead in making, though she had left the bulk of the work to Oso. Kaylie thought that Anara would be quite pleased to learn when he returned to the Highlands that his cooking skills had improved, so long as he suppressed his urge to experiment.

"Tell me, child. Have you been called to the Circle yet?"

"Your daughter Colasa asked me much the same," replied Kaylie.

"Yes, I expect that she would. Sensing the Talent is one of her skills."

"Honestly, I'm not sure. But at the strangest times my mind wanders, and I feel like I'm looking down on a circle of stone monoliths, the largest in the very center. It's most vivid when I'm asleep and dreaming."

"That is one of the signs, child. You see Athala's Forge,

the peak of the tallest mountain in the Highlands. You will be called soon. Do you feel ready?"

"Not yet," replied Kaylie. "I haven't had as much instruction as I would like. Rya has been teaching me, as she could, Thomas as well, but there is so much more that I need to learn."

"Don't fret over it," said the Sylvan Warrior. "No one is ever ready when they are called. You are strong in the Talent. Very strong. You will join our ranks soon. Of that I have no doubt."

"It frightens me, to be honest," admitted Kaylie, scraping the bottom of her empty bowl with her spoon nervously. "Thomas told me some of what he had to go through to become a Sylvan Warrior."

"Your worry is wasted, child. The experience is different for each Sylvan Warrior. As I said, you are strong, and not just in the Talent. When you are called you will do well."

Ariel said the last with such certainty that Kaylie's fears dissolved, and her pride swelled. The Sylvan Warrior's words heartened her and gave her hope for what would be required of her in the future. Kaylie decided to shift the topic of conversation, hoping that Ariel would know more about what they were seeking since Thomas believed that it was located here.

"Thomas explained a bit about why we came here. About what dangers the Kingdoms face from the Shadow Lord. But he wasn't specific."

"It's hard to be specific," said Ariel. "Rynlin said that Thomas was here in search of the Key. Thomas likely told you that as well."

Kaylie nodded that he had.

"The problem is that no one really knows what the Key

of the prophecy is. An actual key? Something else? The details have been lost to history."

"In fact, no one's really sure where the Shadow Lord came from," continued Ariel. "He's also known as Lighteater, Lord of the Dark, Lord of the Night ... there are many names. It just depends on the Kingdom and its stories. Some say that he is a former member of the Sylvana who turned to evil, others say that he is a long dead king who found a book of Dark Magic that corrupted him over time. In actuality, when man first began to use the Talent, what others have often called magic, there were some who used it for their own purposes. For evil purposes. The Talent is a part of the natural world, from which all magic comes. Once it is used, it eventually returns to nature."

"Then the power that the Shadow Lord wields is similar to what a Sylvan Warrior, what I, use?"

"In short, yes. Clearly you have spoken with Rya about this already. But Dark Magic is twisted from its original purpose. It has no place in the natural world, so can't return to it. Over time, the more Dark Magic was used, the more it took on a life of its own. Some say this Dark Magic grew so strong and so profligate because of the desires and demands of weak men and women that the magic itself became the Shadow Lord. The Dark Magic took on a life of its own. As a result, even though the Shadow Lord can take on a human body, it is very much an inhuman thing."

"If that's true, then how do you fight something like that?" asked Kaylie, her fear for Thomas increasing.

"With skill. With will. With courage. There is so much that's needed. But first Thomas must find the Key. He can't get into Blackstone undetected without it, as that dreaded place is protected by an ancient Dark Magic. If he doesn't have the Key, its defenses will kill him."

"So all we can do is hope that he finds the Key, and by doing so puts himself in the position to fight against an evil that has been defeated but never destroyed."

"Yes, an unfortunate twist of fate, is it not?" Ariel patted Kaylie on the knee, recognizing the difficult situation in which the Princess of Fal Carrach found herself enmeshed. "But we can help Thomas when help is needed. You said Rya was instructing you in the Talent. As I said, I can sense your strength. Before Thomas returns shall I show you a new skill in the Talent that might be of use?"

"That would be wonderful! Thank you."

"Tell me, child. Have you learned how to break the link between a warlock or some other dark creature with a similar ability and their Dark Magic? How to cut them off from the source of their power?"

32

THE PULL

Several days of hard but uneventful travel deeper into the mountains had left the Marchers tired but confident. Thomas had provided the direction while Ariel identified the best path for them to take, and when a trail wasn't available, the easiest way through the forest, ravines and gullies that crisscrossed the mountains. As they journeyed higher among the peaks outside Afara, they enjoyed the more temperate weather, as it didn't take long for the sweltering heat and humidity to begin to wear on the Marchers, who were used to cooler climes.

Ariel and Kaylie had used the Talent to scout for leagues around them with nary a trace of dark creatures to be found. Still, the Sylvan Warriors and Marchers were on edge, a sense of anticipation gnawing at their nerves. Perhaps it was because they were so close to achieving their goal, or perhaps it was something else, but a cloak of menace had settled over them. A premonition of attack, but by what and from where they couldn't determine.

At midday, with the sun hidden by the clouds that wreathed the mountain peaks, Thomas stopped abruptly, closing his eyes. The last few days he had worried less about what was around them and more about where they were going, his focus almost entirely on the nagging tug of the Key.

"What is it, Thomas?"

Kaylie stood beside him, never far from his side after he had first wandered off on his own among the trees after speaking with Ariel just a few nights before.

"We're close," he said. "Very close."

The pull was so intense that it verged on pain for Thomas. The Key beckoned to him, demanding that he come, as if it knew the role that it was to play and it was eager to do so. Confident in his bearings, the pull guided him up a steep slope to a well-hidden seam in the mountain. A small ledge at its front, which only he could pick out from where they stood, offered the only hint that there might be a tunnel that led deeper within the stone.

A jolt of energy shot through him as he realized that he was close to achieving his goal. But something bothered him, and his restlessness increased the tension of the Marchers. It felt as if something followed them, watching from the shadows, waiting to strike. Knowing that Kaylie and Ariel had been doing much the same, Thomas took hold of the Talent, searching throughout the mountains for any threat, any sign of peril, just to see if they might have missed something. But there was nothing. No sense of darkness or evil. Then why this feeling of impending attack?

"Do you feel it?" he asked Ariel. She had stepped up next to Kaylie.

"I do, but I don't know what it is."

Once again taking hold of the Talent, Thomas extended his senses. Sweeping his consciousness for leagues around, nothing appeared out of the ordinary. There were no dark creatures that he could identify anywhere nearby. Yet the tickle at the base of his skull, warning of danger, remained. Could this feeling be connected to whatever was protecting the Key?

He debated whether he should wait before continuing his pursuit of the Key, just to see if something happened. Perhaps the sense of danger would go away, though he knew that was unlikely. Besides, he didn't want to leave Kaylie and his Marchers unprotected against something that they might not be able to defend against.

"Thomas, don't worry about us," said Ariel, somehow knowing what was going through his mind. "Do what you need to do. Kaylie and I can manage if trouble appears."

Thomas nodded reluctantly, reaching out to grasp Kaylie's hand, giving it a squeeze. Not satisfied, Kaylie reached for Thomas, hugging him fiercely before kissing him softly on his lips.

"Be careful," she said. "Take no unnecessary chances. Otherwise you answer to me."

Thomas smiled at Kaylie's show of bravado. Taking hold of the Talent once more, in a flash of blinding white light Thomas transformed himself into a large kestrel, winging his way up the steep mountainside. Catching a warm air current, he circled the peak for a few minutes, just to get the lay of the land. The sense of danger remained, but even his sharper senses that resulted from his taking the form of the Highlands' largest bird of prey offered no way to interpret the feeling of peril that continued to plague him.

Frustrated by his inability to identify the source of his unease, he settled his sharp, strong talons onto the ledge that jutted out on the sheer rock face. Shifting back to his human form, he walked through the seam, unperturbed by the utter darkness.

NERVOUS ENERGY

Watching Thomas enter the crease in the mountainside, the Marchers quickly established a defensive perimeter, their backs against the rock of the peak. Aric decided to take a couple of Marchers with him to scout the surrounding area, heeding Oso's warning to stay close. They could all sense that a threat was near, but what that danger could be remained an irritating mystery.

"Some dark creature of the Shadow Lord?" asked Kaylie, who had settled next to Ariel. The Sylvan Warrior scanned the rough landscape regularly, with both the Talent and her eyes, looking for what she didn't know. But still she did it. It was a habit that she couldn't break.

"Who can say?" she replied. "If there were Ogren or Shades on this island, I would know. But that's not what this feels like."

"So no clue as to what it could be?"

"No," she replied. "I sense something in the mountain. A power. But it doesn't seem to be good or evil. It's simply there. I don't believe it's a threat, at least not to us. No, there's something else. I just can't place it and that worries me."

While Kaylie and Ariel had been talking, Oso had made sure that the Marchers had established a strong shield line. Satisfied that they were as ready as they could be, Oso took out his sword and a whetstone, running it across the already razor sharp blade. Several of his Marchers followed his lead, needing to do something with their nervous energy. The tension seeped into their bones, the feeling that something stalked them playing at the very edges of their senses, and they wanted to be ready for whatever might come.

As Ariel huffed in annoyance, she continued to scan the terrain and the skies. Kaylie kept her attention focused on the seam in the rock that Thomas had entered. She had wanted to go with him, but knew that she couldn't. Whatever peril he faced in searching for the Key he needed to deal with on his own, and she didn't want to distract him. If he didn't make it out safely, Kaylie promised herself that Thomas would never hear the end of it. Cursing silently, Kaylie pulled her sword from its scabbard across her back and a whetstone from her pack. Just like the other Marchers, she needed to focus on something else while Thomas searched for the Key, and she feared that she'd have need of her blade sooner rather than later.

34

INVISIBLE SWORD

E ntering a pitch-black cave without a torch would frighten most people, but it had no effect on Thomas. His glowing green eyes allowed him to walk unimpeded through the scar, discerning the rough rock of the tunnel from the gloom as if the midday sun lit his way. The cave itself wasn't very large, no more than forty or fifty feet across from end to end and running just a short distance into the mountain. With his excellent vision, Thomas made out the frame of a doorway cut out of the middle of the wall facing him.

With no other path to take, he moved forward across the threshold. The rough stone gave way to carved slabs as Thomas walked down what became a hallway that led deeper into the peak. He continued on the path for several minutes, taking his time, trying to get a feel for what was around him. He stopped every few steps to listen for any movement. Yet all remained silent. He was alone.

Finally, he came to the end of the passage. The hallway opened into a large chamber carved by ancient hands. A skylight, barely more than a slit in the stone above, allowed the grey light of the day to filter into the room, giving it a murky cast.

Along the edge of the chamber, dozens of statues resembling soldiers wearing ancient armor and holding spears or swords of stone stood guard, their features remarkably lifelike despite the fact that they were cut from the rock of the mountain. He spun around slowly, taking it all in. It was an impressive achievement, and obviously done for a reason. But for what purpose? And what to do now?

That sense of being watched, which had plagued him for the last few days, had grown stronger with each step he took deeper into the rock. But here, in this chamber, that feeling seemed to be vibrating with an added intensity. The cause of it appeared to be centered in this very room. But where could it be coming from? There was nothing here but stone figures.

He approached the wall on the far side of the hall. Whoever had crafted this place had chipped and then sanded the wall down to a glassy sheen. In fact, it was so shiny that it bore a strong resemblance to a mirror, so much so that Thomas could see his reflection in the dim light. There wasn't a mark or imperfection on the gleaming stone, except for one. Right in the middle, about five spans up from the roughened floor, someone had carved a symbol. Taking a closer look at the marking, he thanked Rynlin for being so demanding with his education. It was an ancient symbol, but one that he recognized. It represented the word for "key."

Smiling at his good fortune, Thomas extended his senses. He felt it immediately, the natural magic that radiated from the stone in front of him. His grandmother Rya had told him about something like what he faced now. The wall was an illusion of a sort. Only the right person, the person who was supposed to be here, could walk through the barrier and reach what was beyond the translucent stone. Those who shouldn't, or couldn't, would see nothing more than a stone wall. Thinking of the power of the magic radiating from the stone, perhaps the Key had an even more aggressive defense for those who shouldn't be here. His eyes traveled over the stone guards that lined the chamber as that thought crossed his mind. Was he the person who was supposed to be here? Steeling himself, he knew that there was only one way to find out.

Thomas took a moment to center himself. What he was about to try could be the correct next step or it could unlock a hidden threat. Having no choice but to trust his instincts and be prepared for whatever may come next, Thomas extended his hand, placing it on the symbol carved into the stone. With just a little pressure, his fingers disappeared into the stone. He smiled, pleased that he had been right. Then he pushed his arm farther into the stone, the image shifting much like the surface of a pool of water that rippled when you dropped a stone in it. He pulled his arm out from the image, just to make sure that he was correct.

Satisfied, he extended his hand once more, starting at the carving, then pushed his entire body into the stone. It felt as if he was walking through water, though nothing flowed around him. The stone had simply assumed a more viscous form, much like jelly, that allowed him to slide through it slowly.

Thankfully, he only had a few feet to go, as the grasping nature of the magic unsettled him. As he exited the stone and entered a smaller chamber, he almost fell to his knees on the smooth stone floor, the pull of the Key threatening to overwhelm him. It was here, in this room. He knew it! He had been right. But before he could begin his search, he sensed something to his side, a whisper of movement, though nothing was visible. Allowing his instincts to take hold, the training Antonin and so many other legendary warriors of old had engrained within him governing his actions, he ducked and rolled away from the wall just as sparks streaked across the stone from the slash of an invisible sword.

35

THE SENTINEL

R egaining his feet quickly, Thomas freed his sword from the scabbard across his back. The pull of the Key was insistent, demanding. It was definitely here. But where? He searched through the gloom quickly, his eyes fixing on a long table carved from the rock of the chamber and extending out from the far wall. With his sharp vision he picked out the dozens of actual keys set out on the stone. But he ignored them for the moment, a more pressing concern occupying his thoughts. Whatever had attacked him remained in the small chamber. Although he couldn't see what it was, he could sense its presence.

Feeling the air stir at his back, Thomas dove forward as an invisible blade passed through the air just behind him, barely missing his hip. He glided away from the center of the room, until his back touched the stone wall, reducing his opponent's possible angles of attack. Normally he would have preferred to have more space so that he would have more alternatives for moving, but not now. Not when he couldn't see his opponent. Now he needed to limit his attacker's options. He didn't know for sure what he faced, but it brought to mind something from the past, something that he had learned about when the spirits of the dead warriors had trained him to fight.

Though he could not track his invisible adversary, he could sense the movement around him, the slight shifting of the air. He held his sword at the ready. He guessed that he faced one of the ancient Sentinels, warriors imbued with a magic that allowed them to appear or disappear at will. He stopped his thoughts from wandering to the point of losing concentration as a barely discernible disturbance in the air was all the warning that he received of the next attack.

Rolling to the right, based on a hunch he swung back with his sword, catching the Sentinel's blade on his own. Tired of being the prey and pinpointing his adversary's location, Thomas continued his attack, launching a series of lunges and slashes that forced the Sentinel back. Thomas confirmed his opponent's positioning each time his blade sparked on that of his adversary's. After several seconds, Thomas stepped back, disengaging from the Sentinel.

He could attack all he wanted, but he fought a losing battle. Eventually the Sentinel's invisibility would prove the determining factor in the duel. He needed to even the playing field, and he knew of only one way to do that.

Closing his eyes, he took hold of the Talent and extended his senses. He did it just in time. The Sentinel launched another attack, its curved blade scything through the air, but now, though the Sentinel remained invisible, Thomas could track his movement, his rival's body taking on a ghostly hue.

Keeping his eyes closed much like he did during his many training sessions as a boy with Antonin the Spear, he blocked the Sentinel's strike, then swung his own blade low, hoping to catch the Sentinel across the knee and disable him. The Sentinel dodged the blow just in time.

Thomas continued his assault, eyes remaining closed, as he used the Talent to follow the Sentinel across the room. For several minutes they glided around the chamber. If anyone had been watching it would have appeared as if Thomas were practicing the various fighting forms on his own, if not for the sparks that shot out frequently that confirmed the striking of steel on steel. Finally, sidestepping a lunge, Thomas got inside the Sentinel's defenses. His blade a blur, he forced his opponent against the wall, then drove his steel into the Sentinel's gut.

A roaring sound rushed through the chamber, resembling a gust of wind blowing through the eaves of a house on a stormy night. Opening his eyes, Thomas looked down at the Sentinel, now visible, slumped against the wall. The defender of the chamber had turned to stone, just like his comrades on the other side of the wall.

With the Sentinel no longer a threat, Thomas stood there for several minutes, maintaining his grasp on the Talent just to make sure that there were no other surprises coming his way. Confident that he was alone, he released the Talent and turned his attention to the many keys that lay upon the stone table cut out from the far wall. A final test, he assumed. There were so many, of all shapes and sizes, that he didn't know where to begin. Some were plain, made from wood, others of stone or steel. Some were intricately carved and studded with jewels, or crafted from gold or silver. Some of the designs were so complex that it hurt his eyes to look upon them.

Which one could it be? Which would grant him freedom of access to Blackstone? Which would guarantee a meeting with the Shadow Lord?

Thomas feared the possible consequences of selecting incorrectly. If he picked the wrong one, would the stone Sentinels in the other chamber come to life as well, waiting for him to emerge from the wall that was not a wall before cutting him to pieces?

So he took his time while examining the dozens of keys lining the table. In the faint light, he saw that carved into the stone where the keys rested were the words "Knowledge is the key." Could it really be that simple? Why not? He had entered this chamber by pushing on the ancient symbol that represented knowledge. It had proven prescient. Why not continue down that path?

Thomas studied the many different keys. He ignored the ones made with gold and silver and those encrusted with jewels and other distracting ornamentation. After less than a minute had passed, he found what he sought. Intricately carved and hidden behind many of the more ostentatious offerings was a key made from hardened steel shaped into the ancient symbol for knowledge.

Most would not know what it meant, as the symbol came from the language originally used at the time the Sylvana were formed more than a thousand years in the past. A language that was no longer spoken, but sometimes written, that Rynlin had required him to learn despite his many protestations at having to master a dead dialect. Maybe all that training and education his grandparents had forced on him was paying off, he mused.

When he picked up the steel key, it felt right in his hands. The nagging pull that had plagued him for weeks disappeared, replaced by a warmth that began in the key, flowed into his hand, then arm, and then throughout his body. He had found the Key. All that time and effort, the commitment and sacrifice of so many people, leading to this moment. But there was no time to celebrate. He needed to move onto the next step. Inspecting the Key more closely, he saw that thin veins of what looked to be diamonds ran through the plain steel, which caught the little bit of light that illuminated the chamber. Inscribed in the same language as that on the table, running along one side of the Key, were the words "*When the darkness surrounds, the light will prevail.*"

What that meant, Thomas wasn't entirely sure. Perhaps Rynlin would know. But that was a concern for another day. At the moment, he was more concerned about a more pressing matter. Was the real test to come when he entered the main chamber once again? Were the remaining Sentinels waiting to welcome him or challenge him? Noticing the small oval in the Key's grip, Thomas affixed it to his necklace, the cold steel warming at the touch of his skin as it slid next to his Sylvan Warrior amulet. That done, grasping his blade tightly just in case, he prepared for what might happen when he pushed his way back through the magical wall.

36

GUARD OF HONOR

Not knowing what to expect in the larger chamber, Thomas pushed his way back through the shimmering wall, his sword in hand and the Talent ready for use. The stone statues were gone. In their place several dozen men stood at attention, their captain several steps to their front. When Thomas had exited the magical barrier, the soldiers half-bowed in unison, their leader offering a slight nod of respect.

Thomas spared a moment to take it all in. The men were tall, all with hard eyes who clearly knew how to use the spears, swords and battle axes they seemed to prefer. And their armor was something Thomas had never seen before. It resembled steel mesh, but the pattern in the metal differed for each man, suggesting for one tiny diamonds and another small, interlocking ovals, and so it went, though for all the soldiers the armor was painted a matte black with touches of grey. In the gloom, these soldiers blended into the darkness, so much so that Thomas had difficulty identifying them unless they moved.

"You're Sentinels," said Thomas, his voice sounding

overly loud in the silence as he turned his gaze to the soldier standing in front of the others.

"We are," the man replied in a soft voice. "And you are the Defender of the Light."

"I am," replied Thomas, his voice catching as he acknowledged the title and its responsibility for the first time openly. Thomas' mind worked furiously as he recalled his history. The Sentinels were the first soldiers to reach the Sylvan Warriors more than a thousand years before, offering their skill and blood to slow the Dark Horde before it could escape the Northern Steppes and invade the south. Their sacrifices, along with those of the Sylvana, had given the Kingdoms the time needed to bring their armies to bear on the Lord of the Shadow. Following that, the Sentinels had become the first defenders of the Kingdoms, aiding in the building of the Breaker and then becoming the first soldiers to stand watch atop its broad expanse, always waiting for the return of the one who had caused so much pain and loss in the Kingdoms.

"Your name?" asked the Sentinel captain.

"Thomas Kestrel, Lord of the Highlands." Thomas sheathed his sword in the scabbard across his back and released his hold on the Talent, knowing intuitively that these soldiers would not attack him.

"And your mother's surname?"

Thomas was surprised by the question, so it took him a moment before responding. "Keldragan."

The Sentinel captain smiled. "As I expected. I can see the resemblance. We are kin, Defender of the Light. I am Kincaid, Lord of the Western Isle and brother to Rya West-gard, now known as Rya Keldragan."

What had started out as a strange journey in so many

ways was only getting stranger, the soldier's words shocking Thomas. "You're my uncle?"

"Yes, your great uncle, centuries removed," the Sentinel captain said with a smile. "How is my baby sister?"

Thomas smiled as well, trying to adjust to the surreal nature of the conversation he was having with his just-discovered relative. "She is well. Irascible as ever."

"Yes, that sounds like my sister. More often than not when we were growing up, she was as smooth as a nettle." Kincaid laughed, unable to control his glee. "Rynlin as well?"

"Yes, Rynlin probably is no different than he was the last time that you saw him. Demanding and not one to suffer fools."

"That is an excellent description, nephew. I must admit that when I first met him, I did not think that he was the right one for Rya. But the more I realized that his stubbornness matched my sister's, I knew that they were meant to be together." Kincaid shook his head at the memories that flooded through him. "But we must move on, Thomas. Though I would love to learn more about you and the world beyond this stone, as you know time is short and action must take precedence over talk."

"Can I ask just one question?" Kincaid nodded, willing to humor him at least for a time. "How did you and your men come to be here?"

"The Key," replied Kincaid. "The same reason you're here. When Malachias stole the Key, my men and I were given the task of taking it back. It took us years to locate it, then just as long to steal it back from him. Then we ran. The men you see behind me are just a small remnant of the many who began the quest."

"Why here in the Distant Islands? And why didn't the Sylvan Warriors know about the location of the Key?"

Kincaid studied his nephew, sensing the power and courage within him. Yes, he would do well with the task set before him, regardless of how it may end. "We had nowhere else," Kincaid answered simply. "Malachias and his servants, one in particular, pursued us relentlessly. Those of us who made it to Afara were all who survived. We were hounded across the Kingdoms by the Shadow Lord and his dark creatures, whittled down as we tried to escape. When we finally did, and at great cost, this seemed to be the best place to make our stand. We expected that Malachias would find us eventually. But apparently not. We truly had escaped, no one knowing what had become of us or the Key."

"But why not get a message to Rya or Rynlin? Why not let them know about the Key and where you were?"

Kincaid's eyes darkened, and Thomas noticed the change in his soldiers, the visible anger breaking out on many of their faces, their bodies taut. "There was a traitor among the Sylvan Warriors. Whether there still is, I don't know. That's why Malachias succeeded in stealing the Key in the first place. We didn't know who we could trust. So we remained silent, believing that as the years passed memories would fade, giving us an added layer of protection."

Kincaid raised his hands, stopping Thomas from asking the next question that waited impatiently on his lips. "We knew the prophecy as well. That the Defender of the Light would find the Key. So we decided to remain hidden from the world, guarding the Key, for when the world had need of it again. And it seems that that time has arrived."

Thomas nodded at his uncle's decision-making, which had stood the test of time. "This might not mean much to you and your soldiers, but thank you for your sacrifice. If Malachias still held the Key ..."

"Then all would be lost," finished Kincaid. "You are correct about that. You are welcome. Now that we have completed our task, we can finally rest."

"The Sentinel that I fought in the other room. I didn't ..."

"No," cut in Kincaid, motioning to one of the soldiers at the end of the column, who nodded with the faintest tilt of his head. "You did not kill him. But once you entered the chamber of keys, we needed to test you just to confirm what we suspected."

"What was that?"

"That you're more than a match for the Lord of the Shadow."

Thomas nodded, pleased but made uncomfortable by the praise. "Before I go, may I ask one more question?"

"Of course. You are the Defender of the Light, and my nephew to boot. Ask what you will."

"Do you know how to use the Key to enter Blackstone?"

For almost a minute the Sentinel captain did not respond. When he did it was the answer that Thomas had expected but didn't want to hear. "I am sorry, but I do not."

Thomas nodded, expecting as much. "Again, my thanks. And it was a pleasure to meet you, Uncle Kincaid. I will bring word of you to Rya and Rynlin." He then spun on his heel and began to exit the chamber, but he didn't get far.

"Before you go there is one other thing that you should know." Thomas turned back to Kincaid, the Sentinel's ghostly presence appearing dimmer, as if each passing second brought the spirit closer to the peace that he craved. "There is more to the Key than what's said of it in the prophecy. It will help you enter the Lord of the Shadow's lair, but its power is greater than that."

"What do you mean?"

"The Key negates Dark Magic. Destroys it. You have heard of the Well of the Souls?"

"Yes," answered Thomas, his thoughts returning to a lesson with Rynlin on a very hot day years in the past. His home had been stuffy, the air barely moving, which was rare on the Isle of Mist. All he had wanted to do was finish his instruction and go to Shark Cove with Beluil for a swim. "I was told that the Well of the Souls could be the source, the receptacle, of the Shadow Lord's Dark Magic. That during the Great War the Sylvan Warriors had failed to kill the Shadow Lord because they had not found the Well of the Souls. But Rynlin said that it was only a guess, never confirmed, for no one had ever come across the Well of the Souls. Therefore, the thought that it was perhaps more myth than fact, though he had no good way to judge."

"That is correct again, Thomas," replied Kincaid, the spirit's presence beginning to flicker, its connection to the material world continuing to weaken now that his mission was complete. "But not entirely correct. Remind Rynlin for me when next you see him of that fact. That should annoy him to no end. Remember, if you want to destroy the Shadow Lord, completely and utterly, you must destroy the source of his power, and the Shadow Lord is never far from it for that very reason."

"The Well of the Souls."

"The Well of the Souls," agreed Kincaid. "Use the Key to destroy the Well of the Souls."

"But how ..." Thomas' words caught in his throat. Kincaid and the Sentinels had disappeared.

37

DRAGAS

When Thomas emerged from the cave and peered down from the narrow ledge, he realized immediately that something was terribly wrong.

The Marchers stood in a semicircle with the base of the peak at their backs, Ariel and Kaylie in the middle. Facing them were three huge Dragas. He had last encountered such dark creatures while standing on the Breaker so many months before. Some had thought these massive beasts extinct, not knowing that they had instead remained close to their traditional hunting grounds around Blackstone. As large as a cottage, the Dragas' sharp claws dug into the stone, wings spread wide as the sun glinted off their black and green scaly hides. Maws gaping, their sharp, needle-point teeth dripped a thick saliva that flickered with a greenish tinge. When the saliva dripped onto the ground, steam rose as it burned into the rock like acid, scarring the stone.

The Marchers had kept the dark creatures at bay, which Thomas found strange. Not because he doubted the abilities of the men and women who had traveled so far with him, but because these monsters were not known for their patience, demonstrating a ferocious aggressiveness that could rarely be matched by any of the other servants of the Shadow Lord. Yet the massive creatures seemed to be holding back for something, content to keep the Marchers in place. As if they were waiting for him to obtain the Key and then ...

An ear-splitting screech shattered the stillness of the mountains, giving Thomas the little warning that he needed. He leapt from his perch just in time, the claws of a fourth Dragas digging huge furrows into the mountainside and opening the small crevice Thomas had slipped through into a wide gash as pieces of shattered stone fell to the ground several hundred feet below.

Using the Talent to transform into a kestrel as he fell through the air, Thomas had little time to do anything but evade the massive Dragas that chased after him. Thomas had hoped to go to the aid of Kaylie and his Marchers, seeing out of the corner of his eye the other Dragas launch themselves at their prey now that he had exited the passage-way. But he was too busy with his pursuer to assist. Ariel pulled an arrow from her quiver and shot at the black and green blur streaking after him, but to no avail, as the steel tip of the shaft slid off the scales on the Dragas' foreleg. More arrows followed, again with no effect, the dark creature's armor protecting it from the excellent marksmanship of the Sylvan Warrior.

Thomas dodged through the air, hugging the ground, whipping around trees and rocky outcroppings, all in a frantic attempt to evade the Dragas. Due to its size and strength, the Dragas was more direct, simply plowing through the groves of trees and smaller rock formations that dotted the landscape that Thomas attempted to use as an obstacle. As he curled back around to the small clearing, he was both pleased and relieved to see that his Marchers still stood strong, the three Dragas dead, hacked to pieces. That surprised him, even with Kaylie and Ariel there to help through the use of the Talent. But he didn't have the time to ponder what had prompted such a savage and effective response by his Highlanders.

A shriek of anger brought Thomas back to the problem that he faced. The Dragas, though slowed initially by Thomas' attempts at evasion, still remained behind him and was gaining, the dark creature's needle-sharp teeth nipping at his tail feathers. He knew that eventually his pursuer would catch up to him if he continued in the form of a raptor. So he decided to take a different tack.

Approaching the edge of the clearing, Thomas quickly transformed back to his human form, sliding to a stop on the rocky plateau. The Dragas screeched in triumph, homing in on its prey. With only seconds to react, Thomas grasped the Talent, preparing to shoot a bolt of energy from his hand toward the huge beast that streaked toward him, sharp claws outstretched and ready to tear him to shreds. But before he could do so, a shard of white hot energy sliced through the Dragas from tail to snout.

Temporarily blinded by the flash, Thomas dove to the side, the force of the creature's mass barreling through the air buffeting him, threatening to force him over the edge of the cliff, as he scrabbled away on the rock. Mortally wounded, the beast skidded across the stone, coming to a stop on the very fringe of the precipice. Smoke rose from its carcass where the blazing hot energy Kaylie had released had burned through its armored hide.

"Thomas, are you alright?"

Kaylie ran up, pulling him to his feet and then into a crushing hug.

"I'm fine." He returned the hug, enjoying the closeness. "What happened with the other Dragas? I saw the three charge you and Oso, but I didn't see what happened after that. How did you manage to kill them so quickly?"

Unwilling to let go of Thomas, Kaylie talked into his shoulder, explaining how they were preparing to hold off the beasts for as long as they could while he was in the mountain, but it turned out that they didn't need to. Before the Dragas could close on the Marchers, some mysterious, invisible attackers killed the dark creatures. The only thing the Marchers could make out, other than the practiced butchery of whatever swarmed the Dragas, was the occasional spark when a blade struck a scale and failed to slide between the hardened armor into the creatures' soft under-bellies.

"The Sentinels of the Key," said Thomas. "When I was leaving, the stone statues assigned to defend the Key came to life. They explained a bit of their history. I guess this was their final service to the Kingdoms, making sure that we escaped with the Key."

"Perhaps it was," agreed Ariel, who had approached on quiet feet. She stared at the dead beast just a few feet away with distaste. "Dragas have not flown beyond the Northern Steppes for centuries. We must move quickly now. The Shadow Lord stirs if he has loosed these dark creatures so far to the west."

38

GOOD NEWS

Anara stared into the flames of the fire, enjoying the brief moment of peace. The last few weeks had been constant motion, constant decisions, constant adjustments as the Marchers fought to maintain control of the Northern Highlands against ever increasing numbers of dark creatures seeking to gain purchase in the Kingdom. Renn, Seneca and Nestor, the Highland chiefs responsible for distinct fronts of the Marcher defense and who sat across from her, looked just as tired as she felt. But though exhausted, they were also pleased. So far, the Marchers had held against even the most ferocious attacks, thanks in large part to their allies, a band of legendary warriors who could harness the natural power of the world.

"It appears that the Ogren have pulled back," said Rynlin Keldragan. He stood by the flames, allowing the heat to soak into his body on what promised to be a frigid night in the Highlands.

"Do we know why?" asked Seneca between bites, the grizzled Marcher finishing the first warm meal he had eaten in days.

"No," replied Nestor. "But I'm not complaining."

The others around the fire murmured their assent, thankful for the respite. Anara watched all of them closely. She had grown to know each of them quite well during the last few weeks as they fought together. At first, when Thomas had charged her with leading the defense of the northern Highlands in his absence, she had balked at the assignment. She knew that she could do it, and do it well, but she didn't think that the older war chiefs sitting across from her would accept her authority. Nevertheless, despite her doubts, she had acceded to Thomas' request and taken over responsibility for the Marchers in the north. In the beginning, there had been some tension between her and the Highland chiefs, but that had disappeared swiftly once they saw Anara in action. Whether killing an Ogren opposing her or needing to move Marcher companies over long distances quickly in order to block dark creatures from entering the higher passes, she had proven to be extraordinarily competent at these and any other challenges placed before her. A fact that Renn, Seneca and Nestor had seen demonstrated multiple times, benefited from and now appreciated and respected. So much so that the three Highland chiefs had taken to the orphaned Marcher in a way that she had never expected. Now it seemed like she had three uncles at her back, helping her, guiding her, listening to her, as they held to their difficult duty.

"What's on your mind, Rya?" asked Anara. "I get the sense that you're thinking on something."

"Thomas is returning," she replied, her hand holding onto the amulet carved in the shape of a unicorn's horn that hung from a silver chain around her neck. "He has the Key."

That last comment drew everyone's stares.

"How do you know?" asked Renn.

"We can feel him," answered Rynlin. "Where Thomas is. Where he's going. He's coming home. Rya is right. He has the Key."

"He did it," chuckled Nestor. "I never doubted that he would, but even this appeared to be almost too much for him."

"What does that mean for us?" asked Anara. "Is that why the Ogren are giving us space to breathe?"

"My guess is that the Shadow Lord is pulling back," said Rya. "The attacks were constant for weeks, and now nothing. And no sign of dark creatures crossing the Northern Steppes toward the Highlands."

Rynlin nodded in agreement. "The Shadow Lord will want to ensure that Blackstone is protected now that Thomas has the Key. Perhaps he has given up here as well. His minions have failed to gain any ground in the Highlands. With that route blocked, maybe he will turn his full attention to the Breaker now."

"So what's our next step?" asked Seneca.

"Continue to defend our northern border," said Anara, a dagger dancing between her fingers as was her habit. Thomas had charged her with keeping the Highlands free of dark creatures, and she meant to continue doing that. "At the same time, we prepare to march. When Thomas calls, we must be ready to answer."

39

UNEXPECTED VISITOR

"Is this the right place?"

Kaylie stood at the bow of the ship provided by Dendrick, the Lord of the Distant Islands, at Ariel's behest. The two were great friends, and a quick explanation and request by the Sylvan Warrior had set plans instantly in motion to get Thomas and his Marchers to the east as quickly as possible. Dendrick had provided his fastest ship and provisions for the journey, getting them out of the harbor and into the open sea in a matter of hours. They had avoided the Whorl, which remained fixed just outside the Kenmarian port city of Faralan, by first sailing north and then made good time as they cut east across the Winter Sea, landing at a hidden cove where the Clanwar Desert met the northwestern tip of the Breaker, the towering wall of black granite slabs running as far as the eye could see toward the Highlands that appeared as no more than a hazy smudge far to the southeast. After their experience in the mountains outside Afara, they had expected trouble from the Shadow Lord and his minions on the journey home. But much to their surprise, no attack, not even a hint of danger, had materialized.

"Yes, it is." Thomas scanned the barren shore in the dark of night with his sharp eyes, seeking any sign of movement while he also searched the nearby coast with the Talent. Kaylie did the same and they both nodded when they completed their tasks. There was nothing but the play of the breeze across the sand and the reeds that grew thickly along the shore. Few inhabited the rolling hills that partitioned the desert from the Breaker, which rose just a few leagues to the north. "But let's stay wary, nonetheless. We've come a long way, and I'd hate to lose a step so close to our objective. Our luck has held since leaving Afara, but that might be coming to an end."

Once Thomas was satisfied that all appeared to be well, the sailors brought the sleek vessel as close in to land as possible, lowering several longboats and rowing the Marchers to shore with strong, consistent strokes that rapidly cut through the calm water of the small bay. In the cold of the early morning, the only light came from the bright, shining stars, which made the white sand of the beach glow dimly. Once their passengers were safely ashore, the sailors returned to their vessel, turning back to the west and their home isles. The Marchers hastily spread out along the shore and then into the lowlands, setting up a defensive perimeter. All was calm and quiet, but that didn't mean it would remain so.

Thomas stood calmly in their midst, extending his senses once again. Pleased that no hazard threatened, he turned back to Oso and Kaylie, somewhat surprised. He had located an unanticipated visitor waiting for them.

"Daran Sharban, a Sylvan Warrior, is just up this way. I'll walk up to meet him. There doesn't seem to be any immediate danger near, but my gut is telling me that something isn't quite right. Oso, keep the Marchers sharp."

"Of course, Thomas." Oso scrunched up his face, which made him resemble a cantankerous old man. Clearly, this discovery didn't please him. "Were you expecting to be met?"

Thomas turned to Oso, thoughtful, his mind working furiously to put together several disparate pieces of a puzzle that Thomas feared was about to reveal a nasty truth. "No. That's what worries me."

The large Highlander issued the necessary commands to the Marchers as they followed Thomas off the beach and into the scrub that marked the border between sand and sparse forest that rapidly gave way to a series of knolls. The Marchers remained alert, hands close to the hilts of their swords. They could feel it as well. No imminent sense of danger or threat, but an uneasiness, as if something was about to happen, but what it could be they could only guess.

Kaylie's thoughts remained on what needed to be done. With Thomas having gained the Key, the battle with the Shadow Lord approached quickly. Faster than she would have liked, but she kept that thought to herself. Rallying the Kingdoms to fight at the Breaker was the next step and the only way to keep the Dark Horde on the Northern Steppes. But so much depended on Thomas. She resolved that she would do all that she could to reduce as much of his burden as possible.

Thomas was having similar thoughts, knowing that the time for him to go to Blackstone and meet his fate was approaching. He was resigned to it and realistic about the likely result. But before that he would do all that he could to ensure Kaylie's safety. Fighting the Dark Horde was not something that she needed to do, though he was certain that she would argue otherwise. He needed to find a way to get Kaylie to her father. She'd never forgive him for it, but better that than he be the cause of her being placed in mortal peril.

His thoughts were interrupted as he walked over the final dune and recognized Daran Sharban, his red hair bright even in the darkness of night, standing calmly at the edge of the forest. The Sylvan Warrior charged with protecting this part of the world, he grinned as Thomas approached.

"Well met, Daran. I wasn't expecting you to be here."

"I spoke with your grandfather, Thomas. He asked that I offer what assistance I could when you arrived."

Daran stepped forward jauntily, the smile never leaving his face, though it didn't translate to his eyes, which Thomas interpreted as anxious. The Sylvan Warrior gripped Thomas' hand strongly, then stepped back.

Thomas kept his face impassive, but he studied Daran closely. The feeling of wrongness continued to plague him, in fact having grown more persistent as the Marchers had left the beach, but he still couldn't identify the source of his unease. Yet he did sense a tension in Daran that he had never encountered before. It was distinctly out of character for the Sylvan Warrior and that sent a bolt of warning through him.

"Quite a journey, from what I understand," said Daran, taking in Kaylie, Oso and the Marchers coming through the scrub from the beach. "And all went well? Did you find what you were looking for?"

"As well as could be," replied Thomas, his eyes locked onto Daran, measuring him. Weighing him. Finding something lacking. For some reason, the conversation that he had engaged in with Kincaid about why he and the

Sentinels had never revealed the location of the Key came to mind.

Kaylie stepped up next to Thomas, taking in this tall, red-haired stranger. She noticed the moonlight glint off the silver necklace he wore, identifying him as a Sylvan Warrior.

"The Princess of Fal Carrach, I presume," said Daran, giving her a slight bow and a wide smile. "I have heard much about you. I am Daran Sharban, Sylvan Warrior and protector of these lands."

Thomas stepped in front of Kaylie, his unease blossoming and his instincts warning him of danger. Kaylie noted his movement. At first, she was surprised, but then she understood. Her hand naturally drifted toward her dagger in response.

"No one knew that we were coming in here, Daran." Thomas stared at his fellow Sylvan Warrior, his gaze hard and unwavering.

Daran's always present smile fell for a moment, then quickly returned. "Thomas, why the concern? I'm simply here to help you and your Marchers. It's the least that I could do for a fellow Sylvan Warrior. Rynlin asked that I look out for you. I'm just doing as a good friend asked."

"Thomas, what's going on?" asked Kaylie, her own anxiety growing. She glanced behind her, noting that Oso and the other Marchers were still several hundred yards away.

Thomas studied Daran carefully, his inspection incisive. Even in the dim light provided by the moon, he could pick out every feature of Daran's face. And on this frigid night, he noticed sweat beading on the tall Sylvan Warrior's forehead and running down his temple. Even more telling, Thomas' necklace, once worn by his mother, had grown ice cold. He had used the Talent just moments before to confirm that there was no danger in the vicinity. But he had never known the gleaming silver pendant to be wrong, the icy metal suggesting that he was in peril. In fact, if there was a threat as the magicked amulet implied, it most likely stood in front of him.

"You never answered my question, Daran. How did you know I would be here? No one knew." The hair on Thomas' neck prickled as the tension within Daran built, observing how his friend flexed his fingers nervously and couldn't seem to stand still as he shifted nervously from one foot to the other. "Not even my grandfather."

Daran's smile disappeared for good, his eyes now sharp, his voice cold. "It didn't have to come to this, Thomas. It could have been much easier." He sighed in resignation. "But if this is the way it has to happen, then so be it."

In an instant Thomas felt the pull of the Talent as Daran took hold of the natural magic of the world, enclosing Thomas, Kaylie and himself in a shimmering dome of energy that blocked out the sound of the ocean waves slamming against the shore and the nighttime noises of the forest. The barrier glowed dimly in the night, its light blue radiance catching Oso's attention, the large Highlander remembering what Thomas' grandparents had constructed to keep the Shadow Lord's creature contained during the battle in the Highlands. He and the Marchers sprinted forward, some with their blades drawn. But they had to stop when they reached the magical barrier, unable to break through the glowing dome with their fists or steel to reach Thomas and Kaylie.

Much to his frustration, Daran had raised the dome before Thomas could push Kaylie clear. Now they were both trapped, the pellucid barrier muffling the cries of outrage as

Oso and the Marchers were prevented from coming to Thomas' aid. Kaylie pulled her sword, ready to fight. Thomas simply stood his ground calmly.

"How long since you sold yourself to the Shadow Lord?"

The bluntness of Thomas' question caught Daran off guard. He saw the Marchers trying to break through his magical dome, but he wasn't worried. They could pound on the shield for days and it would have no effect whatsoever. But he did feel some urgency to what he had to do next. He had been given a task to complete, and he would within the specific time frame, but he had always found a good conversation too hard to resist.

"Long enough," replied Daran, a smile back on his face. "It was an opportunity that I couldn't pass up. The Sylvan Warriors were decreasing in number. We all knew the Shadow Lord had survived the Great War and would return eventually. The odds and my desire to live a long life pointed me in this direction."

Thomas' mind worked rapidly, finally piecing all the discordant fragments into a recognizable whole. Little things that didn't seem to fit were coming together to solve the larger puzzle.

"There were fewer Marchers because of you. You provided the information needed to find them when they were alone. You guided the Shadow Lord's creatures right to them. And you helped them follow us when we came out of the Highlands on our way west, guiding them in our direction."

"Guilty as charged," laughed Daran, a glint of desperation sparking in his eyes, then disappearing just as quickly.

"You were at the Roost, and again in the forest before we reached the Clanwar Desert. The cowled assassin."

"Yes," confirmed Daran, giving Thomas a small bow to

acknowledge his deductive skills. "But in my defense, I would have taken no pleasure from your death. It was simply an assignment to be carried out. You got lucky both times, Thomas. If not for that we wouldn't be here now."

"Are you sure about that, Daran? If I recall correctly, you were the one running away both times. What makes you think that you have the strength to face me now?"

Daran stared at Thomas, his expression filling with rage at the slight, yet Thomas identified fear there as well that the tall Sylvan Warrior, try as he might, failed to hide.

"We'll just have to see who is stronger," replied Daran, though his voice wavered, as if the uncertainty resulting from his previous encounters with Thomas had already begun to worm its way beneath his confidence.

"How could you?" demanded Kaylie. "They were your friends. Your brothers and sisters."

Daran laughed again to hide his increasing misgivings. "It was quite easy, Princess. Quite easy, indeed, when you consider the master who I serve."

"Was it worth it?" she asked, her distaste clear.

He stepped forward, looking Kaylie over with a lecherous grin. "You're more beautiful than I expected, Princess. Quite a catch, in fact. If my master gives you to me, then perhaps it will be worth it in the end."

Thomas took hold of the Talent, allowing the energy of nature to flow through him. Daran noticed immediately, stepping back.

"She is already spoken for, Daran. Now what is it that you want?"

"Well, as I said, the Princess of Fal Carrach would be a wonderful gift," Daran replied through a forced chuckle. "But I'm here for a bigger prize, Thomas."

"Me."

"You."

The silence stretched for more than a minute, Daran now serious, the two Sylvan Warriors facing off against one another. Kaylie was afraid to breathe. The Marchers remained outside the magical dome, their frustration clear, not able to hear anything but still watching the standoff intently.

Daran moved first, raising his hands quickly and shooting bolts of black energy toward Thomas and Kaylie. Thomas wove a shield made from the Talent in front of them, the white radiance pulsing brightly every time it deflected the quarrels of Dark Magic.

"Stay down," said Thomas, as he remained in front of Kaylie, holding the shield.

The intensity of Daran's attack increased as the traitorous Sylvan Warrior sought to destroy Thomas' defense right from the start, the black energy trying to envelop the shield. But the barrier held; in fact, it grew stronger as Thomas streamed more of the Talent into it.

"Thomas, I can help," Kaylie yelled.

Thomas grinned at Kaylie's insistence, despite what they faced, drawing her to him even more.

"I know you can. But Daran is almost as strong as I am in the Talent. And he's been practicing since before the Great War. You have the strength, but not the training. If I'm to fight him, I can't worry about you as well."

Kaylie wanted to protest, but his logic made sense. Reluctantly she nodded in agreement.

"Thank you."

Thomas kept his attention on Daran, maintaining his shield. The attack continued, but with no effect other than the bolts of black energy deflecting off the shield to dissipate against the barrier. Thomas actually was thankful for the dome. Though having Kaylie here behind him was a concern, the magical barrier kept Oso and his Marchers safe. For now.

"But there must be something that I can do?" Kaylie growled in frustration.

"There is. You had mentioned that Rya was teaching you how to defend yourself with the Talent."

"She was."

"Did she teach you how to do what I'm doing now? To craft and hold a shield?"

"She showed it to me, but she never had the chance to take me through the process beyond a few attempts."

"No matter," said Thomas, his focus still on Daran, who continued to shoot shard after shard of Dark Magic toward them. "I need you to form a shield like I have. Are you willing to try?"

Seeing no need to answer, Kaylie grasped the Talent, allowing the power to flow through her. She examined what Thomas had done and instinctively tried to imitate the flows. At first, the ball of energy that swirled in front of her didn't resemble anything at all. But gradually it took shape, slowly mimicking the shield that Thomas continued to use to defend against Daran's attack. It was a bit smaller than she would have liked, but she fixed that quickly.

Thomas glanced back. "Excellent, well done."

"What do you want me to do?"

"Stay here, close to the barrier. Keep the shield in front of you."

"What are you going to do?"

"Something that Daran doesn't expect."

40

COMBAT

Daran maintained his assault on Thomas knowing that based on his past efforts trying to defeat the Highland Lord in a duel would be a risk, and perhaps one that could cost him his life. Though the veteran Sylvan Warrior had the edge in experience, Thomas was stronger than he was in the Talent, so he did not take any unnecessary chances. Daran's job was to delay and allow events to move forward as he had been instructed.

Therefore, Daran was quite content to maintain his current position, using his power to keep his adversary at a distance. Thomas' focus on not only the girl but also himself forced him to concentrate on their defense, making Daran's task easier as the minutes passed and the appointed time grew closer. He didn't need to defeat Thomas with the Talent. He just needed to keep him backed up against the dome that he had created.

But then the situation changed, and not for the better. Daran had never known that the Princess of Fal Carrach had the Talent within her, nor that she had any training. He began to worry as he watched her craft a shield similar to the one Thomas was using to hold off his own attack. And then Daran had no time to do anything but defend himself.

Thomas released his shield, sending his own spears of blazing white energy toward the traitorous Sylvan Warrior. Daran's attack faltered as he struggled to protect himself from the ferocity of Thomas' assault. Seeing his former friend scrambling to respond, Thomas pressed forward, hoping to overwhelm his adversary with brute force.

Angry at Daran's betrayal, Thomas fought now in a cold, seething fury. Angry at the loss of so many Sylvan Warriors because of one person's greed. Angry at unknowingly having put Kaylie in danger.

Confident that Kaylie was safe behind her shield, he redoubled his efforts, forcing Daran back against the magical barrier. Bolts of white-hot energy followed lightning strikes, then a blinding swirl of energy rushed toward the red-haired Sylvan Warrior. Each attack pushed Daran toward the far side of the dome, away from Kaylie, which was Thomas' goal.

Abruptly, Thomas stopped his attack. He stood there calmly, staring at Daran with contempt. The only sign of the emotion roiling within him was his tightly clenched hands held down to his sides. The traitorous Sylvan Warrior also released his hold on the Talent, letting his shield drop.

"So was it worth it?" asked Thomas. "To come to this point?"

Daran struggled to catch his breath. Defending against Thomas' attack had drained him. He had attempted to kill Thomas twice before without success, but in this very moment he realized that he could never expect to defeat him in a fair combat. Thomas was too strong. Too determined. Too tenacious. Daran's greater experience in the

Talent, and his additional powers in Dark Magic granted to him by the Shadow Lord, meant nothing in this fight.

Daran laughed, his irrepressible personality forcing its way to the surface despite the dire circumstances that he faced. "Probably not," he replied. "But sometimes in life you make bad choices. Or perhaps they are choices that aren't really choices. Who can really say? No matter. In the end, you pay for them for the rest of your life."

Thomas ignored Daran's attempted rationalization. "You were my grandfather's best friend."

"Aye. Your grandfather's a good man, and I've always liked you, lad. I'm sorry it's come to this. But as I said, bad choices and all."

In a flash, Daran called on his Dark Magic for the first time, crafting a staff made of pulsating black energy and swinging for Thomas' head. Thomas created his own staff from the Talent, blocking the blow. They moved around the dome much like the gladiators of old, attacking and defending often in the same motion, the glowing staffs of energy -- one a pulsing black, the other a blinding white -- sparking whenever the Dark Magic and the Talent connected.

The Marchers watched in fascination, never having seen two opponents move so fast. The Sylvan Warriors fought at such a speed that often Oso and the other Highlanders could only catch the blur of movement, the only sign of engagement the sparks cascading in the moonlight when the staffs struck one another.

Kaylie remained where she was, keeping her shield in front of her to protect against the stray bolts of energy that ricocheted through the dome whenever the two staffs met. She knew that Thomas was stronger in the Talent, but she still worried for him. She desperately wanted to help, but acknowledged reluctantly that attempting to do so in the middle of such a duel could be deadly for Thomas if he were distracted by whatever she tried to do.

The fight continued as the minutes passed, Thomas and Daran spinning and gliding around the dome as they engaged in a deadly dance. Yet those watching could see that Thomas was having the better of it. He had forced Daran back against the dome, his unceasing aggression keeping the traitorous Sylvan Warrior on the defensive. Thomas continued to batter at Daran, knowing that with every blow of his staff, another ounce of strength drained away from his opponent.

"Thomas, enough!" Daran released his Dark Magic, his staff blinking out, and he fell to one knee. Sweat poured off the Sylvan Warrior, soaking his clothes despite the cold. He looked wan and pale, his efforts to defend himself having taken a heavy toll.

Thomas stepped back, though he kept hold of the staff.

"What now, Daran? You have nowhere to go. The only thing keeping me from killing you right now is the friendship that we once had."

"And for that I'm thankful," huffed Daran, trying to catch his breath. "You've proven yourself once again. But unfortunately for you, I assumed that you would make this incredibly difficult. So I figured that I would need some help."

Daran looked up and Thomas followed his gaze. What Thomas saw turned his blood cold.

Thomas hadn't realized that Daran had reshaped the dome, eliminating the top but keeping the walls in place to keep the Marchers out. Streaking through the opening came three Dragas, their huge, leathery wings fully extended as the dark creatures descended through the air until their three-toed claws dug into the rocky soil. Thomas cursed himself for a fool. He should have expected as much from Daran, knowing that his former friend's own survival was always foremost in his mind. Even worse, these Dragas were larger than the ones he and the Marchers had faced when claiming the Key, and this time he didn't have the Sentinels to help him.

41

TAKEN

"Thomas!" screamed Kaylie, as she saw the three Dragas glide through the opening in the dome, venomous saliva dripping from their jaws to scar the earth beneath them.

The Marchers began to pound on the translucent shield once more, seeking to aid their friend and leader. But it was wasted effort. They had no way to break through the magical barrier.

"Malachias, I'm glad you made it," said Daran. "Otherwise this boy would be the death of me." The Sylvan Warrior laughed at his own macabre sense of humor.

Thomas stood in front of the three Dragas, the massive beasts surveying the man who dared to challenge them without a hint of fear. He saw the hunger in their eyes, the stench of their rancid, poisonous breath turning his stomach. Thomas shivered upon seeing the tall man on the back of one of the Dragas, a saddle tied around its belly. The robed figure's bald pate gleamed, his cadaverous face appearing all the more skeletal in the moonlight. Even in the darkness, Thomas couldn't miss the blackness of Malachias' eyes. Yet he refused to back down.

"So once again this is the one giving us so much trouble," Malachias said in a brittle whisper that carried within the silence of the dome.

"Aye. The Lord of the Highlands himself."

Malachias stared malevolently at Thomas for a moment, seemingly assessing him in an instant.

"How did you break free from the collar, boy? No one's ever succeeded in doing that."

"I think I'll keep that to myself."

"Probably a wise decision," muttered Malachias. "It doesn't need to end this way, boy. Chained or not, think about what we discussed when last we faced one another. If you challenge my master, your fate is sealed. There are other paths from which to choose."

Thomas shook his head, a look of determination settling on his face. "There is only one path."

Malachias grunted in disgust. He had expected such a response. The boy was a predictable fool, but a dangerous fool.

"There was no need to kill the Princess of Armagh. She was a useful tool."

"I didn't kill her," replied Thomas. "She killed herself when she threw her lot in with you and your master."

Grunting again in response to Thomas' comment, Malachias finally turned his attention back to Daran Sharban. "For someone as clever as you, you were going about this all wrong, Sylvan Warrior." He bit off the last few words as if they tasted badly.

"Really? How so?" asked Daran, standing unsteadily as the massive pull on the Talent that he needed to form the protective dome and take on Thomas had left him weak and unsteady.

"As we expected, the boy is made of steel. So the key to defeating this one is the girl."

With an unseen command, one of the riderless Dragas charged toward Kaylie, screaming in rage and hunger. Thomas sprinted toward her, but he knew that he couldn't get there in time. The Dragas was too fast.

Having little opportunity to respond, Kaylie's training with Kael and Rya took over. She moved based on instinct rather than thought. Whipping out her sword, she infused the blade with the Talent, thankful that Rya had made her practice this skill hundreds of times before she was satisfied that Kaylie had mastered the task.

The Dragas sped toward her, claws tearing up the rocky ground, mouth agape, teeth the length of a man's forearm shining in the moonlight and large enough to take her in one bite. Kaylie waited until the dark creature was almost upon her before she swung down, then slid to the side. Her blazing blade sliced through the tough hide of the Dragas like a knife through butter, taking off a large portion of its lower jaw.

The beast screamed in anger and pain, rising up on its hind legs to get away from the prey that had chosen to fight back and injured it so grievously. That's when Thomas struck. Using the staff made of white energy, he swung through the back of the creature's hind leg. He heard the satisfying crunch of bones breaking as the dark creature pitched forward, its damaged leg unable to support the weight of its upper body. Thomas then leapt up, using the Dragas' collapsing body as a way to launch himself up into the air so that he could bring the staff down once again, this time on the beast's left wing. Once more he heard the rewarding sound of breaking bones.

The Dragas collapsed to the ground, blinded by a pain that was now accompanied by fear. It had never been bested and had never expected to be. But now it was helpless as it writhed on the dry grass in mind-numbing agony.

Kaylie stepped forward with her sword and brought the blade down on its skull, the magicked steel sliding into its brain and killing the wounded beast.

Yet Thomas and Kaylie had no time to savor their victory. Malachias used the attack by the Dragas to craft his own ambush, pulling on his Dark Magic and sending a shard of corrupted black energy toward Thomas. Focused on helping Kaylie, Thomas turned at the last second. He brought his staff up in an attempt to block the attack, but he was only able to deflect a small portion of Malachias' strike.

The Dark Magic cut into his side and blasted Thomas backward, slamming him against the dome of energy that continued to keep the Marchers from the fight. He slid to the ground and lay there in a crumpled mess, not moving.

"Thomas!" screamed Kaylie. Dropping her blade and releasing the Talent, she sprinted toward him. His clothes and hair sizzled from the Dark Magic that had burned through him. His eyes were closed, parts of his skin scorched, and he wasn't breathing. "Thomas! Thomas!"

Kaylie pulled him into a hug, attempting to wake him, desperate to see his eyes open. But he didn't move, his body limp. The Dark Magic had torn through Thomas, sucking the life from him much like the kiss of a Shade. Kaylie pulled Thomas closer, trying to will life back into him, her tears dripping down onto his face as the realization of what had just happened slammed into her like a wave crashing onto the shore.

"As I said, the boy's weakness is the girl. A distraction, and a useful one at that."

"Indeed," said Daran. "You were right."

Daran stared at the girl, but even more so at Thomas. He had known Thomas since he was a child and had spent more time with him than he could recall through his friendship with Rynlin and Rya. And now that boy was gone, his life taken. One decision on his part, Daran thought. One bad decision, and it had all led to this.

"Take the girl," said Malachias. "She could prove useful still. And find the Key."

For a moment, Daran thought about resisting, of finally fighting back. But he knew that the time for that had come and gone as he pushed that brief defiance from his mind. It was pointless. There was nothing that he could do now. The only thing that he could achieve by refusing was his own death.

Approaching Kaylie, Daran pulled her away from Thomas. Inconsolable, she struggled violently, not wanting to leave him. Using his Dark Magic, a touch to her forehead ended her struggles and put her to sleep. But in doing so, he realized that his worsening weakness was turning into exhaustion, his power beginning to fail. Looking up he observed that the dome of energy had begun to flicker, and through the haze he could see the Marchers more clearly now. Staring at him. Intent. Waiting for the barrier to fail. Waiting to exact their revenge upon him. If the magical shell fell before he was away, he wouldn't have the strength to mount a defense. Acknowledging the risk of the decision he was about to make, Daran quickly looked down at Thomas' body, sprawled in the dirt and grass. Thomas could have the Key on him. Then again, perhaps he did not. Daran tried to convince himself of that possibility, knowing that it was a foolish and unlikely thought. Did he have the time to search the body? A sharp crack to his left decided it for him. The dome of energy was about to fail, the once translucent haze flickering faster and faster. It was only a matter of seconds before it disintegrated.

Shaking his head in frustration, Daran carried Kaylie to the Dragas, laying her across the front of his saddle before hopping onto the beast. As the two Dragas launched themselves into the air, the traitorous Sylvan Warrior released his control over the shield, and the wall of energy dissipated.

Daran didn't bother to look back as they winged their way into the chill of the night. He didn't need to see the Marchers finally come forward in silence to stand around their fallen lord. He had liked Thomas, thinking of him as a nephew. But that was in the past now, better just to let it go. For the Highland Lord was finally dead and the Shadow Lord and the Dark Horde now had an open path to the Kingdoms.

42

IMPRISONED

Kaylie awoke over the northern Highlands, the cold night air scraping across her face and forcing her eyes open. She struggled to regain consciousness for several minutes, fighting through a groggy haze that made it difficult to focus or think, her memory no better than a jumble of disparate impressions. Finally, she recalled what had happened, the terrible events of the early morning all crashing down upon her like a monstrous wave on the shore. The Dragas. The treachery. Malachias. Thomas. When it all returned to her, she jolted from her confused state of mind to one of instant terror. She struggled frantically, trying to escape. Trying to do something. But she could barely move, and she was soon thankful for that. If not for the leather straps Daran had used to tie her to the saddle, she would have fallen to the peaks far below.

She shivered more from her fear than from the cold as the full weight of her predicament struck home. The Dragas glided easily through the sky, their powerful wings pushing them across the Highlands then out over the Northern Steppes. Though the massive dark creatures frightened her, she took solace in the fact that she had killed a Dragas, one on her own in the Distant Islands and one with Thomas' help, but she did nonetheless drive her sword through the beast's skull. So these monsters could be killed. But could her captor? The figure riding to her right, bald and sharp featured, a fetid grey robe flapping in the wind, terrified her even more than a Dragas.

The man whose eyes resembled swirling pools of black gave off a trace of ancient menace. The one named Malachias. He had looked at her the instant that she had awakened, knowing immediately when she had returned to her senses, a predatory glint in his eye. It felt as if the skeletal figure were undressing her, but not in the way Daran did. The traitorous Sylvan Warrior seemed to take particular pleasure in the fact that she rode in front of him. His hands had settled around her waist now that she was awake, and she knew his actions weren't designed to keep her in her seat. She had experience in dealing with that kind of predator, but not with one such as Malachias, whose needs appeared to have transcended the demands of the flesh.

When Daran looked at her, she knew that he saw her as a prize, as something for him to use so long as he desired and then discard when he was done. But when Malachias looked at her he stripped her inner self bare. It felt like he had evaluated her soul and in seconds determined how he could use her to his advantage. If her assessment was accurate, she didn't know if she had the strength or courage to deal with a creature such as him.

Malachias had taken her for a reason, a reason that she didn't want to think about but was all too obvious as the burnt ash of the Charnel Mountains replaced the dead grass and scrub of the Northern Steppes flowing beneath them in the bright moonlight. The hills below her quickly turned into towering mountains that seemed to challenge the soaring peaks of the Highlands for hegemony, her fears increasing tenfold.

She reached for the Talent, desperately hoping to feel its familiar touch, but her anguish only deepened. Her thoughts were still too muddled to do anything but confirm that her skill in molding the natural power of the world remained, but was just beyond her reach. Several times she tried to concentrate, to break through whatever impediment kept her from feeling the familiar warmth of the Talent flowing through her, but her mind continued to drift, as she was still muzzy from whatever Daran had done to her.

Some additional clarity was thrust upon her when the two Dragas began their descent, circling over the withered husk of Blackstone. She had never seen the ancient city of ruins before, believing that it was no more than a relic from an earlier age. What filled her eyes now terrified her and sent a chill down her spine.

A strong wind gusted continuously through the stone metropolis, the black ash caught in its grasp and swirling uncontrollably. As a result, what was visible one second was hidden the next, but she had glimpsed enough. Camped in the midst of that charred landscape was the largest army she had ever seen, one brought together for a single purpose. To conquer the Kingdoms. She had fought Ogren and Shades with Thomas. Through those experiences, she had thought that she had learned to control her fear. But this was a discovery that frightened her to her very core. A terror that she had never experienced before.

Ogren marched through the barren city, forming into their war bands. Shades led them, the massive beasts following the silent commands of the Shadow Lord's captains. Off in the distance, at the very border of the ruined city, she caught sightings of swiftly moving shadows, no more than flits of movement at the edge of her vision. Fearhounds, she guessed. Perhaps even Mongrels, judging by their massive size.

The Dragas slowly circled a monstrous keep before settling onto a huge balcony that extended out over the largest square she had ever seen, which now contained thousands upon thousands of dark creatures. Daran quickly dismounted, but not before running his hands from her hips to her thighs and resting them there, suggesting what her future might hold if he had a say in it. She cringed at his touch as he removed the straps that had kept her in her seat.

Dropping to the ash-covered stone, Kaylie fell to her knees as her legs gave out beneath her. Unconcerned by her weakness, which was a continuing aftereffect of the application of Dark Magic upon the Princess of Fal Carrach, Malachias stepped forward, grasping her arm firmly. He helped her up, but not from any kindness. Rather, he felt the press of time, and he pulled her through two massive doors into a murky chamber. The only light came from the dimness of the early morning, the clouds covering the city placing it in a perpetual murk. The chamber awed her with its checkered floor of white and black stone and in the middle of the design a large disc with a carving caught her eye, but she couldn't make out its etchings in the dark.

"Who have we here, Malachias? I wasn't expecting visitors."

The menacing whisper sent a petrifying chill through Kaylie's body. Her instinct for survival told her to run, to get away as fast as she could. She tried to back out of the room in an awkward stumble, seeking the dim light of the day just beyond the entry. But Malachias' grip only tightened around her arm and held her fast.

"Something of value, master. The King of Fal Carrach's daughter."

A cowled figure wearing black, flowing garments glided across the checkered floor to stand before her. The wispy robes shifted in the light breeze in a way that suggested that they had no weight, more mist than substance.

Kaylie wanted to look away, to run, to hide, to do anything but stand there, but she couldn't. Her captor wouldn't allow it. As the shadowy figure approached, head hidden, all she could make out were the eyes, which burned a bright red. At first, she thought those eyes resembled the flames of a fire. But then she realized her mistake. Not a fire, but rather blood.

The figure stood before Kaylie for several minutes, not saying a word. His examination unnerved her, even more so than Malachias'. Yet she refused to be cowed, and though her fear sent her whole body shaking, she forced herself to stare into those blood-red eyes.

"You are right, Malachias." The whisper echoed in the circular chamber. "We can use this one against her father. He will have little desire to fight if he knows that the life of his daughter hangs in the balance. It will make our assault on the Breaker that much easier."

The shadowy figured turned his gaze away from Kaylie, much to her relief. Her limbs, previously frozen in place, felt like her own again. She hadn't realized that she had been holding her breath. She forced herself to stand up straight though her body fought against her.

"And our brave Sylvan Warrior. What have you to say?"

Daran's normal smirk was nowhere to be found. He shuffled his feet, trying to hide his unease but failing.

"They were exactly where you said they would be, master."

The cowled figure who appeared to be more spirit than man stared at the Sylvan Warrior, his blood-red eyes boring into him. The silence grew too much for Daran.

"He's dead, master. Malachias can confirm it."

The words tore into Kaylie's heart. The haze that covered her mind had kept the past night a blur, taking away her ability to hold onto anything solid. When she thought of Thomas, she had felt an inordinate grief. But Daran's words burned through the mist, driving a stake into her heart. She let out a moan as her legs gave way, her sorrow all encompassing, but she remained in place, Malachias' strong grip easily holding her up.

"I haven't sensed the boy for some time, so you may be speaking truthfully, but that's no guarantee. Malachias?"

"Dead, master."

A small laugh erupted from behind the darkened cowl, sounding like a snake slithering through the sand. "You've done well, my traitorous Sylvan Warrior. Better than I expected."

"Thank you, master."

"And the Key?"

Malachias and Daran glanced at one another, both unwilling to meet the Shadow Lord's gaze. Both seemed to hope that the other would reply first as the silence dragged on. Finally, Daran could contain himself no longer, the building stillness setting his nerves on edge.

"No sign of it, master."

The Shadow Lord turned his blazing eyes upon Daran, the Sylvan Warrior finding it difficult to look into that penetrating stare.

"Malachias?"

Even the forbidding, normally unperturbed right hand of the Shadow Lord appeared uncomfortable. "I could not sense it, master." Malachias shifted his feet, the only visible sign of his agitation. "If it was there, I would have known. I would have located it. Besides, with the boy dead, the Key is no longer a concern. The boy is the only one who could have made use of it."

The Shadow Lord remained silent for quite some time. Malachias kept his body still, hoping his posture displayed a sense of confidence, false though it may be. Daran couldn't stop himself from fidgeting.

"As you say," the Shadow Lord finally said. "Malachias, take the girl to the cells. We'll make use of her later." The Shadow Lord turned and glided back into the dark gloom of the chamber. "Sylvan Warrior, return to your place. You have done well, but you still have a role to play."

43

DRAWING POISON

I nitially stunned by what they had seen, Thomas having fallen in front of their very eyes, and they unable to do anything but watch helplessly, the Marchers had stood guard around the Lord of the Highlands in silent vigil, overcome with sadness and grief when the magical barrier finally disappeared. Oso had leapt forward, trying to help his friend. His brother. But he could find no visible wound to treat. Just a few scorch marks the color of black ash along his side as if he had been burned. The large Highlander knelt down, searching desperately for a pulse or a breath. He thought that he detected a very shallow inhalation every few minutes, the time lengthening between each movement, but neither he nor Aric could be certain, the rise and fall of Thomas' chest barely perceptible.

Oso placed a blanket under Thomas' head and over his body, hoping to make him comfortable and keep him warm in spite of the bitterly cold wind. He ordered the Marchers to set up a small camp and establish a rotation of perimeter guards. Then he sat down next to Thomas, not knowing what else to do as the sun began to rise in the east, its appearance still an hour or so off because the Breaker and Highland peaks blocked its strong rays. A knife wound or a slash from a sword, Oso could care for an injury such as that. That was straightforward. But this? This, he had no clue what to do. His first thought was that Rynlin or Rya could help, but how was he to reach them from here? He had no way to communicate with them. There was nothing that he could do. Nothing but wait for fate to take its course.

When Oso's sorrow began to mix with his feeling of helplessness, that's when the wolves began to appear. First in ones and twos, then a dozen or more at a time. Black and grey, some streaked with white or brown, the large animals padded silently toward the Marchers, trotting out from the forest and scrub. Their bright eyes sparkled as the darkness turned to light. Some turned away from the Marchers, their gaze tracking anything that moved beyond the small camp as if they had established their own guard. Others settled on their haunches, just a few feet from Oso, their eyes locked onto the unconscious Highland Lord.

As the minutes passed, even more wolves arrived, dozens appearing at a time. At first, they set the Marchers on edge. A few kept their hands close to the hilts of their blades, wary of the massive animals despite knowing that they were allies of the Highland Lord and were performing an important service in defense of their homeland. But the wolves made no move toward the Marchers, so the men and women of the Highlands relaxed, if just a bit. Oso barely noticed them, his focus so intent on his friend, trying to will his own life force into Thomas, who had risked so much for him when they had first met.

The number of wolves continued to increase, until at least four packs had settled around the Marchers. The wolves knew who lay in their midst. The Raptor, brother to their leader, enemy of the Dark One. They knew his deeds. They knew him. And they knew that they needed him if they were to destroy the dark creatures that plagued their lands.

All was quiet for almost an hour, no one, man or beast, daring even to move, and then much to the surprise of the Marchers, all the wolves rose from where they had sat or lain down and a path opened up among them, leading from the forest directly to where Oso sat with Thomas. A shadowy blur sped from the trees, followed by another pack of wolves streaming behind. This wolf was larger than any other, the size of a small horse, its fur black but for a streak of white across its eyes.

The huge wolf stopped behind Oso, then nudged him in the back. Oso had been so intent on Thomas that he had no idea what had been occurring around him.

"Beluil. I'm glad you're here."

The large wolf stepped around Oso, turning his sparkling eyes to Thomas. He sniffed from head to foot, growling the whole time. Though Oso did not know what had happened to Thomas, Beluil apparently did, and the large wolf was clearly upset.

Beluil's resulting howl, echoing off the peaks to the east, shattered the stillness. Then all the wolves raised their muzzles and howled to the sun as it finally peeked over the Highland mountains and lit up the small clearing. The sound of anguish and sorrow resembled that from a horn before charging into battle, carrying along the Breaker and then into the Highlands to echo among the white-topped peaks. When the silence returned, the last of the echoes having played out, Beluil lay down next to Thomas, his massive head resting protectively over Thomas' legs. The wolf's eyes stared to the east, toward the mountains, never wavering, as if he expected something to come from that direction.

It wasn't long before Beluil's patience was rewarded. As the sun rose just a bit higher in the sky and the Marchers maintained their silent guard, still unsettled by the number of wolves that had taken up residence around them, an angry squawk turned every eye to the sky. At the sound, Beluil rose to his haunches, his eyes still fixed on the mountains. He howled again, a call of pain and anger that all the wolves once again lent their voice.

As the cry dissipated, Oso stared at the brightening sky, finding two massive hawks shooting down toward him. If he had not known what was about to happen, he would have drawn his sword like some of the Marchers did. But the hawks were not interested in attacking. Instead, they landed deftly right next to Thomas, and Oso closed his eyes to protect against the expected glare.

After two bright flashes of white light, Rynlin and Rya stood before him.

"Thank you, Beluil," said the tall Sylvan Warrior, his dark eyes grim, his hand running affectionately through the large wolf's black fur. "We knew Thomas was in danger, but we could barely feel him through his necklace. You helped to guide us here."

"Can you help him?" asked Oso.

Rya immediately dropped to her knees and began to examine Thomas, placing a hand on his chest as she closed her eyes. Oso kept his eyes on Thomas' chest, but through the entire time he waited for some sign of life, any type of movement, there was nothing at all. Rya pulled her hand away an instant later, hissing under her breath. She studied her grandson, seeing something that no one else could. "I don't know," she whispered, a tremor of fear in her voice.

Rynlin bent down and grasped her shoulder, giving her an affectionate and supportive squeeze. "I will do what I can to help, but you must fight, Thomas," Rya continued, the normal steel in her voice returning. She turned her sharp gaze to Oso. "The Dark Magic is in him, trying to consume him. But the darkness hasn't won, not yet."

Crouching down, once more she gingerly placed her hand on Thomas' chest. She remained in that position for several long minutes. Rynlin stood behind her anxiously, scratching Beluil's massive head absently to calm his nerves. Whoever had done this to his grandson had much to account for, and the enraged Sylvan Warrior already knew what he would do when he found the one who had caused his grandson's injury. That thought, continually running through his mind, kept his growing fear for Thomas from overpowering him.

"Rynlin, give me your hand," said Rya, her voice anxious. "Thomas is still with us, but just barely. I need your strength if we're to help him."

Rynlin dropped to his knees, reaching out and taking hold of Rya's left hand as she kept her right on Thomas' chest. A white glow began to emerge from her palm, dim at first, flickering, before settling into a consistent stream. The glare increased in intensity, growing so bright that no one could look at it directly, having to turn away or shield their eyes. Once Rya had the power that she needed, she began to direct it into Thomas' body, searching and cleansing, trying to drive out and cauterize the taint that sought to eat him alive.

At first it was a straight-forward task as she applied the Talent, but then she met the resistance that she had expected and been searching for. It was then that she knew she had found the source of Thomas' malady. Gripping her husband's hand even more tightly, to the point where Rynlin gasped in pain, she redoubled her efforts, calling forth more of her Talent and what she was harnessing from Rynlin, waging a battle within Thomas that sent his body at first into a fit of shaking and then into convulsions as the power of the natural world scoured through him.

"Hold him down, Oso!"

Rynlin couldn't move as his wife drained him of the Talent, taking more and more from him as she struggled with the Dark Magic that tried to devour Thomas. The wolves and Marchers looked on anxiously, all having sensed that they had reached the climax of the fight.

A cold wind began to blow across the clearing, unhindered by the bright, warm sunlight that streamed down upon them. That wind soon took shape as a twisting darkness began to seep slowly from Thomas, then faster and faster as Rya pulled the Dark Magic from her grandson, much like a poison being drawn from a wound.

The swirling blackness quickly gained speed, whipping around haphazardly for a moment before a form began to appear within the mist. But Rya refused to allow the evil to become substantial. Having extracted all the Dark Magic from her grandson, she turned her attention to the swirling mass that was beginning to take the shape of a man, initially wispy in form, ephemeral, though the blood-red eyes were unmistakable. Maintaining her hold on the massive amount of the Talent that she had used to cleanse Thomas, she directed her power toward the blackness. The blazing white light that streamed from her hand burned into the dark, swirling cloud, the white-hot energy raging through the inky darkness and leaving behind a black ash that drifted away on the wind. In seconds, with a terrifying shriek that sent a bolt of fear through many of the

Marchers, the evil was gone, and all was quiet in the clearing.

Oso looked down at his friend. Thomas lay comfortably on the ground. He was no longer shaking, and he appeared to be breathing normally. His color also had improved as the cold that had seeped into his body had been replaced by a natural warmth. Beluil stepped forward, licking his friend's face with his broad tongue, leaving a trail of saliva in his wake.

"Will he be all right?"

"Yes, Oso," said Rya, finally releasing her husband's hand. His wife had been holding on so tightly that Rynlin had to rub his crushed fingers in an attempt to regain some feeling. "Dark Magic had settled into Thomas. I don't know how he fought it for so long, but he has always been a stubborn boy. If we hadn't gotten here when we did to extract it, he would have died within the hour, the evil of the Shadow Lord consuming his spirit."

Rya peered down at her soundly sleeping grandson, her hand trailing in his hair. She had almost lost him, but thankfully not. Then her tears began to flow down her cheeks.

Rynlin would have comforted his wife at such a time, but his mind was on other matters. His normally grim expression had become murderous.

"Tell me what happened, Oso. Tell me who needs to pay."

44

PAWN

It had only been a few hours, yet to Kaylie it felt like years since she had arrived in the Shadow Lord's lair. When told that she would be put in the dungeon, she had expected something damp, dank and moldy. But apparently the ash and dry winds that shaped the landscape above-ground had much the same effect belowground. The black ash that covered everything in Blackstone had found its way down here as well. She took solace in the fact that at least it was dry, not a drop of water to be found. The cell that she was in contained a small slit of light in a top corner of the stone ceiling far above her that kept away some of the ever-present shadow from which she could never escape entirely in this dismal place.

She sat on a stone bench, the only amenity in her cell, and tried desperately to fight against the dark, terrifying thoughts that plagued her. Despite her best efforts, her fears and failures, her losses and limitations, threatened to crush her. When she finally succeeded in forcing those percep-tions to the back of her mind, her grief pushed its way to the forefront and tried to overwhelm her.

Tears coursed down her cheeks as her mind drifted to Thomas. He couldn't be dead. He just couldn't! Yet she saw what had happened. She had held him when he fell. He had been cold, lifeless. His spirit consumed. Simply gone. Strong and stubborn as Thomas was, he couldn't have survived Malachias' attack.

She allowed herself only a few minutes to grieve before turning her mind to what Thomas would do if he were in her situation. Wiping her tears from her face with a sleeve, she studied her cell once again, looking for a way to escape. To keep herself sane, to keep her dark thoughts at bay, she turned her mind solely to that task.

Reaching for the Talent, she struggled to grasp it. The natural magic of the world was there, she could feel it, but it spilled through her fingers like water rushing through a stream. She could sense it but do nothing with it.

"It won't work, child. The Shadow Lord's Dark Magic is too strong. You will not be able to make use of the Talent here."

Malachias stood in front of the bars of her cell, his hypnotic gaze fixed upon her. Chertney and Rodric had arrayed themselves slightly behind him.

A shiver of fear ran through her, but she ignored it and steeled herself to engage with the right hand of the Shadow Lord. Her fear of Malachias had grown with Thomas' murder, yet Chertney and Rodric had little impact on her now. Chertney had withdrawn within himself, likely smothered by Malachias' presence and power. Rodric had become a shell of his former self. Never truly vibrant, the former High King now resembled someone who floundered and flopped around in his constant attempts to maintain his sanity. His stringy, greasy hair fell to his stooped shoulders.

The desire for power, the yearning for control, still burned in his eyes, but his energy had diminished, as if he were beginning to understand the true price that he paid for his allegiance to the Shadow Lord.

Kaylie curtailed her efforts to grab hold of the Talent, frustrated by her lack of success, and turned her attention to Malachias with a fierce gaze.

"What do you want?" asked Kaylie, pleased that she had asked the question in a strong, commanding tone, preventing the tremor of fear that ran through her from escaping in her voice.

"You, child. I want you. But not in the way Daran made plain." He stepped closer to the bars, his black eyes sucking in the shadows of the cell. "You have a role to play now. One you can play willingly, meaning things go easier for you. Or not, depending on what you decide. Regardless, you will play your part as my master requires. There is no point in attempting to resist. It is better simply to obey."

"I will not be a pawn for your master. My father will fight for the Kingdoms no matter my fate."

"Your father will die for his treachery!" Rodric pushed himself forward, just inches from the bars. "For what he has done to me!"

Spittle dribbled down the lips of the former High King as he tried to control his rage. He blamed the Highland Lord and many others for the loss of his throne, and Gregory of Fal Carrach was among them, in fact near the top of the list.

"He has done nothing to you," Kaylie replied calmly. "You have done it to yourself." For a moment, Kaylie considered telling the former High King his daughter's fate, then thought better of it, not knowing how the obviously mad Rodric would react.

"Control yourself, Rodric, or you may leave." Malachias' soft, scratchy voice made the former High King cringe, and he stepped back to stand beside Chertney. He turned his eyes once more to the Princess of Fal Carrach. "You need to understand the power that you seek to obstruct, child. A power that none can stand against. A power that I will set upon you to achieve my master's ends, if need be."

Biting off the last of his words, Malachias flicked his fingers toward Chertney. A thin trail of black mist surged down Chertney's throat and his nose before he could defend himself. The inky cloud worked quickly, not even giving the black-clad lord time to scream as it surged through his body and sought to destroy his life force. His eyes bulged in shock, his hands clawing at his chest, tearing apart his clothes, to get at what was ripping through his insides, but to no avail. In seconds, it was over, the light leaving Chertney's eyes as his frantic movements became sluggish, then stopped altogether as he collapsed to the ash-covered floor. The powerful warlock was no more than a desiccated corpse that resembled a mummy that had been unearthed from an airtight chamber after a thousand years of slumber. Rodric stared in horror, terrified. Malachias had just killed one of the most powerful users of Dark Magic in all the Kingdoms with barely any effort, a fact that was not lost on Kaylie.

"As I was saying, you have a choice to make. Your father and your Kingdom will be crushed. You must think of more than yourself now that your love is dead."

"You don't know that!" protested Kaylie, though her words sounded hollow, even to herself.

"Don't play with me, child. I am more than a man. I can see your heart. The boy is dead, and I will use you to get to your father." Malachias turned quickly for the exit, Rodric trailing after as if tied by a string. "You do not want to end up like Chertney."

"The end is near, child," he continued, his voice drifting back from farther down the murky hallway. "A new world is taking shape, and it begins tomorrow."

45

VENGEANCE

D aran walked down the steep trail cautiously, stopping at odd moments for several minutes at a time to listen and watch for anything out of the ordinary, his eyes scanning his surroundings warily, his senses attuned to the normal goings on of this part of his protectorate. All seemed as it should be as he gazed down upon the hidden valley that was his home. The small cottage that he had built at the very edge of the woods that lined the glade was invisible unless you knew where to look or stumbled upon it by mistake.

He could have hurried back from his audience at Blackstone. In fact, he desperately wanted to. But he chose to take his time, leaving the Charnel Mountains as quickly as possible by changing into the shape of a hawk and flying across the Northern Steppes but then slowing his journey by transforming back and hiking through the wilderness for several hours, wanting to get a feel for what was around him and needing the time to recover from what had been a terrifying, unsettling experience. He hadn't actually lied about the Key, but neither had he been entirely truthful. Yes, he had not found the Key. Then again, with his magical barrier collapsing and the Marchers intent on reaching Thomas, even with two Dragas at his back he hadn't put much effort into looking for the artifact, afraid that it would take too much time and leave him vulnerable to a sword in the belly. He was grateful that the Shadow Lord had accepted his explanation and was surprised that Malachias had supported him. Moreover, he had no doubt that word of his betrayal would spread, the only question being how fast. Would he have time to complete his other tasks before he was discovered? He hoped so. Regardless, he was certain that this would be his last visit to the cottage that he had called home for centuries. Now was the time to move on and not be tied to any one place for long, as no doubt his former friends would be intent on exacting their revenge upon him, assuming any survived the coming onslaught.

When he reached the valley floor, he stood at the fringe of the forest for almost an hour. Silent, unmoving, he searched for anything out of place with and without the Talent, anything that would suggest that he wasn't alone. That his master may have decided on a different course for him, a deadlier course, passed through his mind repeatedly. But he told himself that was foolish, that there was nothing to worry about. If his master wanted him out of the way, there was no better time to do it then when he stood before him in Blackstone.

Finally satisfied that all was as it should be at his home, Daran breathed a sigh of relief. He stepped from between the trees, walking quickly toward his cottage. He needed to find out when the Sylvana would gather, then share that with his master. Once the Shadow Lord had that information, his master could address the only real threat to his plan for conquering the Kingdoms and, with luck, eliminate the Sylvana with a single blow. If Daran didn't succeed in obtaining the desired information, well, then maybe his fears would come to pass. Perhaps his usefulness would come to an end in the eyes of his master. But there was no point in worrying about that now. He had work to do.

Using the Talent, Daran removed the magical protections that he had placed on his cabin, pleased to discover that nothing had disturbed his wards during his absence. His traps would have alerted him. When he pushed open the door and stood backlit in the waning afternoon light, he realized his mistake too late.

"Have you been here long?"

"Long enough."

"How did you get past my defenses?"

"An easy task. Remember, I was the one who taught you the ways of the Talent. I was the one who showed you the ways of the Sylvana."

"And for that I'm thankful."

"But that wasn't enough for you."

Daran closed his eyes in resignation, sighing. "No, it wasn't."

Rynlin Keldragan rose from the bench he had waited upon, his tall presence filling up the small cabin. He looked at his former protégé with disgust, his eyes burning brightly with anger, his posture menacing.

"Thomas lives, Daran. Your master will not be happy."

"No, he won't," Daran agreed. A bolt of cold fear shot through the red-haired Sylvan Warrior. He shook his head in acceptance of his failure. That news wasn't really as surprising as it should have been. He had watched Thomas grow up, he knew his strength. If any could live through such an attack, it was him. But that information was more than disheartening. It was a death sentence for Daran, and it sapped his will like wine draining from a newly opened cask. He was stuck between the Sylvana and the Shadow Lord, now having betrayed both. His death was assured. It was just a question of which threat would get to him first.

Daran thought to lie, to extricate himself from what was an unwinnable situation. But he saw no escape route. No way to turn the situation to his advantage. No way to push the blame somewhere else.

"What did he promise you?"

For several long moments, Daran refused to look at the forbidding visage that stared down at him. It took all of his strength to force his eyes to his former mentor. But still he couldn't speak.

"Riches? Power? Everlasting life? After all these years I would think that you would know the truth of what you have committed yourself to. What you have betrayed your brothers and sisters for."

"It was a losing cause," whispered Daran, suddenly tired, as if he finally felt the many years of betrayal weighing down upon him. "The Sylvana are decreasing in number. It's just a matter of time before all are destroyed. You've seen what power the Shadow Lord holds! You've seen the forces that he controls!"

Rynlin looked at his former pupil with pity. "You've been consumed by your fears, Daran."

"I have been consumed by reality, Rynlin! No one can stand against the Dark Horde! Not this time! Rather than die in some pointless battle, I shall live and enjoy the bounty the Shadow Lord has promised me. Or at least I would have." With this last outburst, it seemed that all of Daran's strength fled him, his body sagging as if he were about to collapse to the rough-hewn floor.

"Yes, we are fewer in number." Rynlin's voice was quiet

but harder than steel. "We have lost several Sylvan Warriors in recent years. I believe we have you to thank for that."

Daran cringed at the claim, not bothering to rebut the charge. There was nothing he could say that would change the truth of his former mentor's words.

"But that doesn't mean we will give up. That we will surrender to a fate over which we have no control." Rynlin's voice was filled with contempt. "We will not do as you have done, placing your fate in the hands of a creature that cares only for itself. That views you simply as a pawn, as a means to an end."

Daran laughed. "You think you can win? That you can defeat the Shadow Lord and his Dark Horde?"

Rynlin looked at Daran with a cold smile, now questioning why he had taken such great pains to help Daran achieve his goal of becoming a Sylvan Warrior so many centuries before. The betrayal hurt, but Rynlin refused to let it show. The harm sustained by his grandson made him hurt even more and filled him with a rage that he could barely contain.

"Who can say?" said Rynlin. "The only certainty is that we still retain our free will, something that you have given up. We still have the ability to decide for ourselves how our end might come. Yours has already been determined, whether you know it or not."

"Maybe so," replied Daran with a weary resignation. "But that doesn't mean I have to die today."

A blast of Dark Magic shot from Daran's hand, straight for Rynlin, who took hold of the Talent just in time, crafting a swirling mist of white energy that took in the darkness. The two magics spun around each other, sparking when they touched, until slowly the white light of the Talent exerted its dominance over the Dark Magic, changing it, consuming it, until the black disappeared. Through it all, Rynlin's stony eyes stared at Daran.

"That's the best that you can do?" asked Rynlin, contempt dripping from his voice. The deadness in his tone made Daran's blood run cold. He had hoped that a sudden attack would give him an advantage, but it was not to be.

"No, I can do much better," snarled Daran, realizing that the next few minutes would determine if he lived or died.

In a matter of seconds, Daran released more than a dozen shards of black energy aimed for his adversary. But even that couldn't break through the shield that Rynlin had created. Each fragment of Dark Magic slammed into the swirling white energy with no effect, but the speed of the assault meant that Rynlin couldn't do as he had done previously, seeking to convert Daran's Dark Magic for his own purposes. Instead, all he could do was deflect the continuous attacks, and because of that Daran's cottage paid the ultimate price. Each shard of black energy that struck the shield was deflected and slammed into the house, destroying walls, windows or ceiling, whatever it came into contact with. Within seconds, two walls had collapsed, and the roof had been blown off, leaving gaping holes that allowed in the last light of the day.

Daran knew that he had no choice but to continue his attack, having no good means of escape. If he wanted to live, he had to defeat his opponent.

"You were always so full of yourself," said Rynlin. "Always so sure of yourself, as if the rules of the world never really applied to you."

"Stop talking, old man. I don't need to listen to your pronouncements anymore. The lectures that would drag on and on. Stupefyingly so. How much of my life I wasted having to listen to you drone on I can't even measure. So much of my life stolen from me."

Rynlin smiled at Daran, knowing what his former pupil sought to do. Irritate him. Distract him. Daran wanted to see if his goading could lead him into a mistake. But not now. Not when thoughts of his grandson remained foremost in his mind.

"True," agreed Rynlin. "You have wasted your life. But you have only yourself to blame."

The sharpness of Rynlin's words seemed to strike the traitorous Sylvan Warrior like a physical blow. Before Daran could respond, a stream of white energy surged from Rynlin's hands, cascading over Daran, who formed a shell of Dark Magic around himself right before the Talent struck.

"You cannot defeat me, old man," screamed Daran, as he fought to maintain control over the thin barrier of Dark Magic that he had formed around himself for protection. "I learned everything you taught me. And then the Shadow Lord gave me even more power and knowledge. More than even you can comprehend." Despite his taunt, it was all that Daran could do to withstand Rynlin's attack. The shell that he had crafted so quickly had begun to shrink, tightening around him.

"There's where you're wrong," said Rynlin, his deep blue eyes sparkling with malice. "Because I didn't teach you everything that I know."

Rynlin's gaze turned to stone as he increased the power that he commanded through the Talent, expanding the stream of energy that surged around Daran so that it compressed the shield until it began to crush down upon the red-haired traitor, forcing him to his knees. Daran tried desperately to maintain his defenses, but there was nothing that he could do. Rynlin was too strong for him, too knowledgeable, too implacable. Slowly, inch by inch, the blazing white energy ate into his shield, tightening around him even more, until he started to feel the first few pinpricks of pain as barely visible darts of white energy slashed through his shield and cut into him. That first jolt of pain shook Daran's concentration, and that one second of lost control proved to be the end, as those initial pinpricks became a swarm of daggerlike thrusts of white energy into Daran's body. First in his chest, then his back, his thighs, his arms. Rynlin refused to let up, the white-hot energy blasting through the last few remnants of Daran's shield until the only thing that could be seen was a man-shaped figure that had collapsed to the floor of the cabin surrounded by a blinding white nimbus.

Daran wanted to scream, pain wracking his body, every prick of energy making him feel as if he were being torn apart one cell at a time. Terror rose up within him as he realized that his own demise was near. And it was then that Daran understood his mistake. He had always thought that in the end the Shadow Lord would be the cause of his death. He had just never considered that it could happen in this way, at the hands of a man he had once considered to be his mentor and friend.

46

WATCHING EYES

Catal Huyuk lay quietly among the burnt rocks, tired and worn from his exertions of the last month. As each day passed the stress had increased. The hours, sometimes days, of hiding, knowing that a single wrong move would mean his demise. Several escapes that brought him closer to death than he would have preferred. Such as the time when an Ogren had risen from where it had been sitting against a tree, Catal Huyuk having stood right next to the dark creature for almost an hour while hidden in the brush, barely breathing, his hand gripping the handle of his axe, not wanting to kill the beast since that increased the chances of his being discovered. It had been the longest wait of his life, and he had breathed a huge sigh of relief when the massive creature had finally moved deeper into the forest. But he didn't have time to think about all that had occurred. It had seemed a blur that began in the mountains of Kenmare with Thomas and his Marchers and had concluded here at the doorstep to the Shadow Lord's domain.

It had all started when he had held that tight, twisting

path for several hours, keeping back the Mongrels, Ogren and Shades to give Thomas and his Marchers time to escape the mountains of Kenmare and continue on their quest to the west. Once the Shades realized the futility of attacking him in such a defensible space, and that they had little hope of catching the Marchers, the dark creatures had withdrawn, allowing Catal Huyuk to make his own escape and head back to the Charnel Mountains to continue with the task that Rynlin had assigned him.

His leathers camouflaged him from searching eyes, and there were many of those to worry about. First it was the Dragas, a flight of six drifting in lazy circles, followed by a pack of Mongrels, the monstrous beasts the size of ponies and sprinting through the pass he monitored every hour of the day. Had been watching, in fact, for more than a week.

He knew that he had made the right decision, thinking that the pass that offered the most direct route from Blackstone to the Northern Steppes would be the one used, the one that the Dark Horde had used once before. The Knife's Edge. The pass led directly south from Blackstone through a gorge the sheer sides of which rose thousands of feet in height. Once in the pass the Dark Horde would be protected from attack until they exited where the trail narrowed to a tip that led from the border of the Charnel Mountains to the lowlands. From there, it was just a daylong hike onto the Northern Steppes. Rynlin had told the massive Sylvan Warrior that he expected the Shadow Lord to release his Dark Horde in a matter of days. Unfortunately, his friend had been right. He had seen the signs of increased activity, Ogren and Shade scouts following the trail. And then a few Ogren war bands to test the way. Only a few more minutes passed before he saw the vanguard of the Shadow Lord's host. The war party of Ogren, led by their Shades, tramped through the pass almost a half mile below him in a steady, earth-shaking pounding, their rusted, blackened sword blades and spear points barely gleaming in the weak light of the Charnel Mountains.

Catal Huyuk waited just a few more minutes for the next Ogren war party of several thousand dark creatures to march below him, satisfied now that the Shadow Lord's primary assault had begun, that this wasn't a diversion, for he had no doubt that the Shadow Lord knew that the Sylvana were here in the mountains, watching all the approaches that led to the Northern Steppes.

Yet that didn't seem to matter to the Lord of the Shadow. Based on the size of the main host Catal Huyuk now watched begin to make its way through the pass from his position on the slope looking down into the gap, apparently the Shadow Lord didn't fear watching eyes. He probably didn't fear much of anything.

Staying low, Catal Huyuk slowly slid behind the lip of his hiding place, not standing until he was certain that the creatures in the pass could not see him from below or the Dragas flying in tight circles over the Knife's Edge from above. He would need to be careful of the Dragas and the Mongrels, but he wasn't worried. He had been fighting dark creatures for centuries, and he was already well versed in the terrain surrounding the Knife's Edge thanks to the last few weeks and his adventures when he was younger, when the Shadow Lord first attacked the Kingdoms.

It was the sound of rocks skittering behind him that saved his life. Catal Huyuk ducked and then rolled, the rusted black blade slicing through the air where his head had just been, cutting instead into the rocky slope the Sylvan Warrior had just scrambled down. But that didn't stop the Shade from continuing its attack, its milky white

eyes tracking the large fighter's movements as the dark creature twisted around like a snake and lunged, slashed, then
lunged again, each time Catal Huyuk evading the assault
with a speed that no man his size had the right to attain.

The Sylvan Warrior fought the urge to take a quick
glance over his shoulder, fearing that Ogren might be
preparing to stab him in the back, for where there was a
Shade there tended to be several of the monstrous dark
creatures. But he couldn't take the risk. The Shade, its movement sinuous, fluid, almost mesmerizing, was too fast, too
deadly. Catal Huyuk sought to gain some space to catch his
breath and pull free his battle axe, but the Shade wouldn't
permit it. Following after the Sylvan Warrior with a dogged
tenacity, the Shade forced Catal Huyuk to continue to
retreat farther down the steep slope. As the speed of the
dark creature's slashes and lunges increased, the blackened
blade, from which a single touch meant death, came closer
and closer, the Sylvan Warrior dodging, weaving as best as
he could as he jumped down onto a narrow trail that limited
his options for escaping the Shade. The dark creature
dropped down after him, his blade a web of swirling steel
that sought to cut into the Sylvan Warrior's flesh as the
Shade tracked him along the tight path. Catal Huyuk knew
that eventually, and likely sooner rather than later if the trail
continued to tighten, his luck would run out. He needed to
turn the tables quickly. Otherwise, he was a dead man.

The loose rock beneath his feet gave him the idea for
what to do. The next time the Shade lunged, its blade skim-
ming across the leather armor that protected the Sylvan
Warrior's left side, Catal Huyuk allowed his left foot to slide
back, then continued the movement to fall to one knee. The
Shade, its milky white eyes showing no emotion, sensed
victory with the stumble, turning the blade inhumanly fast

to slash down on the Sylvan Warrior's exposed neck. But Catal Huyuk had been expecting that, had wanted the Shade to do just that. As soon as the blade came sweeping toward his head, he collapsed to his side and swung his left leg behind him. The impact of Catal Huyuk's boot slammed the Shade into the rock wall that lined the trail. Before the dark creature could recover from the shock of the blow, Catal Huyuk was up on his feet, a foot-long dagger driven into the back of the dark creature's neck.

The Sylvan Warrior remained standing behind the dead Shade, his dagger keeping the dark creature in place, as he listened. Other than the screech from a distant Dragas, the only sound Catal Huyuk heard came from the wind whistling along the trail and kicking up the blackened ash for which the peaks he was among had been named. Satisfied that the duel had not attracted the attention of any other scouts of the Dark Horde, he stepped back and allowed the Shade to slide to the ground. Kneeling down, the Sylvan Warrior used the Shade's cloak to clean the blood from his dagger and then return the weapon to its sheath on his thigh.

Catal Huyuk breathed deeply several times, trying to release the adrenaline that ran through his body. He said a silent prayer to a long forgotten god, thankful not only that he had survived, but also that the clash of steel had not drawn the attention of any other dark creatures serving in the advance screen for the Dark Horde.

Picking a fight hadn't been his goal, but sometimes it couldn't be avoided. He trotted down the slope to the south, his mind once more focused on his most important task. He needed to get to the Breaker before the Dark Horde and rally the Kingdoms. For the first time since the Great War, the Dark Horde marched for the south.

47

THE HORDE MARCHES

Rynlin stepped from the trees, a tall, gray shadow in the fading evening light. The Marchers Oso had placed on guard normally would have shown more concern if such an imposing figure had simply appeared in their midst. But they knew Rynlin was Thomas' grandfather and that he had many of the same unique skills as their lord. Besides, several wolf packs now surrounded their small camp at the verge of the mountains as an additional guard, the large animals ranging for leagues around, so Oso had little fear of being taken by surprise.

Rya stood when her husband approached, appearing strangely uncertain. She had been forcing Thomas to sip from a light broth so that he could regain his strength. Though no physical wound showed from his combat with Daran and Malachias, he was exhausted, coming so close to dying that he was halfway over the edge and about to slip down into a pitch-black abyss from which he'd never emerge if not for his grandmother's intervention. Rya kept telling him that the only way to recover was to eat and rest. Good advice, but it didn't appeal to him knowing that

Malachias had taken Kaylie. He didn't have time to wait until he felt stronger. He could sense events speeding up, and he needed to get ahead of them. He needed to move. The tug, the unseen force that was pulling him toward Blackstone, had increased with such intensity that it felt like an ache in his chest.

"Daran?" she asked hesitantly.

"No longer a threat," Rynlin said quietly. His voice was hard, though Rya detected a note of regret. The statement saddened Rya, but she knew that Daran's end was necessary and deserved. "There's something else."

Thomas had pushed himself up to a standing position from where his grandmother had made him lie down. Rynlin didn't even notice, still surprised, after all this time, of how quietly his grandson could move.

Rynlin sighed. He had hoped for more time. More time for Thomas to recover. More time for the Kingdoms to prepare. But in his mind the words of the prophecy kept running as if on a broken reel, gaining speed and force with each passing second.

Thousands of years of predictions, of truths shaded in mystery, were hurtling rapidly toward a point of impact. Toward a specific time where no further predictions or prophecies had been made. Where the result of this one event, the meeting between the Lord of the Shadow and the Defender of the Light, would set a new course for the history of the Kingdoms. Whether the result would fall in black or white, as one of the lines of the prophecy foretold, lay balanced as if on a scale. The slightest push to either side would lead to a distinct future. But which future? That was the greatest, most frightening unknown.

"I got word from Catal Huyuk. The Dark Horde comes.

The Shadow Lord's army will be through the Charnel Mountains by daybreak."

"So it comes to pass." Oso had joined them, Beluil coming up as well, nudging Thomas with his snout, almost as if in admonition for not obeying his grandmother.

Thomas stood there silently, leaning against his longest friend and running his fingers through Beluil's thick fur. He turned his gaze to the northeast. He could sense the Shadow Lord, knew that his nemesis remained secure in his mountain fortress in the once vibrant but now dead city of Blackstone. He fingered the Key, which he had attached to his Sylvan Warrior necklace. Using the Talent to conceal it from those who might seek to regain it had worked better than he had expected, as neither Daran nor Malachias had sensed the magic that he had applied to the steel Key to hide it in plain sight. A trick he was quite familiar with and had employed for the first time during his escape from the Crag when he stood in the river and hid behind a screen made of the Talent from the reivers who pursued him. He pushed those memories to the side, recognizing that their popping into his thoughts now was a sign of the fatigue that plagued him, a heavy weariness having settled into his mind and body. He admitted reluctantly that his grandmother was right. He needed to rest. But not now. Not with the Dark Horde on the march and preparing to descend on the Kingdoms. He knew what came next, what he had to do. He understood the risk as well. But perhaps even if he couldn't save himself, he could at least save Kaylie.

"The Shadow Lord thinks that I'm dead. I'll have to disabuse him of that notion."

"Even if you make it to Blackstone safely," said Rya, her concern obvious, "you're not strong enough right now to use the Talent to transform into a kestrel and fly. And even if you could make use of the Talent in that way right now, by the time you arrived, you wouldn't have the strength to fight the Shadow Lord, at least not with any chance of surviving the encounter."

"He won't have to," interrupted Rynlin.

He had seen the movement among the wolf packs, the large wolves shifting, creating a path out of respect for the animal that trotted toward them now.

Acero, the unicorn that had selected Thomas following his elevation to Sylvan Warrior, came to a stop just a few feet away. Thomas stepped forward, gingerly, his legs still finding their way beneath him. He rubbed Acero's nose with affection, enjoying the calm that filled him as he massaged the massive animal's black coat. Acero nuzzled Thomas, then stepped back. Carefully, Acero lowered his twisting black horn, almost nine feet in length, Thomas reaching out with his fingers and touching the sharp point.

Instead of the flash of memories as had happened when the two had first bonded, Thomas instead felt a jolt, like a sharp charge that filled the air during a thunderstorm in the Highlands. A feeling of warmth swept through him, draining away his exhaustion, replacing it with a renewed energy, as his friend shared his own power with him. Though still not back to full strength, Thomas felt more like himself now. Reaching out for the Talent, the natural magic of the world surged within him, giving him the confidence that he needed in his weakened state that he could take the next step, the one that would put the prophecy to the test. Thomas smiled, hugging Acero's broad neck in thanks.

"Thomas, you still don't need to rush off," urged Rya. "I know why you want to. I understand. I truly do. But don't allow your emotion to get in the way of your reason."

"I do need to," Thomas replied, smiling softly. "I can't

leave Kaylie there. You're right. That is a key motivation. But, as I said, the Shadow Lord likely believes that I'm dead. Malachias and Daran would not return to Blackstone if they didn't believe it to be so. I need to make use of that belief for as long as I can."

Rya closed her eyes in reluctant acceptance. Not because of how Thomas had answered her. She had expected that, knowing her grandson. And he was right. He did need to take advantage of the unforeseen opportunity that he'd been given. What upset her was that time had run out. The day that she had been dreading ever since Thomas had confirmed that he was the Defender of the Light was almost upon them, and she was afraid that as a result she was going to lose her grandson.

"You're right, Thomas. I just don't like it."

Thomas stepped away from Acero, giving his grand-mother a long hug before turning his gaze back toward the Charnel Mountains and Blackstone.

"In the past, the Sylvan Warriors have defended the Kingdoms, using the Breaker as their primary defense," said Thomas. "But not this time."

Rynlin grinned wickedly. "No, this time we'll take the fight to the Shadow Lord and give you the distraction that you need. The Kingdoms can hold for a time without us. Gregory knows what he needs to do."

Rya nodded, agreeing with the logic of the plan, though the worry for her grandson stayed with her.

"When do you leave?" asked Rya.

"As soon as the sun sets."

"We'll be there when you need us," said Rynlin. "Have no fear of that."

48

DEFIANCE

Kaylie leaned her head back against the hard rock of her cell, the dark penetrated only by a grey ray of light from the slit high above her that offered her the only evidence that there was life beyond her stone and steel enclosure. She sat there miserably in the quiet and cold, but thankfully alone. When Malachias had left, Chertney's body had remained, a reminder of the power that the Shadow Lord's servant wielded. But as the hours passed that reminder had faded until only a pile of black ash clumped on the floor. She had pulled her knees to her chest, making herself as small as possible. She told herself that it was to keep warm, but she couldn't lie to herself, not completely. She knew, in part, that it was her reaction to the fear that coursed within her and threatened to paralyze her. A fear that she struggled to control.

All the terrifying stories that she had heard about the Shadow Lord ran through her mind on a continuous loop. They played upon her fears, eating away at her. No matter what she tried, she couldn't force them out, couldn't lock them away. Only her thoughts of Thomas interrupted the flow, and then only briefly. When that happened, sadness and grief crushed the breath from her.

"You don't have to be here, child." The whisper sounded like a shout because of the silence of the cell.

Kaylie looked up sharply. The Shadow Lord stood before her, in the cell, his looming, dark presence sucking all the light from the room, but for the blood red of his burning eyes. She averted her gaze, fearing to look for more than a second.

"Your love is gone, yes, but your father remains. So all is not lost."

Her fears increased as his words washed over her. How did he know what she had been thinking? Once again, she reached for the Talent, yearning to feel the warmth of the natural magic of the world flow within her. But as with every other time that she had tried to grab hold of the Talent during the past day, she failed. It was as if a glass wall had been built around her. She had assumed that the Shadow Lord's Dark Magic was the reason, and it was. But she didn't realize that the Shadow Lord was also the true cause of the fears and uncertainties that threatened to paralyze her. That he was seeking to turn her to his purpose through the subtle manipulation of his Dark Magic playing with her mind.

"Your father will want to help you, child. I know that he loves you. He'll want to keep you safe. Keep you healthy and whole."

Kaylie closed her eyes, trying to push his words away. But they seeped through her, finding breaks in the walls that she tried to erect around her consciousness.

"He won't accede to your wishes, no matter what you do to me," she replied with some heat, trying to ignore the pressure building in her head that was turning into a debilitating pain. "He won't sell his Kingdom, himself, for me."

Kaylie lifted her eyes, defiance blazing in her strong gaze. She remembered how Thomas had acted when he was Rodric's prisoner not so long ago in Tinnakilly. The calm attitude and hard stare. The lack of emotion. She adopted it for her own.

"A brave face, child. You are to be commended. But I know what's in your heart."

The Shadow Lord drifted closer, his wispy robes almost touching her, blood-red eyes peering down at her. Kaylie cringed inwardly, fighting desperately to maintain her calm outward demeanor.

"You have power, child. I can feel it. It would be a pity to waste it. It would be a pity to waste your life. To give up all that you could attain. All that you could become."

The Shadow Lord enjoyed toying with people, having a unique knack for finding their weaknesses, then turning those chinks to his advantage. Though Kaylie was tired and worn, and clearly she struggled to maintain her composure and focus, the Shadow Lord had yet to find what he needed to break through her defenses. He had been playing with her fears for the past day in an attempt to soften the Princess of Fal Carrach but with little success. Now he tried a different tack.

The visions in Kaylie's mind changed. The fear fled from her. At first Kaylie thought that she had succeeded, that she had won. But then she realized that wasn't the case. That her fears had been replaced with something else. The visions began again, but this time they filled her with hope and pleasure. She saw herself at the height of her powers, a master of the Talent, stronger even than Thomas. Able to do things that no one else had ever tried or thought to do with the natural magic of the world. The visions increased in pace, her future triumphs and victories speeding through her consciousness.

"Think of it, child. The power you currently control. What it could be. What I can show you. What I can teach you. You could be the most powerful woman in the Talent in the history of the Kingdoms. Think of what you could do. What you could accomplish for Fal Carrach. For your people. For yourself."

Her defenses became brittle, threatening to shatter, the Shadow Lord's words sliding across her walls, seeking a crack, searching for a way through. Kaylie shut her eyes, biting her tongue. She knew what the Shadow Lord hoped to accomplish, understood it in her heart and soul, yet her desire to fight back waned. Her resistance began to fracture, to fail, but then she relaxed, allowing the tension to subside within her. An image of Thomas came to mind, strengthening her, calming her, giving her the inner faith she needed to rebuild her defenses.

"Your promises are no more solid than the wind," Kaylie whispered, refusing to look into the Shadow Lord's eyes. "You will never have me."

The Shadow Lord stood there quietly, staring down at the Princess of Fal Carrach for several minutes, letting the silence build, his blood-red eyes blazing in the darkness.

"We shall see, child. We shall see."

49

AMBUSH

The Ogren war party, more than a thousand strong, and one of dozens now trotting across the burnt grasslands of the Northern Steppes, felt the rumble beneath their feet, the land seemingly protesting their passage, but they ignored it. Instead, the beasts focused on the orders of the Shades that led them, the men, or what once had been men, covered in black, their faces hidden, only their milky white eyes visible beneath their black cowls. The Shades had a simple purpose. Force the Ogren toward the Breaker and the lands of men. One or two of the Ogren looked back and saw the rays of sunlight that shot down toward Blackstone, hidden in part by the peaks of the Charnel Mountains, the beams of white coinciding with the shaking ground. But just as soon as the light appeared, it was gone, swallowed up once more by the murky grey and burnt ash that dominated the landscape.

The tall grass, dry and dead where Ogren and other dark creatures had passed before, green still visible where the minions of the Shadow Lord had not yet trod, rose to the chests of the towering Ogren, some of the dark creatures almost ten feet in height. The Shades always followed the Ogren on the Northern Steppes, in part to maintain control, but also so that the Ogren created a path through the tall grass, making their passage that much easier. The problem for the dark creatures was that such an approach limited their vision as they made their way across the Northern Steppes, the Shades unable to see to the front beyond the broad backs of their charges or to the sides because of the encroaching veld. That fact was well known by their enemies, who planned to turn it to their advantage.

The movement within the high grass that tracked the Ogren war party was virtually invisible. The strong wind playing across the grass masked their approach. Moreover, the attackers were patient. There was no need to rush. Mortal enemies of all dark creatures, they knew what they were about. They knew the weaknesses of their prey, how to kill the beasts while minimizing the risk of injury to themselves. Perhaps most important, they knew that they had the edge.

The two Shades assigned to this war party trotted behind their charges, enjoying the ease of their passage, the massive Ogren flattening the tall grass for them. They concentrated on maintaining order among these unruly beasts, keeping them pointed toward the massive wall that could just now be seen off in the distance as a black smudge that gained greater clarity with each passing league. They were the advance of the Dark Horde, charged by their master with scouting the Steppes as the other, larger war parties followed after them.

The Shades were so intent on their task that they missed the flash of motion to their flanks, and by then it was too late. Two large shapes leapt out from the grass on each side onto the backs of the Shades, driving them into the soft earth. Before the dark creatures could raise the alarm, sharp teeth bit into their necks, killing them.

The two wolves, one grey, the other white, shook their bloody maws in an attempt to remove as much of the dark, bitter ichor as possible. The blood of dark creatures left a terrible taste. They watched as the Ogren war party continued to push forward through the grass, unaware that their leaders had been eliminated. The two wolves trotted after the Ogren, sensing their brothers and sisters in the grass around them, moving closer, preparing to strike.

Their leader, Beluil, had been explicit on how to attack the war parties. Take the shadow men first, the massive wolf had communicated. Then the Ogren would not fight together. Instead, they would fight on their own, making the wolves' task that much easier. The wolves had listened to Beluil. He was brother to the Raptor, and all the wolves knew of the Raptor. The man who killed dark creatures with a savagery that matched their own. The man who was likely part wolf, they liked to think.

A roar of fright broke through the quiet, interrupting the sound of the wind sifting through the tall grass. Then another, and another, followed by even more until the ragged cries seemed to form into a single shriek that tore across the grassland. The Ogren war party, once so orderly, had stopped, dozens of the large beasts having disappeared, wild thrashing taking place in the long grass and then stopping suddenly. The Ogren still standing had pulled their weapons. They knew that they were in danger, but they had yet to identify the threat. As more and more Ogren disappeared, pulled down in the tall grass, the massive beasts began to swing their weapons wildly around them whenever they caught a sign of movement, many striking their compatriots in their panic and aiding their attackers in their work.

The two wolves that trailed the Ogren sprinted forward, using the long grass to hide themselves as they joined the fray. Their brothers and sisters had sprung the trap, the fear of the Ogren making their work easier. Now the two wolves wanted more kills, and they knew that they only had a few minutes to achieve their objective, for their wolf pack was thorough when faced with the task of killing dark creatures. Beluil had given them the responsibility of destroying as many Ogren war parties as possible before they reached the Breaker, and they would do that with a speed and violence their prey could not defend against. The Raptor had asked for their help, and they would give it. Besides, killing dark creatures was in their blood.

50

BROKEN TRADITIONS

Dusk approached, long shadows stretching out from the stone columns that ringed the plateau named Athala's Forge, all seeming to connect at some point to the east. Rynlin stood on the Pinnacle. The stone in the center of all the others, steps cut into its base, towered over the columns. He waited. Perhaps not patiently, but he waited, nonetheless.

He had called the Sylvana to the Circle, and they had come from all the Kingdoms, from the Distant Islands in the west to Benewyn in the east. Now he needed them to act, to do something that they had never done before, for time was short and the future of the Kingdoms hung in the balance. When the sun touched the western horizon and began to sink below the peaks, Catal Huyuk finally emerged from between the stone columns, his massive battle axe strapped to his back along with his sword. He looked tired, worn, but that was to be expected. He had been given a dangerous task, and he had accomplished it.

"My friends," said Rynlin. "The time is upon us. The Kingdoms who remember have been roused. Their soldiers either stand at the Breaker or make their way there now, for the Shadow Lord's Dark Horde approaches. Now it is time for us to once again take up the responsibility that has been ours for more than a thousand years, to defend against the Shadow Lord and his minions."

"You have seen the Dark Horde?" asked Tiro, the portly Sylvan Warrior agitated.

He had learned of Daran's treachery upon arriving at the Circle, and it had struck him in his very soul. If their greatest enemy could corrupt a Sylvan Warrior, what could they do to defeat the Lord of the Shadow?

"I have," rumbled Catal Huyuk. "Rynlin gave me the task of watching the Charnel Mountains. The Horde began its march yesterday through the Knife's Edge. I would think that by now the advance war parties are halfway across the Northern Steppes."

"Then we go to the Breaker," said Brinn Kavolin, a tall Sylvan Warrior with a short, pointy beard. "The Kingdoms will need us."

"They will need us, yes," said Rya, who had stepped up next to her husband at the top of the Pinnacle. "But one of our own needs us more."

"What do you mean?" asked Brinn.

"Thomas has found the Key," said Rya. "He goes to Blackstone as we speak to challenge the Shadow Lord."

Murmurs rose up around the Circle, the Sylvan Warriors startled by the news. They knew of the Key, what it supposedly allowed you to do. But to go to Blackstone on his own? No one had ever survived an encounter with the Shadow Lord. Why was the newest and youngest Sylvan Warrior so anxious to press the matter?

Sensing their unease, Rynlin quickly stepped forward, his voice clearly heard throughout the Circle.

"We all know the prophecy, that the fate of the King-doms hangs in the balance. And we know that the Defender of the Light is the only one able to fight the Lord of the Shadow and have any hope of success, no matter how small it may be. Thomas has found the Key, so he can gain access to Blackstone. It confirms that Thomas is the Defender of the Light."

"Yes, as we expected he was. But even if Thomas gets into Blackstone, he can't take on the Shadow Lord by himself. No one is strong enough to do that. And he'll be surrounded by enemies. Even with the Dark Horde crossing the Northern Steppes dark creatures will remain in that cursed city. They'll cut him down before he can challenge the Shadow Lord." Tiro shook his head in dismay, already having worked out in his own mind Thomas' inevitable demise, and with it the hopes of the Kingdoms.

"That's why if he is to succeed, he needs our help. Thomas enters Blackstone at first light. We must be there with him."

"What do you mean?" huffed Tiro, unable to contem-plate such an unorthodox suggestion. "Attack Blackstone? Attack the Shadow Lord with the Dark Horde descending upon the Breaker? That's madness."

"That's necessity," responded Rynlin. "Gregory of Fal Carrach leads the Kingdoms at the Breaker. He knows what must be done, and he will do it. He will hold for as long as he can. But we must help Thomas. We must help the Defender of the Light."

"But that is not what we have done in the past," said Tiro, still clearly flustered by the idea that Thomas had presented to him months before. "That is not part of our tradition."

"We have held to our traditions for too long," argued

Rynlin. "Times have changed. The Shadow Lord has changed his strategy. He has corrupted the rulers of several Kingdoms. He has the former High King in the palm of his hand. And he has turned one of us to his evil ways." The last reminder ended the murmurs that had begun below the Pinnacle, the expressions of the Sylvan Warriors darkening. "The Shadow Lord expects us to fight at the Breaker. That's why he sends the Dark Horde. We must change our strategy if we are to succeed. It is time for us to play our part. It is time for us to take the battle to Blackstone. We must act!"

"It sounds to me like you're simply trying to protect your grandson," Tiro replied weakly, seeking any excuse to keep the Sylvana to what they had done before to defend against the Shadow Lord.

"Indeed we are," said Rya coolly, her eyes burning brightly with anger. "And we are trying to assist the Defender of the Light. You know the prophecy, Tiro. We all do. Whether we like it or not, the time is upon us. There is no prophecy for what comes next. No one has defeated the Shadow Lord in single combat, so I do not know if my grandson will survive. But I will do everything possible to ensure that he does. Remember, in addition to my grandson's fate, the fate of the Kingdoms rests on what occurs tomorrow. History can no longer be our guide. We must make a new history."

"Would you ignore a Sylvan Warrior in need?" asked Rynlin, his quiet voice carrying across the small plateau. "Would you leave him to his doom knowing that you could have done something to help?"

"We would not," grumbled Catal Huyuk, staring daggers at Tiro, who wilted under the gaze. Catal Huyuk usually said little during these councils, so when he felt the need to speak the others listened. "We have all seen the signs. We know what is coming even if we don't want to acknowledge it. We must help Thomas. What I saw of the Dark Horde this morning reminds me of what we faced in the Great War. But that doesn't matter. Thomas is our only hope against the Shadow Lord. Waiting at the Breaker as we've done in the past does nothing for him. Even if we hold the Dark Horde for a time at the Breaker, if Thomas doesn't destroy the Shadow Lord, if he can't even fight the Shadow Lord, it won't matter. We must make for Blackstone. Otherwise, we are doomed."

"We barely stand a chance now," complained Tiro. "Our numbers continue to dwindle."

"That can't be argued," said Catal Huyuk. "But though our numbers have decreased, our power has increased. Have you not sensed the strength in Thomas? The opportunity that he creates for us? We must use his strength and combine it with our own. We must help him."

The other Sylvan Warriors nodded their heads or murmured their agreement, believing in the truth of their massive friend's words.

"Then what would you suggest?" asked Tiro, turning his attention to Rynlin.

"We do what we do best," he replied simply.

"And what would that be?"

"We kill dark creatures," said Catal Huyuk. "We ride for Blackstone."

"So you want us to attack the Shadow Lord in his lair!" demanded Tiro. "We're not ready for that. That has never been done before. Thomas or no, this still seems madness to me."

"Traditions are made to be broken," said Rya. "And now is the time. Just because we've never done it doesn't mean it can't be done."

Tiro was about to offer another excuse, but the words died in his mouth. Always before when the Sylvan Warriors were to ride into battle, they would summon their mounts from the Valley of the Unicorns, which was hidden not too far from the Circle. Such had been the way since the Sylvan Warriors first came to be. But to Tiro's shock and amazement, the unicorns were trotting up from their valley of their own volition.

The other Sylvan Warriors followed Tiro's gaze, also astounded by the sight. The unicorns stopped at the edge of the Circle, finding their Sylvan Warrior and standing next to him or her. Their gazes were insistent, their eyes demanding. They wanted to ride. They wanted to fight.

Tenlin, a brown unicorn, stepped toward Tiro, then bent his head to lower his massive, eight foot horn. Tiro stood there too surprised to move. As the seconds passed, he stared into Tenlin's eyes and then realized what the great steed wanted. Reaching out his hand, Tiro touched Tenlin's horn.

Images immediately flashed across the Sylvan Warrior's mind. Tiro saw the fearsome dark creatures pouring out of the crevices that dotted Blackstone, preparing to march on the Kingdoms. He saw the Ogren war parties making their way across the Northern Steppes and breaching the Breaker. He saw the burning and the slaughter, the agony and the heartbreak that would befall those beyond the towering wall. And he knew that Rynlin and Catal Huyuk spoke the truth.

If the Sylvan Warriors did not engage in battle now, there would be no battle in the future. It would be a slaughter, and the Shadow Lord would win even if Thomas, the Defender of the Light, succeeded in entering Blackstone with the Key. The young Sylvan Warrior needed their help.

He needed a distraction. He needed time to fight the Shadow Lord without fear of being slaughtered by their enemy's servants.

Tiro withdrew his hand from Tenlin's horn and sighed in resignation. He had blinded himself to reality to protect against what was to come. But that was a fool's errand, he acknowledged, berating himself silently. The Sylvana were warriors, fighters, men and women born to act. And now was the time.

"Thank you, Tenlin," said Tiro, patting the unicorn's flank. "You have reminded me of something that I had forgotten over the long centuries."

"We fight," said Catal Huyuk.

"We fight," said Tiro, nodding. "Rynlin, I assume you have a plan?"

"Indeed I do," replied Rynlin, grinning wickedly. "The Shadow Lord won't know what hit him."

51

BREAKING IN

The journey through the sparse forests lining the southern side of the Breaker and then north from where the Clanwar Desert met the western Highlands had gone faster than expected. Acero, Thomas' unicorn, never flagged, galloping at a pace that no horse could attain, the landscape passing in a blur. Beluil and the wolves his friend had selected, based on their strength and stamina, had kept up. The wolves served as an honor guard for Thomas, prepared to defend against any dark creatures if the need arose because of the large number of Ogren war parties beginning to make their way across the Northern Steppes. But the goal was stealth, slipping by any threats without being noticed or having to engage.

Thomas had been reluctant to use the Talent so close to Blackstone, fearing that the Shadow Lord would sense his presence if he did, and he wanted to stay dead for as long as possible, so they had crossed the Northern Steppes at night. But there was no need for concern. Beluil and his pack steered them safely across the plain, avoiding the many Ogren that trudged through the high grass toward the

Breaker. Along the way, they also found the remains of several dark creature war parties that much to their misfortune, and to Thomas' pleasure, had been the target of Beluil's wolves.

When they reached the lowlands of the Charnel Mountains, Thomas, Beluil and their escort continued up into the higher peaks, staying away from the Knife's Edge and any other routes that the Shadow Lord's dark creatures might use to make their way down to the Northern Steppes. Even with the many detours required in order to maintain the secrecy of their approach, they made excellent time through the dark of night. The sun was still a distant thought when Thomas and Beluil settled among the rocks lining the crest that looked down on Blackstone, the dead city just a mile away. Acero and the wolves had found a safe place to wait just a league away, wary of any dark creatures that might protect the Shadow Lord's sanctuary. As they gazed down upon the ruins, Thomas turned his mind to the next challenge and the most pressing. He had the Key, but he had no idea how it worked. Was the bearer of the Key the only person able to break through the Shadow Lord's deadly wards safely? Could the bearer bring along any who were with him? Would the Key disable all the magical traps or just those near the bearer? And if the Key disabled the magical traps, would the Shadow Lord become aware of that fact? So many questions, all critical, but no answers and no way to obtain them. If Rynlin and Rya were able to convince the Sylvan Warriors to attack Blackstone, there was nothing he could do but hope that his passage into the city with the Key would disable the defenses so that they could enter as well.

He and Beluil watched the dead ruins for almost an hour, trying to become accustomed to the rhythm of the place. Despite the fact that it was early morning, they both saw a great deal of movement. Shadows slipped through the darkness, breaking up the gloom. Shades and Ogren, and perhaps some other foul dark creatures, set on some task. There were no fires. The dark creatures didn't need the warmth or the light to see. As the minutes passed, Thomas' mind worked furiously, trying to puzzle out how the Key worked and what could happen when he tried to set foot in the Shadow Lord's home. But no matter which direction his mind wandered, no good solution presented itself. Having grown accustomed to the meanderings of Blackstone's inhabitants, Thomas decided on a course that would hopefully limit any chance of discovery. He needed to act, and time was of the essence. The Dark Horde approached the Breaker, and before Thomas challenged the Shadow Lord, he hoped to free Kaylie first, if he could.

Thomas began to push up from the black ash when he felt a nudge in his side. He settled back down, scratching Beluil's large head.

"I know, my friend. I'll be careful."

Beluil stared at him intensely, Thomas reading the images going through the large wolf's mind. His friend was afraid for him, worried of what could happen, and he wanted to go with him.

Thomas tried to ease his concerns. "I'm afraid, too. But I have to do this on my own. I don't know what will happen if you're with me."

Beluil continued to stare at him, his eyes mournful. Thomas sighed, then hugged his best friend.

"Don't worry, brother. I'll be careful. Just be prepared. I don't know what will happen, but if I can get Kaylie free, I'll need you to help protect her."

The massive wolf nuzzled Thomas a final time, letting

him know that he would be ready. Beluil then nudged Thomas forward before settling beneath a rocky crag that would allow him to continue to gaze down upon Blackstone and still keep him hidden from any prying eyes when the black of night turned to the daily grey gloom so common to the Charnel Mountains.

Thomas trotted down the slope, the blackened ash muffling his already silent steps as he easily avoided any obstacles or dangers lurking in the darkness thanks to his sharp eyesight. He stayed hidden as much as possible, knowing that Beluil tracked his movement from his perch on the ridge. When he reached the boundary of the dead city, he slowed, making his way even more carefully. Every few steps he stopped to listen, wanting to ensure that the way was clear and that nothing hid in the shadows. He didn't want to run into any dark creatures by mistake as he contemplated the ruins of Blackstone just a few feet to his front.

He didn't know what would happen when he tried to enter the city proper, but there was nothing that he could do but go forward. Any who were not a slave to the Shadow Lord would likely die without the Key, unable to avoid the many traps made of Dark Magic set to defend the Shadow Lord's city. But how did the Key work? Not knowing worried him, but there was nothing for it. Thinking about it for most of the ride from the Winter Sea had gotten him nowhere. Unbidden, the relevant lines of the prophecy ran through this mind:

> Drawn by faith,
> He shall hold the key to victory in his hand.

PERHAPS IT WAS as simple as that. He had found the Key through his faith and belief that he could. Perhaps once again it was simply a matter of having faith.

Knowing only what he didn't know, Thomas didn't have the time to consider what could happen if the Key didn't function as he hoped. The Dark Horde would be at the Breaker by midday, the Shadow Lord's minions preparing to invade the Kingdoms. And Kaylie was locked away somewhere in this city. He knew his likely fate when at last he faced the Shadow Lord, but he hoped that he could at last free her before having to take on his nemesis and give her a chance to make her escape. Thomas shook his head to clear it, tired of the same concerns and questions playing through his mind in an unbroken loop.

As Thomas stepped hesitantly into the city, he began to feel it. There was a sharp, forceful push against his senses, as if the Dark Magic tested him, trying to determine if he were friend or foe. Thomas pulled the Key out from beneath his shirt. It was warm to the touch and growing hotter as he moved slowly into the city. Not knowing what else to do he continued to walk forward. With each step, the resistance increased just a bit more, as if he were pushing against a bubble that hadn't burst yet and was folding around him instead.

Thomas stopped, gathering his thoughts. He was still alive, but each step forward was becoming more difficult, the Dark Magic not attacking him yet, but beginning to resist more aggressively, pushing back, reluctant to yield. An idea suddenly came to him, and with nothing else to go on, he put it into practice. He focused his mind on the Key, taking in its design, the craftsmanship. For no particular reason, he gently took hold of a tiny amount of the Talent, just a sliver of nature's real power, barely felt by any who might be able to sense such things. He fed that minute stream of the Talent into the Key.

The talisman grew warmer and then brighter, the small diamonds set into the stone glowing strongly with a dazzling white light. And then it happened. The bubble that Thomas sensed he was pushing against popped silently. The magical defenses of Blackstone dissipated, pulled into the glowing diamond that pulsed blindingly for several seconds, then winked out. The Key had consumed the wards of Dark Magic and cleansed the city's perimeter of the Shadow Lord's evil. The city was now open not only to Thomas, but also to any who wanted to follow in his path.

Thomas smiled. A good sign, he thought. And a bit lucky. But he knew that he would need luck if he were to survive the next few hours, if not the day. Tucking the Key beneath his shirt, Thomas continued silently into the city, bent on his task and still wary of crossing paths with the many dark creatures roaming about the dead metropolis.

52

FINAL TASK

For more than a thousand years the Shadow Lord had sought to gain mastery over the Kingdoms. But his efforts to date were all for naught, as the Sylvan Warriors had thwarted him time and time again. He had tried many different schemes in the past, but he generally favored seeking to obtain power indirectly by using puppets to accomplish his goals. He had found, however, that this rarely worked for any lengthy period of time because of the weakness of the men and women he selected to serve as his pawns.

The primary case in point now rode across the Northern Steppes next to Malachias, trailing behind an Ogren war party several thousand strong with the Breaker just now becoming visible as the sun began to rise at their backs. Initially, the Shadow Lord had thought to turn Rodric into something more than just the ceremonial High King, but rather the actual ruler of all the Kingdoms exercising real power. Intricate plans had been laid, pledges kept, resources acquired and spent, yet it had all failed despite the years of meticulous planning, all because of a boy who was supposed to have been killed a decade ago but wasn't.

As a result, Rodric's usefulness was coming to an end, and whether he knew it or not was of no consequence. The Shadow Lord had given the former High King a final assignment. Lead the Dark Horde across the Northern Steppes and issue the Shadow Lord's ultimatum to Gregory of Fal Carrach, the new High King. Surrender the Kingdom forces and swear fealty to the Shadow Lord, or his precious daughter would be put to death, after she had been used by the Shadow Lord's servants as a plaything. Rodric was to give Gregory a few hours to mull that possible fate before the Dark Horde attacked the Breaker.

As Rodric considered the task set before him, he found it harder and harder to concentrate. His eyes were watery, his cheeks sunken, his skin sallow. The crown of Armagh, although he had lost that Kingdom, remained perched precariously on his head. Every so often, Malachias glanced across at the former High King in disgust, unable to decipher Rodric's constant mumbling nor understand why his master had kept him alive. In his opinion, the man had lost his mind, driven mad by his failures, and should have been eliminated long before.

Malachias didn't know that the scene from the night before, when the Shadow Lord had summoned the High King for an audience to give him his final assignment, continued to play through Rodric's mind, never stopping, never changing pace, an endless loop of terror. The fear that had taken root in Rodric remained, for it was last night that he finally realized the real consequences of the bargain that he had made with the Shadow Lord so long ago. He knew his end was near, his usefulness to his master having run its course. And now he finally realized that he was no more than a dupe, a piece to be played as needed. When his master's need disappeared, so would he.

Now finally having recognized the precariousness of the situation in which he had placed himself, he could find no avenue for escape. He had no choice but to do the Shadow Lord's bidding. Assuming that the blasted Gregory Carlomin refused to stand aside for the sake of his daughter, something that Rodric expected knowing the King of Fal Carrach and his sense of honor, an attack on the Breaker was all but inevitable.

But as the former High King allowed his horse to carry him after the Ogren war party, the Breaker growing larger with each step, he thought that perhaps there was an opportunity here. One last gasp to prove his worth. In the battle that would follow, the Dark Horde would win. The Shadow Lord's forces were too many; the forces of the Kingdoms too few, even with the massive barrier aiding their defense. It was simply a matter of time before the servants of the Shadow Lord broke through and ran rampant into the eastern Kingdoms. If he played this right, perhaps he could arrange the circumstances of the Dark Horde's inevitable success so that he was viewed as the victor of this battle. Perhaps he could rebuild his position with the Shadow Lord and give his master a reason to keep him alive.

Rodric sat a little straighter in his saddle, his crown almost sliding from his head because of the unexpected movement. Yes, there was a chance, slim though it might be. For the first time in weeks he smiled, his mind, or rather what was left of it, turning to the task of survival and what he would need to do to make what could be his last scheme work.

53

AN OPEN PATH

"Has he passed through?" asked Tiro. His hesitation at the course suggested by Rynlin at the Circle had been replaced by determination once the Sylvana had made their decision.

Rya held onto her amulet tightly, her thoughts focused on her grandson. The warmth that she felt when looking down upon Blackstone from the ridge above it gave her a brief flicker of joy.

"He has," she replied. "He's almost to the center of the city."

"And the defenses?"

"There are no defenses," answered Rynlin. While his wife had searched for their grandson, he had used a tiny stream of the Talent to push into Blackstone. He had done much the same thing more than a thousand years before, and then he had felt a deadly resistance, the Shadow Lord's Dark Magic waiting, ready to strike at any fool who dared to enter his domain but had not sworn allegiance to him. This time, unlike the last, nothing pushed back. The Dark Magic was gone. "When Thomas entered Blackstone, the Key must have disabled the traps."

Smiles broke out on the faces of the Sylvan Warriors upon hearing that. They had ridden their unicorns down from the Circle, through the Highlands, across the Northern Steppes, then into the Charnel Mountains from where those burnt peaks met the Sea of Mist, sticking to the eastern coast to avoid the Ogren war parties before turning to the west and heading for the Shadow Lord's seat of power. They had hoped that taking such a circuitous route would get them where they were now without being detected. So far, their strategy had worked, arriving just outside the city with what passed for morning light in the Charnel Mountains just an hour above the horizon. Rynlin nudged Militus forward, his massive unicorn barely winded from the long gallop through the night.

"My friends," he intoned, his voice quiet but heard by all. "The Defender of the Light has entered Shadow's Reach. He seeks to challenge the Lord of the Shadow."

More than a hundred Sylvan Warriors brought their unicorns to the lip of the ridge. The anticipation of the men and women who had sworn to defend the Kingdoms against the Shadow Lord flowed down into their mounts. And as those Sylvan Warriors with the innate ability to make use of the Talent reached for the natural magic of the world, their unicorns' horns glowed a bright white.

"We ride to the Defender of the Light!"

The unicorns responded to the urging of their riders, leaping down from the crest, their hooves digging deeply into the ash-covered ground as they charged toward the outskirts of the Shadow Lord's lair. A few Ogren burst out from the ruins once the Sylvana broke the city's boundary, but the dark creatures realized their mistake too late. The unicorns facing the Shadow Lord's beasts simply dipped their heads and drove their spearlike horns through the creatures' chests. Those few sentinels eliminated, the Sylvan Warriors split into several groups, taking different paths through the ruins as they rode for the center of the city, intent on eliminating as many dark creatures as possible along the way.

54

CROSSED BLADES

Thomas moved swiftly but quietly deeper into Blackstone, Beluil tracking his movements as he watched his friend dodge carefully through the ruins, often appearing as no more than a shadow himself as he skipped away from the Ogren, Shades and other dark creatures that periodically appeared in the ash-covered streets. Never having been in Shadow's Reach, Thomas trusted to fate, allowing the Key to pull him toward the Shadow Lord, believing that if he found his nemesis, he would locate Kaylie as well. The Key appeared to function much like his Sylvan Warrior amulet, as the magical artifact seemed intent on guiding him safely and secretly through the warren of streets and alleys cluttered with debris that made up this husk of a city.

At first, Thomas worried that the path the Key selected for him would lead him into a pack of dark creatures. Though the Dark Horde had emptied much of Blackstone of the Shadow Lord's servants, many dark creatures still ran about obeying whatever orders they had been given. But the

Key apparently took this into account, steering Thomas on a winding route that kept him clear from any threats.

With the sun beginning to rise in the east, turning the black of night into a murky grey, Thomas came to a stop in front of two huge, black doors made of steel. He looked around quickly, satisfied that no dark creatures approached from behind. Off to the side he glimpsed the main square of Blackstone, the wind blowing the black ash into dozens of small dust devils that spun across the large, flat courtyard. He waited for several minutes to ensure that nothing approached that could take him by surprise. Then he put his right hand against where the doors met. Not unexpectedly, a mass of sparks shot out in response to his touch. Dark Magic held these massive gates closed.

The Key had steered him to this entrance, which he gathered led into a large domed chamber from what he could see of the outside of the keep, and was urging him to enter the hall. The pull was growing more insistent and with it his nervousness. It felt like a swarm of butterflies flitted about in his stomach. Therefore, Thomas took a moment to regain his composure, taking several deep breaths and attempting to clear his mind as he tried to calm himself. He had known his possible destiny for quite some time, yet he had distracted himself from it by focusing on all the steps that needed to be taken to reach this point. By concentrating on the process, on what he had to do, he had kept himself from thinking about the likely result of all his actions. He couldn't do that anymore. Now, he needed to take the final step. He needed to accept his fate.

For just a moment, he was afraid. The terror of what was to come almost incapacitated him. But then he forced his fear down, his surging anger taking its place. For ten years, he had been hunted. He had fought off assassins and almost died countless times. He had sought to protect his friends and those who were perhaps more than friends. He had faced the burdens of needing to free his homeland and meet his responsibilities as a Sylvan Warrior. He was tired of it. Tired of it all. It was time to end this. If he didn't survive, so be it. But he would make the Shadow Lord pay a steep price for his death. He would pay the evil that had plagued him for the last decade what it was owed, and he would do all that he could to help the Sylvana, the Kingdoms and, perhaps most important, Kaylie.

Steeling himself, he stepped up to the doors. Thinking that he could do as he did with the Key when entering Blackstone, he pulled the artifact from beneath his shirt and directed a small stream of the Talent into the diamonds that ran the length of the steel. He had hoped that the Key would then allow him to push open one of the doors quietly so that he could slip into the room without being discovered. But the Key seemed to have something grander in mind. Even though he had infused the artifact with barely any of the Talent, the two doors, just seconds before magically sealed, blasted inward, slamming against the inner walls, one of the doors sliding off its hinges as it bounced back from the stone.

The blast reverberated throughout the chamber and echoed across the city. So much for an unobtrusive entrance, thought Thomas. Stepping on silent feet into the chamber, he tucked the Key back beneath his shirt.

Surveying the room quickly, though he had never been here before, he felt like he had. Then the realization struck him. The chamber was exactly as it had appeared in his dreams. The shadows flitting to and fro at the edges of the chamber. The black and white tiles on the floor. The disc in the center portraying two figures he couldn't quite make out in the gloom without getting closer.

"Thomas!"

Thomas pulled his sword from the scabbard on his back at the scream, finding the source at the far end of the room on a balcony that looked out over the square. Kaylie stood there, a tall, dark shadow next to her. He couldn't discern any real shape to the creature that towered over the Princess of Fal Carrach, its misty, black robes disappearing now and then into the swirling shadow, clearly identifying only the brightly glowing red eyes. Eyes that burned the color of blood.

Thomas realized that the time had come. His true enemy stood before him. Surprisingly, he felt lighter. The stress and worry that had plagued him for years flowed out of him, the often crushing weight on his shoulders lifting, leaving him relaxed and ready.

The Shadow Lord turned his blazing eyes toward the intruder. He had had the Princess of Fal Carrach brought up from her cell, wanting to continue what he had started the day before. Testing her. Probing with his Dark Magic. Seeking to find her weaknesses in order to break through her defenses. Trying to determine how much effort it would take to turn this young woman strong in the Talent into a tool that he could use to his advantage. But he had barely gotten started before he had been so rudely interrupted.

"So boy," whispered the Shadow Lord, his sibilant voice carrying throughout the circular chamber. "You live. I had been informed otherwise, but I should have expected as much. My congratulations on a small victory, but it shall be short-lived. The time has come for us to end this."

Thomas stood there with his sword drawn, his expression hardening. Despite the fear that thudded in the very pit of his stomach, the sense of foreboding that threatened to overcome him, he maintained control of his will and determination, allowing his anger to drive him. His green eyes flared.

"Yes, the time has come," he said calmly, his hand tightening on the hilt of his sword.

"Thomas," whispered Kaylie, still finding it difficult to believe that he was alive. Tears trickled down her cheeks, her joy at seeing him mixed with her fear for his well-being.

"Step away from him, Kaylie."

She struggled to shift her feet, trying to run toward Thomas, but she found that she couldn't move a muscle in her body. The Shadow Lord had used his Dark Magic to hold her in place. The best that she could do was turn her head from side to side.

Recognizing what the Shadow Lord had done, Thomas' eyes flashed once again, his anger increasing. With one glance the Shadow Lord deciphered the truth.

The Shadow Lord's wicked laugh echoed around the circular chamber. "This will be a very good day, boy. I am glad that you've joined me here. After all, the requirements of the prophecy must be met. I'm not going to kill you quickly. I'll do it slowly, so your love can watch you die. Won't that be fun?"

The Shadow Lord continued. "First, my Dark Horde will crash upon those who oppose me like a wave upon the rocks, killing your people who now hide behind a wall. They will discover that a bunch of forest weaklings are no match for one of my power. Then, and only then, once you've experienced the breadth of your loss, will I kill you. If you behave yourself, it will be quick. If not, I can make it last a very long time. Either way, you will die."

55

AS YOU COMMAND

G regory of Fal Carrach sat his horse with the Breaker at his back. The massive wall rose three hundred feet into the sky, the black stone appearing sheer as it caught the gleam of the rising sun, but he knew better. He had spent the last hour walking his mount along the base of the towering barrier, a few times running his hand across the stone. By the look of the barricade he expected it to be smooth, but that was a false assumption. There were nooks and crannies throughout, which he assumed ran all the way to the top. Perhaps the stone had been slick and smooth at one time, but centuries of rain and wind had scoured its surface. That could be a problem in the battle that fast approached, but he would worry about that later, when he hoped that he could do something about it.

Sarelle of Benewyn had followed him the entire time, not saying a word. She simply stayed with the King of Fal Carrach, tracking his eyes, what Gregory examined, whether it was the Breaker or the land that stretched out in front of the towering wall. He had been charged with defending this place against a host that far exceeded his own. So any detail, any finding upon his inspection of what would become the battlefield, could be all important to their success or failure.

"They will come here?" Sarelle finally asked, as the two faced the long grass rippling at the soft touch of the wind in front of them. The plain extended for a mile across the front of the Breaker, rolling hills and thickets bracketing the space on both sides.

Gregory took a moment before answering, surveying the landscape one last time. "They will," he replied. "Our scouts report that the first Ogren war parties are no more than an hour away. Though the many war bands are traveling separately they should all be coming together right about here. This is where we will fight."

"Are we ready?"

Gregory turned in his saddle, stretching his neck to look up at the crest of the Breaker. He could see the movement above him. He couldn't pick out individual soldiers, but he knew that with Kael managing the defenses atop the imposing barrier, they would be as prepared as they could be for the onslaught to come.

"No," Gregory replied with a smile. "But we will do the best that we can."

"That's all we can ask for," said Sarelle, satisfied, and glad that Gregory had not tried to lie to her simply to make her feel better. She was a realist. She knew what they faced. The Breaker would help, it would give them time, the time Thomas needed to do what was required of him, she hoped. But if the Dark Horde truly was as large as the scouts reported, then the Breaker could only do so much. If Thomas failed at his task, and admittedly history was against him, then in the end the defense of the Breaker wouldn't matter. Eventually the soldiers who stood atop the black, granite wall would be overrun, and the Dark Horde would swarm into the Kingdoms. Rather than allowing her thoughts to drift down a dark path, she instead turned her attention to something that she had been thinking about for quite some time, the circumstances of the day only adding to her perceived urgency. "You know, Gregory, there is something that we must discuss."

"What would that be, Sarelle?" Gregory turned to face her, taking in the breastplate that fit her perfectly, her red hair streaming behind her because of the gusts of wind. She was radiant. He would have loved to take her away from here, to be with her if only for a day, but he couldn't. Such was the curse of leadership. Responsibility to others took precedence over all else.

"When we have pushed back the Dark Horde -- and we will push those evil beasts back because I have no doubt that Thomas will succeed; he is too stubborn not to -- there will be no more dancing around between us."

"What do you mean?"

Sarelle's eyes burned brightly as she captured Gregory's with her own. "I mean that you are mine, Gregory Carlomin. We may rule separate Kingdoms, but you are mine. We will rule together. As one."

Gregory smiled, unable to hide his pleasure. "As you command, my Queen."

56

CRUEL HOPE

Thomas stood in the gloomy chamber wrapped in shadow, his emotions roiling within him as he stared at the Princess of Fal Carrach, who was stuck in place. He closed his eyes, trying to settle himself with several deep breaths. The time had finally arrived. All the training, the education, the effort, the sacrifice leading to this one moment. Having fixated on this single event and its consequences for so long, the connection in his mind with the Shadow Lord growing stronger in recent years, the dreams of death and suffering plaguing him night after night, his worries for his family and friends intensifying as he wondered whether he had the courage to do what he had to do … as he breathed in deeply and exhaled slowly, it all dissipated as he cleared his mind of anything that could distract him. He discovered that a calm had settled over him. A peace. Even a small pleasure, knowing that one way or the other, the pressure and expectations, all the burdens that he had lived with, fought against, consigned himself to for so long, finally were going to be relieved.

Thomas opened his eyes, a smile of contentment

breaking out. He stepped through the gloom, walking from black tile to white, white to black, before stopping at the edge of the disc in the center of the floor. Testing the weight of the Sword of the Highlands in his hand, the steel blade flickered even in the pall, catching what little light there was streaming into the chamber through the open balcony and the broken skylight centered over the stone etchings in the floor.

Thomas raised the blade, his eyes finding the inscription that ran the length of the steel: "Courage and honor lead to freedom." Now he truly understood. Now he knew why his grandmother, Rya, liked to tell him so frequently, "*You must do what you must do.*" The best way to fight your fear was to accept it, to allow it to be there, to know that it was a part of you, and then to use it. And that's what he would do now.

"You still don't understand, do you, boy." The Shadow Lord glided forward, leaving Kaylie by the balcony. His quiet, grating voice echoed off the circular wall of the chamber. "No one has ever defeated me. Not even the combined might of the Sylvan Warriors when their numbers were ten times larger than they are now. Not Athala, the founder of your cursed band of fighters. Not Ollav Fola, the first High King. No one! No one can stand against me. Yet still you choose to defy me? You run toward your own death needlessly."

The Shadow Lord stopped at the edge of the disc, standing across from Thomas, his black robe swirling in and out of the shadow, his blood-red eyes burning with a devilish delight.

"Think, boy. Think of what you could have if you saw the truth for what it really was. Think of what you could have if you acknowledged reality instead of trying to perpetuate a dying order. The Kingdoms are crumbling, and only I will stand tall when they collapse. You could be there with me. You have the power, the strength that's needed. You could help the Kingdoms join my new world."

"You think that I would so easily betray my family, my friends ..."

"Think, boy! Your family and friends? What of them? They have done nothing but use you!" The Shadow Lord's whisper erupted into a harsh growl. "Your grandparents and their Sylvan Warriors have sought a pawn for centuries to oppose me. They have trained you so that they could send you to your death. They were not driven by love. They were driven by greed! They think of themselves. The power they had. The power they've lost through the centuries. They hoped that you would help them to regain that power. Why take on this thankless task so willingly when you have so much to live for?"

Thomas glanced sharply at Kaylie. She stood there utterly still, silhouetted on the balcony by the grey light that streamed into the chamber. Tears trickled down her cheeks. The Shadow Lord held her with his Dark Magic, and there was nothing that she could do but watch and hope.

"Yes, I see it. The love you have for her." The Shadow Lord chuckled softly. "Would you really give up that love, that opportunity for happiness, just because you were given an impossible task that could only lead to your death and you feel the need to try to fulfil it? Look on the Princess of Fal Carrach, Thomas. You can see it in her eyes as well. She wants a future with you. She wants to be with you. But she knows that she can't have that if you remain focused on the task given to you by those who only sought to use you for their own purposes. Are you truly willing to let that future go? That one chance for happiness? It is a rare thing and not to be given up lightly."

Thomas pulled his eyes away from Kaylie, looking once again at the inscription on his blade. He could understand now why so many fell within the grasp of the Shadow Lord. The men and women who were seduced by his words, the half-truths, the lies, the promises that would not be kept. Yes, he would have liked the chance at a life with Kaylie, but not on those terms. Not on the Shadow Lord's terms. If he was to have a future with Kaylie, it would be on their terms or not at all.

"Do you really think that I'm as weak as all the others?" asked Thomas, his green eyes blazing in anger. "That I was no better than Daran or Rodric? That I cared more for myself than for others? That my interests always have to come first?"

"You're making a mistake, boy. You will miss your one chance …"

"No!" Thomas' shout resounded throughout the chamber then out into the dead city and the mountains beyond. "Your promises mean nothing to me. Your words are only that, no more solid than the black ash covering this city that swirls at the slightest whim of the wind. If Kaylie and I are to have a future, it will be one of our own making, not something given to us by you."

The Shadow Lord stood in the gloom, not saying a word. Silence settled over the room, seeming to last forever, but really only held for a few long minutes as the Shadow Lord appeared to be running calculations behind his blazing eyes, new ways to try to turn Thomas, to make him an ally, to have him see things in a different light. Yet just as fast as a thought came to him, the Shadow Lord rejected it. Until finally the master of Blackstone realized that there was only one course left to him.

"So be it," said the Shadow Lord. "You will have your

wish. Perhaps you are right. Perhaps there is no way around it. The prophecy requires us to contend against one another. No matter my best efforts, it appears that the demands of the prophecy must be met."

Thomas appeared startled at the Shadow Lord's reference. The Shadow Lord chuckled scratchily in response.

"Yes, I know the prophecy. I know it quite well, in fact. You think your grandparents were the only ones to pay it heed? Look where we stand."

Thomas eyed the disc that separated him from his opponent. It looked exactly as it did in Thomas' dreams. The carved stone showed a young man with a burning white sword fighting what appeared to be a shadow, though the faint outlines of a man in black were visible within the carving, a soul-eating black sword consuming the light. The image of Blackstone rose behind the two combatants.

"I had it crafted more than a thousand years ago," said the Shadow Lord. "Knowing what could come to pass. Knowing what would come to pass. To remind myself every day that we would stand here like this. To remind myself of what would be my greatest victory. You see, boy, you're not the only one who has prepared for this moment, for I, too, know what's truly at stake."

Catching the faint shift of the Shadow Lord's robes, Thomas jumped back. Grabbing hold of the Talent, he infused the Sword of the Highlands with the natural magic of the world, raising his weapon above his head. Sparks flew as the Shadow Lord's blade, darker than night, slashed down and struck Thomas' blazing white steel. More sparks showered down as steel met steel in a rapid series of strikes, revealing the determination in the eyes of the two combatants as they glided across the tiles.

The Shadow Lord had moved faster than a viper, seemingly crafting his blade from nothing before attacking Thomas. And now all Thomas could do was defend as he moved around the chamber, blocking, parrying and avoiding the Shadow Lord's incessant assault. Each time the two blades met -- one black, one white -- a shower of sparks lit the surrounding shadows before falling onto the checkered floor.

Kaylie watched agonizingly, wishing that she could help. But knowing that even if she weren't held by the Shadow Lord's Dark Magic, her interference could only hinder Thomas, who appeared to be hanging on by a thread.

Thomas fought valiantly, but the Shadow Lord was faster than any opponent he had ever faced, even the spirits of the many warriors from the past that his grandfather had raised from the afterlife for his training. All he could do was concentrate on protecting himself, on keeping that cursed black blade from slicing into his flesh, and that was becoming more and more difficult by the second. Each of the Shadow Lord's slashes, cuts and lunges kept him off balance, oftentimes Thomas' blade coming up barely in time to keep his adversary's black steel, a steel that he could only see because it was darker than the gloom of the room, from burying itself in his body.

He realized that he needed to change his tactics rather than continue as a practice dummy for the Shadow Lord. Otherwise, his fate was sealed. He thought back to his instructors, the spirits of warriors' past. All had given excellent advice. Yet one stood out. His first blademaster. Antonin, First Spear of the Carthanians. He had fought more than a thousand duels, and he had admitted that there were times that the opponents he faced were better fighters than he was, either faster, stronger, more skilled, or all three. Nevertheless, Antonin had always prevailed. Not because he was a better fighter, but because he was more flexible. His opponents knew one way to fight, but Antonin was not chained to any one method or style. He would use all that he had learned from the men and women he had fought in single combat to his advantage.

Thomas remembered something that Antonin had explained to him during one of their first lessons together, the words offered by his reticent instructor having stuck with him: "You are a Kestrel, and you are a Keldragan. The families have two histories, yet you are the connection between the two. You can take the best of both and make it work for you. So it is in the training circle. Do not stay wedded to a single way to attack or defend. Be flexible. Take the best of what you face in the circle and make it work for you."

Thomas raised his blade one more time, taking the full weight of the Shadow Lord's steel on his own sword, the sparks caused by the metal meeting brightening the chamber for just an instant with each flash. But instead of backing away as he had been doing, Thomas ducked and drove forward with his shoulder, catching the Shadow Lord in the chest and pushing him back. Thomas followed that with a quick slash, forcing the Shadow Lord back once more, before launching himself forward, a quick lunge turning into a sweeping cut for the Shadow Lord's legs.

The Shadow Lord slid back, shocked by the turn of events. His irritation increased as he caught sight of Thomas standing there calmly, watching him, measuring him, and apparently not too concerned by what he saw. The Shadow Lord's simmering anger built to a roaring fire of rage as the boy who stood before him, the boy who should have died so long ago, had the audacity to smile.

The Shadow Lord leapt to the attack once more, black

blade seeking Thomas' heart, his speed incredible, so fast, in fact, that from Kaylie's perspective the Shadow Lord's onslaught was no more than a blur, her eyes scarcely able to follow the movement. To her amazement, Thomas easily stepped aside. Then he did so again. And again. As the Shadow Lord continued his futile assault, his blade striking out faster than a snake, and only catching air, Thomas dodged and weaved across the black and white tile of the floor, looking as if he knew what the Shadow Lord was going to do before the Shadow Lord did. Rather than defending, he simply sought to evade, not having any need to raise his blade.

Frustrated after a series of useless lunges and slashes, the Shadow Lord growled and charged once more, raising his blade for a downward blow that should have taken Thomas' head. But his quarry wasn't there. Thomas had already moved, raising his blade simply to deflect the strike. Again and again, the Shadow Lord sought to plunge his steel into Thomas' chest, but his black blade never reached its target. And each time he missed, the Shadow Lord's fury boiled all the more, for he saw that this boy who played at being a Sylvan Warrior had closed his eyes and had the gall to taunt him, to play with him like a child with a toy.

The Shadow Lord did not realize that Thomas had expanded his use of the Talent during the duel, not only infusing his blade, but now also using the natural magic of the world to extend his senses much like he did when he battled the Sentinel for the right to bear the Key. Thomas had been so fixated on the Shadow Lord's black blade, remembering his dream of that very sword being driven into his side so many times in the past, that he had almost lost the combat before it had begun.

But he had remembered his training and the times that

Antonin had required that he fight with a scarf tied around his eyes, forcing him to rely solely on his senses and intuition. And he remembered that when he did so, he had fought better because he no longer thought, which took too much time against some opponents, but instead simply acted, permitting his instincts and the Talent to guide him.

As he did that now, he could tell much to his satisfaction that the Shadow Lord's frustration was building, which meant that Thomas had chosen the right course. Waiting. Being patient. Allowing the Shadow Lord to enrage himself. Seeking that one opening that would give him a chance at victory.

Relying only on the power flowing within him and his senses, Thomas drifted across the chamber. His eyes closed, his impulses leading him, Thomas found that he could easily avoid the Shadow Lord's unceasing attacks. Whether a lunge or a sweeping cut, Thomas danced away, sometimes raising his blade to defend, sometimes not. But always watching for that one opportunity that he needed.

Then he saw it. The Shadow Lord had overextended his last thrust, trying to cleave Thomas in half with a two-handed blow. His adversary was off balance, the black blade striking a white tile and gouging it deeply, sparks flying and illuminating the shadows for just a second.

Instead of moving away as he had done so many times in the past, Thomas ducked and rolled, then immediately lunged forward himself, the Shadow Lord barely deflecting the blazing white blade as Thomas sought to bury the steel in his heart. The Shadow Lord stumbled back, no longer gliding effortlessly across the chamber, as Thomas continued to press his attack.

Now, it was Thomas' blade that was a blur, the Shadow Lord raising his own just in time to stop the blazing white steel from connecting. Lunging, slashing, jabbing, Thomas refused to let up, knowing that this could be his only chance. His only opportunity to defeat his adversary. His only possibility for survival. His blade was getting closer and closer to the Shadow Lord, who struggled against the speed of Thomas' assault. Sparks flew with every strike, the white and black blades meeting time after time as Thomas pushed the Shadow Lord around the circular chamber, forcing him back against the chamber's stone wall, never giving his nemesis the time to recover.

Then Thomas opened his eyes in shock. He had moved instinctually, not thinking, simply doing. The Shadow Lord stood right in front of him, the Sword of the Highlands driven into his chest, the power of Thomas' lunge so strong that the burning white blade had sunk a foot into the wall.

The Shadow Lord's blazing red eyes had dimmed, now no more than banked cinders. As the seconds passed and Thomas' shock turned to realization, the Shadow Lord's softly burning embers gradually turned to black, the fire gone.

Thomas stood there for a moment, trying to comprehend what had just happened. Then he pulled out his blade from the stone, allowing the Shadow Lord to slide off the point and slump against the chamber wall. The Shadow Lord, his greatest enemy, his greatest fear, was no more.

57

BLAZING WHITE LIGHT

K aylie ran to Thomas, the Shadow Lord's demise releasing her from the Dark Magic that had held her in place. She threw her arms around him, burying her face against his chest.

"Thomas, I can't believe you ..." She couldn't find the words that she wanted, still too shocked by what had happened. Thomas had killed a creature that supposedly couldn't be killed.

"I know. Neither can I." He held her tightly, relishing the feel of her body against his own.

Hands on his chest, Kaylie pushed back from Thomas, gazing up into his bright green eyes that glowed in the murky dark. "You defeated the Shadow Lord. You did it." Gripping his shirt tightly, Kaylie pulled Thomas closer, kissing him deeply.

For a moment, Thomas lost himself in the feel of Kaylie's lips. Then he smiled. "Later. We need to go."

Thomas looked one more time at the Shadow Lord's body, slumped against the wall. In a matter of minutes what had once been a terrifying face had become all too human, the blood-red eyes closed. The remains brought to mind what happened through a Shade's kiss. The energy had been sucked from the body, leaving a dry, desiccated husk in its place. Yet despite his success, Thomas didn't feel victorious. Rather, he felt like his work was incomplete. That there was still more to do, and it had nothing to do with the Dark Horde marching toward the Breaker and the Kingdoms beyond, but he didn't know what it was that bothered him. He turned to leave, sword still in one hand, his other hand in Kaylie's, when a harsh laughter filled the chamber. Thomas' blood ran cold.

"You thought it would be that easy, boy?" The deep, bloodcurdling voice echoed around the Shadow Lord's throne room. "You are more of a fool than I thought. You have taken my body, boy, but not me. Never me. Our duel is not yet done."

Thomas looked up toward the chamber's obscured ceiling, finding the source of the voice. A roiling black shadow darker than the surrounding gloom swirled angrily above him.

"You thought that a steel blade could kill me?" asked the raspy voice. "After all that I have survived? I have lived for millennia. Steel can't kill me. You can't kill me!" In the midst of the swirling mass, two blood-red pinpricks blazed fiercely. "But I can kill you!"

Having a good idea of what the Shadow Lord was about to do, Thomas grabbed hold of the Talent. Pulling Kaylie close, he formed a shield of white energy that expanded around them. It resembled the dome barrier that his grandparents had constructed when he battled the ancient dark creature the Shadow Lord had set upon him when his Marchers fought Rodric and the Armaghian army for supremacy in the Highlands. The barricade took shape just in time. The mist and shadow that the Shadow Lord had become, his corporeal body destroyed, surged down toward them. The blackness tried to consume them, smashing itself against the shield, pushing and probing incessantly along its length, looking for a weakness, searching for a way through the barrier. It took all of Thomas' strength and focus to maintain their protection, understanding the likely outcome if he failed.

For several minutes, the battle raged. The Shadow Lord explored and prodded, whipping around Thomas' defensive shield faster and faster, seeking a crack or weakness that he could exploit. Yet Thomas' protective barrier held, flashes of bright white revealing when the Shadow Lord sought to force a way through with his Dark Magic.

"Well done, boy," said the Shadow Lord, the black mist pulling back from its attack after several minutes of failure. "But you won't be able to hold me back forever. As you weaken, I only grow stronger here. Here my power cannot be challenged. You will die this day. Both of you."

It was then that a dark shadow detached itself from a column behind Thomas and Kaylie. Thomas couldn't turn to see what approached, needing to maintain his complete concentration on his shield in order to keep the Shadow Lord at bay. But Kaylie did glance behind them, catching the movement, and watching the smoky form materialize into Ragin Tessaril, son of the former High King. Although the robed figure's face was waxy and pale, the terrible, disfiguring scar was unmistakable.

"You are mine, coward!" he shouted at Thomas' back. "You will pay for what you did to me!" The former Prince of Armagh ran a hand across the weeping scar that started where his right eye used to be and ended below his jaw.

A shard of black energy shot from his other hand, aimed

straight for the distracted Thomas. Kaylie reacted without even thinking, placing herself in front of Thomas' unprotected back and forming a small shield of white energy on her forearm that she used to deflect the Dark Magic.

"No!" raged Ragin. "The old man stopped me once before. Try as you might, Kaylie, you cannot stop me. If you do not step away, I will destroy you and then him."

Maintaining her shield, Kaylie rose to her full height, placing herself squarely between Ragin and Thomas.

"You cannot have him," replied Kaylie coldly. "If you want him, then you must come through me first."

"So that's the way of it," hissed Ragin. "You're more of a fool than he is."

A pitch-black fog began swirling around Ragin's hands, faster and faster, the constant motion almost spellbinding. Then a black ball of energy no larger than Ragin's fist shot toward Kaylie. Using the shield on her forearm, she deflected the attack, the sphere of black energy crashing into the wall, blowing out several of the large stones and allowing more of the dim grey of the morning into the chamber.

"That's the best that you can do?" asked Kaylie contemptuously. "You sell yourself to the Shadow Lord and that's all you received in return?"

A maniacal laugh burst from Ragin's throat. "Actually, no. I can do so much more."

Another ball of black energy shot from Ragin's fist, and then another, and another, until it seemed to become a constant stream of hand-sized spheres that shot toward Kaylie. The Princess of Fal Carrach stood there calmly, confident in her knowledge and abilities. She used her shield to take the brunt of the attack, parrying each ball of energy as she did the first, the Dark Magic blasting more and more holes through the walls and the resulting light brightening the Shadow Lord's throne room. But she quickly grew tired of the game, Ragin demonstrating a singlemindedness and lack of creativity that had plagued him well before the Shadow Lord had granted him the ability to use Dark Magic. Kaylie then smiled as she made a critical discovery. She was stronger than Ragin and more skilled. Even with his Dark Magic, he was no match for her.

That realization filled her with a strength of will and purpose that she meant to put to good use. Turning the angle of her shield, the next ball of black energy Ragin shot toward her rebounded right back at him, forcing him to dodge out of the way, the Dark Magic blasting through the column behind him and then out through the far wall. Shocked, Ragin shot another ball of black energy toward Kaylie, which she just as quickly sent right back toward him, Ragin once again diving out of the way just in time.

"You made a mistake, Ragin."

"What would that be?" he wheezed, rising to his feet with some effort and then dusting himself off.

"You've made me angry."

A stream of white-hot energy burst from Kaylie's hands, surging toward Ragin, who formed a swirling shield of black to defend against Kaylie's attack. Unimpressed with his response, she maintained her assault while increasing its intensity, thereby requiring Ragin to focus solely on maintaining the integrity of his shield. Kaylie used that to her advantage now that she had his undivided attention, walking toward Ragin, the strength of her attack increasing with each step, until she stood no more than a few feet from him. She could see the strain on his face as he struggled to hold back the power that she threw against him. And then she did something that drained what little color remained from Ragin's sickly countenance, leaving him stricken as if he had just lost the most important thing in the world to him. Because he had.

Making use of the skill Ariel had shown her just weeks before on the Distant Islands, she used the Talent to cut Ragin's link to the Dark Magic gifted to him by the Shadow Lord. Ragin's face fell, shock his only visible emotion. But the former Prince of Armagh's hate remained. Ragin reached for the sword at his hip, but Kaylie was faster. Pulling the dagger that Thomas had given her from where she had hidden it in the side of her boot, she drove the blue steel into Ragin's stomach, then stepped back.

Ragin's frantic efforts to pull his own blade free from the tangle of his robes stopped, his hands going to his belly as he tried to keep the dark red blood from spilling out onto the tiled floor. But he was destined to fail. What little color remained in Ragin's face drained away as he dropped to his knees, his life seeping out to stain a large white tile.

"You can't ..." It was all that Ragin could say as his eyes glazed over, his world beginning to go dark. Everything that he had sacrificed for this one chance to kill his tormentor, selling his very soul, all for naught. First, stopped by an old man, and now by a girl. It wasn't fair. It just wasn't ...

"I did," said Kaylie quietly, at first unsettled by what she had just done, but then pushing that remorse to the side, knowing that she had no choice. That Thomas would be dead otherwise.

Thomas hadn't been able to track Kaylie's duel with Ragin, needing to focus his full attention on the Shadow Lord. He worried for her, wanted to help, but there was nothing that he could do. When her hand gripped his shoulder, giving him a squeeze of reassurance, he knew that she had won and he smiled, but only briefly because of the effort of doing so. Sweat dripped down Thomas' face, the effort to maintain control of such a large amount of the Talent rapidly draining his energy. Though Acero had helped Thomas with his recovery by sharing some of his strength, his body's fight against the darkness that Malachias had set within him could not be dealt with so quickly or easily. He needed time to rest and recuperate, time that he didn't have.

Sensing Thomas' flagging strength, Kaylie reached for his hand. Seizing control of the Talent once again, she offered her power to him, and Thomas gladly accepted. He wove Kaylie's Talent into his own, strengthening the shield and lessening the strain that was weighing on him from the Shadow Lord's continuing assault.

After several minutes, the Shadow Lord drifted away from Thomas' shield, frustrated by his inability to break through. Thomas closed his eyes, breathing deeply, enjoying the respite, no matter how brief it might be. He held on to Kaylie's hand tightly, thanking her with a quick squeeze of his fingers.

"You are both stronger than I thought," whispered the Shadow Lord. "But it will only be a matter of time. Even combined you do not have the strength to stand against me."

Thomas opened his eyes, smiling. His hearing was better than most, and the sounds that started to drift in through the open balcony and the holes dotting the walls hardened his will.

"We don't need to hold for much longer," answered Thomas.

The angry swirl of the Shadow Lord stopped, the black mist hanging in the air. The master of Blackstone could hear it now as well. Roars and screams, the scrape of steel on steel, drifted up from the courtyard just beyond the balcony. Every so often the chamber brightened as a blast of white flashed through the gloom, dust cascading down from the damaged ceiling as the ground rumbled in response to every lightning strike. The cries of battle drew even closer and became more intense. The Sylvan Warriors had breached Blackstone, and the Shadow Lord's servants were faring poorly against them.

For a moment, the Shadow Lord didn't understand what had happened. His defenses around the city crafted of Dark Magic were stronger than any Sylvan Warrior could have hoped to endure. It must be the Key, he thought angrily. This whelp had used it to enter Blackstone secretly, and its passage into the city must have weakened or eliminated his magical traps.

That conclusion set his mind racing. If that could happen, what else might be possible? The Shadow Lord knew that he was stronger than any who opposed him. This boy, the so-called Defender of the Light, was strong in the Talent. But was he strong enough to truly challenge him? And what was the likelihood of success now that he had joined with the girl? Moreover, what would happen if the boy's grandparents joined the fight? Or any of the other Sylvan Warriors with skill in the Talent? Who was to say what the result would be if all three Keldragans and some of the others faced off against him? Once before the Sylvana had combined their strength to combat his Dark Magic. They had defeated him, and it had taken more than a thousand years for him to recover from that failure. Could the Sylvana do the same again? Or worse? For the first time in centuries, the Shadow Lord felt two emotions that were almost foreign to him. Fear and doubt. They combined to create an unease that gave him an urgency he hadn't felt before.

The Shadow Lord shot down in a blur, hoping to catch Thomas off guard. But the Sylvan Warrior was ready, and his shield remained intact, holding back the Shadow Lord. Thomas held tightly to Kaylie's hand, continuing to manage the flow of her additional strength, working it through his shield constructed of the Talent to wherever the Shadow Lord probed and sought to shatter his defenses.

The encircling black mist that was the Shadow Lord swirled faster and faster, blotting out what little light there was in the room until it seemed that Thomas and Kaylie stood in a perpetual night that blasted against them like a gale-force wind.

"You cannot defeat me, boy!" shrieked the Shadow Lord, his Dark Magic pressing intensely on Thomas' magical barrier, pushing it closer to him, shrinking it in size.

Thomas knew what would happen if the shield became too small. That it would only be a matter of time until the Shadow Lord destroyed their only real protection. Even combining his strength in the Talent with Kaylie's, Thomas still worried that the Shadow Lord could overwhelm them with his Dark Magic. The fate that Thomas had feared for so long seemed to be coming true. As the darkness came closer and closer, pushing incessantly against his defenses, compressing the natural magic of the Talent, Thomas struggled to maintain his control as his shield flickered uncertainly in response to his wavering strength.

He had come to terms with his own death, but he could not allow Kaylie to suffer the same fate. There had to be something that he could do. But what? As his mind searched desperately for an answer, his eyes were drawn to a tiny speck of light that burned brightly in the tightening space that he and Kaylie shared. It came from the Key that hung around his neck, a single surge of brightness in a sea of black. Perhaps that was the answer, he thought, a final option available to him.

As the Shadow Lord increased the potency of his attack, the black mist pressing closer and closer, turning the bright white of their shield into a worrisome grey, Thomas focused on the Key that hung around his neck. He had sensed its power when he had first found it, and he had used that power to enter Blackstone. Yet now it seemed to be calling to him. Telling him what it wanted.

Having no other choices to consider, Thomas complied, allowing his instincts to guide his actions. He began to focus the Talent he controlled on the Key, first in just a small stream of power, then more and more as his confidence grew. The shield that he had created began to flicker faster and faster from white to grey to black, then back again, bulging inward in some places as the Shadow Lord continued to push and Thomas pulled the Talent away from the barrier and transferred it to the Key.

Kaylie watched in fear and fascination, worried that what Thomas was doing would give the Shadow Lord the break in their defenses that he so desperately needed. But she saw as well that the Key was shining more and more brightly as Thomas wove the Talent that they controlled into the artifact. The Key began to pulse with a blinding light, the flashes coming more rapidly as it pulled in more and more of the Talent that Thomas sought to infuse it with. The surging energy became more intense, hotter, almost eager, until the physical Key could barely be seen within the blazing white energy.

That's when Kaylie noticed the change that had occurred. The Shadow Lord had halted his assault, pulling away from them. The black mist and shadow continued to swirl, but the Shadow Lord was hesitating, apparently undecided about what to do next. As if the Shadow Lord didn't know what to make of what Thomas was doing with the Key. As if it could be a threat to him.

With his barrier no longer under attack, Thomas pulled in more and more of the Talent, combining his and Kaylie's strength into a single flow that flooded into the Key. The diamonds that were a part of the stone pulsed brighter and brighter, each flash illuminating the chamber in a dazzling light. And with each pulse the white energy began to destroy the darkness that had lurked in the chamber for millennia.

That's when Thomas realized what he had to do.

"You're right," said Thomas in a quiet, confident voice, a small smile playing across his lips. "I can't defeat you on my own. Even with Kaylie's help I can't. But with the Key, I can destroy you."

Drawing out the very last bit of the Talent that he could from both himself and Kaylie, Thomas grasped the Key in his free hand, raising it toward the black mist that twisted and turned above them. Then with a single thought he released the tremendous magic that the Key held. What burst from the ancient artifact was more than the natural power Thomas had infused it with as the ancient relic magnified the strength of the energy it held a thousandfold.

The blazing white light blasted into the Shadow Lord, illuminating the chamber with a brightness that rivaled the sun. For a moment, nothing happened. The light and the dark appeared to be at an impasse, two unstoppable forces having slammed into one another. But slowly, ever so slowly, the tide turned as the stream of white light swelled, becoming stronger and stronger, and more and more demanding. Thomas released even more of the energy that the Key had amplified, putting all the strength that remained within him into his task as he knew that this was his only chance to defeat the Shadow Lord once and for all.

The white light began to eat at the edges of the darkness, biting at it. Destroying it. Obliterating it. The Shadow Lord struggled to defend himself, to find some way to combat the boy's assault. The ancient creature drew on more and more of his Dark Magic, attempting to hold back the white light. To stop it from wrapping itself around him. But no matter what he tried, the stream of white energy hungrily consumed all the Dark Magic that the Shadow Lord offered, taking it in and extinguishing it, and with every cut the swirling black mass that was the Shadow Lord shrank.

"Release me, boy!" shrieked the Shadow Lord. "Release me and I can give you everything that you desire. Release me and I can give you the Kingdoms!"

Faster and faster the white light from the Key devoured the darkness. The blood-red pinpricks of light began to flicker in the black mist, the struggle between the opposing forces tearing at the very essence of the Shadow Lord.

"I don't want the Kingdoms," Thomas answered calmly.

"Then what?" screamed the Shadow Lord, the creature's pain seeping into his voice as the white light continued to devour him. "What do you want? I can give you anything you want!"

"You're giving me what I want," said Thomas calmly. "I want you to pay for what you have done. I want you to pay what is owed."

With that, Thomas offered a final surge of his strength, a final blast of the Talent. The Key gratefully accepted it, then turned its full force on the Shadow Lord. The pinpricks of blood-red flickered faster and faster, the swirling black growing smaller and smaller in size. The fiery white light ripped into the Shadow Lord, eating away at what remained of an evil that had plagued the Kingdoms for thousands of years. Destroying an evil that had threatened nature itself.

The pure white light shot into and through the Shadow Lord, shredding the creature. Sensing its impending victory, an enormous bolt of energy burst from the Key. With the resulting blinding flash, a thunderous boom rocked the chamber. Dust and small pieces of stone fell to the floor, the reverberations of the explosion rippling out to the very edges of Blackstone.

For the first time in centuries, sunlight streamed into the chamber unimpeded. The grey clouds that hung over the city slowly dissipated, replaced with a clean bright light that lit up the entire room, leaving no place for the unnatural darkness of the Shadow Lord. With a final flicker of red, the black mist, now no more than a tiny, swirling mass of darkness, disappeared with a sharp crack and a final screech of terror.

Thomas released his hold on the Key, allowing it to fall against his chest. The artifact no longer pulsed, but a spark of bright, white light continued to shine within the diamonds embedded in steel.

Thomas smiled. They had done it. They had won. But even though the Shadow Lord was destroyed, he knew that there was still more to do, the pull of the Key requiring more from him. But first things first. Reaching down he took Kaylie in his arms. He had asked for more and more of the Talent from her, and she had gladly given it. But it had weakened her past the point of exhaustion. Holding her carefully, he stumbled out of the chamber.

58

ATOP THE WALL

The Breaker stretched from the Winter Sea to the western Highlands, a monstrous wall of black stone that rose several hundred feet from base to top. It was so wide, in fact, that several dozen men could ride their horses side by side across the parapet, which provided enough space for catapults, huge buckets for burning oil and pitch, and other weapons of war. At regular intervals sally ports dotted the base of the wall, though all remained barred and guarded and had been crafted within the stone in such a way so that they weren't identifiable when looking at the barrier from the direction of the Northern Steppes until they were opened.

Gregory strode atop the Breaker emanating a confidence that he didn't feel. With each step, a Fal Carrachian soldier, or a soldier from Benewyn or Kenmare or Armagh, saluted, demonstrating their respect for the High King. He nodded, smiled or gave a few words of encouragement, locking away the nervousness that roiled within him.

He had placed the fighters of Fal Carrach, Benewyn, Armagh and Kenmare at the top of the wall, rear guards protecting the sally ports. The warriors of the Desert Clans had arrived just the day before, prepared to venture out from the Breaker at a moment of opportunity or need, but for now those skilled horsemen would remain in reserve, joining the Marchers who waited impatiently for word of the Highland Lord.

Looking out over the top of the wall, Gregory saw nothing but the dark creatures of the Shadow Lord. Thousands upon thousands of Ogren, corralled by Shades, stood near the Breaker and stretched across the Northern Steppes with more war parties appearing every hour, to say nothing of the Mongrels, Dragas and other monstrous beasts that many of the soldiers of the Kingdoms had never seen before.

In their midst sat Rodric Tessaril, former High King and ruler of Armagh, and apparent general of the Dark Horde in the Shadow Lord's absence. Though Gregory bet that Malachias, the tall, bald man who rode at Rodric's side and radiated both a malevolence and sense of command that the former High King could never achieve, was the one really in charge.

The Dark Horde had assaulted the Breaker three times so far that morning. The first two were just probing attacks, testing the defenders, seeking a weakness. Rodric had demonstrated a singular unimaginativeness that had played into the hands of the Kingdom soldiers. Each time the former High King had sent dozens of Ogren war parties against the towering barricade, the huge beasts screaming in rage as they charged toward the stone wall. Their cries were short-lived, as the defenders atop the Breaker launched thousands of steel-tipped arrows that tore through the ranks of the dark creatures. Those that had reached the base of the wall had little time to enjoy their success, as vats of boiling pitch spilled from above, followed by flaming torches that set the Ogren and other beasts ablaze, the stench of burning meat almost overpowering as it drifted to the top of the wall.

After the first two failed attempts, Malachias had argued with Rodric for quite some time before the deposed High King tried something different for the third attack. He had called forward an Ogren war party wearing spiked armor on their arms and legs. The massive beasts, their upper bodies heavily muscled, had climbed the wall with ease, driving the spikes on their armor into the wall and pulling themselves up the roughened stone. The resulting skirmish atop the Breaker had been spirited but short, the defenders over-whelming the single Ogren war party in just a few minutes by using long pikes to keep the dark creatures from scaling the parapet and attacking the beasts while they still clung to the stone, expelling them from the wall like a leech stuck to the skin and allowing gravity to do the rest.

But Gregory worried about what would happen when multiple war parties attacked in such a way, believing that this latest effort by Malachias was simply another test, and a successful one at that. He doubted that his soldiers could hold the top with such facility against a larger number of Ogren. So, in his mind, it was just a matter of time. Either Thomas succeeded in Blackstone, the odds for which were not in his favor, or the Kingdoms fell when the Dark Horde scaled the Breaker and then descended on the lands beyond like a swarm of locusts.

To say nothing of the fact that the Shadow Lord held his only daughter, having received word just before he climbed to the top of the Breaker that Rodric sought to offer terms for her safe release. Gregory had refused, suspecting what the Shadow Lord would require in return. He loved his daughter more than life itself, but he could not put her above the needs of all the Kingdoms. He would have to trust in Thomas and hope that the enterprising Highland Lord found a way to free her. Gregory growled in irritation, pushing those dark thoughts from his mind and knowing that he could do nothing about his many worries. But he could do something here.

"My lord, to the north."

Kael Bellilil, Highlander by birth and Swordmaster of Fal Carrach for more than two decades, called Gregory over. Kael had been working with a ballista crew to target the weapon correctly.

Gregory looked to where Kael pointed. For a moment, Gregory thought that his eyes were playing tricks on him, because he was seeing something that he had never seen before. The grey clouds that normally hid the Charnel Mountains from view had disappeared, sunlight now streaming down onto those mountain peaks for the first time in centuries.

He stared for several long minutes, trying to decipher what this unexpected occurrence might mean. Had Thomas succeeded? Was his daughter safe? A light touch on his arm pulled him from his wonderings.

"What is it, Gregory? You seem distracted."

Sarelle Makarin, Queen of Benewyn, stood next to Gregory, her hand now on his arm.

"I was just thinking," he replied, enjoying the feel of her touch.

"After our conversation earlier this morning, I was thinking about what I would do after we defeat the Dark Horde. After Thomas succeeded and my daughter was safe."

"And what would that be?" she asked, a mischievous glint in her eye.

Gregory turned to face Sarelle, capturing her eyes with his own. She noticed that they glowed with an intensity that she had never seen before.

"Find a wife."

Gregory's response left Sarelle speechless. Though she had made her intentions clear, she worried that Gregory would never marry again. Unfortunately, she didn't have time to probe Gregory's response more deeply.

The battle horns of the Dark Horde once more blasted across the Northern Steppes. Gregory gazed down at the chaotic mass of dark creatures, watching Malachias, this time Rodric trailing after him reluctantly, issuing orders as several Ogren war parties approached the Breaker, all wearing the spiked armor that would allow them to climb to the top. Kael had already started bellowing orders as soldiers scrambled to their positions, ensuring that the boiling pitch was in place in an effort to reduce the number of beasts that made it to the top of the parapet.

Grasping Sarelle's hand gently, then giving it a squeeze, he left her, seeking the place that he thought would have the hottest fighting. High King he may be, but he was a fighter at his core, and he would do everything that he could to give Thomas the time he needed to save his daughter.

59

A BRAVE GIRL

"Thomas!"

Thomas turned at the sound of his grandmother's voice, which came from the far end of the square. He held Kaylie carefully in his arms. She had gone in and out of consciousness when he had walked out into the light on unsteady feet. She was exhausted, having given him every bit of strength that she had to help defend against and then defeat the Shadow Lord.

He moved as quickly as he safely could across the courtyard. Surveying the ruins that stretched out before him, Thomas realized that the battle had almost reached its conclusion. The Shadow Lord had left behind a small force of several thousand Ogren led by a cadre of Shades. He had sent all his other dark creatures to the Breaker. Thomas' enemy had never expected the Sylvan Warriors to try to make it past Blackstone's defenses, not understanding the real power of the Key that Thomas still wore around his neck. That lack of knowledge had contributed to the undoing of an evil that had plagued the Kingdoms for thousands of years.

The Sylvana had made quick work of the Ogren and Shades charged with protecting Blackstone. A few Sylvan Warriors continued to ride their unicorns around the wide perimeter of the dead city and then through its deteriorating streets, searching for any dark creatures that may have survived the onslaught of steel and lightning. But it appeared that the legendary warriors were wasting their time after having been exceedingly thorough with their attack. The only movement in Blackstone that the Sylvan Warriors now saw came from the gentle breeze swirling the burnt ash that covered the city. A city that began to resemble, if only just a very faint reflection after more than ten centuries of neglected corruption, what it had looked like in the past, before the arrival of the Shadow Lord, as the ever-present grey clouds vanished, and the sun blazed gloriously in the sky.

Thomas stepped around the bodies of a few dead Ogren and one Shade, which was still twitching as it completed its death throes, a sword stroke having taken off almost all of its head with only a few strands of sinew and flesh keeping it attached at the neck.

"I'll take her."

Rynlin appeared at Thomas' side, recognizing his grandson's own fatigue and gently taking Kaylie from him, then bringing them both over to Rya. Rynlin carefully lay Kaylie down on a makeshift litter of cloaks. Rya hovered over the Princess of Fal Carrach for several minutes, her hand resting gently on Kaylie's head. Using the Talent she scanned for any injuries, thankfully finding none. Satisfied with her examination, she was pleased that her student would suffer no lasting harm. When she looked down again, Kaylie's eyes were open.

"You did a dangerous thing, girl," said Rya sharply, her

fear at the risk taken by the young woman she had begun viewing as a daughter getting the better of her. "You almost gave too much of yourself."

"It was necessary," said Kaylie. She reached out and found Thomas' hand, squeezing tightly. The Lord of the Highlands had found a seat next to her. He passed her a flask of water, and she drank deeply.

"Maybe so," said Rya, not yet finished with her upbraiding. "But you could have gotten yourself killed. You almost did. I have not spent all this time instructing you in the Talent simply so you could burn yourself out."

"If she hadn't done as she did, we wouldn't be here," said Thomas. "Without Kaylie's strength, we wouldn't have survived. The Shadow Lord would have destroyed us."

"A brave girl," said Rynlin with a smile, understanding his wife's concern but suggesting with a glance that she leave off for now. "Stubborn as well. I expect that she'll be joining us at the Pinnacle shortly."

"Did we lose anyone?" asked Thomas.

"No," replied Rya. "The Shadow Lord never expected us to be here. He thought that he would catch us at the Breaker. Maden Grenis and Catal Huyuk are conducting a final search, just to make sure that there are no more dark creatures lurking about. But the city is ours."

"And what of Gregory and the armies at the Breaker?"

"Likely engaged at this point," said Catal Huyuk, who trotted forward on a unicorn name Brutus, a massive grey whose horn extended almost nine feet in length. When Catal Huyuk leapt to the ground, he barely came up to the unicorn's shoulder, so great was the animal's size. "Although I expect that the battle has probably just begun. The Dark Horde would not have made it to the Breaker until midmorning at the earliest, and noon is still an hour off."

Thomas nodded. That was good news. If Gregory could hold for just a few hours more, they had the opportunity to end the threat presented by the Dark Horde for good. He stood as Acero and Beluil approached. The pony-sized wolf trotted forward, rubbing his large head against Thomas' chest. Thomas dug his hands into his friend's fur, glad that the large wolf had made it through the battle unharmed.

Acero took his place, allowing Thomas to rub his nose. The massive unicorn stepped back and bent his head. Thomas reached out a hand. As soon as he touched the sharp point of the horn, images of what had occurred during the last few hours passed between them; Acero learning of Thomas' exploits, Thomas of Acero's role in the fight for Blackstone. Both were impressed with the other's efforts.

"There's more to do," said Thomas. "The Shadow Lord is gone, but he can still return. His Dark Magic still survives." The Shadow Lord's words prior to their final combat played through his mind: "*As you weaken, I only grow stronger here. Here my power cannot be challenged.*" His thoughts turned to his conversation with Kincaid, the leader of the Sentinels charged with protecting the Key and an uncle that he had never known until just recently. He pulled the Key from beneath his shirt and read the inscription: "When the darkness surrounds, the light will prevail."

"The Well of the Souls," said Rynlin, noticing the glint in his grandson's hard eyes. "You can feel it."

"I can. The Key is pulling me toward it, just as it did when I first entered Blackstone and it guided me to the Shadow Lord. It seems to be suggesting that there is some unfinished business that needs to be completed."

Rynlin stared at the Key that Thomas now held in his hand, the steel appearing to glow because of the brightly shining diamonds embedded along its length, the rocks pulsing with an insistent, white light.

"Do what you need to do. We'll wait for you here."

Kaylie watched the exchange with some confusion. The water helped to revive her, though she still felt incredibly weak. Rya had whispered to her to just give it some time. Her strength would return, but slowly. Nevertheless, she could still barely push herself up to a sitting position without Rya's help. After everything that they had been through, she could tell by the expression on his face that Thomas clearly meant to do something dangerous. This despite the fact that he couldn't be feeling much stronger than she was, his exhaustion plain as well.

"Thomas, what are you ..."

Thomas gripped her hand tightly, smiling down at her. "I'll be back shortly. There's one last thing that I need to do."

Nodding to those around him, Thomas jogged back the way they had come, entering the gloomy doorway that led into the Shadow Lord's chamber.

"Thomas!" Kaylie yelled weakly. "You can't ..."

Rya knelt down by the Fal Carrachian princess. "There's nothing you can do, child. This is something that he must do alone."

"What must he do? He just killed the Shadow Lord."

"I know, child. If Thomas hadn't succeeded, with your help of course, we wouldn't be here now. The Shadow Lord would have had his final revenge on the Sylvana."

"But where is Thomas going?" she asked, the worry clear in her voice.

"The Shadow Lord is dead, but given enough time he can return to the world if the Well of the Souls -- his source of power -- isn't destroyed," answered Rynlin. "It's not something that we can ignore, not if there's any chance that the

Shadow Lord could rise once more. This is something that only Thomas can do. Only the bearer of the Key has the power to combat the Shadow Lord's Dark Magic and extinguish the evil that it harnesses."

"What is the Well of the Souls?"

"A repository, some say source, of the Shadow Lord's Dark Magic. Destroy the Well and the Shadow Lord cannot return. He won't be able to use the foul power of the Dark Magic residing there to reconstitute himself. Leave it intact ..." Rya didn't feel the need to complete her thought, the implication obvious. Her worried eyes were fixed on the doorway Thomas had just entered.

Turning away from Rya, Kaylie peered through the smoke to where Thomas had run back into the keep, trying to send what little of her strength remained to aid him.

60

DESCENDING DISC

As Thomas ran back into the now crumbling chamber in which he had fought and defeated the Shadow Lord, the words on the Key ran through his mind on a continuous loop: *"When the darkness surrounds, the light will prevail."*

When the Shadow Lord had first come to Shadow's Reach, making the capital of what had been called the Northern Peaks his lair, the once beautiful city had begun to change. Previously a place of bright colors, the grey clouds and fog had taken up permanent residence over the metropolis. The flowers and trees stopped blossoming, their withered remains replaced by weeds, and the soft earth that had once been perfect for farming became a dusty, black ash that enveloped the city and became a plaything of the wind. Within a century the once thriving capital was no longer recognizable. The people who had populated the mountains had either left or become prey for the Ogren and other dark creatures that had quickly swarmed among the peaks, preferring the dark crevices and caves that surrounded the city to the houses and pavilions that fell into decay and disrepair as the centuries passed. What had once been known as Shadow's Reach, taking into account the shadows that played across the city when the sun set in the mountains, had been renamed Blackstone.

Some had said that the change that had caused the transformation of this mountain city was the arrival of the Shadow Lord. Thomas didn't doubt that his former adversary's appearance in these northern mountains had been part of the cause. But he believed that there was more to it than that. It wasn't just the Shadow Lord that had initiated the change.

The myths that his grandfather had taught him, in which there was always a kernel of truth, referenced the Well of the Souls. It was said to be the cause of all the Dark Magic in the world -- whether there was just one well or many no one really knew since stories from other lands told of similar receptacles -- and the source of the Shadow Lord's power. The Shadow Lord did cause the change to Shadow's Reach, setting it on a path to become Blackstone. But the Shadow Lord also had ensconced the Well of the Souls somewhere within the labyrinth of caves and hidden tunnels that lay beneath the city. And it was the Well of the Souls that gave the Shadow Lord the power that he needed to move forward with his plans to gain control of the Kingdoms and, in the process, destroy the world around him. Moreover, the Well of the Souls gave the Lord of the Shadow the opportunity for rebirth if ever there was need.

Based on those myths, Thomas believed that though he had defeated the Shadow Lord, he could not destroy him completely as long as the Well of the Souls continued to exist within Blackstone. That belief had only been confirmed by Kincaid, the Sentinel commander. Therefore, with his final task clear in his mind, Thomas scanned the circular chamber, looking for some hint of how to find the Well of the Souls. The Shadow Lord had spent a great deal of time in this room, making it his base of operations, so Thomas guessed that there was a reason for that, beyond just looking out over the square and watching his Ogren parade in front of him. The only distinct aspect of the chamber that caught his attention was the disc in the center of the chamber, the image of the Defender of the Light fighting the Lord of the Shadow etched into the large, circular stone.

He walked over to the disc, examining it closely. The pull of the Key became more demanding, the diamonds glowing more intensely, when he stepped onto the very center of the stone. Thomas studied the carving for quite some time until his sharp eyes identified something that might be of use. Where the blades of the two combatants met, there was a scarcely visible indentation. Pushing down with his foot, the small stone collapsed into the disc. All was quiet for a moment, and then a grating sound of stone on stone rasped throughout the chamber.

Thomas pulled his sword from its scabbard on his back as the circular carving sank into the floor, taking him into darkness as it dropped into the earth.

61

ATTACK FROM ABOVE

The flight of Dragas, a dozen in all, flew across the Northern Steppes, the peaks of the Highlands rapidly approaching to their west. The dark creatures, their leathery wings extended as they glided through the air toward the Breaker, scanned the skies with an arrogance born of their dominance as a predator. Few creatures had the courage or wherewithal to fight a Dragas, the scaled, winged beasts having few weaknesses thanks to their needle-sharp teeth, poisonous saliva and armored hide.

Thus it was with some surprise that the lead Dragas felt a wrenching, searing pain as a razor-sharp claw sliced into its leathery wing, followed by another, and then another. The monstrous beast had little time to react as another talon tore through its soft underbelly, the wound so deep and so long that the dark creatures' guts began to gush out as the beast dropped toward the plains far below, its tattered wings unable to keep it aloft.

Many of the other Dragas faced a similar end, knocked from the sky as dozens of kestrels shot down from the thin air above, claws outstretched, ripping into the most vulnerable parts of the dark creatures. The Dragas that survived the initial assault attempted to fight back, but had little chance of success, as the raptors swarmed the beasts, four or five working together to attack from multiple directions at once and eliminate their blood enemies with their overwhelming numbers.

The kestrels had waited for these dark creatures in the colder air well above the Highlands, knowing that they would come. Knowing that the Dragas would seek to invade their homeland once they were done with their work at the Breaker. And they understood as well that their coloring made them virtually invisible when they attacked from above. Something that they did with great effect against the Dragas, decimating the dark creatures in a matter of minutes and ensuring that the defenders on the Breaker had one less threat to worry about.

62

WELL OF THE SOULS

As the circular stone descended beneath Blackstone, Thomas used the Talent to extend his senses, searching for any danger, but finding nothing but a weak taint of corruption as he dropped through the pitch black. Thomas' eyes glowed a bright green as he sought to pick out anything around him that could give him a hint of what he might face, but even with his excellent vision this darkness gave him nothing but a faint, barely discernible view of the chiseled rock that passed by as he traveled deeper beneath the Shadow Lord's city.

The disc continued its slow descent, the fresh air gradually giving way to a dry, musty smell. A cold breeze that wafted up through the vertical tunnel chilled him. After several minutes, the stone finally came to a stop, settling noiselessly into a large circular chamber.

A soft green glow beckoned from the open doorway that stood before him. But Thomas remained where he was, feeling the need to be cautious. He extended his senses once more. Still no sign of an immediate threat, but something tickled at the edge of his awareness. It was familiar, but he couldn't place it. A warning, though faint.

Having no other path to take, he stepped through the doorway, his path lit by a green moss that covered the stone and glowed brightly in the dark. The luminescence gave everything a sickly greenish tinge, though he welcomed the change from complete darkness.

As he walked down the short passageway, Thomas saw another open doorway carved from the rock that led to a smaller chamber lit even more brightly than the hallway. Yet with each step what had bothered him at the very edge of his consciousness became even more persistent, a prickle of warning running down his spine. His senses revealed to him that danger lay straight ahead, but the Key also told him that he needed to keep moving in that direction if he hoped to achieve his objective. With each step, the pull grew stronger.

When he reached the doorway, he stopped. He detected the danger now. An ancient evil lurked inside the room ahead, but what it was he didn't know. He could see nothing from the threshold. Steeling himself for what was to come and trying to be cautious, Thomas had stepped halfway through the entrance when the hair on the back of his neck bristled. He dove and rolled forward, the blade that would have removed his head missing by only a hair.

Rising to his feet straight from the roll, sword at the ready, he was now able to identify what had disturbed him when he had first reached the bottom of the tunnel. Arrayed before him were four ghostlike fighters. The feeling that radiated from them was similar to what he experienced every time his grandfather had him train with the spirits of the great warriors, but with these four there was something more. A feeling of rot and wickedness oozed from the figures and permeated the rough-hewn chamber.

The evil spirits surrounded him immediately, gliding noiselessly through the green light coming from the moss covering the walls. Thomas examined each one carefully. The guardians of the Well of the Souls, he assumed, four individuals with the darkest names in the history of the Kingdoms, and all easily identified. Thomas assumed that the Shadow Lord had done what Rynlin had done for him for his weapons training, summoning these spirits for a specific task. But unlike his grandfather, the Shadow Lord had never released them, instead chaining them here with Dark Magic, giving them the responsibility for protecting the Well of the Souls.

Salacin, ruler of the Tenghos, a people that once dominated the Northern Steppes. He invaded what had not yet become the Kingdoms several times, conquering great swathes of territory and killing hundreds of thousands of innocent people in the process. Urala, one of the first High Kings, who slowly grew mad during his reign. As his insanity worsened, he took to torture, using it for no other reason than his own pleasure.

Cleowna, once thought of as the most beautiful woman in the Kingdoms. Married to the High King, she fell in love with another who rejected her advances, unwilling to betray the trust of her husband. Angry at being spurned, she tricked her husband into starting a war that led to the death of her unwilling lover and the destruction of his Kingdom. And Arian, a giant of a man, standing almost eight feet tall. Once the greatest champion of the Desert Clans, he turned to cannibalism, eating his opponents after killing them in battle, becoming no better than an Ogren.

Understanding now what he faced, Thomas glanced

quickly around the room. The moss completely covered the chamber, ceiling and wall, thus the strength of the illuminating green light. At the far end, past his four opponents, rose a small well containing a dark black liquid that churned ceaselessly as if at war with itself. Thomas didn't have time to examine anything else.

Relying on his training, Thomas jumped forward, avoiding Cleowna's quick stab at his back. But that only brought him face to face with Arian, the massive ghost swinging a hammer toward Thomas' head. Dodging the blow, Thomas brought his sword up, catching Salacin's blade on his own, before twisting away from Urala, who attempted to drive a short sword into his side.

Thomas wanted to attack, knowing that it was the only way to survive against these fearsome adversaries, but he had little chance to do so. The next several minutes involved a singular effort simply to stay alive. Though his opponents were spirits, their weapons were real enough when they struck his own, sparks brightening the green gloom every time he parried a blade.

The struggle continued for several minutes more, Thomas dodging and weaving throughout the chamber, never getting close to his primary target, the Well of the Souls, and not caring at the moment. His attention remained focused solely on staying alive as the four spirits sought to corner him. Once up against a wall, they would overwhelm him quickly. Thus the need to keep moving, staying away from the walls if at all possible, and ensuring that he had room to maneuver. But it was becoming more and more difficult as his strength ebbed, his exhaustion growing, making his normally crisp movements slower than he would have liked, and thereby increasing the danger that eventually the blade of one of the evil spirits opposing him would find its mark.

Suddenly, and much to his surprise, through some unseen command the four spirits stopped their attack and arranged themselves in front of Thomas, staying between him and the Well of the Souls.

"You fight well, boy," said Salacin. Standing next to him Mad King Urala giggled uncontrollably. At what, Thomas didn't know. "So well you would have been a welcome soldier in my army."

"And good looking as well," murmured Cleowna, eyeing Thomas up and down.

"Isn't that what got you into trouble in the first place?" asked Arian, the giant warrior's huge hammer resting on his shoulder.

"Can't blame a girl for looking," replied Cleowna. "Besides, I've been stuck in this chamber with the three of you for centuries. A handsome new face is a welcome change compared to having to listen to the Mad King year after year."

"Enough, our task remains the same." Salacin turned an angry glare from Cleowna toward Thomas. "Leave, boy. Your bravery and skill have earned you that right. We will offer you this opportunity only once."

Thomas stood his ground, using the passing seconds to catch his breath. "I have a task as well, a duty that can't be ignored."

Salacin nodded. "I expected as much. But know this. Your death is inevitable. Granted, you may defeat one or two of us, your fighting skills suggest as much, but not all four. We are too strong for you. Too strong for a weakened Highland Lord."

Thomas stared at Salacin with some surprise, not

expecting these spirits to know who he was. He didn't dwell on it as he had work to do, and he could feel the sands running through the hourglass with Gregory holding the Breaker.

"You're right," replied Thomas. "I can't defeat you on my own, and perhaps I won't have to."

Before Salacin could respond, Thomas took hold of the Talent, calling forth four spirits from the underworld, who coalesced next to him.

Antonin, First Spear of the Carthanians, stepped forward. The spear he held gleamed brightly, its seven-foot length catching the green glow of the moss.

"Worthy opponents, I see," said the Carthanian.

"Indeed," replied Fergus Steelheart, a gleaming sword in his hand. The leader of the Golden Blades eyed the four spirits who stood before them. With a wicked gleam in his eye, he announced, "I get the giant."

"Not if I get him first," said Ari the Archer, the tall man materializing next to Antonin. He held his bow in his hand, arrow already nocked, his fingers tickling the string and itching to pull back and release the shaft.

"Boys never change," said the final spirit who appeared next to Antonin. Camilla, Keeper of the Staff, stood taller than all three and matched Arian the Giant in height. Her staff appeared to be a small tree that had been smoothed down by a great deal of use. "If anyone gets the giant, it's me."

Thomas grinned confidently. "I can't defeat you on my own. But I have no doubt that my friends can."

"Thomas, leave these villains to us," said Antonin. "You have a more important task."

With that, Antonin, Fergus, Ari and Camilla charged forward, engaging the evil spirits arrayed against them.

Thomas watched for just a moment, waiting for a space to open up, then ran toward the source of the Shadow Lord's Dark Magic, weaving his way between the four separate combats that erupted within the chamber.

With the guardian spirits engaged and kept away from him, Thomas finally was able to approach the Well of the Souls. The roiling black water bubbled and hissed, churning with an anger that seemed almost palpable. Thomas pulled the Key from beneath his shirt. When he had first obtained the relic, he had seen the tiny inscription in the diamond set within the stone: "*When the darkness surrounds, the light will prevail.*" He hadn't really understood what it meant at the time, but he thought that he did now.

Thomas knew that he couldn't destroy the Well with his own power, so instead he focused his Talent on the Key, drawing in as much of the natural magic of the world as he could and infusing the diamonds that ran the length of the steel with it, much as he did when fighting the Shadow Lord. The diamonds began to glow more intensely and soon pulsed with a tremendous, flaring white light.

"No, you can't!" screamed Salacin.

Only he and Cleowna remained, Arian and Urala having already been dispatched. The two evil spirits attempted to fight their way past Antonin, Fergus, Ari and Camilla, but it was no use. Thomas' friends easily kept the two guardians of the Well of the Souls at bay.

Ignoring the cry and trusting in his spirit protectors, Thomas continued to stream as much of the Talent into the diamonds as he could, throwing all his power into it. When he could offer no more, his strength waning, he dropped the blazing Key into the roiling Well of the Souls.

At first, nothing happened. Then the black liquid began to churn faster and faster, as if it tried to expunge what

Thomas had placed in it. But then the liquid began to change, the black becoming grey, then black once more. Then grey again with bits of white shining through. Thomas watched the struggle intently, enthralled by the battle raging within the pool of black.

The inky liquid continued to boil, and then something happened that suggested that the struggle had turned. The white light that infused the diamonds shot out from the Well, growing brighter and brighter as the water boiled even more, threatening to escape from the receptacle of evil.

The ground started to tremble, gently at first, then more violently. Moss covered rocks began to break loose from the walls and the ceiling, small ones at first, but soon the larger stones shook free as well. As the ceiling collapsed, Thomas dodged the falling stones. The Well of the Souls became a geyser of pure white light that shot through the hole, revealing the massive tunnel that Thomas had traveled through while on the stone disc. The blazing geyser lit up the length of the tunnel, then blasted its way through the floor in the chamber above, and then through the roof of the keep, tons of rock crashing down all around him.

"Thomas, you must go!" commanded Antonin. Thomas' four spirits had defeated the Guardians of the Well, and they stood there watching him, eyes filled with pride and concern.

"Hurry, Thomas! It's all coming down around us," warned Camilla. The spirits had nothing to fear, but Thomas did as the fall of rock and stone increased in pace, the cloud of dust and dirt fogging the chamber despite the ray of light.

Thomas considered making use of the disc that had brought him here in the first place, but then thought better of it. He'd be a sitting target as the Shadow Lord's former palace fell on top of him with few options for escape.

Gathering the last of his rapidly failing strength, Thomas grabbed hold of the Talent, encasing himself in a gleaming ball of white light.

63

STONE AND LIGHT

Rynlin and Rya continued to look after Kaylie, though their attention was split as they glanced regularly at the crumbling keep, hoping for some sign of their grandson. Maden Grenis and Catal Huyuk had just returned from their latest circuit of Blackstone's environs, finally satisfied that the Shadow Lord's guards were dead or gone. They had confirmed that no dark creature remained alive in the city. The Sylvana had captured Blackstone.

It was then that the ground started to sway and shake violently. Many of the decrepit buildings began to collapse if they hadn't done so already over the long centuries, the old stone structures unable to withstand the violent motion of the earth. Even the massive hall from which Kaylie and Thomas had escaped began to shudder. Stones on its edges plummeted first, taking with them the gargoyles and other monstrous beasts carved into the parapet, and then the western wall disintegrated in a cloud of grit and other debris. To the amazement of the Sylvan Warriors, a stream of blinding white light shot through the roof of the castle, signaling its demise. It was only a matter of time before the entire structure fell in on itself.

"Into the square!" shouted Rynlin. "Stay away from the buildings!"

The Sylvana and their unicorns quickly heeded his command, taking advantage of the relative safety of the large open space as the ground continued to heave to and fro.

Kaylie looked imploringly at Rya. "What about Thomas?"

"He will be all right, child. He always is."

But this time, Rya found it hard to believe her own words, and Kaylie could decipher the worry in her eyes. Rya sensed Thomas through the necklace around her neck, but it was a faint feeling and rapidly fading. As they watched from the square, huge pieces of the fortress fell inward, burying the massive structure in its own stone, the ground around it torn apart by the angry earth. And through it all a blazing stream of white light shot into the sky, destroying the murk and the shadow and allowing the bright sunlight of the morning to illuminate the square for the first time in a thousand years.

Rynlin stared for a moment at the collapsing keep, shaking his head in frustration, hands gripped tightly at his sides, before he started walking toward the worsening destruction, intent on finding Thomas.

Rya's words checked his progress. "You can do nothing for him. He will get out if he can."

Tears formed in Rya's eyes. Rynlin stood stock still, overcome with emotion, wanting to aid his grandson but hearing the truth of his wife's words. Finally he nodded, then walked back to them just as several more towering geysers of white light rising thousands of feet into the air burst through the rubble of what was once the Shadow Lord's sanctuary. Many of the Sylvana watched in astonishment, glad to see the change occurring in Blackstone, but saddened by what that might mean for their fellow Sylvan Warrior. Kaylie's tears streamed down her cheeks as Rya tried to comfort her.

"Look!" shouted Rynlin, pointing to the sky.

Kaylie and Rya turned just in time to watch a massive kestrel shoot between the falling rubble, the large predator weaving its way up and around the disintegrating stone and the streams of white energy. The raptor circled once over the destroyed keep, then banked toward the Sylvana waiting in the square, screeching out a cry of victory.

Rynlin laughed with joy, recognizing the shape his grandson had taken. Rya smiled broadly.

"Thomas," Kaylie whispered.

"Yes, child," said Rya, stroking her hair while watching the kestrel soar free in the sky. "You should know by now that he is not one to die without a fight."

64

CALL FOR HELP

The morning had drifted unknowingly into early afternoon, a dark haze from the hundreds of burning fires dampening the bright sunlight of the day. The swirling smoke and ash fell prey to the wind, obscuring or revealing what occurred on the battlefield according to its caprice. Gregory stood atop the Breaker, having stepped back for a brief moment from the soldiers who continued to fight bravely, to fight with conviction and determination, but with the glimmer of fear beginning to show in their eyes. At first controlled and disciplined, with the Dark Horde's continuing attacks, the soldiers' actions became more frantic and desperate as the Ogren and other dark creatures tried to scale the parapet. The men and women who struggled so valiantly understood what the result would be if the Shadow Lord's servants breached the Breaker.

They had resisted two major assaults already, pushing back the Ogren that had climbed to the top of the Breaker. During the second attack the defenders had been required to sweep the parapet clear in a half dozen places, preventing the dark creatures from gaining a toehold on the wall. The struggle had been hot and intense, seesawing for several minutes, as the Ogren that had scaled the wall threatened to overwhelm the soldiers who struggled to contain the many attempted breakthroughs. It wasn't until Gregory had been able to turn several dozen archers away from the task of shooting down into the milling mass of dark creatures far below that the soldiers on the wall forced the tide to turn. The King of Fal Carrach had formed the archers into companies charged with scouring clean the bulwark of dark creatures and allowing the hard-pressed defenders to pull back and regroup. Sending their steel-tipped arrows scything into the Ogren at close range slowed the beasts, the defenders on the Breaker then charging into their towering adversaries with pikes and lances, skewering the Ogren or sending them back over the wall to fall among the dark creatures screaming for blood at the base of the stone barrier.

But this third attack was the largest and most dangerous yet. Looking to either side, Gregory saw several thousand Ogren streaming up the massive stone wall, their spiky armor cutting into the carved rock and giving them a means to pull themselves up, his weary and dispirited defenders preparing to hold the parapet once more even though the odds were turning against them. There seemed to be no end to the onslaught. No matter where he checked -- left, right, to the front -- the dark creatures of the Shadow Lord came into view. And in the midst of the undulating Dark Horde that swayed like an ocean of hate and hunger from the foundations of the Breaker out onto the long grass of the Northern Steppes, a former High King, hunched over and shrunken in size, remained within the shadow of a balefully grinning Malachias.

Wiping the sweat, dirt and blood from his brow, Gregory

realized that he asked too much of his soldiers. But what else could he do? He had been given a simple but virtually impossible task. Hold the Breaker and give Thomas the time that he needed to kill the Shadow Lord, despite the odds against him, and, if possible, save his daughter at the same time. After the first two assaults, Malachias had offered Kaylie to him once again in exchange for safe passage beyond the Breaker at the cost of obeisance to the Shadow Lord. The offer was much like fool's gold, all glitter and no substance. Gregory had refused, though doing so had almost torn his heart out. He told himself for the hundredth time that he could not put the life of his daughter before those who had already died in defense of the Kingdoms, and those who still fought for and believed in the necessity and justness of their cause.

Gregory smiled mirthlessly, pushing his fears for his daughter from his mind. Thomas was a brave young man, perhaps the most courageous person he had ever met. But no one had ever defeated the Shadow Lord. Defender of the Light or no, the odds were stacked against the Lord of the Highlands. Just as they were now lined up against him and his fighters.

He and his soldiers had given all that they could, and he knew in his heart that no matter how bravely they fought they would not be able to hold back this current assault. Their enemy was too great in number. They could only delay the inevitable. Once the Ogren gained a foothold on top of the Breaker, the dark creatures could sweep down its length in both directions and open the path to the Kingdoms. The battle would be done.

Not knowing what else he could do to prevent the defeat of his army, Gregory reached to his belt, pulling free the Horn of the Sylvana. Thomas had given it to him shortly after being confirmed as the Lord of the Highlands, and Gregory had kept it safe and close ever since. His instincts told him that now was the time to use it. Centuries ago, when the Sylvana were many and played a more active role in the Kingdoms, every ruler held a coveted Horn. If dark creatures threatened the Kingdoms, Sylvan Warriors answered the call. It was the bond that the Sylvana had with the Kingdoms, but would they answer it now? Could they? Had they succeeded in Blackstone? Or had the Shadow Lord been triumphant, his Ogren surging up the Breaker as a symbol of that success? Gregory had seen the blast of bright sunlight in the Charnel Mountains, watching in shock as the clouds that had blanketed those mountains for centuries dissipated. But what did it mean? Nothing else had happened since other than the incessant attacks against the Breaker by the Dark Horde.

With all of his other options gone, Gregory didn't have a choice. He was out of ideas. Even the reserve that he continued to hold back could do little against a host of such size and ferocity. If help was to come, it had to come now. Raising the mouthpiece to his lips, he hesitated for just a moment, then blew strongly into the instrument. The note blasted from the Horn, drowning out the sounds of battle and echoing off the Charnel Mountains far to the north. For almost a full minute, Gregory stood there in silence as the fighting stopped along the length of the Breaker. His soldiers caught their breath as the Ogren climbing the black stone and milling around its base looked around in confusion. Even the war parties that trudged across the Northern Steppes toward the massive wall had halted. It seemed as if time had stopped, man and dark creature alike all across the battlefield waiting to see what would happen next.

Gregory brought the Horn of the Sylvana to his lips

again, then once more, blowing two more strident notes that carried all the way to the Winter Sea. The silence and stillness stretched on along the Breaker and the bloody and charred ground below it. Not even Malachias, so intent on breaking through to the Kingdoms, had moved since Gregory had blown the first note from the Horn of the Sylvana.

Absolute quiet ruled as the seconds slipped by, and then the minutes, even the gusts of wind from the Charnel Mountains having stopped for a time. Gregory had hoped for an immediate response, some guarantee that the Sylvan Warriors came in answer to his call. He could use that to bolster his soldiers, to keep them fighting just a little bit longer and perhaps push the Ogren back from the Breaker one final time.

But there was nothing. Had the Shadow Lord killed Thomas and then destroyed the Sylvana? As the minutes dragged by, the silence gradually dissolved. The dark creatures began to stir once more, the Shadow Lord's servants realizing that perhaps the legends of the past were not about to appear. That perhaps the Sylvana were no more and that there was nothing but the soldiers atop the Breaker to keep them from taking the Kingdoms for their own.

65

ANSWERING THE CALL

The Sylvan Warriors heard the first blast from the Horn as they headed down into the lowlands that bordered the Northern Steppes. Kaylie sat behind Rya on her unicorn, Acero pleased to have Thomas on his back once more. Beluil and his wolves had ranged ahead, having already reached the tall grasses that led toward the Highlands and the Breaker, planning to warn of any danger and eliminate any dark creatures that got in their way.

But so far, no obstacles had appeared to their front. The Shadow Lord had never considered the possibility that the Sylvana might attack Blackstone, instead expecting his cursed enemies to make their stand at the Breaker as they had in the past. As a result, the Shadow Lord had sent all his Ogren war parties and other dark creatures toward the massive wall. The Sylvan Warriors now had an open path to come up behind the Dark Horde undetected, something that Beluil and his wolves confirmed.

"That's got to be the Horn I gave Gregory," said Thomas, his weariness plain in his voice though he continued to push himself, the battle not yet done. "He wouldn't have blown it unless there was need."

"That he wouldn't," confirmed Rynlin, having known Gregory for decades and immediately approving of the King of Fal Carrach upon taking his measure. "What shall we do, Thomas?"

Thomas was taken aback by the question, not expecting it. He glanced around quickly, seeing the eyes of the assembled Sylvan Warriors watching him. But they weren't weighing him, not like when he took the tests to join their hallowed fellowship. He had been an untried boy then. Then, they knew of him, of his potential, but they didn't know him. That was no longer the case. They knew him now. What he could do and what he had accomplished. And they respected him. It was clear in their eyes and their postures. Dispatching the Shadow Lord had changed the dynamic. He recognized it in Catal Huyuk's expression and even in that of Tiro who had always been so cantankerous. Thomas was the Defender of the Light. He had defeated the Shadow Lord. As a result, the Sylvan Warriors now looked to him for leadership.

Thomas turned Acero quickly toward the south, urging him to a trot, the other Sylvan Warriors nudging their unicorns forward to keep up.

"We do as we always have!" shouted Thomas over his shoulder, as Acero picked up his pace, moving from a trot to a gallop.

Yet the gallop of a unicorn did not compare to that of an ordinary horse. The natural magic that flowed through the unicorn allowed the massive equines to sprint faster than any other animal in the Kingdoms. When they reached the edge of the Northern Steppes, having traversed the last gullies and hidden valleys of the Charnel Mountains, Acero and the other unicorns sprinted even faster, to the point where they appeared to be no more than a streak of color shooting through the tall grass of the desolate plain.

"We answer! And woe to any who stand against us."

Many of the Sylvan Warriors smiled now, knowing what was to come, craving the battle to be fought. They had struggled for so long to keep the evil of the Shadow Lord at bay, and now they finally had the chance to eliminate that wickedness completely. They had the opportunity to destroy the Dark Horde.

66

BOLT OF FEAR

"What was that?"

The former High King Rodric Tessaril danced his horse nervously in circles among the Ogren and Shades of the Dark Horde, barely able to control the animal. Just a minute before these terrifying, massive dark creatures had strode inexorably toward the Breaker to join their brethren seeking to scale the imposing wall and force their way past the Kingdom defenders. His success was guaranteed. It was only a matter of time before the Shadow Lord's servants overwhelmed their foes.

Then, once beyond the Breaker, Rodric could ride straight back to Eamhain Mhacha and claim what had been taken from him. More important, he could have his way with the many people who had betrayed him. Gregory of Fal Carrach first, then Sarelle of Benewyn ... well, perhaps he would take his time with Sarelle. She was a beautiful woman, after all. But Gregory, the man who had become High King at his expense, the man who stood atop the Breaker at this very moment leading its defense, would be the first put to the sword.

Malachias stared at the former High King in contempt, guessing at what ran through the fool's mind. The man was oblivious. He was nothing more than a figurehead at the moment, one who would be disposed of shortly. As soon as the Dark Horde overran the Kingdoms, Rodric's utility would come to an end. The Shadow Lord had promised Malachias that he could be the one to put down the incompetent fool for good.

"A horn from atop the Breaker," replied Malachias distractedly. "Nothing more, and nothing to worry about."

The horn sounded once more from the top of the huge wall and then for a third and final time.

An unwelcome shiver ran down Malachias' spine as the shocking realization dawned upon him. The Dark Horde had stopped. Even the beasts scaling the Breaker hung there in anticipation. He realized why in an instant, and his blood ran cold. The Ogren, Shades and other dark creatures remembered, even though they, and he, had not heard a Horn of the Sylvana for centuries. An ancient, instinctive fear settled over the Dark Horde, adding an uncomfortable weight to the unnatural quiet. The silence dragged on, but with each passing second Malachias' smile grew. Always in the past there was an immediate response. A Horn of the Sylvana responding, warning that the Sylvan Warriors had heard the call and prepared to unleash their fury. Always. But nothing this time. Nothing at all.

Malachias' smile shifted into a raspy laugh. He was about to order the Shadow Lord's servants to begin the assault once more, but the command stuck in his throat. A note sounded from the Northern Steppes, crystal clear and carrying on the thin air of the north. A note that sent a bolt of fear straight through his heart.

67

THREE NOTES

The resumption of the Dark Horde's assault on the Breaker wavered, the creatures of the Shadow Lord continuing to hesitate, indecision and worry freezing them. Initially confident that the three blasts from atop the Breaker would go unanswered after so many minutes had passed, most of the beasts still kept their heads turned to the Charnel Mountains, listening. A nervousness settled within the dark creatures, setting the stage for fear. They saw that the clouds had disappeared to the north, no longer hiding the jagged landscape. Bright sunlight now streamed down onto the barren, burnt peaks for the first time since the arrival of the Shadow Lord so many centuries before.

The strange silence lengthened, beginning to wear on the nerves of all the combatants. Then to the north, at the very edge of Gregory's hearing, came a sound that sent a jolt of energy through his body. An answer to his call. The note was soft but strong, rebounding against the black stone of the Breaker to hang in the air over the hushed battlefield.

WE HEAR.

The silence continued, for some dragging on interminably though it was only seconds. Could it be? His hope, extinguished just moments before, blazed back to life. A second note followed, this one louder than the first, closer. It cracked like a bolt of lightning striking the earth.

WE COME.

Looking to the north once more, from atop the wall Gregory could see that something was happening at the very edges of the Dark Horde which stretched out for more than a mile onto the Northern Steppes, some kind of confusion. The order of their advancing war parties had been disrupted. There were flashes of light visible through the smoky haze of the battlefield and grumbles of thunder, even though the sky was clear, followed by the rumbling of the ground that made him think of an earthquake. For the first time since his early morning ride with Sarelle, Gregory smiled. He sensed that the battle was about to turn.

Then a third, final blast echoed off the Breaker and the Highland peaks, the call so loud and ear-splitting that many of the Ogren fell from their perches on the wall, their serrated armor sliding free from the cracks and crevices as the stone shook.

WE CONQUER!

The Sylvan Warriors had returned.

68

THUNDER AND LIGHTNING

The Sylvana burst out onto the Northern Steppes from the Knife's Edge, the primary pass leading out of the Charnel Mountains. Thomas rode Acero in the middle of what was becoming a wide line that began to take on a new shape as they raced across the tall grass.

The Sylvan Warriors knew their business. Rynlin and Rya, with Kaylie riding behind her, made up the point of the wedge with Thomas. The Sylvan Warriors without the Talent spread out to either side, while those with skill in the natural magic of the world held their surging unicorns back to form a second wedge just a few yards behind the first.

Normally the journey from the Charnel Mountains and across the Northern Steppes to the Breaker could take as long as a week by horse. But such was not the case with the unicorns of the Sylvan Warriors. The Sylvana's mounts sped across the grasslands in a blur. In just a matter of minutes the Breaker became visible, towering above the land. And just a league ahead, Thomas' sharp eyes picked out the straggling war parties of the Shadow Lord that were just now joining the rear guard of the Dark Horde.

"Thomas!" shouted Rynlin, who rode beside him. "You will be the focal point. Remember, do not take in too much of the Talent at one time. Conserve your strength. You still haven't recovered from the last few days, even with Acero's assistance."

Thomas nodded. And then, as if through some silent command, the horns of the unicorns began to glow with a searing white light. Glancing behind at the second wedge of Sylvan Warriors, Thomas confirmed that Tiro, Maden Grenis and the others had taken hold of the Talent.

Reaching out tentatively, Thomas hesitantly touched the massive build-up of the natural magic of the world, a huge reservoir of the Talent provided by his peers and held in the horns of their steeds. He was more than tired after his duel with the Shadow Lord and then the destruction of the Well of the Souls. So he heeded his grandfather's warning, knowing that if he took in too much of the Talent, he'd leave himself nothing but a charred crisp.

Therefore, he decided on a different approach, grasping hold of the Talent gently and weaving a connection to each of the unicorns. Their horns pulsed even more brightly, blindingly so as he began to manipulate the power contained within them.

The final Ogren war parties to arrive had reached the last of the dark creatures that made up the Dark Horde. The Shades that led them sought a way through the mass of Ogren and other monstrous beasts that blocked their way as all the dark creatures tried to find a path to the Breaker. They didn't know what was sprinting toward them from behind, and for that they would soon pay a terrible price.

Faster and faster the Sylvan Warriors approached, the thunder of their unicorns' hooves masked by the milling mass of Ogren, Shades and other dark creatures. Finally, with the charging Sylvan Warriors no more than a hundred yards away and closing at an incredible speed, some of the Ogren had the sense to turn toward the Sylvana. But by then it was too late. Their fates had been sealed.

As the Sylvan Warriors in the front wedge drew their swords and spears, preparing to strike, Thomas released the Talent. Streaks of white light shot from the tips of the unicorns' large horns, blasting into the back lines of the Dark Horde, incinerating the dark creatures and leaving behind burned-out husks and piles of ash. Those few Ogren and Shades that survived that first assault met a bloody end as the leading wedge of Sylvan Warriors swept through the survivors with sword and spear, their unicorns using their horns as lances to skewer any dark creatures that tried to oppose the charge.

Recognizing that the sheer number of dark creatures could be a major impediment to the Sylvan Warriors reaching the Breaker, Thomas adjusted his strategy. He began to stagger the spears of energy, first from the front wedge, then from the trailing wedge. The bolts of lightning from the first line struck to the front, seeking to clear a path, while the bolts from the second wedge shot up into the air and slammed down fifty yards beyond the first line, opening up space so that the Sylvan Warriors could continue their charge.

Sensing the opportunity, Acero and the other unicorns dipped their horns and surged forward, slamming into the rear of the Dark Horde.

69

LULL

The Ogren scaling the Breaker hung from the wall precariously, their spiked armor dug into the stone, as they stared to the north, having forgotten the defenders that waited for them above. They were trying to determine what was happening at the back of the massive host of dark creatures.

Gregory followed their gaze. He had taken advantage of the small break in hostilities to rally his defenders, making sure that archers were resupplied with arrows, the soldiers with pikes and lances had regained their formations, that those manning the catapults were restocked with boulders and pieces of stone, and the soldiers tasked with releasing boiling oil and pitch reheated the fires and pulled out new stocks, preparing for the attack to begin once more.

Flashes of light caught Gregory's attention at the rear of the Dark Horde, the streaks of white continuing at a consistent pace and the ground protesting with each strike. As the lightning came closer and closer to the Breaker, slicing through the Dark Horde with an almost inhuman precision, the King of Fal Carrach noticed the change in his troops. A building confidence had replaced their fears and doubts, and what had once been viewed as a desperate last battle to save the Kingdoms had turned into something that was different and altogether unexpected, but quite welcome. A chance to destroy the Dark Horde.

Grinning wickedly, Gregory turned to a smaller man who stood at the back of the action, a man from the Desert Clans who had been placed there for this specific purpose.

"Get to Chuma. Tell him to be ready to ride!"

70

PATH OF DESTRUCTION

The Sylvan Warriors, attacking in two wedges, tore through the Dark Horde like a sharpened scythe through fall wheat. The flow and ferocity of the offensive terrified the dark creatures. The Ogren and Shades in the front ranks realized too late what was happening. But with the Sylvana slamming into the Shadow Lord's host from behind and the Breaker to their front, they had nowhere to go, trapped in a slowly closing vise. The dark creatures, thousands upon thousands, were pushed back into one another, their movements and options limited as they were forced together into a tighter and tighter space. Panic began to set in. Many of the dark creatures desperately sought a path to escape, but only those beasts on the very edges of the Dark Horde had any chance of success. The Sylvan Warrior attack was too methodical, too efficient, too deadly.

Thomas maintained his control over the Talent, Rynlin and Rya riding next to him and protecting him as he directed the massive amount of natural power that was available to him thanks to the efforts of the Sylvan Warriors and their unicorns. To Kaylie, the continuity of the assault

resembled a dance with a distinct rhythm, the first strike
tearing through the ranks of dark creatures in front of the
Sylvan Warriors, the second falling just beyond to sow
confusion and fear and provide the attackers with space to
drive their unicorns into the massive host of dark creatures.

The strikes of white lightning slammed into the ground,
causing great geysers of dirt and rock to be blasted hundreds
of feet into the air along with dozens of Ogren and Shades
each time a bolt hit. The leading wedge of Sylvana swept
through the few servants of the Shadow Lord that remained
standing, swords slashing down to bite into flesh, lopping
off heads, arms and legs, and driving their blades through
chests. When there were too many dark creatures for the
unicorns to skewer with their blazing horns, the colossal
equines, which rivaled an Ogren in height, simply lowered
their shoulders and trampled the dark creatures as they
strove to maintain the momentum of their charge.

In a matter of minutes, the Sylvan Warriors had left a
wide swath of destruction in their wake, the broken, dead
and dying Ogren, Shades and other dark creatures littering
the grass of the Northern Steppes. A small but organized
band of several hundred riders, making use of the Talent,
steel and an overriding purpose and strength, had deci-
mated the once overwhelming power of the Dark Horde.

Yet as the Sylvan Warriors drew inexorably closer to the
Breaker, its intimidating expanse towering above them,
Thomas realized that the utility of their current strategy was
diminishing as the chances of getting bogged down in the
midst of the confused and terrified dark creatures increased.
The decreasing space in front of the Sylvana, combined
with the dark creatures packed within it, had begun to
impede their assault. And Thomas understood that
continued movement was essential. If the Sylvan Warriors

became mired in the seething mass of dark creatures, they would lose the advantages that they enjoyed presently and risk defeat. Thomas quickly decided on a new approach when he caught the glint of steel reflecting off the sun at the very fringes of the battlefield. Guessing at what Gregory had planned and hoping that he was right, Thomas issued new orders.

"Rya, swing right, push to the hills! Rynlin, swing left! We have some friends there who'd like to join the fun."

Thomas' grandparents, having a good idea of what their grandson had in mind, moved quickly to comply. With a dastardly grin Rynlin issued the necessary order, the two wedges on Thomas' left swinging more sharply in that direction; the two on the right doing the same under Rya's command.

The creatures of the Dark Horde were slow to respond as the Sylvan Warriors broke their two wedges in half, each now charging away from the other and pushing for the hills and thickets lining their flanks. The Ogren and Shades struggled to reform their defensive lines on each side as the Sylvan Warriors slammed into them. Yet the maneuver had done more than take the dark creatures by surprise. It had also opened a path toward the Breaker as Malachias tried to split his own force to respond to the change in tactics with the hope of using the knolls that bordered the battlefield on each side as an additional barrier.

But it was Malachias' corresponding adjustment that played right into Thomas' hands. Releasing his hold over the Talent, he returned individual control of the natural magic of the world to his peers, who quickly made use of it to continue their attack. Thomas communicated silently with Acero, who galloped forward, head down, massive horn leading the way, driving through any dark creature too slow to escape his charge.

Rynlin and Rya could spring the trap. Thomas had a different objective now. Malachias and Rodric sat their horses just a few hundred yards to his front with nothing but a few Ogren in his way.

71

FROM THE FLANKS

C huma, appointed leader of the four Desert Clans, had watched the expanding battle with increasing worry, as he and his fighters hid among the hills and sparse forests that flanked the battlefield on each side. The Dark Horde had grown larger and larger with each passing hour and with each attack had demonstrated that eventually the Breaker would fall. It was inevitable. At first, he thought that whoever led the Dark Horde would send scouting parties down the flanks of the ground selected for the assault to ensure that no enemies lay in wait for the arrival of the Shadow Lord's servants. But then he realized that wasn't going to happen, in large part because of those few Sylvan Warriors tasked with helping the defenders of the Breaker using the Talent to help maintain the illusion that the barren and desolate knolls and barrows remained no more than that. Besides, who would be foolish enough to try to ambush dark creatures on this side of the Breaker? Yet as the hours passed, and he saw the Ogren wearing their specially made armor begin to scale the towering wall and exert greater pressure on the soldiers atop the parapet, his worry only intensified.

How could King Gregory and his fighters hold against such a powerful force? Chuma cursed himself for his doubt. There were no other choices left to them. There was nothing to do but fight. If the Dark Horde broke through, it was only a matter of time before every single Kingdom fell, including the Clanwar Desert. The empire of old would return, but this time ruled by the creatures of the dark.

When the horn blew from the top of the Breaker, his consternation almost got the better of him as the following silence stretched on, each passing second feeling like a year. His worry vanished when he heard the Sylvan Warriors respond. Thomas had survived! Confirmation of his young friend's success came quickly with the sounds of battle coming from the rear of the Dark Horde. For the first time in centuries, the Sylvan Warriors had answered the call.

Knowing that the time to engage was fast approaching, Chuma sent orders down the line to his riders, who remained carefully secreted within the folds and nooks of the hills. Using a mirror, one of his men flashed his commands to the Desert Clans waiting on the far side of the battlefield. As a result, his men were already moving into position before the runner sent by Gregory of Fal Carrach reached him. Then they waited anxiously for several more minutes. The Dark Horde's attack on the Breaker had faltered and then come to an end, the dark creatures focused on what was coming at them from the rear, their thoughts shifting from victory and conquest to sheer survival.

Chuma sat his horse as calmly as he could, refusing to allow his increasing tension to show in his features. His men struggled to do the same. From where they now sat their mounts, hidden from view, they had a clear line of sight to the fight enfolding on the plains, watching with great interest and itching to join the battle and strike into the heart of the Dark Horde.

That desire only increased when they saw the Sylvan Warriors come into view, the two wedges of legendary fighters driving through the Dark Horde in an unstoppable charge. The desert soldiers were amazed at the damage that so few could cause and were energized by the success of their allies.

Yet Chuma still waited. Outwardly calm but for his fingers tapping unconsciously on the horn of his saddle, inwardly his guts turned flips. After several more agonizing minutes, Chuma smiled. Thomas had seen them. The Sylvan Warriors had split their wedges into two lines that now pushed the Dark Horde toward the hills flanking the battleground, forcing the dark creatures to set their rear to his front. It was the perfect opportunity, his enemies completely unaware of the new danger that lurked behind them.

Chuma ordered another message to be sent to the Desert Clans on the other side of the battlefield, then he pulled his sword from his scabbard and raised it above his head. His bellow carried all the way down the line of impatient fighters.

"Ride soldiers of the desert! Ride to victory!"

Urging his horse forward, he was at a full gallop within seconds, and he knew that thousands of desert soldiers rode at his back. He was no more than a few dozen yards away from the unsuspecting dark creatures when he lowered his sword and lined it up with the back of a huge Ogren, and then he issued his final command.

"Ride to the Highland Lord!"

72

TIGHTENING VISE

The Sylvan Warriors wasted little time in continuing their assault as the attacking wedges split into two wings. Once again in control of their Talent, the second line of riders called forth their natural magic, using the horns of their unicorns to magnify the power that they could control a hundredfold. The swarm of dark creatures reeled in shock and dismay, more and more of their number destroyed as each second passed. Now was the time to finish the fight, and the Sylvan Warriors had more than enough strength to accomplish that task.

Following a similar approach as during their initial assault, some of the Sylvan Warriors called down bolts of lightning. Others used their mounts' horns to release bolts of white-hot light that tore through the Ogren and Shades that had little choice but to stand against the continuing onslaught because they were pressed so tightly together. Crushed into a single mass, the dark creatures had nowhere to run and barely any space to fight, the only openings appearing when those skilled in the Talent destroyed the front rank of dark creatures so that the first line of Sylvan

Warriors could ride through and attack with steel, forcing the creatures closer and closer to the hills at their back.

That's when disaster struck and any hope for a coordinated defense by the dark creatures fell apart. The Desert Clans burst forth from their hiding places, cutting into the surprised and unprepared Ogren and Shades from behind, the skilled horsemen slicing through the ranks of monstrous beasts with their curved blades as they sought to meet the Sylvan Warriors coming the other way.

Any attempt at defending themselves quickly evaporated as the servants of the Shadow Lord broke under the increasing pressure of the vise now being applied. Their thoughts turned entirely to escape, frantically seeking some way to break free and make a run for the Charnel Mountains. But much to their terror, the trap only closed more tightly around the dark creatures, the Sylvan Warriors sustaining their inexorable charge to the hills, the Desert Clans pushing from the other direction, and neither group willing to allow any dark creature to slip away.

73

FOCUS

"I know you're tired, but you can do this. Focus!" Rya shouted, struggling to be heard over the pounding hooves of her unicorn Bella. The huge animal ran over the dark creatures that survived the Sylvana's initial attack with the Talent, dropping her head every so often to drive her horn through a minion of the Shadow Lord, then shaking the body free with undisguised contempt.

Kaylie, perched behind Rya and holding tightly to her mentor's waist, would have laughed if she didn't need to concentrate not only on holding on to the Talent, but also on trying to stay on Rya's steed as they galloped through the Dark Horde. Leave it to Rya to use the most important battle since the Great War to continue Kaylie's instruction.

Forcing everything going on around her to the back of her mind, she set to her task. Kaylie reached for the Talent once more, and then again, and again, yet each time she was about to grab hold, a jolt or knock from riding among the dark creatures would throw off her concentration, to say nothing of the exhaustion that had settled within her bones from helping Thomas fight the Shadow Lord.

"This is impossible!" Kaylie screamed in frustration.

"Remember what I told you," urged Rya. "Use the Talent to steady yourself first. Once that's done, you can move on to the task at hand. You need to be able to do more than one thing at a time with the Talent."

Kaylie grunted in irritation. The battle raged around her and Rya wanted her to focus, despite her worry for Thomas. She knew that after everything he had gone through in Blackstone that he was just as exhausted, if not more so, than she was. He needed to rest. But that fact had not stopped him from leading the Sylvana toward the Breaker at the call of the Horn and then charging right into the middle of the Dark Horde.

And now he had split the Sylvan Warriors into two separate fighting forces. She understood the strategy, applauded it as she saw the fighters of the Desert Clans stream down from the hills on either side of the battlefield and cut their way into the dark creatures from behind. But Thomas had kept going forward, his eyes focused on Malachias and Rodric, giving her no chance to follow or assist as Rya pulled her wing of Sylvan Warriors to the west to push the dark creatures' backs toward the attacking desert fighters.

"Thomas needs to do this on his own," said Rya, interrupting Kaylie's thoughts. "And he can, but not if he's worrying about you. So focus on what you need to do!"

Rya's words felt like a kick in the backside. Doing as Rya instructed, albeit reluctantly, Kaylie forced everything else from her mind but her feeling for the Talent, which she grabbed hold of with a will. Weaving the natural magic around her, she anchored herself to the saddle, realizing that once that was done, she no longer had to worry about getting thrown off.

"Very good!" said Rya. "Now why don't you see if you can make Thomas' task a bit easier."

Smiling in anticipation, Kaylie pulled in more of the Talent. Though still tired, she could manage more of the Talent at one time than many of the Sylvan Warriors riding with her. Having watched Thomas and the other Sylvan Warriors, she knew exactly what to do, weaving the natural magic she controlled into the horn of Rya's unicorn, thereby increasing exponentially the power of what she was about to unleash.

As the first bolt of white energy shot from Bella's horn, Kaylie reveled in the feeling. Thomas had his own charge to complete, and she would make sure that he had nothing else to worry about but that.

74

NASTY SURPRISE

"Oso, leave off. We don't have time for this." Anara tightened her horse's saddle then vaulted onto her mount. She wore worn leather armor to give her the protection that she needed, but it was so supple that it wouldn't slow her down. She was fast with a blade, faster than any other Highlander except for perhaps Thomas, and she meant to put that skill to use today as the Marchers made their final preparations behind the Breaker, waiting for King Gregory's command.

"But Anara ..." Oso tried to protest, but Anara, her red hair flaming in the sunlight, cut off the large Highlander before he could offer the same argument that he had been repeating for the last hour.

"While you were galivanting across the Kingdoms with the Highland Lord I was killing dark creatures and defending the Highlands just like every other Marcher. Moreover, I'm really good at it. Ask any of those old timers over there enjoying the spectacle that you're making of yourself, and they'll tell you true."

Rather than be offended by Anara's description of them, Coban, Renn, Seneca, and Nestor tried not to smile as they sat their mounts, talking quietly and working out the final details of their strategy. They tried to be as inconspicuous as possible, though it was proving difficult as Anara became more exasperated. The Highland chiefs weren't ready for this argument, and they didn't want to have any part of it. If they engaged in the discussion, they would get bitten no matter what perspective they offered, and they didn't need the aggravation at a time like this. Or a close encounter with the dagger that danced deftly across Anara's fingers.

"I just don't want you to get hurt," explained Oso.

"Don't you think that the same thing goes through my mind every time you're with Thomas? I don't want you to get hurt either."

"Anara, it's just …" Oso was going to say more, but he didn't know how, the words catching in his throat.

Anara's eyes softened when she looked at him. She knew what he was trying to say. "I love you, too, Kylin. But you can't expect me to hide away. I am just as capable as you, and I have and will continue to take the same risks as you. I will fight, just like you, to protect the Highlands. That's who I am. You need to accept that."

Oso's shoulders slumped, realizing that he had just lost the argument. She was right. He knew it. She was more than capable. But he was afraid. Not for himself, but for her. He didn't know what he'd do if he lost her.

"It was a good try, lad," said Coban quietly, who nudged his horse up on Oso's other side. "But it was a losing battle to begin with. Anara is a Marcher to the core. Get used to it. It'll be better for both of us if you do."

Oso knew that Coban was right. Shaking his head in frustration, he resolved to stay by Anara's side during the fight. They would be together, fight together, on this day, and every other day thereafter if he had his way. Oso's thoughts quickly turned to the battle to come as a shout sent a ripple of excitement through the Marchers.

"Prepare the sally gates!" ordered Gregory, as he appeared at the base of the massive wall, confident that all would go well with Sarelle in charge along the parapet. The command spread like wildfire among the troops waiting at the bottom of the Breaker, and his soldiers moved to obey.

The King of Fal Carrach had remained atop the huge wall for as long as he deemed necessary, ensuring that his soldiers completed the task of dislodging the remaining Ogren that had attempted to scale the stone before he moved on to the next step in his plan. Only a few dark creatures remained, clinging to the Breaker haphazardly as the charge of the Sylvan Warriors had distracted them.

Gregory and his soldiers had taken advantage of the momentary lapse in the Ogrens' assault to rebuild their defenses. Wherever an Ogren attempted to climb the wall, a squad of soldiers with massive pikes waited, prepared to use their deadly weapons to keep the creature at a distance if it reached the top as another squad of soldiers, these archers, stood behind the first, ready to pepper the beast like a pin cushion if need be.

But the most important squad was the one charged with heating the oil or pitch that was poured down the stone of the Breaker and then set afire, forcing the dark creatures to make one of three choices before they could breach the top. The beasts could either be burnt to a crisp, fall to their death or try to descend the Breaker before the fire caught them. And now, after the respite, the strategy was working, as more and more of the Ogren fell from their perches, unable and unwilling to suffer the boiling oil and pitch that covered their bodies and too slow in their efforts to dislodge themselves from the rough stone, the fire streaking down toward them faster than they could reach the ground.

For good measure, some of the archers dabbed their arrows in the oil and set them alight, then shot at the creatures hanging onto the rough stone, setting several ablaze. This practice had deterred many of the Ogren tasked with scaling the Breaker as the large beasts ignored the commands of the Shades. Several of the dark creatures, covered in flame as they fell to the grass below, started fires at the base of the Breaker that spread quickly and consumed many other dark creatures thanks to the defenders on top of the wall dropping barrels of oil and pitch to feed the burgeoning inferno.

More than satisfied with his soldiers' work and confident that they could hold the parapet as Sarelle assumed command, Gregory relished the opportunity that now presented itself. The Sylvan Warriors had been exceedingly effective at their work, slicing the Dark Horde in half and pushing the dark creatures toward the hills to the east and west. The Desert Clans had formed the other side of the vise, charging from their hiding places to catch the Ogren, Shades and other loathsome beasts by surprise.

Now was the time for the final push that would break the Dark Horde once and for all. He could feel it in his bones. Looking down the length of the back of the Breaker, Gregory saw that all was ready. The time that he had been waiting for had come.

"Open the gates!" commanded the King of Fal Carrach as he pulled himself up onto his horse. Kael appeared next to him, and just down the line, Coban, Oso, Anara and the other Marchers found their places. Thinking of the murder of his friend Talyn Kestrel a decade past, which had set in motion the events that brought them to this very moment, it seemed only appropriate that the fighters of Fal Carrach and the Highland Marchers would ride out to face the Dark Horde together this day.

The soldiers at the base of the wall scrambled in response to the command. When constructed so many centuries before, the Breaker had appeared to be an unending wall of stone running from the coast of the Winter Sea to the Highlands. But in those places along the Northern Steppes where it seemed most likely that the Shadow Lord's dark creatures would attack in their efforts to ravage the Kingdoms, the builders had included a useful and nasty surprise.

Through feats of remarkable engineering, along the base of the Breaker in a handful of locations massive pulleys and winches pulled back on the wall, then lifted multiple sections of the weighty stone into gaps carved out of the inside of the Breaker. Because of the thickness of the wall, the process took a few minutes, as a succession of large openings in the base of the Breaker appeared.

"The final block is moving now," said Kael Bellilil, who sat his horse calmly next to Gregory.

The Ogren and Shades didn't even notice as the dark creatures remained focused entirely on the Desert Clans and the Sylvan Warriors. This would be a nasty surprise, indeed. Gregory urged his horse a few steps forward, Kael and all the other riders near him doing the same. When the light began to appear underneath the Breaker, the last section of the wall moving out of the way, he knew that it was time.

"Ride for the Kingdoms!" shouted Gregory, spurring his horse forward. "Ride to victory! Ride to the Highland Lord!"

As the Highland Marchers and the soldiers of Fal

Carrach emerged from the hidden gates of the Breaker, the men and women remained silent, eyes fixed forward, lances and swords at the ready, the Dark Horde completely unaware of what was about to drive into them from the south.

75

RODRIC'S END

With the Sylvan Warriors pushing to the east and west and creating a gap to his front, Thomas burst into the open space. Acero needed no urging, their close connection telling the massive steed exactly what Thomas intended. The unicorn approved, knowing that cutting off the head of the snake was the fastest way to kill it. With their quarry just ahead, Acero lowered his head and used his horn and shoulders to eliminate several Ogren and Shades that had moved to block their path.

Almost too late in identifying the approaching danger, Malachias turned his horse to face the Highland Lord just in time. Rodric watched in surprise, his fear palpable, as his adversary of the past decade charged toward him, the Sword of the Highlands in his hand. The once mighty High King had fallen far, and he realized quickly that there was farther still that he could go as he nudged his horse behind the Shadow Lord's right hand, hoping to benefit from Malachias' protection. He had no desire to end up in a shallow grave in the tall grass of the Northern Steppes thanks to a boy who didn't know when to just roll over and die.

"Malachias, the boy!" screamed Rodric, his horse prancing nervously because of its rider's obvious and escalating anxiety. "You must do something!"

"That's certainly my intention, you fool!" hissed Malachias. "But I can't deal with the boy with you still hanging around my neck."

Rodric stared at Malachias, his fear rising as a terrifying realization swept through him. "What? No, you can't ..."

"I should have done this long ago," said Malachias, all of his pent-up anger directed at the former High King. "Your usefulness has come to an end. Now you're simply in the way."

Using his Dark Magic, Malachias sent a black mist streaming toward the High King, who didn't take note of the danger until it was too late. The swirling darkness spun around him at first, almost tentatively, like a shark circling its prey to gauge its strength before attacking. Identifying nothing but weakness, the mist surged forward, covering Rodric in a whirling black mass.

The High King tried to scream, but the mist wouldn't allow it, flowing into his open mouth and attacking from within. Rodric's eyes bulged, his body shaking uncontrollably, as the Dark Magic surged through him. In seconds it was over. The once powerful High King was no more, the black mist, now dissipated, sucking the life from him, the formless mass of Rodric's body sliding off its horse and collapsing in the long grass.

Pleased that he had removed the stone that had weighed him down for so long, Malachias felt lighter as he focused his full attention on the Highland Lord.

76

THUNDERCLAP

Thomas stopped his charge, seeing the Dark Magic in play. He watched dispassionately as the former High King met his ultimate fate. Although he felt a tinge of disappointment that he had not played a direct role in Rodric's demise, he had little to complain about as the result was the same. After so many close escapes the deposed King of Armagh was dead and at the hands of a supposed ally no less.

"Are you ready to try again, boy?" whispered Malachias, his raspy voice carrying easily across the distance. The Dark Magic formed once again, swirling in a black mass above Malachias much like a waterspout of evil. "I let you off easy the last time that we met. I should have finished you then, but now will do."

Exhaustion taking its toll and his strength failing after the struggles of the last few days, Thomas knew that he didn't have the energy to engage in a lengthy duel with the Shadow Lord's general. To stand any chance of victory, he needed to end this quickly.

Sending his thoughts to Acero, the massive unicorn whickered in understanding, then leapt forward, charging toward Malachias. Thomas took hold of the Talent, pulling in as much as he could hold and using Acero's horn to continue to draw on the natural magic of the world.

Pulling the Sword of the Highlands from the scabbard across his back, he infused the steel blade with the augmented power contained in Acero's horn, setting the steel glowing a blinding white.

Surprised that his opponent had not hesitated to attack, Malachias realized that something wasn't quite right. The Shadow Lord's servant began to think of escape, but it was too late. So confident of his abilities and believing that he could overpower the upstart boy with his Dark Magic, Malachias had never considered all the possibilities, such as a massive, black unicorn charging toward him. By the time that he realized his error and that his continued survival depended on his ability to get away, Acero was almost upon him.

Not knowing what else to do, Malachias released the black mist, which swirled in a cloud for a brief second then surged toward Thomas.

Raising his glowing sword, Thomas cut through the billowing, pitch-black murk with ease. The Dark Magic sought to evade the white light of the blade, but there was no escape. The infused steel was too powerful, pulling in the black mist, consuming it and then making its power its own. The evil fog destroyed, Thomas raised his blade as Malachias turned his mount and tried to flee. But another burst of speed by Acero kept Thomas breathing down the neck of the rattled Malachias until the right hand of the Shadow Lord had no choice but to stop.

"Thomas, hold!"

Responding to a silent command, Acero skidded to a stop. Rya appeared out of the slowly disintegrating chaos of battle, Kaylie riding at her back. His grandmother stared at Malachias with a gaze that could melt steel.

"Malachias and I have unfinished business. Centuries old, in fact."

Thomas studied his grandmother for just a moment, noting the iron in her voice. Nodding to her in respect, he lowered his shining blade and nudged Acero next to Bella, then offered his hand to Kaylie. She gladly scrambled across to sit behind Thomas, wrapping her arms around his waist. Acero then circled away, giving Rya the space that she would need.

"You couldn't beat me at the manor," hissed Malachias. "What makes you think that you can defeat me now?"

"I didn't defeat you before," said Rya contemptuously, "because you ran. Just as you've done every time that we've faced one another."

Not having the patience for Malachias' usual taunts, Rya took hold of the Talent and charged toward the Shadow Lord's servant, Bella's hooves digging up the grass and dirt. From both hands, Rya flung a stream of what appeared to be blazing, white daggers toward Malachias. Stunned by the speed of her attack, Malachias barely got his shield of Dark Magic in place. But the strength of Rya's assault staggered him as he barely deflected the strike, and he didn't have time to avoid the unicorn's charge as Bella swiped her shoulder into Malachias' horse. His mount crashed to the ground, Malachias flinging himself clear just in time to avoid being caught beneath the flailing horse.

Malachias pushed himself up, his legs unsteady beneath him. "You will pay for this, woman!"

"I'm tired of your prattle," replied Rya, Bella circling

Malachias in the space that had opened up around them. "You've plagued me for more than a thousand years. All because you couldn't stand the fact that I didn't want you."

"You were meant to be mine," hissed Malachias. "Think of what we could have had if you had not played the fool. The power we could have shared. You were given to me. You belonged to me!"

"This was why I had no interest in you, Malachias. For you there is nothing but power. I was simply another means to achieve it. To be just another of your possessions."

"You are still a fool. This is not over, woman. You will still be mine."

"Threats and words, but no action. Just as always. Your time has come to an end, Malachias."

"You can do nothing against me! Nothing! You are only a woman who ..."

Malachias' words died in his throat as Rya sent a stream of glaring white energy toward him. Malachias tried to defend himself, raising his arms and making a last gasp effort to shield himself with Dark Magic. But the attempt was doomed to fail. Rya's attack was too strong, her power too much, her anger too pure. The stream of energy struck Malachias' shield and blasted through to strike the malevolent creature in the chest. A massive thunderclap sounded across the battlefield with a flash of white lightning that momentarily blinded all who were looking in its direction.

Where Malachias had once stood, the charred imprint of a man appeared in the trampled grass. Rya rode up to the mark on the ground, satisfied that she had succeeded in finally eliminating the Shadow Lord's servant who had been a thorn in the side of the Kingdoms since the Great War and a personal antagonist of hers for just as long. Thomas approached from the other side, Kaylie's hands still around his waist.

"Thorough as ever," he said with a grin. "He certainly did like to jabber, didn't he? I don't know how you put up with it for all those years."

77

FINAL CHARGE

Riding past the burnt grass where Malachias had stood just a moment before, Thomas didn't bother to look back, relieved that his grandmother was all right and had eliminated the last great danger presented to the Kingdoms. The silence that had descended on the battlefield during Rya's short-lived duel gave way to a resounding cheer that rose up from the armies of the Kingdoms, soldiers on the Breaker and those engaged at the base of the barrier with the Dark Horde shouting madly, raising their swords and spears to acknowledge the combat's victor, a petite woman with the aura of a queen.

Thomas pulled Acero to a halt a few hundred yards from the Breaker, Kaylie riding behind him, and watched Gregory emerge from the hidden sally ports with his cavalry right behind him. In the lead, Oso and Coban and the other Marchers pushed their horses to the front, forming into an honor guard as they charged through the mass of Ogren and Shades toward their Highland Lord. At the same time, the Sylvana, having crushed the Dark Horde against the warriors of the Desert Clans, had circled around and formed once again into two wedges behind Thomas.

Smiling with pleasure, Thomas turned Acero toward the right flank of the Dark Horde closest to the Breaker. The massive unicorn began at a trot, then moved to a gallop as the Marchers caught up. A portion of the cavalry streaming from beneath the Breaker followed the Marchers, the other half, led by Gregory, focused its attention on the Horde's left flank nearest the massive wall. Now surrounded on three sides, the surviving dark creatures, their numbers greatly reduced, milled about in fear and confusion, some fighting for their lives, others looking for a path to escape the maelstrom of power, steel and death.

Thomas raised the Horn of the Sylvana to his lips, blowing a clear strong note that echoed off the Breaker and traveled across the Northern Steppes.

WE HEAR.

The Ogren and Shades still alive on the battlefield were momentarily stunned, never expecting such a turn of events. Their fear at how easily the Sylvan Warriors had cut through them had become an immobilizing terror as Thomas and Gregory led their forces toward them.

Thomas blew another note from the Horn, clear and true.

WE COME.

And then a third, the loudest of all, a blasting note that carried well beyond Blackstone, the former lair of the Shadow Lord.

WE CONQUER.

The remnants of the Dark Horde fled to the north, desperate to reach the relative safety of the Charnel Mountains, yet knowing as well that the Northern Steppes, which they needed to cross first, would give them no place to hide. In a swift and unexpected turn of events, all that the dark creatures that had once formed the Dark Horde could do now was flee for their lives.

78

DECISIONS

The armies of the eastern Kingdoms pursued the remnants of the fleeing Dark Horde across the Northern Steppes, decimating the Ogren and Shades seeking to escape. The Sylvana assisted, following the dark creatures into the Charnel Mountains well beyond Blackstone in an effort to eliminate the beasts as a threat to the Kingdoms. Likely just a wish, they knew, but in Rynlin and Rya's opinion, a worthwhile exercise.

Several months after what became known as the Battle of the Breaker, the rulers of the various Kingdoms met at Eamhain Mhacha in a hastily called Council of the Kingdoms. With Killeran's death, Loris, King of Dunmoor, believed that there would be no proof of his alliance with Rodric and Armagh. He spent several days apologizing profusely for not getting his troops to the Breaker in time, offering different excuses to whomever would listen.

Gregory, King of Fal Carrach, and now officially the High King despite his protests, allowed Loris to dig his own grave. The King of Dunmoor had forgotten how meticulous Rodric was with respect to treaties and agreements. Tired of the lies, Gregory pulled out the signed treaty between Armagh and Dunmoor that divided the Eastern Kingdoms between them once the Highlands had been conquered. The response from the other rulers was swift as they sentenced Loris to death with a new ruler to be selected for Dunmoor.

Gregory proclaimed that if he were to serve as High King, he would not do so from Armagh. He would remain in Ballinasloe and the biennial Council of the Kingdoms would move from one Kingdom to the next, seeking to draw all the rulers more closely together to the benefit of all.

Not wanting to have to deal with a potential problem in Armagh, the gathered monarchs named Brennios, former general of the Home Guard, King of Armagh. Having displayed his character and allegiance to his homeland rather than to Rodric, he was the logical, though perhaps unwilling, choice. But being the soldier that he was, he accepted the duty solemnly.

Many of the Kingdoms sought to thank the Sylvana for their help, but the members of the legendary band of warriors had little time for it. Though the Kingdoms were now free of dark creatures, the Sylvan Warriors continued their efforts to push the beasts out of the Charnel Mountains. Perhaps a hopeless task, but any success in continuing to reduce the size of what remained of the Dark Horde benefited the Kingdoms. That and the fact that a permanent force, drawn from all the armies of the Kingdoms, would be stationed at the Breaker as had been done centuries before. A new First Guard would stand on the parapet of the massive wall once again.

79

WEDDING

"I understand Asmera chose Denega, and he accepted," said Kaylie.

She stood in the rebuilt Hall of the Highland Lord, marveling at its simple beauty. The Highlanders had replaced the stained glass windows and repaired the other damage caused by disuse after the Crag had fallen that fateful night Talyn Kestrel, Lord of the Highlands and Thomas' grandfather, had been murdered and the Highlanders betrayed. After the Battle of the Breaker, the Marchers had returned home, and Coban and Oso had led the effort to rebuild the Crag under Anara's watchful gaze.

With the day's events scheduled to start in just a few hours, workers were completing the final preparations for the nuptials.

"She did. I almost feel sorry for Denega. He never stood a chance."

Thomas had approached silently, as was his way, to stand beside her. But Kaylie had sensed him as soon as he had slipped into the room.

"You look very nice," said Kaylie, taking in his clothes.

She was used to the brown breeks and green shirt with a cloak hanging about his shoulders. Now he wore the formal ceremonial dress of the Highland Lord, his pants white and his high-collared coat a deep green, though an unadorned, steel dagger remained sheathed on his belt. Thomas was willing to be flexible with his attire, but would only go so far.

"Thank you. I was told that I had no choice."

"The life of a monarch," laughed Kaylie. "Supposedly free to do what they want, but actually always at the command of someone else."

"Yes, a frustrating lesson." Thomas took in Kaylie's flowing blue dress, which brought out the brightness in her eyes. "You look beautiful."

Kaylie blushed and tried to change the subject. "I haven't seen you for the last few weeks."

Since the destruction of the Dark Horde, Thomas had made it a point to spend as much time with Kaylie as possible, despite all that he had to do in the Highlands and with the Sylvana. Yet for the last fortnight he had been absent.

"I needed to take care of some things for Oso," explained Thomas. "He's a little nervous."

"On his wedding day? I can't imagine why?"

Thomas laughed. "Oso was much like Denega. He didn't stand a chance with Anara."

"That's a good thing, don't you think?"

"For Oso? Absolutely. He needs someone like Anara with him. He's been on his own for so long, it's a good change for him."

Kaylie turned to Thomas expectantly. "And you, Thomas? Do you need someone?"

A squawk echoed in the chamber. A massive kestrel that looked exceedingly familiar to the one that had appeared so many times in the past sat on the open windowsill, staring down at him. With the Marcher victory over the Armaghian army, the raptors had returned to the Crag, reclaiming the fortress as their own. This one, in particular, had made the Roost its preferred perch and was often seen shadowing Thomas.

Thomas smiled, then reached out, taking Kaylie's hand in his own.

"I do."

If you really enjoyed this story, I need you to do me a **HUGE favor – please write a review.** It helps the book and me. I really appreciate the feedback. Consider a review on Amazon or BookBub.

∼

Follow me on my website and join my newsletter at **www.kestrelmg.com** to learn about new releases ... or perhaps even a new story.

∼

Keep reading for **the first few chapters of my latest book.**

THREE CHAPTERS OF THE PROTECTOR

Following is an excerpt from *The Protector*, the first book in my new series, *The Tales of Caledonia*.

About the story

A man sold into slavery as a child is forced to serve a Kingdom to which he owes no allegiance.

A woman born into power holds the key to the Kingdom but only if she becomes the strongest Magus in the history of Caledonia.

Will the two be able to work together to battle the Ghoule Overlord, a creature intent on the complete and utter destruction of Caledonia?

∽

THE PROTECTOR

By Peter Wacht

Kestrel
Media Group, LLC

Book 1 of The Tales of Caledonia

Copyright 2021 © by Peter Wacht

Cover design by Ebooklaunch.com

Published in the United States by Kestrel Media Group LLC.
ISBN: 978-1-950236-19-0
eBook ISBN: 978-1-950236-18-3

SETTING THE STAGE

The Protector is set more than one thousand years before the events that occur in *The Sylvan Chronicles* and takes place in a separate land of *The Realms of the Talent and the Curse.*

Caledonia, though a monarchy, functions more like a loose confederation of Duchies, much to the displeasure of the crown. It is during this time that some of the more adventurous members of the Caledonian nobility have accepted King Corinthus Beleron's territorial grants and begun to colonize the Territories far to the west on the other side of the Burnt Ocean.

These Territories will eventually become the Kingdoms. In Caledonia, as in the other realms, the ability to use the Talent sets apart the person gifted with that skill. But being able to use the Talent is only part of the dynamic. For if a Magus chooses to follow a darker path, the Talent becomes the Curse.

CHAPTER 1. IN THE PIT

Bryen jumped back just in time, the black dragon's claw raking his arm rather than his torso. The sight of his blood, the red drops sprinkling the bright white sand, sent the crowd to a higher level of viciousness. That's why these thousands of people were here, after all. For some, it was an opportunity to gamble on the outcome and perhaps walk away with more than they had wagered. For others, it was a distraction from the mundaneness or the misery of their everyday life. While some simply enjoyed watching the weekly spectacle of man killing man, man killing beast, beast killing man, woman killing man.

It really didn't matter to those drawn to the gladiatorial games in the Colosseum, because no matter why they chose to attend the contests, they were bound by one single, simple principle: someone or something would die, and it wouldn't be them. Because of that, all who attended had cause to celebrate.

Judging by the jubilant screams that echoed down into the Pit when his blood splattered the sand, Bryen guessed that most of those watching expected the black dragon to kill him. He didn't blame them. No one had ever faced a black dragon in the Pit and survived.

Black dragons were uncommon creatures, rarely seen in Caledonia, and they were deadly beasts. They lived in the Trench, and for one to have been captured and brought more than a hundred leagues to the south suggested not only a huge investment, but also that the King felt the need to raise the level of entertainment that he was providing to the people of Tintagel. For that's what the gladiatorial games had become, a tool for the monarchy to distract the people from the challenges, irritations, and burdens placed on them, often by the crown itself. The fact that the King had gone to the trouble and expense to acquire such a unique creature suggested that the rumblings of unrest that Declan had reported during his wanderings through the city had grown more worrisome to the good King Marden Beleron, who seemed more interested in maintaining a reality crafted of smoke and mirrors than addressing the needs of his people.

Bryen pulled his mind away from his political ponderings and back to the very large and hungry adversary that stood before him, the dragon having pushed itself up onto its hind legs and stretched out its leathery black wings. The creature was as tall as a two-story tower, its wings blotting out the sun and putting Bryen into a shadowy twilight. He struggled to keep his feet in the blood-soaked sand, barely escaping another swipe of the beast's sharp, curled talons when he rolled to the side, feeling the hardened claws slide past him by no more than a whisker. Sensing victory, the dragon raised its head to the sky and shrieked in triumph, the ear-splitting noise rising above the din of the fifty thousand spectators crammed onto the wooden benches circling the Pit and extending all the way up into the farthest reaches of the Colosseum.

The tall gladiator, his long, prematurely white hair still flecked in a few places with light brown, retreated from the beast, taking a moment to study his opponent. He ignored the wound on his arm as best as he could, locking away the waves of fiery pain in the back of his mind. He had never fought a black dragon before. In fact, he had never even seen one before, and that ignorance had almost cost him his life. Though the dragon wasn't as large as some of its cousins, growing only to about twenty to twenty-five feet in length, it was just as dangerous. Black scales as hard as rock covered most of the animal, and sharp spikes ran down the length of its spine, functioning as a natural armor which had proven impervious to Bryen's sword and short spear. Initially, Bryen had concluded that his only chance for success was to go for an eye, but much to his dismay he had found that to be next to impossible. The creature was too fast. Unlike many of the bulky, brawny gladiators who fought in the Pit, Bryen had a surprising strength with his wiry frame, which often gave him an advantage during his combats. But not today. Today, he had met his match when it came to speed and agility. Several times Bryen had attempted to attack the beast from behind, yet with each assault it had proven to be a losing strategy. The black dragon tracked him with a frightening intensity as it moved with an almost unnatural celerity, keeping Bryen in front of him at all times.

Even worse, the dragon's sharp claws weren't the only danger he faced. If he got too close to the beast, the dragon also had the option of spitting out a venom that ate through steel and burned through flesh to the bone. Bryen had learned of that unnerving ability the hard way, losing his shield in a futile effort to put out one of the dragon's eyes. If he hadn't gotten the shield up in time, he'd either have been blinded or killed.

So what was he to do? Declan and the other gladiators had taught him a great deal about how to fight in the Pit, but this combat was like none of the hundreds of others that he had survived.

The dragon lunged forward, teeth the size of Bryen's forearm streaking toward his head. Bryen spun out of the way and slashed down with his sword. He struck a hard blow across the dragon's snout, but the steel had no effect, simply clattering off the beast's scales and leaving his sword arm numb. The dragon's head whipped around, the beast clearly irritated that it had missed its prey once again, and that's when Bryen saw his chance. He lunged forward with his spear having aligned the tip of the steel with the dragon's right eye. But, once again, he was too slow. The dragon turned its head just enough so that the point of the spear skittered across its scales. Bryen recognized the danger immediately with the dragon's head now lined up with his chest and no more than a few feet from him. He dove to the side just as a stream of acidic venom shot from the dragon's mouth. Though most of the blast missed him, a few tiny droplets splattered his left arm and leg. Pinpricks of agony shot through his body, and he feared that he would seize up from the pain.

Bryen could have given up. He had given more of himself to the spectators crowding the stands in blood, sweat, and tears during the last decade than they deserved. There was no known way to kill a black dragon. So what was the point? He had nothing left to prove and no way to escape the Pit other than to be dragged through the sand. But one of Declan's many sayings ran through his mind as he continued his roll through the sand, putting several more feet between him and the beast that stalked him. He heard the words in his head in the Master of the Gladiators' gruff voice: "Everyone dies. Not everyone dies with honor." That brought a smile to his lips and the spark of an idea to his mind.

Rather than patiently wait for the dragon's next attack, he decided to change his tactics. Bryen sprinted forward, faking a lunge for the dragon's eye, then jumping into the air and flipping over the beast's head. Before landing in the sand, he jabbed with his short spear toward the animal's other eye. Based on his experience of the last hour, he knew before he even attempted the attack that it wouldn't work, but that was fine with him. Having seen the dragon already tilt its head to defend against the strike, he pulled back his spear and instead swung down into the beast's maw with his sword. Yet even this proved futile. Though his sword struck hard and true against the dragon's front fangs, it was like striking one of its scales. His steel blade bounced backward off the hardened tooth.

Despite his failure, he kept pushing himself forward, cutting, stabbing, and swinging with blade and spear, seeking any of the weak spots that he had used so many times before when fighting other animals. Still, nothing that he tried worked. His anger getting the better of him, he feinted once more to the left, the dragon's eyes tracking him, before he leapt into the air again and tried to drive the point of his sword through the dragon's snout. A gasp went up from the crowd when they saw the blade shatter into hundreds of pieces, the steel no match for the dragon's scales. For a moment, all Bryen could do was stare at the broken blade in shock. Then, sensing the dragon turning toward him, he threw the remnant of his sword at the beast and dodged out of the way, the dragon's claws slicing through the air where his chest had been just a moment before.

Bryen stepped back for a moment, breathing deeply to calm his nerves. His shield and sword now gone, he was left with only his short spear. There had to be a way to get by the dragon's defenses, Bryen told himself. There had to be! Otherwise his time in the Pit would be coming to a hard end.

He resumed circling the dragon, keeping a good distance away as he struggled for a solution. Any solution. Because time was running short. He had been fighting for almost an hour, and he was down to a single spear point. Even worse, he knew his several wounds would begin to slow him down. And when they did, it would all be over. The dragon finally would have its meal.

The cheers and screams from the crowd washed over him, shaking the Colosseum to its very foundation, but it had little effect on Bryen. He was tired of it, tired of everything -- the cheering, the fighting, the killing, the pain, the blood. The crowd wanted to see blood. That's all they ever wanted to see. Every time he stepped onto the white sand of the Pit. Whether it was his blood or the dragon's, it really didn't matter to them. No matter how appealing the thought of escaping from the Pit might be, he decided that it wouldn't be his blood that colored the white sand red on this day. If Death wanted to take him, he would fight for every last breath.

Declan stood at the gate leading into the Pit, his hands clasped tightly to the steel bars as if he were going to pull them free from the bolts connecting them to the stone wall and rush into the Pit to join the fight. The Master of the Gladiators was a hard man, which only made sense since he had lived a hard life. He had broken free from the poverty he had grown up with as an orphan by joining the army. Once in the military, he had risen quickly, his tenacity and lack of fear serving him well, but even more so his ability to gain the trust of the soldiers he led. He treated the men and women he was responsible for as his family, because he didn't have a family of his own. They respected him for that, and when he asked them to risk their lives, they did so, because they knew that he would be risking his life right along with them. He never asked his soldiers to do anything that he wouldn't do himself.

The life that he had built for himself had all fallen apart because of an arrogant halfwit. When a young lord seeking to make a name for himself had ordered Declan and his troop to capture a village, they had done so with an efficiency that had earned him a great deal of praise. But when that same arrogant halfwit then had ordered Declan and his soldiers to slaughter all the village's inhabitants, he had balked. The lord argued that the villagers supported the bandits that they had been charged with removing from the Dark Forest. Eliminating the people who aided the brigands would make their task that much easier. Declan had told the lord that they had no evidence that these villagers were assisting the bandits; in fact, it seemed more likely that they were victims of the raiders, who took their livestock and stole their crops on a regular basis. Moreover, even if the people living at the edge of the wood had some sympathy for the bandits, and Declan had been quite clear that he didn't think that was the case, that was not cause to murder them.

Upon hearing Declan's refusal to execute his order, the lord had made the mistake of drawing his dagger and placing it at Declan's throat, telling him that if he refused to obey, he'd kill him then and there. Declan didn't take too kindly to the threat. Before the lord knew what had happened, Declan had taken the fool's hand and used it to drive his very own dagger into his throat. The inquiry that followed found Declan guilty with cause to be removed from the army, but the lord's father wanted him dead. So the commander of the Royal Guard, demonstrating some mercy for a soldier who he had respected, had instead sentenced Declan to the Pit. He had become a slave, a gladiator forced to fight in the Colosseum, but he was alive. And after ten years of surviving both man and beast, he had been named Master of the Gladiators, relieving himself of the need to fight on the white sand. Still a slave, but more likely to remain alive. Since then he had done as he had when he was a soldier in the army, looking out for the men and women compelled to share his fate. He was hard on them, because that was the only way he knew how to lead, but even more so he wanted them to live. For that, they respected him.

Which was why he felt a wave of shame surge through him as he watched the dragon pursue Bryen around the Pit. Declan had trained the boy to be a gladiator, to fight anything that might stand across from him in the Colosseum. But he had not prepared Bryen for a beast like this. How could he have? Black dragons had never been put in the Pit before, at least not since he had been enslaved. No one had ever been foolish enough -- or so desperate -- to try to capture such a deadly beast. Until now.

"I'm going to gut that fat fool," growled Declan. Not very tall, the Master of the Gladiators was stout with broad shoulders and arms the size of most men's legs. He was built as solid as an oak tree, his body hardened by his years as a gladiator. His strength had served him well in the Pit, but now it offered him little advantage. He could only watch as the boy he had raised battled for his life.

"Beluchmel did this?" asked Lycia. The tall gladiator stood next to him, her eyes never leaving Bryen as he glided across the sand. He had done better than she had expected. Although the black dragon was winning the combat, Bryen continued to move across the sand with that agility and grace of his that seemed almost freakish in a person as tall as he was. She was only a head shorter than Bryen, and though she was quicker than any other gladiator in the Colosseum, her movements never flowed so smoothly as his.

"Aye, lass," replied Declan. "He felt the need to bring that wretched beast from the Trench. How he did it, I don't know."

"But why?" asked Davin. The tall gladiator with spiky red hair stood behind the Master of the Gladiators. Normally he had a smile on his face that often appealed to the fairer sex, even when he fought in the Pit, but not now. Not when his friend had been sentenced to death.

"The King is with us today," grumbled Declan.

Davin cursed and then spit behind them. "He wanted Bryen to die. I have no doubt that he still holds a grudge."

"No," corrected Lycia. "You may be right, but that wasn't his goal today. He wanted to put on a show."

"Right, lass. Doesn't matter to Beluchmel whether Bryen lives or dies, only that the King of Caledonia enjoys the spectacle that plays out before him."

"So Bryen is the sacrificial lamb," muttered Davin. "The

blood needed to quell the mob and satisfy the urges of our blockhead of a monarch."

"That he is," said Declan. They all knew the odds were stacked against the young gladiator, regardless of how fast or skilled he may be. They had watched for the past hour as their friend had used every bit of knowledge that he had learned fighting in the Pit to keep himself alive, but nothing he had tried had affected the black dragon. Bryen had only succeeded in angering the beast and delaying the inevitable.

"He's survived worse," offered Lycia, who pushed her braid of long, red hair back over her shoulder. Davin and Lycia were brother and sister, forced into the Pit for stealing food while homeless in Tintagel.

"He's never fought worse," said Davin quietly. "None of us have."

There were many reasons to stay out of the Trench, but the black dragons that had made that grim terrain their own topped the list. The beasts, almost mythical in nature because they were so rarely seen, were known to take those foolish enough to enter that primeval land in a single bite. And as the red-haired gladiator watched his friend struggle to stay alive, he saw that the dragon hadn't tired. It seemed that the beast was intelligent as well, allowing Bryen to wear himself out, waiting patiently until he made a mistake. Then the dragon would have its victory, and Beluchmel would have the end to the story that he was seeking.

"Let's not give up on him just yet," snapped Declan, his worry getting the better of him. "I didn't waste all my time teaching that scrawny lad to fight just to see him end up in a dragon's gullet."

～

During the past decade Bryen had spilled gallons of blood, some of it his own, on the white sands of the Pit. All with the goal of entertaining the crowd, to allow them to forget their problems and worries for a few hours, to let them bet on who or what would survive, to give them the pleasure of seeing death firsthand without having to risk their own lives. At first, the cruelty of it all had horrified him. Now, he barely paid any attention to it. He had seen too much death, been the cause of too much death, for it to affect him. Now he viewed fighting in the Pit as a way to escape. But he didn't think that he had the courage for that -- not yet.

He had first stepped onto the sand a day past his ninth birthday, weighed down by a short sword that he could barely hold with both hands and a foot-long dagger strapped to his thigh. He was to be that day's entertainment, matched against a veteran gladiator from a western Duchy who was built like a rock and wise to the ways of the Colosseum. The huge gladiator, muscles bulging, face contorted by a series of bloodcurdling screams, soaked in the cheers and adulation of the crowd, playing upon the desires of the onlookers. When the combat began, the experienced gladiator toyed with Bryen to start, nicking him first in the arm, then the leg, then the other arm, letting the crowd see the blood, savor it, and thereby incite them into a frenzy.

At first, Bryen had been terrified, never having fought another person before, and still not sure why this was happening to him. He had only received a few weeks of training from the Master of the Gladiators, and when Bryen had been told to walk down the dark passageway lit at the far end by the sun gleaming off the white sand, the irascible Declan seemed to have little hope that he would be walking back this way at the end of the combat. Bryen had no choice then, just as he had no choice now, and he realized that he would die as soon as the veteran gladiator grew tired of his sport. That thought had enraged Bryen, filling him with an anger that he had never experienced before, an anger that burned away the fear of fighting for his life in front of tens of thousands of screaming people that had almost frozen him in place. It was as if a door had been opened for him, a door that allowed him to see the world as it truly was -- kill or be killed. Discarding his sword because he knew it would only be a detriment to try to use it against his much larger opponent, he had attacked the gladiator with his dagger with a speed and ferocity that surprised his adversary and had drawn gasps of shock and disbelief from the crowd.

Deftly dodging the larger man's sword thrust, Bryen had rolled past the gladiator, dragging his dagger across the back of the man's legs and slicing cleanly through a hamstring. The gladiator had fallen to a knee, one leg useless. Rather than giving his opponent a chance to regain the initiative and perhaps decide to kill him quickly rather than tease the crowd, Bryen had made the decision for the veteran fighter by mercilessly cutting across the back of his other leg, disabling him completely. Unable to believe what had happened, the gladiator barely felt Bryen's dagger sink into his back in search of his heart.

When it was over, Bryen had risen to his feet, his eyes locked on the now lifeless body. The pool of blood grew larger as it seeped onto the white sand. He had studied the gladiator for several seconds, still not sure why it had all happened, and where he had found the strength and courage to fight back. But then he realized that thinking about it too much served no purpose. He was simply happy to still be alive. Much to his surprise when he looked up from the fallen gladiator, after scanning the stone rows that rose above him, he saw nothing but surprise and shock on the faces of the people staring down at him. Silence reigned in the Colosseum as the crowd also tried to figure out how he had succeeded.

Slowly, the clapping had begun, followed by the cheers, as the crowd acknowledged the little victor. When Bryen raised his bloody dagger to the sky, the cheers had erupted into a roar, a few screams of Volkun, or the wolf, raining down upon him. Bryen had walked from the Pit to thunderous applause, the Colosseum swaying back and forth. Reaching Declan, he retched what little was left in his stomach and then almost passed out. The entire experience had sickened him. Yet it was only the beginning.

The Kingdom of Caledonia, located on a peninsula of the same name with a northern boundary of almost impassable mountains that connected to the Trench, had become addicted to the gladiatorial games during the last few centuries. The capital city of Tintagel was known the world over for it, with many people traveling hundreds of leagues simply to catch a glimpse of the ultimate human struggle. In the beginning, criminals, slaves, or prisoners fought one another. Then volunteers began to fill their ranks, trading their freedom and risking death in search of glory and riches by binding themselves to the owner of a gladiatorial troupe. Sometimes these gladiators achieved it. If they performed well, they were entitled to a share of their owner's winnings. And after earning a certain amount, they could buy back their freedom, their reputations' intact and their fortunes made. More often than not, however, they fought until they died, living at the owner's school until they fell in the white sand of the Pit. They had realized too late that slavery was simply that -- slavery.

Eventually, the King of Caledonia, in search of a new revenue stream that would not require another tax on the people, confiscated the gladiator schools and the combats in the Colosseum became the royal sport. Since then, no one in their right mind considered selling their freedom to fight in the Pit, reserving that place for the dregs of society, the criminals who willingly chose a gruesome death rather than wasting away in a cell and the unfortunate who had no say in the fate that had befallen them. But the crowd cared little about who struggled on the white sand; though, of course, they did have their favorites -- it was a money sport, after all. Their main concern was blood. They wanted to see the white sand turn red.

Bryen understood that better than anyone, having spent the past decade surviving animal or man, fighting on the days of the four principal lunar phases -- the new moon, first quarter, full moon, and last quarter -- since he had first arrived at the School of Gladiators located behind the Colosseum. An orphan forced to survive on the hard streets of the capital city, he had been caught stealing food. Sentenced to death or slavery, Declan, the Master of the Gladiators, had plucked him from the gibbet or the pleasure houses -- the bidding when he was on the slaver's block had been leaning toward the latter -- giving him instead a life in the Pit. At first, he had been terrified, not knowing what that really meant. But he had learned quickly, taking in every-thing that Declan sought to teach him. And of the many lessons that the Master of the Gladiators had imparted, Bryen had learned perhaps nothing more important than the fact that life revolved around a simple proposition: kill or be killed. Declan had drilled that understanding into him relentlessly. So much so that it had become a part of him.

But now Bryen was thinking less about survival and more about death. What if he died? Did it really matter? The thought had filled him with an overwhelming fear for years. When he was younger, he would wake up screaming in the middle of the night because he remembered his first combats when his odds of survival had been slim at best. But as he grew older, his perspective had changed. Death was the easiest form of escape. He would no longer be forced to entertain the bloodthirsty crowd of nobles, merchants, tradespeople, and others who could afford the admission fee to the Colosseum. And after so long a time on the white sand, after so many deaths, the thought of his own bothered him little. What if he didn't fight to the best of his abilities? What if he allowed his opponent to slip past his defenses in a brief moment of weakness?

Though he thought about it frequently, he knew that it would not be a satisfying escape, and he could never bring himself to do it. Declan had influenced him greatly over the years, and whenever his thoughts wandered to this dark corner of his mind, the Master of the Gladiators' words burned through his soul as a reminder, a reminder that he seemed to hear far more than he would like: "Everyone dies. Not everyone dies with honor."

He regained his focus as the dragon slithered forward, its jaws searching for his head once again. Bryen dodged out of the way, rolling to the ground to avoid the lunge, his spear once again skittering harmlessly against the scales near the dragon's right eye. Gathering some sand in his hand, he threw it into the face of the beast, blinding the creature for a time and winning a moment's respite to search for some way to take down his adversary. Every creature -- man or beast -- had a weakness. He knew that. He had found it hundreds of times before. Bryen simply had to find the dragon's. Yet, it was easier said than done. The beast was remarkably fast, and its sharp claws gave it excellent traction in the sand. Further, based on his lack of success during the past hour, there seemed to be no way to break through the animal's armor. Bryen could spend an entire day hacking at any part of the dragon's scales without a tangible result, but he couldn't even do that now because he had already broken his blade, having been reduced to a single spearpoint. No, there had to be a better way.

With an angry growl, the dragon lashed out again, its vision clear once more, and again Bryen jumped out of the way. He had barely avoided the lunge, but the beast didn't give him a chance to recover. The massive head rose up before him, unleashing a stream of venom that sizzled as it discharged from its teeth-filled maw. Tired from the long struggle and his wounds beginning to affect him, Bryen moved slower than usual. Though he escaped the full force of the venom, several large drops landed on his left leg, sending a fiery agony from his toes to his core as the acid burned into his skin. His scream of pain, the first sound he had made since he had entered the Pit more than an hour before, energized the crowd, sending them to a new level of hysteria. Sensing the end, the inevitable conclusion brought the thousands upon thousands of spectators to a fever pitch, their voices a dull roar that mimicked rolling waves of thunder on a stormy night.

Bryen continued the roll that brought him safely out from under the stream of venom, but the dragon maintained its attack, the beast charging across the sand with its jaws open in anticipation of victory. Bryen came to his feet quickly, separating the pain in his leg from his consciousness. He then dodged to the side, allowing the dragon's head to slip past him. That's when he saw it. It was an opportunity that he simply couldn't pass up. Stabbing with his spear, the steel tip plunged into the dragon's exposed ear. He couldn't thrust the steel as deeply as he would have liked, but it was enough at least for the moment. The strike disoriented the beast and stopped its charge, the dragon rearing up once again and shrieking in pain. For the first time since the dragon had been released in the Pit, Bryen had drawn blood. But he knew that what he had done wasn't enough. Time was quickly running out. Still, his chances had improved at least somewhat, as Bryen had finally found what he was looking for.

Much to the crowd's surprise, Bryen charged directly toward the rearing black dragon, a cry of anger and pain escaping his lips. Bryen's tactic startled the dragon, but the beast recovered quickly, attempting once more to catch its prey with a stream of venom from its maw. As soon as the dragon began to open its mouth, Bryen realized that his plan would work. Before the first drops of venom flew toward him, Bryen pulled his foot-long dagger from the sheath on his thigh and changed his grip on the blade so that he held the tip between the fingers of his left hand. Just as quickly, he released it, sending the sharp blade spinning end over end through the air.

The dragon never saw the dagger as it slid through the just beginning stream of venom, the steel plunging deep in the back of its throat. The dragon's terrible screech of pain drowned out the thunderous roar of the crowd, which shockingly became silent. They had never expected the duel to turn so quickly. The dragon fell on its side, trying to tear the blade from its mouth with its claws, Bryen momentarily forgotten. And that's when the gladiator struck. Bryen dove forward, driving his spear into the soft belly of the black dragon with all his might, and then again, and again, and again, until finally he found the beast's heart and the dragon's magnificent head flopped to the sand, its eyes glazed over by death, a pool of bright red blood stretching farther and farther away from its steaming body and staining the white sand the color of the setting sun.

Bryen had been right. The dragon's weakness lay in its underside. He stood over the beast, offering his own private apology and a nod of respect to a worthy competitor. He had not wanted to kill such a magnificent creature, but he had little choice in the matter. Kill or be killed. That was his life. Weary of the fight, Bryen backed away from the dragon, an animal much like him -- forced to fight for the pleasure of others. A feeling of regret rose up within him, whether because the dragon had died or because he survived, he could not say. Ignoring the thunderous applause of the spectators and the pain of his injuries, many of the people in the stands howling like a wolf to acknowledge his victory or screaming for the Volkun, Bryen walked slowly across the Pit toward the large steel gate that had just opened. A familiar figure stood before him.

"A good fight," said Declan, his short, grey hair standing straight up.

"A useless fight," answered Bryen, as he walked across the gladiators' stockade and entered the dim light of the training rooms beneath the Colosseum. The roar of the crowd thankfully dissipated as the door closed behind him, but not before a man a hand taller than Bryen with flaming red hair saluted him, three long spears clutched tightly in his hands, as he strode out toward the Colosseum. It was Davin's turn to test his luck in the Pit.

Declan studied his charge for a time before replying. The grizzled veteran tried to keep a distance from his charges. Why get close to someone who was going to die? But he had found it impossible to follow that stricture with Bryen. The frightened, willowy boy with the unkempt hair, the youngest person to ever fight in the Pit -- much less survive for so long -- had grown up before him, becoming a tall, lean young man. Declan understood that Bryen's experience in the Pit had scarred him, both inside and out. Three long slashes that had healed with time but never disappeared marred his left cheek and neck. His sharp grey eyes were hard, and his long brown hair and beard were almost overcome by a premature white. Though Declan would never admit it to anyone, he saw Bryen as a son, so he had trained the boy harder than he had trained any other gladiator to ensure that he had every chance of surviving in the Pit. Seeing the emptiness in Bryen's eyes when he passed by him tore through Declan's heart. The thought that he could do nothing to help Bryen escape from this life nagged at him constantly. He understood that Bryen had tired of his weekly struggles, and he knew what happened as soon as the hope for freedom, for a better life, disappeared. He had seen it too often in other gladiators. But what could he do other than give him the best chance at surviving? To train him. To teach him. To give him the tools that he would need to live, even if the life he lived wasn't the one that he wanted.

"You need to be faster next time," Declan said gruffly, unsure of what to say, so he fell back into his more comfortable role as Master of the Gladiators. "Otherwise, you may not be as lucky. If your aim had been off by just a hair, you would have died."

"Probably," said Bryen as he dropped heavily to a wooden bench and closed his eyes. Declan noticed the grimace that played across his face, so he told one of the boys who worked at the Colosseum to find the physick. The slash and burns Bryen had suffered needed treatment.

The expression on Bryen's face told Declan that his young charge simply didn't care anymore. Declan cursed the boy's luck. Bryen didn't deserve to be here. None of the gladiators did. But few could challenge fate and win. There was nothing that he could do about it, nothing except teach them everything he knew, all with the hope that something he gave to them would allow them to live -- if only for one more week.

"Well done, Bryen. For a moment I thought the sand would turn red."

Bryen looked up and grinned, seeing Lycia standing in the doorway. Just a few days after Bryen had arrived in the Colosseum, Declan had explained what the saying used so frequently by the gladiators meant, as it referenced a gladiator dying on the white sand of the Pit, his or her red blood soaking into the feathery, soft, pure white crystals.

"So did I."

"But not yet."

"No, not yet," Bryen confirmed.

"Death doesn't choose us ...," began Lycia.

"We choose our death."

Bryen finished the saying that was a mantra among the gladiators. They clasped arms and then Lycia walked off with a grin, giving his shoulder an affectionate squeeze as she headed toward the steel gate to watch her brother fight. She understood that she had to give him the space that he needed to release the tension of the duel, from the fight that in all his time in the Pit had brought him closest to death.

CHAPTER 2. DEMANDS

"Are you enjoying the combat, Duke Winborne?" The question was a simple one, yet it held several meanings in the slightly mocking tone with which it was offered. "I understand you have a unique perspective on the games."

"Quite the spectacle," replied the Duke of the Southern Marches, who hesitated just a moment before responding. He chose to ignore the attempted insult. "I'm quite impressed by this gladiator. A lesser fighter would not have survived for so long against such a beast."

In actuality, Kevan Winborne despised the gladiatorial combats. They showed a lack of respect for human life, for the people compelled to participate. The Caledonian Kingdom had abolished slavery hundreds of years before, yet a form of it still remained here in the Pit, something that was simply accepted and overlooked, and it left Kevan somewhat sickened. The privileged classes viewed the Colosseum as a place of sport and an opportunity for their own amusement or distraction. They cared little for the wellbeing of those forced to perform on the white sand, ignoring the hypocrisy of such a practice, as they were only concerned about the quality of the show. They wanted drama, excitement, bravery, skill, and a heroic end, having no concern for the people or creatures placed on their sandy stage.

"Very true," replied the handsome young man. Long black hair ran to the nape of his neck, and more often than not it fell into his eyes. His regular attempts to move the unruly strands amused and excited the many young, eligible ladies who sought to attract his attention. He had an easy smile, though the ladies pursuing him tended to ignore the fact that it tended to curl into a sneer when he failed to obtain what he wanted, or he believed that the person he was interacting with wasn't worth his time. When you sought to catch a king, the little things could be disregarded. "Very true. Tell me, Tetric, has anyone ever survived an encounter with a black dragon? I believe we haven't had a beast as dangerous as this one in the Colosseum for decades."

"Not to my knowledge, your Majesty. And you're right. The last time we had a creature such as this was well before your father's reign. Six gladiators fought it together. All six died." Tetric's words came out as a hiss. His intense black eyes, which had an almost hypnotic quality, added to the man's formidable appearance. Wiping a few drops of sweat from his bald head, then stroking his short, pointed beard, he turned the full force of his gaze on Duke Winborne. "Of course, no man can escape his fate, no matter how hard he might try."

"Yet this young man continues to do so." Kevan understood Tetric's reference quite well. Having to pay his respects once a year to the young King Marden, ruler of Caledonia, was a chore that he dreaded but couldn't avoid. To also have to deal with the likes of Tetric, the King's Chief

Advisor, almost made the experience unbearable. The Duke of the Southern Marches sighed in weariness. He was still a young man, or at least he liked to think so, but the last few days in Tintagel had aged him. As soon as he and his contingent of soldiers had ridden under the gates of the Corinthian Palace, named for Marden's late father, a battle had ensued. Not one of steel or magic, but rather of words. Insinuations, threats, and promises that could be just as deadly as a dagger in the ribs. "No man can escape his fate, Tetric. I will agree with you on that. But no man has to accept it willingly. No man has to give in. Though a man may be placed on a certain path, that man can still fight it. In fact, some would say that allowing others to choose your path is worse than fate. You never know what will come of the choice until it's too late."

Tetric flinched as if he had been struck a physical blow, yet he quickly recovered with a menacing glare. Kevan was pleased to see that his jab had hit home. Rumors buzzed around Tetric like buzzards circled a wounded animal. And everyone knew that in any rumor there always was some hint of the truth.

Marden's chief advisor had appeared mysteriously in Caledonia a decade before, quickly inserting himself as a confidant and advisor to King Corinthus, Marden's father. At the time of Tetric's arrival, Caledonia prospered. The harvests flourished, the Kingdom was free of the pirates who often marauded along the coast, and the Dukes and Duchesses of the various provinces had learned to settle their differences through diplomacy rather than war -- all aided by the King's wise and just leadership. Yet soon after Tetric had wormed his way into the Tintagel court, cracks began to appear in the Kingdom's foundations. The crown began to ignore the requirements of long-standing treaties, impinging on the rights of the provinces. New taxes were forced on the Duchies, and thus on the common folk, making it harder for the average worker or farmer to pay their debts. The argument was often much of the same. There was a need for more soldiers in the Royal Guard. The Corinthian Palace had to be expanded. The navy required more ships. More, always more. While at the same time the commoners suffered and Tintagel, the capital of Caledonia, began to fall into disrepair. No one could trace these problems or crises directly to the new Chief Advisor, because it was King Corinthus who signed every order or approved every action, but Tetric's influence over the King was clear and increasing by the day. Then Corinthus' health began to wane.

In consequence, as time passed, Tetric rather than Corinthus appeared to be ruling Caledonia, yet there was little that the Duchies could do, if only because now several of the provinces were frequently at odds with one another, and individually no Duchy had the strength to stand against the much larger Royal Guard. The King's health continued to fail and after several years of deterioration the old man died. With a young, ambitious, and impressionable Marden following his father to the throne, in just the last three years Tetric had strengthened his grip on the Kingdom -- surreptitiously, of course -- along with his influence over the mercurial and short-tempered king.

"I disagree," replied Marden. "A man can be forced onto a path he hasn't chosen for himself. It simply requires a certain incentive. For example, just the other day I had a man drawn and quartered because he refused to admit his crime, proclaiming his innocence to the very end. If he had retracted his statement of innocence, then perhaps I would have been more lenient. Maybe a beheading instead. But that was his choice. He chose to fight, to deny. To try for a different path. In this instance, the man's decision to resist led to a more painful death."

Marden settled back in his chair, his attention once again on the combat that continued to play out before him. The gladiator now circled the black dragon, searching for an opening. Ah, well. No matter how good a fight the man put up, it was all for naught. If he fought in the Pit, he was a man condemned and his sentence eventually would be carried out. Even if he survived his struggle on this day, and that likelihood was slim, fate would catch up to him on another. "And then just yesterday a merchant accused of smuggling was brought before me. He had a cart full of finely woven rugs, jewels, even some spices, all from the Western Isle. He was given the choice of turning over his contraband to the crown and leaving the Kingdom peacefully or having his head chopped off. Though he, too, proclaimed his innocence, stating that he had paid the required taxes on the imports, he wisely chose the former course, losing his contraband but escaping with his head, though he will be spending a good bit of time in prison for his crime."

"May I ask, your Majesty, what these examples have to do with me?" asked Kevan. He knew exactly what they had to do with him, but he had to play along, if only to massage the ego of this young, impetuous ruler. "I know you asked me to attend you here for a specific purpose. I'm curious as to that reason."

"You are the most direct, straightforward of my vassals, Kevan," said Marden, leaning forward now, his black eyes focused on the Duke of the Southern Marches. "Whether that's good or bad, we shall see. I should have expected you of all people to cut to the chase." Marden nodded toward his advisor. "I told you he would do such a thing, Tetric, did I not?"

"You did, your Majesty," confirmed Tetric, twirling the pointed end of his beard in his hand. "As you said, Duke Winborne is one who goes straight to the heart of a matter." Tetric eyed Kevan with a malicious intent in his eyes. Kevan's pointed comment had obviously struck closer to home than he had thought possible. Moreover, it had stayed with the advisor, who was known for holding grudges and meting out retribution when the time was right.

"You see, Kevan," began Marden, "I'm faced with a problem." He clenched his fist and sneered as he watched the gladiator's blade shatter on the black dragon's snout. It wouldn't be long now. The gladiator's heroics would soon be lost to history. "I've sat on the throne of Caledonia for three years now. And the Duchies are growing restless. I'm sure you're quite aware of that."

Kevan shrugged and nodded his head noncommittally. The provinces were always restless these days because of the crown's usually self-serving decisions. Before Tetric had arrived, King Corinthus had usually put the interests of the Kingdom before his own. With the King's Advisor and the coronation of Marden Beleron, that dynamic had been reversed. As a result, there were rumblings that several of the Dukes and Duchesses were interested in removing Marden from the throne. But none were willing to take that risk on their own. Yet. No Duchy on its own had the strength to defeat the King's Royal Guard, and the distrust sown by Tetric during the last decade had weakened the former bonds between the Duchies. As a result, none of the Duchies but for a few trusted any of the others enough to form temporary alliances to achieve their goals. Thus, the Dukes and Duchesses spent half their time looking at their peers, worrying about what they might be planning, while spending the rest of their time trying to hinder Marden's many schemes. For Marden, it was an effective way to rule, keeping his greatest threats off balance, and Kevan gave Tetric full credit for engineering the current situation.

"To help soothe the Duchies, Tetric advises me that it's time to select a bride. Isn't that right, Tetric?"

"Yes, your Majesty. Absolutely correct. By picking a bride you can solidify your position on the throne and remove any questions with respect to an heir, once the lucky bride is with child. Then the Duchies can turn their attention to more important matters rather than questions of succession."

Kevan listened to Tetric with half an ear, his mind having outpaced the conversation. An icy chill ran down his spine. He knew immediately what was coming next.

"I've thought about this for some time, Kevan. Marriage is not something that you simply jump into." Marden sat back in his chair, a broad smile on his face. "Your daughter Aislinn is a beautiful young lady, don't you think? And with the Southern Marches the most powerful of all the Duchies, I believe it only fitting that Aislinn become the Queen of Caledonia. Don't you agree?"

Marden said the words with such nonchalance, as if the proposal was simply a topic of idle conversation and carried little import. Yet for Kevan the words drove a stake through his heart.

"Your Majesty is very kind for suggesting Aislinn as a possible match, but I must admit that I'm somewhat surprised by the choice." Kevan cleared his throat, trying to buy some time to think. "Aislinn is still just a young girl, and not yet ready for marriage. I would even suggest that she's a bit rough around the edges. Would you not, your Majesty, do better by selecting a young woman of greater maturity? A young woman who would have a much better understanding of how lucky she would be to marry into the House of Beleron?"

"Kevan ..."

"Keep in mind as well, your Majesty, that though I may rule the strongest of the Duchies, my House is still relatively young compared to some of the others. Choosing Aislinn is a great honor for me, I certainly can't deny that, but her selection may cause you ill will with some of the other Duchies."

Marden opened his mouth to reply, his face scrunched up slightly in anger, as his temper, which was never very far from the surface, threatened to erupt. He was the King! When he made a decision, there was no discussion or debate. No questions or resistance. There was only action. With an effort, he forced down his irritation. If he had learned one thing in his three years on the throne, it was that patience and cleverness at times trumped the application of force and unnecessary confrontation. And this was one of those times. Having regained control of himself, Marden was about to take a different tack, but before he could say what was on the tip of his tongue, Tetric interrupted him.

"King Marden is well aware of the political ramifications of his choice," said the King's Advisor, leaning forward so that Kevan could smell his acrid, musty breath. It reminded the Duke of the Southern Marches of a newly opened crypt and sent a shiver down his spine. "And though your daughter is young, she is still of an age to marry. She offers more to our good king than any of the other eligible young women in the Kingdom. So much more."

With the Advisor's last comment, Kevan realized immediately that Tetric was much more dangerous than Marden, a thought that worried him, yet wasn't a surprise.

"As King Marden has said, he has given much thought to his decision," continued Tetric, his voice an unsettling hiss. "An alliance between Tintagel and the Southern Marches would strengthen the Kingdom, so he asks for your daughter in marriage. It is not just a gracious request, but one to be valued and appreciated. What say you, Kevan?"

Kevan shot Tetric a hard glare, well aware of the insult offered by the King's Chief Advisor. Or rather the warning. To address a Duke of Caledonia with such informality was almost unheard of, occurring only between equals. Yet Kevan got the impression that Tetric saw himself as more than equal to Kevan or Marden. Kevan looked down briefly at the combat still taking place in the Pit. The gladiator was holding his own, having survived for more than an hour. He seemed to be quite capable, and the young man's patience was impressive as he waited for his opening, waited for the right moment to strike. Though almost everyone in the crowd believed that the black dragon would eventually kill the young man, Kevan knew the truth of it. The gladiator had become the hunter in just the last few minutes. It was only a matter of time before he proved victorious. Turning his gaze back to Marden and Tetric, an uncomfortable lump in the pit of his stomach suggested that unfortunately for Kevan, he was now the quarry, a position that he detested. As a military leader, he was used to taking the initiative. To advancing forward. But now, all that he could do was attempt to build up his deteriorating defenses as quickly as possible. Perhaps if he exercised the same patience as that of the gladiator fighting for his life, he could extricate himself and his daughter from this trap, at least for a time.

"Your Majesty, I must apologize. Truly, your request is

overwhelming. I had never expected it." Tetric smiled slightly at the statement. Kevan was now certain that this entire plot was Tetric's idea. More important, it was clear that Tetric held more sway over the son than he ever did over the father, and that was a frightening realization.

"It is overwhelming," answered Tetric in his quiet rasp. "But the King still needs your answer. He needs his bride."

"Your Majesty, obviously you know my decision, for there is no choice but one to be made. However, as I noted, my daughter is young and strong-willed. She will most likely not understand what is going on between us, between the crown and the Southern Marches. With your permission, I would like to speak with her first and present your proposal to her. I will then send you my reply, which of course is simply a formality." Kevan held his breath, waiting to see if his delaying tactic would work. He expected Tetric to see through his maneuver immediately, and, in fact, he sensed that the Chief Advisor was about to quash his attempt at deflecting the request, but this time Marden beat him to it.

"Of course you may, Kevan. I must have your official response by the fall Council of the Kingdom, so you have a few months to educate your daughter on the role she is to play. And I expect no further delays. If I don't receive word of your daughter's acceptance by then, I will, of course, be sorely disappointed, and we will have a much more serious conversation."

Tetric's face turned bright red, his rage barely contained, but control it he did. The fool! They had maneuvered Kevan into a corner from which he could not escape, but Marden had just given him a small path he could use to slip away.

"Of course, your Majesty. Thank you for your generosity. If I may, your Majesty, it is a long ride back to the Southern

Marches. The sooner I am off, the sooner this matter can be settled to both our satisfaction."

"Then off with you, Kevan. I will wait on your reply. And remember ... Father ... don't keep me waiting."

"Thank you, your Majesty." Bowing at the waist, Kevan exited the royal box just as the crowd burst into a thunderous roar. He glanced down toward the white sand and saw exactly what he had expected. He had been right. The gladiator had won. As had he, at least for a time, having escaped Tetric's trap for the moment. But only for the moment. Kevan cursed his luck under his breath. What was he to do?

KEVAN TOOK his time as he made his way to the stable at the bottom of the Colosseum, used for the horses and carriages of only the richest and most powerful men and women of Caledonia, as he wanted to think a bit more about what had just happened and how to evade the net Marden and Tetric were attempting to throw over him and his daughter. It was there that he found Tarin, his Captain of the Guard, already in the saddle, the reins of Kevan's horse held firmly in his hands. Tarin seemed to have the ability to read minds, knowing that Kevan wanted to leave quickly. But he hadn't foreseen the dilemma that now plagued the Duke of the Southern Marches.

"Not yet, Tarin," said Kevan. "There is something that I must do first."

Tarin shrugged. "I had expected as much." He had served Kevan for more than a decade. He was well aware of his lord's moods and habits, and he could tell that Kevan's mind was working on a problem at a furious pace.

"Is it as we feared?" asked Tarin, sliding off his saddle and tying the reins of both horses to a gate.

"Worse, I'm afraid," replied Kevan. "Much worse." Kevan stood there for a minute, until finally the path that he needed to take formed in front of him. It just might be the solution, or at least part of the solution, that he was looking for. Besides, there was little risk to what he had in mind. "Who is responsible for the gladiator who just defeated the black dragon?"

Tarin gave his lord a quizzical look, not expecting the question. "I believe Beluchmel," replied Tarin.

"Did you watch the combat, Tarin?"

"I did." It had been an impressive display for someone with little or no military instruction. True, gladiators were taught to fight. But Tarin was a career soldier and came from a family of career soldiers. His prejudices favored those with a military upbringing, seeing a distinct difference between that and the training to be a gladiator.

"And your thoughts?"

The Captain of the Guard waited a moment before answering. Tarin rarely answered anything right away, for he was a man of caution, a trait that certainly benefited him as a soldier, yet could also prove a hindrance at times. "He fought with intelligence, with a patience and skill rarely seen in gladiators. Usually they come charging across the Pit, looking to end the combat as soon as possible, often not caring if they live or die. This one let the fight come to him, and his decision making is beyond dispute. He picked the perfect moment to make his move."

"Let us go in search of this Beluchmel," decided Kevan, nodding his head in agreement. "We have business to conduct."

~

"WHAT DO YOU THINK, Tetric? Will my soon-to-be father-in-law try to back out?"

"It will be hard for him to do so," replied Tetric. "Though I doubt that he has any intention of allowing his daughter to go through with it if he can avoid it. His responses were quite vague, you know. He didn't commit to anything other than speaking to the girl about the proposal." He and Marden had watched Kevan walk quickly from the royal box. They both suspected the decision that Kevan wanted to make. Therefore, they needed to ensure that he had but one option to select from, a choice that favored their plan.

"I agree," said Marden. "Still, do you think he will break if we apply the right amount of pressure?"

"No. He will not."

"We need him or his daughter, not both." Marden tore his gaze away from the opened doors and glanced back to the white sand of the Pit. The attendants had already removed the dragon's body and the next combat was about to begin, this one pitting a tall, red-haired gladiator against two starved lions. He already had guessed the outcome, so he turned his attention back to his advisor. "We need to find some other way, Tetric. Some other way to ensure that the Duke of the Southern Marches does our bidding."

"Yes, your Majesty, we will. I will make sure that everything is in place."

CHAPTER 3. A DEAL

"This is most unusual, Duke Winborne," said Beluchmel, his massive frame shaking as he pounded with a large fist on the oak door wrapped in steel bands. His size was deceptive, as the luxurious silk robes that he preferred to wear hid more fat than muscle. "Most unusual. In fact, I can't even remember when a request such as this has been made, and I've been Master of the Colosseum for the last three decades."

Kevan ignored the chatter coming from the large man. The bright sun gleamed brightly off Beluchmel's bald pate, long stringy hair near his ears running down to his shoulders. Serving as the Master of the Colosseum had its obvious perks, so long as you didn't bring too much attention to yourself. The fact that Beluchmel had survived in his position for such a long time, and had obviously profited from it, testified to his abilities, no matter how nefarious they may be. Based on his large, red, bulbous nose, the veins thick and obvious, Kevan assumed that much of the fortune the man had acquired was used to keep the Master of the Colosseum in drink and other pleasures.

"What's the price?"

An eyehole opened before them, then closed just as quickly, the grunt heard from the other side of the large gates acknowledging Beluchmel's authority, though clearly with some reluctance. Slowly, the gates began to open, winches on both sides pulling them apart. Beluchmel squeezed his bulk through, stomping into the training ground, followed by Kevan and the always cautious Tarin, who laid a wary hand on the hilt of his sword.

Practice yard it may be, but to Kevan's eyes, it looked more like a prison stockade. A ten-foot wall made of brick and mortar surrounded the entire complex, and ten feet beyond that wall rose a twenty-foot wall. Ten feet beyond that barrier, a wall thirty feet in height loomed above the complex, blocking much of the late afternoon sun. Along each wall at fifty-foot increments a bored guard stood looking down at the activities below.

Tarin's soldierly eye took it all in, guessing that something unpleasant waited between the walls of varying heights for any gladiator foolish enough to try to escape. Even a full-scale revolt would fail, he concluded. The gladiators' compound lay against the back of the Colosseum. On the remaining three sides just outside the walls was the permanent headquarters for the King's Royal Guard. If the gladiators somehow succeeded in escaping from their small enclosure, and the likelihood of that appeared to be poor at best, they still had to fight their way through a small army. All in all, it was the most effective prison Tarin had ever seen constructed.

On each side of the field, a long, ramshackle barracks stood in disrepair, the paint peeling off as the stone baked in the noonday sun. In several places, holes were visible in the roof. Obviously, Beluchmel had done his best to siphon off as much of the money directed toward the upkeep of the gladiators' compound as possible.

A field several hundred feet long lay before them, more dirt than grass. Markers divided the field into distinct areas. The gladiators assigned to each space trained with specific equipment, honing their skills in order to improve their chances of surviving in the Pit. Tarin immediately noted that none of the gladiators were very old with perhaps just a handful beyond their early twenties. Try as the gladiators might to sharpen their abilities, he wasn't surprised that their efforts could only take them so far. He understood that once a man or woman set foot on the white sand their death was assured, for most in a matter of months. When you were required to fight four times a month, it was inevitable that eventually your luck would run out. No matter how skilled a gladiator may be, all it would take would be a momentary lapse in concentration, a single poorly timed lunge or a slip on the white sand, and the end would come. Nevertheless, he was impressed by their diligence. Some balanced on a thin pole while trying to stave off the jabs of their compatriots' spears. Others lifted stones that he guessed weighed several hundred pounds, and then those same gladiators tried to run through sand placed there to mimic the fighting floor of the Pit. And still more worked to master a dozen other tasks, all designed to extend the time until their unavoidable death.

"The price will depend on the gladiator you select," answered Beluchmel, leading them quickly across the field toward the main building that squared off the compound. Though this structure was in a better state compared to the gladiators' quarters, its age was apparent. Mortar crumbled slowly between the stones, and the roof, this one made of wood shingles rather than hay, sloped dangerously toward the ground on one end.

Beluchmel pushed his bulk through the opening, his sides scraping against the stone. The door had long since been removed, or most likely it simply had disintegrated over time, mused Kevan. He and Tarin followed the Master of the Colosseum into a small room in which a man sat quietly behind a desk made of two sawhorses and what Kevan guessed was the missing door. The solidly built man, his grey hair shorn close to his scalp, ignored them, continuing to work through a stack of papers. He didn't seem to be a man who enjoyed his task. He had the hardened appearance of a gladiator, a man who had survived many combats in the Pit, and he had the scars on his arms and legs, revealed by the shirt and training shorts he wore, to prove it. Though the man was older, Kevan suspected that he could return to the Pit right then and still emerge victorious, though he doubted that the man had fought on the white sand for quite some time.

Beluchmel, obviously uncomfortable in his surroundings, cleared his throat a few times, hoping to gain the quiet man's attention. But the serious-minded fellow continued to ignore them. "Declan, I bring with me prestigious visitors. Rise and offer them the appropriate courtesies."

The man failed to lift his head as he continued to sift through the papers on his makeshift desk. "I am busy, Beluchmel, and I have no time for visitors. I barely have time for anything but trying to keep my men and women alive." Having completed what he had been working on, finally Declan looked up from his papers, his sharp eyes giving a glimpse of the quick temper that lay just beneath his outward calm. "Now where is the fresh hay you promised me for the roofs? And the other building materials, Beluchmel? Where are they? We've waited for months. If the King feels the need to put on this bloody show, then he needs to take better care of the men and women consigned to play a role in it."

Declan rose from his chair and walked around his desk. Though Beluchmel towered over the shorter man, that was of little import. Beluchmel wouldn't last a second alone with Declan. "How am I supposed to train my gladiators to fight in the Pit if I can't even give them habitable quarters and good, healthy food? And tell me, Beluchmel, how will you fill your pockets with gold if you have no gladiators fighting for the King's pleasure? How will you keep that large head of yours on your portly body if the good King Beleron doesn't have his favorite entertainment to keep the people's minds off their own troubles?"

Beluchmel gulped loudly, a sheen of sweat appearing on his forehead. Kevan and Tarin now understood why their guide had seemed so uncomfortable entering the gladiators' compound. Though Beluchmel managed the Colosseum, this kept man ruled the gladiators.

"You will have everything I promised you, Declan, everything. The shipments have simply been delayed. A few more weeks is what I have been told. Surely you can wait that ..."

"I'm tired of your excuses, Beluchmel," said Declan, stepping closer to the Master of the Colosseum and causing the larger man to step back in fear. "If I had half a mind, I'd break you in two and leave you for ..."

"Although that would truly be an interesting sight," interrupted Kevan, stepping between the two men before Declan could make good on his promise, "I have a bit of business to discuss with you first. And since we must leave within the hour, we need to take care of it now. Once that's concluded, you can do whatever you want to this one."

Kevan pointed to Beluchmel, who clearly welcomed the interruption and had begun to sweat profusely despite the chill of the late afternoon. "I'm assuming that you are the Master of the Gladiators?"

"I am," replied Declan, the anger leaving his face, if only for a moment.

"Excellent. I am Kevan Winborne, Duke of the Southern Marches. And this is Tarin Tentillin, Captain of my Guard." Tarin and Declan eyed one another, judging strengths and weaknesses in an instant. It was a common habit when two soldiers met for the first time. Satisfied by what each one saw in the other, they nodded a wary greeting.

"Duke Winborne," said Declan, giving the lord a perfunctory nod of his head. "You mentioned business. We have few visitors to the training ground. What can I do for you?"

"I am in need of a gladiator, Declan."

Declan chuckled softly. He had heard that some of the wealthy and powerful had strange tastes, yet this seemed a bit out of the ordinary. Declan picked up on much of what was going on in the Kingdom during his wanderings through the Colosseum and the city, but he had never heard anything unique, unseemly, or untoward about the Duke of the Southern Marches. In fact, from what he could tell from the various pieces of information that he had gathered, this Duke was more austere than most of his colleagues. Of course, not every rumor made its way to the Colosseum, Declan admitted, and every man was entitled to his private fancies, within reason, of course.

"May I ask the reason why you require a gladiator?" asked Declan.

"It's none of your concern," answered Tarin, who stepped forward, his hand caressing the hilt of his sword.

The insolence of this Master of the Gladiators, former soldier though he may be, irritated the Captain of the Battersea Guard.

"It is my concern," grated Declan, his face red with anger. "I've trained these men and women, some since they were children, to be fighters, survivors. Fate gave them a bad hand sending them here to die, but I've done everything I could to ensure that they die with honor, and more importantly, that they delay their deaths for as long as possible. I will not release a single gladiator until I know your purpose, Duke Winborne. It is that simple."

"You will not release ..." sputtered Tarin, his blade half out of his sheath. Kevan quickly grabbed his captain's hand, forcing the blade back into the scabbard. Tarin was a stickler for everything in life, whether protocol or his own appearance, as seen by his usually spotless uniform, perfectly parted hair and waxed mustache. But Declan didn't appear to be flustered by Tarin's display. In fact, he seemed to be less than impressed, obviously believing that he'd have little trouble dispatching Tarin if there was cause to do so.

"Declan, don't be a fool," said Beluchmel, worried that his business deal was about to fall through. "If the Duke of the Southern Marches requires a gladiator, then he will have one, even if I must bring a company of the King's Royal Guard in here to ensure that he gets one."

"Then you'd finally be giving me the opportunity that my gladiators and I have been waiting for," said Declan quietly, his eyes glowing with a hard anticipation. Beluchmel took another step away from the Master of the Gladiators, quivering with fear.

During the entire exchange, Kevan had studied Declan, sizing him up. He saw loyalty there, and honor, and, perhaps his most noble trait, compassion. He cared about the men and women whom he trained. That alone earned Kevan's respect.

"Enough of this," said Kevan in a thunderous voice, quelling the three men into silence, even the feisty gladiator. "Declan, I admire loyalty. It is a trait rarely seen these days, in even the best of men. You ask a fair question, and you will have an answer. I have a daughter, a teenage daughter. As the Duke of the Southern Marches, there are certain risks that I have to worry about, and it seems that those dangers are becoming more real, not only for me, but also for my daughter."

Declan nodded his head knowingly. Slave he may be, but he was not a fool. Duke Winborne was the leading contender for the throne should anything happen to King Beleron. Based on what he knew of the Duke of the Southern Marches that could be a good thing for Caledonia, though he doubted that the man would live very long if he ever demonstrated any interest in the throne, not with Tetric lurking in the shadows.

"I require a gladiator to serve as her Protector."

Declan studied the Duke of the Southern Marches for almost a full minute, until he was satisfied that he had spoken truthfully. Serving as a Protector was an honorable task, though much like a gladiator, a Protector had no personal freedom. But Declan was surprised by the admission. It was an archaic practice. No one had served as a Protector for at least five decades. "And I'm assuming that you've already selected a gladiator to serve as your daughter's Protector."

"I have," answered Kevan. "The gladiator who defeated the black dragon."

Declan's heart rose in his throat, choking him for a

brief moment. Of course, he shouldn't have been so shocked. Bryen was one of the best gladiators to ever fight in the Pit, despite his relative youth. Why wouldn't the Duke of the Southern Marches want the best to serve as a Protector for his daughter? He searched furiously for a way to prevent the deal, but nothing came to mind. There was no legitimate way that he could stop the sale of a gladiator. Then again, perhaps he was looking at this from the wrong perspective. Perhaps this would help Bryen in some way. If nothing else, it would release him from the Pit. Bryen clearly wasn't interested in glory, the only thing attainable to a gladiator now. True, slave he would remain, but his life wouldn't hang in the balance based on the changing moon. And serving as a Protector couldn't prove to be a worse fate than the one that awaited him on the white sand, regardless of the threats Duke Winborne may have been concerned about. If Bryen could survive the Pit for ten years, then he could certainly endure watching over the Duke's most likely spoiled daughter. After struggling a few seconds more with what he knew had already been decided, he nodded his head in acquiescence, then quietly left the room through a doorway at the back of the office.

"Well, my lord, despite the trouble put up by our honorable Master of the Gladiators, it looks like you will have the gladiator that you require." Beluchmel rubbed his hands in anticipation. Matters were finally getting interesting, in his opinion -- another contribution of golds to his pocket.

"Your price?" Kevan asked the question sharply, clearly not interested in the drawn-out haggling so much a part of the general marketplace in Tintagel. Though some enjoyed it, and Beluchmel appeared to relish it quite a bit judging by the brief turn of disappointment on his face, Kevan did not.

"Fifty golds," answered Beluchmel with a straight face, his eyes sharp. They had entered his arena now.

"Fifty!" objected Tarin. "For a gladiator? That's robbery."

"Done," answered Kevan, judging the price cheap after having seen the gladiator in action. The cost of protecting his daughter was nothing to him, and based on this gladiator's performance, Kevan knew that he was buying the best.

"But Duke Winborne!" protested Tarin.

"The golds, Tarin," commanded Kevan.

Knowing from experience that arguing with his lord once he had made up his mind was a bad idea, Tarin began pulling out the pieces of gold from a large purse hidden beneath his cloak.

"Oh, my apologies, Duke Winborne. But I forgot the transfer fee required by the crown. That's an additional ten golds, for a total of sixty." Beluchmel grinned mischievously, knowing that he had won. The cost of this gladiator was obviously not a concern to Duke Winborne, so why not try to extract as much as possible.

Tarin was about to protest once again, but Kevan cut him off. "So be it. Sixty."

Throwing up his arms in mock despair, Tarin placed the heavy, thick coins in a smaller leather bag. The Captain of the Guard shook his head in frustration. The boy they were buying may be a fighter, but he was not a soldier. Hopefully that fact wouldn't cause the Duke of the Southern Marches to rue his decision.

~

"STOP MOVING AROUND. How am I supposed to take care of your wounds if you flop about like a small child with a splinter in his finger?"

Bryen couldn't help but smile at Lycia's command, though her touch was anything but light as she first checked the slice on his arm from the black dragon's claw and then rewrapped that wound once she was satisfied that the physick had done good work with the sutures. She then turned her attention to the burns on his left arm and leg caused by the animal's venom. For those there was little that she could do other than make sure that Bryen continued to apply the healing ointment that sat next to him on the wooden bench so that they didn't become infected.

"You're babying him, Lycia," said Davin. "Leave him be. He's had worse injuries than these."

"I'm making sure that he's well, that's all," said Lycia, her voice turning hard. Her brother had a knack for getting a rise out of her, often for the most innocuous of comments.

"You never show so much concern for me," protested Davin. "Besides, I had the harder fight. Two starved lions are much more difficult than a black dragon."

"The only reason it was a harder fight," corrected Lycia, "was because of those skinny legs of yours. You spent more time tripping over yourself than actually fighting those poor beasts. Besides, you weren't even hurt. Not even a scratch."

Bryen closed his eyes for a moment and settled the back of his head against the brick wall. The bickering between brother and sister washed over him, and he allowed his focus to waver for just a few minutes. After all that he had been through that afternoon, this being the closest yet that he had come to his own death, he found the incessant wrangling between Davin and Lycia relaxing.

Brother and sister had arrived in the Colosseum three years before, and Bryen remembered the day clearly. They had entered through the gates arguing with one another and it hadn't stopped since. When he had first seen Lycia, he had thought that she was the most beautiful girl he had ever laid eyes on, and he and Davin had become fast friends, one of his few here in the training barracks. There was a great deal of respect between him and the other gladiators. He had survived the longest of any of the men or women forced to bleed on the white sand, other than Declan himself. But because the prospect of death was always near that mutual respect rarely turned into friendship. Not when you might be charged with killing a friend in the Pit. Thankfully, Bryen had not yet had to fight Davin or Lycia. Next to him, his two friends were the best gladiators in Tintagel, and Beluchmel had no desire to interfere with the stream of money he earned whenever one of the three entered the Pit. The Master of the Colosseum was a greedy, soulless man, but he was not stupid. He would not do anything that would affect his potential earnings negatively.

Bryen was drawn from his peaceful reverie by the silence that settled suddenly within the gladiators' quarters. He opened his eyes and saw that both Lycia and Davin were staring at Declan, who stood in the doorway. Bryen took in Declan's serious expression. Though Declan was always serious, this time his eyes suggested something else. There was a touch of sorrow and anger at the edges of his flinty glare and perhaps even a hint of hope. "What's the matter, Declan?"

The Master of the Gladiators was about to answer, but he couldn't find the words, his emotions threatening to erupt, and that wasn't something that he knew how to manage effectively. So as he'd done all his life, he simply pushed the feelings roiling through him to the back of his mind and locked them away. "I'm sorry, lad, but there was nothing that I could do. Come along."

Declan walked out of the gladiators' changing room,

shaking his head in what Bryen took to be disgust but was actually sorrow.

Bryen had no idea why the Master of the Gladiators was acting this way. He looked to Davin and Lycia for guidance, but his two friends were just as surprised and confused as he was, both shrugging their shoulders in response. Declan could be moody at times, but they had never seen anything like this from him before.

Shrugging his shoulders as well, Bryen exited the room and hobbled after Declan as pain flared in his leg with every step that he took, a sense of unease settling within his stomach. He hadn't felt this nervous even when he was fighting the black dragon.

ONLY A FEW MINUTES had passed before Declan reappeared, and behind him came the gladiator from the Pit. He was younger than Kevan had expected, perhaps only a year or two older than his daughter, but his struggles on the white sand had aged him. His hair and short beard were mostly white, a few strands of light brown peeking through, and his grey eyes that contained faint specks of green held the haunted expression of a man who had seen the worst that life had to offer. Yet, there was something else there too, something that had confirmed for Kevan that this gladiator would defeat the black dragon -- an intelligence, or perhaps cunning, tempered with a self-confidence that displayed true character, not arrogance. All in all, Kevan was quite pleased with his selection.

"Bryen," said Declan, "this is Duke Kevan Winborne of the Southern Marches. He has a need for a gladiator, and he has chosen you. You are in his charge now." The words seemed to physically injure Declan, the vigorous, strong man shrinking in upon himself. The Master of the Gladiators couldn't bring himself to look at Bryen while saying them.

Bryen was clearly shocked by the statement, Declan not having prepared him for the announcement. The gladiator stared painfully at the Master of the Gladiators, then examined the other men in the room. His eyes passed over Beluchmel with barely a pause -- someone who was not a threat, at least not directly, surmised Kevan -- then rested on Tarin for a moment, sizing him up. Kevan thought that he could read the gladiator's mind. A soldier, skilled and experienced, but then just as quickly, another kill if need be. Finally his gaze fell on Kevan, and a cold shiver ran down his spine. For an instant, Kevan thought that he saw a flash of hate within those hard eyes, but then just as quickly it was gone, replaced by a deceptive calm. This gladiator did indeed have the appearance of a volkun, a wolf in the old tongue, waiting calmly, confidently, for its prey, pretending a lack of interest. But when the time was right, the volkun would strike quickly and with an uncontrolled ferocity. The moniker that Kevan heard being hurled down upon this young man after his victory over the black dragon certainly fit him.

Beluchmel reached for the bag of gold that Tarin had dropped on Declan's desk, but Kevan stepped in front of him -- no easy task considering the large man's bulk -- before he could grab it with his fat, greedy fingers. "I'm sure you can make better use of this than Beluchmel can," Kevan said, speaking to the Master of the Gladiators.

"But ..." Beluchmel's attempted protest was cut short by a sharp glance from Tarin, whose hand was once again on the hilt of his sword.

"Yes, Duke Winborne, I can. Thank you. But it is a hard price to pay." Declan's eyes remained on the stone floor, still unwilling and unable to look at Bryen.

Kevan nodded his understanding, then motioned for Tarin to come forward. The Captain of the Guard pulled wrist restraints and a short chain from his belt. Having no good reason to resist, and still a bit astonished by what was happening, Bryen held out his hands, his eyes boring a hole through the far wall. Tarin was careful to avoid the bandage on Bryen's right forearm, a reminder of the black dragon's sharp claws. Satisfied that the shackles were secure, Tarin stepped away and nodded to Duke Winborne.

Kevan immediately walked out of the small room, Beluchmel following after, trying to figure out some way to get a fair share of the gold now resting in Declan's hands.

"Time to go," said Tarin, giving Bryen a shove to his shoulder. Much to his aggravation he had to do it again, this time harder, as his initial effort had no effect whatsoever, the gladiator simply looking down at him with those eyes that revealed nothing. "You may be leaving the Pit, but that doesn't change your place in the world. Remember that. You're still a convicted criminal. Still a slave."

"Free he may not be," said Declan harshly, his eyes finally lifting off the ground and burning with their customary fire. "But he is not a slave. He is a gladiator. A fighter. Treat him as such, Captain."

Though Tarin knew that he should be insulted by Declan's outburst, he was more surprised than anything else and somewhat taken aback.

Bryen smiled grimly, locking eyes with his former trainer. There was no need for words as the master and the student studied one another for the last time.

"Thank you for giving me the skills to survive, Declan,"

said Bryen quietly, his soft voice sounding more like that of a poet than a man accustomed to the blade. He then shuffled out the door, slowed by the burns on his left leg from the dragon's venom, now wrapped in a loose bandage that Lycia had fiddled with until she had gotten it exactly how she wanted it. Tarin followed him outside, seeking to intimidate Declan with a glare, but failing miserably.

Declan nodded to his young charge, struggling to restrain the tears that threatened to fall as he watched the boy who had in many ways become his son take his leave.

I HOPE you enjoyed the first three chapters. To keep reading, **order your copy today at www.amazon.com**.